THERE GOES THE
NEIGHBORHOOD

THERE GOES THE NEIGHBORHOOD

JADE ADIA

HYPERION
Los Angeles   New York

Copyright © 2023 by Jade Adia
All rights reserved. Published by Hyperion,
an imprint of Buena Vista Books, Inc. No part of this
book may be reproduced or transmitted in any form or
by any means, electronic or mechanical, including
photocopying, recording, or by any information storage
or retrieval system, without written permission from
the publisher. For information address Hyperion,
77 West 66th Street, New York, New York 10023.

First Edition, March 2023
1 3 5 7 9 10 8 6 4 2
FAC-004510-23020
Printed in the United States of America

This book is set in Centennial LT Pro / Linotype
Designed by Zareen Johnson

Library of Congress Cataloging-in-Publication Data
Names: Adia, Jade, author.
Title: There goes the neighborhood / Jade Adia.
Description: First edition. • Los Angeles ; New York :
Disney-Hyperion, 2023. • Audience: Ages 12–18. •
Audience: Grades 7–9. • Summary: "In order to stop the
destructive forces of gentrification, three best friends use
social media to create a fake gang and get justice for their
South LA community" —Provided by publisher.
Identifiers: LCCN 2022007108 (print) •
LCCN 2022007109 (ebook) •
ISBN 9781368084321 (hardcover) •
ISBN 9781368084338 (ebook)
Subjects: CYAC: Gentrification—Fiction. • Gangs—Fiction •
Social media—Fiction. • Murder—Fiction. •
African Americans—Fiction. • Hispanic Americans—Fiction. •
South Los Angeles (Los Angeles, Calif.)
Classification: LCC PZ7.1.A245 Th 2023 (print) •
LCC PZ7.1.A245 (ebook) • DDC [Fic]—dc23
LC record available at https://lccn.loc.gov/2022007108
LC ebook record available at https://lccn.loc.gov/2022007109

Reinforced binding
Visit www.HyperionTeens.com

SUSTAINABLE FORESTRY INITIATIVE
Certified Sourcing
www.sfiprogram.org
SFI-01681

Logo Applies to Text Stock only

To Leslie, of course.
Every page, every time. It's all for you, Mom.

To all the Black kids raising a finger to the status quo.
Your fury and creativity are beautiful, and I cannot
wait to see what you do.

AIGHT, so I know how it looks—bad—but I can tell you for damn sure that we didn't do it. Everyone thinks the gang did it, which I guess makes sense given that gangs tend to have a reputation for stuff like this, but I know for a fact that it wasn't the gang because the gang is fake. I made it up.

Well, me, along with Zeke and Malachi. And we'd never kill anyone. That would defeat the whole purpose of it all. We invented the "gang" so that we could *live*. I know that might not make sense now, but it will soon.

I just need you to trust me on this: we did not kill that white man.

PART ONE

*The rulers of this country have always considered
their property more important than our lives.*
—ASSATA SHAKUR

ONE

"Swear to god if this happens again, I'm gunna scream." I pull my forehead back from the glass and use my fist to wipe away the condensation.

"Yeah, I'll walk straight to the mayor's mansion, and he better be ready to catch these hands," Zeke says. He forms two fists and throws a couple of fake punches in the air.

Malachi laughs, gripping the number on his classic Kobe jersey. "Bruh, you're not gunna fight anyone."

This much is obvious to me and anyone who knows Zeke. The boy once told me that he could never imagine himself fighting someone, unless it was in space and he had a lightsaber.

"Okay, *fine*," Zeke relents. "But I will send a strongly worded email. And write a bad Yelp review."

"I don't think you can write Yelp reviews for the City of Los Angeles," I mumble. It's only July 1, but when I try to count up the number of mom-and-pop shops to bite it this summer alone, I give up after ten. Jugos Azteca was the last place in the neighborhood where you could still get a giant thirty-two-ounce Styrofoam cup of agua fresca at any hour for only $2.

But now it's gone too.

The global spice mart was the first to go. Some corporate stooges bought it last year and turned it into a boutique Pilates studio. And the Liquor Bank where we used to buy sour belts and chile mango pops? That was shut down for a health code violation, and now there's an artisan coffee shop where you can paint a ceramic mug while you wait. Last year, someone took over the fish fry restaurant next to that, and now there's a goddamn taco shop run by a couple of white boys, and their only salsa option is pico de gallo. *Pico-de-fucking-gallo.* Not a bottle of Valentina or Yucateco in sight. Not even any Tapatío or weak-ass Cholula. We went there once to see what the deal was, but between the three of us, we only had enough cash for one taco to split. When the corny dude brought it over to us, we asked for hot sauce and he gave us SRIRACHA. Fuck outta here with that ketchup shit. That would *never* have happened back in the day.

So yeah, things in South LA are changing, to say the least.

"We could walk on Western Avenue until we find the elote guy?" I suggest, more so as an excuse to get as far away as possible from this depressing-ass empty storefront than out of an actual craving for street corn.

"Rhea, it's too hot to walk. Like *Mad Max* slash *Dune* slash that *Star Trek* episode when Kirk fights that desert lizard level *hot*." Zeke uses the seam of his graphic tee to wipe a line of sweat from underneath his sheepdog haircut.

"Well, unless you magically learn to drive, I don't know what our other option is," I say. I'm usually the one good for thinking of the plan for the day, but between the heat and yet another spot biting the dust, I got nothing.

"When I get my permit, I'll be charging y'all for rides," Malachi says proudly.

"Boy, please." I bop the back of his head. "As if you can even buy a car." At fifteen, the three of us can barely afford snacks, let alone a whole-ass vehicle.

The sun kicks it up a notch. Trippy waves of gas rising from the steaming concrete do a little dance for me before melting away. Across the street, something catches my eye. *If this looks like what I think it does . . .* I fight the urge to gag.

"Wait, guys, hold up," I say, holding a hand above my eyes to block out the sun.

For the past six months, the city's been building this high-speed Metro rail to slice through our neighborhood. The construction site is almost always empty, but today, it looks like there's a "special" new addition.

Cars honk as I dodge traffic, but I couldn't care less. When I hit the other side of the street, I lace my fingers around the wire of the chain-link fence to get a better look.

You've got to be kidding me.

Zeke catches up and puts on his CNN newscaster voice to read the brand-new billboard staring at us. "*Kofa Park: Los Angeles's Newest Up-and-Coming Hot Spot!*"

I roll my eyes. "Gimme your backpack," I say to Malachi.

"Why?" He pulls the straps of his space-themed JanSport close to his chest.

"You don't trust me?"

"Hell no!" He backs away all dramatic at first, but there's a faint trace of a smile beneath it all. I lunge forward to snatch it but miss. He laughs and tosses me the backpack.

I snag a Sharpie from the front pocket. "Watch out for a security guard, aight?" I dig the rubber toes of my Converse into the gaps of the fence and climb over. My shoes hit the concrete with a sting.

The marker squeaks as I rub its felt tip against the Plexiglas. The future train stop shelter has two side panels, so I hit those real quick before focusing on the backside, which is the most important because this is what faces the street.

This is the shit that people see.

We've had bullshit billboards like this popping up all over South LA for the past couple of years, so normally I wouldn't have even noticed. But something about this particular one caught my eye:

All the people in the ads are white.

Well, at least they were until a minute ago.

I use the brown Sharpie to fill in one last face.

The guys hop the fence to join me on the forbidden side. Malachi with his long legs does so much easier than Zeke, who sort of half scrambles, half falls his way over.

The hood of the train stop structure casts a thin strip of futile shade covering only half of the metal bench, which by now has already absorbed hours' worth of summer heat, so it's way too hot to sit on. But that doesn't stop Zeke from trying. Twice.

"Rheaaaa," Zeke complains to me after burning his ass once again. He rubs the seat of his jeans. "Can you just let this go?"

"No." As a Black girl, I know how shit works: we're either hypervisible or invisible. I'm not gonna pretend that I personally don't fall in that second category, but I don't need a goddamn billboard rubbing it in my face. Let alone erasing the entire hood into obscurity along with me.

My hand cramps and I accidentally color outside of the line.

"I'm too young and too cute to get a rap for breaking and entering," Zeke complains.

On the other side of the fence, a white twentysomething woman with a cat on a bedazzled leash crosses the street to avoid walking past us. She clutches her phone all dramatic, the panic button locked and loaded as if we've been lurking here waiting to mug her. She avoids my eye contact as I stare her down.

Apparently, we don't look very young to her.

I ignore Zeke and keep coloring. He groans and grabs the cluster of neon-yellow caution tape from the floor, walking over to Malachi. Even while leaning against the fence, Malachi towers over Zeke, so Zeke has to rise up on his toes to wrap the "Do Not Enter" tape around Malachi's neck. Zeke arranges the makeshift boa and smiles. "You look fabulous."

"Y'all play too much," Malachi says, hiding a smirk. He adjusts the caution tape scarf and takes the wave brush from the back pocket of his jeans, compulsively rubbing it across his head, fresh from the barber with a new fade. The new cut works for him. A little too well. I've seen the way that other girls have started to look at him this summer. He's all height, glowing brown skin, and perfect teeth since the braces came off. Not like that's any of *my* business—how other girls look at him, I mean. As his oldest friend, I try not to notice the changes. Plus, it's not like I've glowed up in any way to match.

Zeke, Malachi, and I have been best friends since Pampers. Our moms became tight when they'd volunteer at our day care together. As we got older, that turned into waiting for us at the bus stop after school, which was always late because we'd mess with the driver so much that he'd have to pull over to yell at us to stay in our seats and shit. So our moms had plenty of time to bond and gossip about the other parents. Eventually, the three of us became accustomed to impromptu playdates on the patch of grass at the street corner while our moms kept raising their gelled nails at us, telling us to chill out for "five more minutes." And let me tell you, when Black and Latina moms get into full-on chisme mode, you know for damn sure that they ain't gonna be just "five minutes." So, Zeke, Malachi, and I leaned into our crew. We gradually transitioned from school friends, to bus friends, to friends-friends.

These days, my mom doesn't hang out with the others anymore. Or anyone, really, except her newest husband. Even I didn't make the cut. So Zeke and Malachi aren't just my best friends, they're my tethers—the ones who keep me from feeling like I could drift away at any moment without anyone noticing, the ones who make me feel at home in the world. Not like I'd ever straight-up *tell* Zeke's sentimental ass or Malachi's smug self how much they mean to me, but whatever, they know. And the fact that they ride-or-die so hard with me, hopping a fence to watch my back, no questions asked, means it's mutual.

"Incoming security guard." Malachi tilts forward like he's ready to bolt. Little diamond-shaped impressions run down his spine where he had been leaning against the fence. "You done yet?"

"Nah, hold on." The guys hover over my shoulders, but I cover my work. "I said I'm not done yet."

Malachi sucks his teeth. "C'mon, let us see."

"It's not finished."

"Sis, relax," Zeke says. He swats away my hand and takes a sharp inhale.

Malachi doubles over in laughter. "They look like they're in blackface!"

"No, they don't!" I protest. I take a step back but realize that they low-key do.

Not my best work.

"This somehow feels even more racist than the original ad," Zeke cackles.

"Ay, yo, STOP!" On the opposite side of the track, a skinny security guard pulls up on some bootleg Mall Cop bullshit. He leans over the handlebars of his bicycle, but his helmet is slightly too big, so it sags to the side, making him look even younger than he is. I recognize him because he works the night shift at Wing Stop. It's probably just in my head, but swear to god, I can smell the lemon-pepper seasoning lingering on his uniform from over here.

"The penalties for a conviction of misdemeanor graffiti are up to three hundred sixty-four days in county jail, a thousand-dollar fine, or both," the guard shouts, tryna make his voice big. The dark skin of his chicken legs glisten with sweat and cocoa butter.

"And what's the penalty for rockin' shorts that tight on a Wednesday afternoon?" Malachi clowns as he hops the fence back to the street. I take the moment of distraction to add my final touch: I scratch out the "newest up-and-coming" part of the ad.

"You know what?" The skinny guard whips out his busted Android with a screen crack deeper than the San Andreas Fault. "Names and addresses! I got y'all on tape!"

With that, Zeke and I catapult ourselves over the fence. I kick out a kink in my leg from the fall as we watch the goofy Mall Cop nigga round the corner, pedaling straight toward us.

Malachi's big brown eyes go wide as he claps in my face. "Yo, let's go, let's go, let's go!"

We sprint by the men in suits who hand out copies of the local paper every afternoon and the mural of the dark woman whose afro holds a spaceship above the words "Free Your Mind." A group of girls, maybe four or five years younger than us, double Dutch in the empty parking lot where a woman selling tamales laughs with a customer who hangs out of their car window, delicately grasping a plastic bag steaming from the heat of the corn husks. I can smell the masa even after we dip into the alley, leaping over empty boxes of backwoods and lost wads of braiding hair from the salon above the black-and-gray-style tattoo parlor.

Our sprint slows to a jog, which slows to a walk. We emerge on the other end and lose the guard at last.

"Your bad attitude is gunna screw us all over," Malachi says between deep gasps for breath. "I'm cutting off your Sharpie supply, Rhea."

Recently, there's been something about the way he says my name that makes my stomach do a slow somersault. I clock the feeling but push it aside. "Whatever, bighead," I reply, knocking my sandal against his Jordans, but being careful not to scuff them up.

The heat catches up to us, so we practically crawl the final two blocks to Zeke's apartment, which is where we hang most of the time because his mom, Lupe, keeps the fridge stocked with hella snacks. Within minutes of piling inside, the three of us are arguing over who gets the last cheese-and-loroco pupusa when Lupe comes in.

She's crying.

"Ma?" Zeke asks softly, relinquishing the tiny bowl of curtido that he had been threatening to withhold if we didn't share with him.

"Can you get this out of the way, please?" she asks me, pointing at a chair that we had knocked over earlier. I stand and move it to its proper place at the table so that she can move her wheelchair around our mess. We all stare at the open envelope and crinkled letter lying facedown in her lap, but none of us dare to ask about it. She shuts her bedroom door gently, and Zeke sinks back down onto the carpet.

"What do you think that's about?" Zeke asks, clenching his hands together.

"I don't know." I tread carefully, because Zeke's one of those real sensitive, empathetic guys. He's the type who'll get choked up by those corny commercials where someone earns their degree from an online university and their kids try on the graduation cap. When things get dark for real, he can fall apart easily. I never really cry on my own, but with Zeke, his tears are annoyingly infectious. Once he gets started, it's Game Over for me—straight kryptonite. Unlike Zeke, though, I'd rather keep the feels to a minimum, so I throw myself into "Operation: Zeke Cry Prevention" at all costs.

"Do you think it's health stuff?" Malachi asks cautiously. Zeke's mom has been some type of sick for practically our entire lives. A few years ago, though, her nervous system stopped working well, which made it hard for her to walk, until, eventually, she couldn't walk at all. The doctors never figured out exactly what happened, but she's been able to manage with the chair and hasn't been to the hospital in over a year.

Lupe has one of those wild, uninhibited laughs that makes it easy to forget that she's often in pain.

"Nah, man. She was at the doctor last week and everything was chill. They spent most of the appointment talking about how the doc's bratty son ruined his niece's quince photo shoot."

"How'd he ruin the photo shoot?" Malachi asks. I flick the side of his head to remind him to focus on the actual issue at hand.

From behind her closed door, Lupe calls out to us, "Why don't you all go to Malachi's house? I need a bit of space to work this afternoon." Lupe is the part-time billing manager for a semiretired dentist, so she's always contacting someone's insurance or returning a patient's phone call.

"Sure, no problem," we reply in unison, though the chorus of our voices comes out more apprehensive than eager.

Malachi and I get up, but Zeke's still glued to the floor. I reach out my hand. "Just give her a minute, it's probably nothing," I whisper. He grabs my wrist, and I pull him up, careful not to knock over the collection of porcelain crosses on the bookshelf behind me.

Zeke locks the door behind us as Malachi and I attempt to see who can jump high enough to touch the hallway ceiling. I'm centimeters away from swiping the stucco above our heads when a familiar voice yells at us from down the hall.

"Cut that shit out!"

"Not this asshole again," Malachi murmurs.

Right on cue, Vic comes waddling down the hall. He's one of those short, pudgy white dudes who's thicc with lower body curves honestly not unlike my grandma.

"Here comes the Evil Landlord and his signature body odor fragrance . . ." I say to the guys. We cackle, which only makes Vic more pissed.

"Hahaha laugh all you want, cretins. In thirty days, I'll be the one laughing." He haphazardly waves a scroll of paper at our faces like a fire extinguisher. "I'll never have to see you three spilling Arizonas and stomping all over my units ever again."

"'Cause you're gunna kill us?" I chime in with a devious grin.

"As much pleasure as that would give me, no. I won't have to. Didn't you hear the news?" He runs his french-fry-grease-soaked hands across his mouth and nods at Zeke. "Acne-ridden wannabe Carlos Vives over here is moving." Vic makes his pale fingers into the shape of a gun and pretends to fire it at Zeke's chest.

"What are you talking about? We're not moving," Zeke pipes back.

Oil mixed with sweat glistens above the self-satisfied grin smeared across Vic's face. "Oh yeah? So, you're saying that you personally have the money to afford the sixty percent increase in rent, then?" A fly buzzes through the hallway, filling the silence that falls between us. Vic moves to swat it. He misses.

Look, I don't know how much the rent is, but I got an A in math last year—a 60 percent increase is no joke.

"You see this?" Vic theatrically unrolls the scroll that he's been wielding and reveals a set of blueprints. "The shithole that you're standing in now—which was run into the ground by all of *your people*—will soon be renovated. Out with the old tenants, and in with the new ones." I've seen enough changes on the block recently to know what he means. Read: millennials with tech jobs and hipsters with trust funds. "And this apartment complex"—he knocks on the wall—"is going to house them."

"You can't do that!" Zeke shouts. His voice cracks in a way that under different circumstances would have been fair game for ridicule. "We're under rent control."

"News flash: the rent control ordinance expired, kiddo. And I've already got an investor lined up. We're expected to close the deal by the end of the month. Now, if you'll excuse me." Vic pushes past a stunned Zeke to start taping notices of eviction to each of the doors.

Nuh-uh, fuck that. First they close our shops, now they're full-on tryna displace us? I throw my arm in front of the door that Vic is preparing to plaster. "Do you *really* think you can get away with this?" The rage that's been building inside of me all afternoon, all summer, pops off. I knock the stack of eviction notices from his grimy hand. "Well, go ahead. Try it. I fucking *dare you.*" I get all up in Vic's space, so close that I can feel his soggy fast-food breath soak the air between us. I lower my voice to a cold whisper. "Because guess what? When all this shit passes, we'll be the ones left standing . . . not you."

His beady eyes narrow. "Is that a *threat*?"

I cross my arms. "It's the truth."

Vic sneers and gathers the papers from the floor. "Thirty days. That's all you got."

"Is that a *challenge*?" I clap back.

I stare Vic down and he stares right back. No matter where Zeke moves, there's no way he'd stay nearby—not with prices surging across the city. He could end up all the way out in the valley or even the Inland Empire, both of which are far as hell. Moving out there is practically like going out of state—we'd *never* see Zeke.

I break away to look over at Zeke, who's glued to his door,

mist gathering over his eyes. I grab his wrist and pull him down the hallway with Malachi while the ghost of Vic's sick laughter bounces off the concrete walls against our backs. "Change is inevitable, kids. Better get used to it now."

The door slams, and we're left standing outside, looking in.

"To Live and Die in LA . . ." Zeke says, eyes red. "That was the plan."

I clench my fists until the knuckles crack. Our crew is not falling apart. Not like this, not on my watch, not ever.

We have to stop him.

"It still is."

TWO

"I feel like we should just stay in and play Catan tonight." Zeke's head hangs off the edge of the couch as he scrolls through the list of unwatched anime shows. We ended up at Malachi's house after spending the afternoon wandering around the block.

"Hell yeah, Imma come at y'all with the vengeance!" Malachi rushes to the bookshelf to remove the game box. He moves a little too eagerly, a little too desperate to cheer Zeke up after this afternoon, or at the very least distract him. "Y'all screwed me over blocking off all the wood last round. But I'm not gunna let the Longest Road slip away from me this time."

"We literally play board games every weekend. Can't we go to the block party?" I beg. Every summer during the week leading up to the Fourth of July, there's a steady stream of turnups across the surrounding neighborhoods. For the adults, it's a time to drink beer, get sloppy, and do the Electric Slide. For everyone our age, it's the perfect opportunity to hang out late, swapping fireworks and phone numbers beneath the hazy glow of half-busted streetlights. "We're not going to make any progress on"—I try to choose my words carefully—"Zeke's *situation* by staying home all night."

"I don't know, Rhea," Zeke says. "I don't feel like being around anyone but y'all." He selects our favorite episode of *Samurai Champloo* as background noise. "If I'm moving—"

"You're *not* moving!" I shout. Zeke's eyes go wide, startled by my lack of volume control. I take a breath and start over, more gently this time. "I'm not letting anybody separate us."

"Zeke, don't worry about Vic's punk ass," Malachi huffs. "You're not about to leave us right before sophomore year. No way in hell . . ." He starts pacing back and forth, throwing his hands in every which direction as he talks.

As much as he likes to dig at Zeke sometimes, they're brothers in a way that runs deeper than blood. At first glance, they're opposites: Malachi's this tall, wiry Black kid who's ten months into what we all assume is gonna be a massive growth spurt (his dad is six foot six). His primary passion is basketball (though he's real average at it), but watching cartoons is a close second. Zeke, on the other hand, is this averaged-height Salvi kid who'll always be averaged height, who only likes playing sports virtually and is all about sad music and sci-fi. But when you look closer, it's clear they're tight. Zeke has always been the most captive audience for every single one of Malachi's drawings, even the ones that are an "acquired taste." And when our classmates are shitty at school, I'll often come across the two of them in a corner with Malachi's hand on Zeke's shoulder as he whispers to him in a stern voice: *"You're a good fucking guy, Zeke, those other dudes are just jealous—you're a real man and they don't get to tell you otherwise. Nobody gets to tell you otherwise."* I can't imagine what one would do without the other.

Can't imagine what I'd do without them both here with me.

"I just want to stay in tonight," Zeke repeats quietly.

His baby face falls and casts a spell of depression around the room.

"I hear you, but we gotta make some moves," I beg. "There will be tons of people out tonight. I feel like we can maybe get some ideas. Or at the very least—" I want to say that if Zeke really does have to move at the end of the month, we might as well spend our time going out and making new cliché memories, but I can't bring myself to say it out loud. I open my mouth, but choke up and instead end up clearing my throat.

Zeke gives me a sympathetic frown and moves from the couch to hug me. "I get it," he says softly into the tangle of curls mangled into a ponytail at the base of my neck. Zeke always gets me, even when I can't get any words out. He pulls back, holding on to my shoulders at arm's length. "One hour," he says firmly.

"One hour." I break into a smile and watch a bit of lightness spread across his face too. "Aight, Bighead, get up. We're going," I call out to Malachi.

"If we're gunna go out, I need to wear a different pair." He points to his shoes, as if the need for a wardrobe change is obvious.

"Nuh-uh, you're gunna take too long," I say. Mind you, this boy has approximately fifty-two pairs of Air Jordan 1s that he stores in their original boxes.

"Matching the right A1s for the right occasion is an art. Like wine pairing. Real classy shit, which you wouldn't know anything about." There are few things that get Malachi more irritated than being asked to attend an event in what he considers the "wrong pair" for the occasion. I don't get it at all.

"Nigga, all your shoes are low-key the same, you're fine," I say.

"The same?!" he screeches.

"Oh my god, Rhea, why must you always do this?" Zeke rolls his eyes and grabs his keys.

I laugh to myself and walk toward Zeke, offering him my arm. "Shall we?"

"We shall," Zeke replies in a posh voice, daintily hooking his arm with mine as we stride out the door.

———

When we pull up to the block party, the scene's already lit. Food truck vendors line the street selling meals so fire that they'll make you weep when you have to look into your own pathetic fridge the next day. On one end of the block, there's a bounce house full of screaming kids and balloons. At the opposite end, a folding table with two mismatched speakers has been transformed into the DJ station. Girls in braids chase after little boys in white undershirts, zipping between clusters of parents throwing back red Solo cups. "Juicy Fruit" plays from the speakers, followed by banger after banger of Black barbecue classics.

There's no place like home.

We put our money together to snag an extra-large horchata to split three ways. The boys and I follow the signs toward the makeshift outdoor movie setup in the mini park off the main strip. *Friday* projects onto a large inflatable screen. Everyone's already seen it a million times, so the area's almost empty, with the exception of two couples making out on different sides of the row closest to the screen. Even in the dark, I can recognize one of the guys with some girl's ornate nails wrapped around the back of his head.

Diego.

I stomp past him, straight to the far back corner so that I don't have to look at him sucking someone else's face.

Malachi takes the foldable chair on the end of a row while I sit in the middle with Zeke on my left. We empty our pockets and distribute the bags of Sour Patch and Hot Cheetos that we had copped from 7-Eleven on the way over.

"You know why this is happening, right?" Zeke begins, and takes a sip of the horchata. "It's because of all the new coffee shops."

"And the frozen yogurt bars," Malachi adds.

"And the boutiques selling three-hundred-dollar jeans only available in tiny mannequin sizes," I groan.

"Like, what's the point of all these new stores if we can only afford to window-shop?" Zeke says as he passes me the Styrofoam cup. "They're pushing us out."

"I mean, I knew that vibes were changing, but I didn't know that it'd, like, really affect us, you know?" I admit. "Like, we've all *been here*. Our parents have *been here*. I didn't know that *here* could just stop being ours."

"We can't afford to pay more rent," Zeke sighs. "Mom can only work part-time and take care of Stella and Kiké." Lupe had Zeke pretty young, so she waited a while before having his little brother and sister—they'll be starting first grade this fall. "Her disability checks don't do much, and the EBT card never pays for a whole round of groceries anymore. She always has to use cash to cover the difference when we go to the store." The horchata makes it through the rotation back to Zeke, who takes an overly long sip. "We're totally fucked."

"What if we get jobs? Maybe we could pay for the rent increase?" Malachi suggests.

"We couldn't work that many hours even if we tried. There's, like, child labor laws for that," I say.

"Or you know that Lacy got the hookup with her fake ID. . . ." Malachi's big sister is a senior at our school, Bayrex Charter High, and is the quintessential LA Cool Girl: a baddie with a tiny tattoo behind her ear, never seen at a party without her edges laid and an immaculately rolled joint between her elegantly long fingers.

"That's adorable that you think you're slick enough to sell weed," I say, truly laughing at the thought of Malachi's loud mouth trying to be subtle about anything at all.

"Bruh, you're not about to start dealing for me. I appreciate the suggestion, but that's not you, man." The boys reach over my lap to exchange the signature dap-handshake that they made up in fourth grade. "And even then, Mom wouldn't accept our money."

"Could we find y'all another cheap apartment nearby?" Malachi asks.

"Doubt it," I say. My internet stalking skills are top-notch, but even I know that I can't get us out of this situation just by working some magic on Zillow. "The rent's rising everywhere, man."

"Plus, there are barely any wheelchair-friendly units in the first place," Zeke adds. "Mom says we're 'priced out' of the city. When people without money get evicted, there aren't a lot of new housing options. So, when we move—"

"Zeke, you're *not* moving. I told you to stop saying that shit." If I could, I would reach into Zeke's brain and rip the thought of defeat from the fabric of his mind. We can't start thinking like we've lost before we've even put up a fight.

"Fine. *If* we move, there's no chance we'd get to stay in the city, let alone the neighborhood, now that everything's gentrifying. Landlords all over are doing the same thing as Vic— kicking people out and raising rents like crazy. It's happening to shop owners too. Like Jugos Azteca. I'm sure that's why they bit it." Zeke kicks the chair in front of him in frustration. "White people didn't even *like it here*. How can they go from being afraid to even drive through South LA to wanting to open up açai bowl stands in less than one generation?"

"My grandma told me about the Rodney King uprising in the nineties and how white people were freaked *out*. Avoided these parts like the plague for years," Malachi offers.

Zeke presses his hands to his temples. "We shouldn't have to watch the hood burn to keep it as our home."

Burn, no. But maybe some heat could work in our favor. . . . White people round here still see the color of our skin and cross the street or call the cops—that's never changed. Racism is surely alive and well. The only difference is that now there's enough *other* white people around to make them feel "safe," which is why they're so obsessed with colonizing the neighborhood. It's crazy, I know, but maybe there's a way to work with their racism. To use it against them.

I just don't know how.

We all sit in silence and briefly tune in to the movie playing on-screen, which is somehow even funnier than I had remembered, but I can't laugh. It's like there's an emotional tapeworm in my stomach, leeching all the light out of me. I watch for a solid five minutes and get to the iconic scene where Ice Cube and Chris Tucker lean back in their chairs in unison, but still—no gas.

Plus, it doesn't help that I can still see Dumbass Diego with his tongue down that chick's throat.

I angrily chomp down on a Cheeto. "If they're gunna come to the movie to make out, then why would they pick the first row, where everyone can see them?" I kick my Converse up onto the dingy seat in front of me. It shudders and almost collapses beneath my heels. The thing is, Dumbass Diego was my first (and only) kiss. It happened last winter break behind the wall at the edge of the skate park and lasted only a second. It was okay, sweet even . . . until he went on to tell everyone that I touched his dick.

The worst part of it was that I actually liked Diego. Or at least I thought I did.

"That's probably what gets them off," Malachi says. He knows about the kiss and the rumor, obviously, but has always pretended that he doesn't. Never bringing it up—not even to joke about—was the nicest thing a friend could do given the circumstances.

"Gross." Zeke sticks his tongue out. "Hey, why do we bother getting three straws if we always forget which one is which?" Zeke picks a red straw at random for one last sip before passing Malachi the horchata.

"I bite mine, so I know which one is which," Malachi says confidently.

"We all bite ours," I say flatly.

Malachi brings the cup close to his face so that he can examine the three, equally crooked plastic tubes. "Hm."

We lean back in our chairs and let the stale evening air press down on us. Zeke closes his eyes, his hand still caked in the red dust of Hot Cheetos. Malachi makes strange faces of equal parts cringe and amusement at the events unfolding on-screen. I find myself staring at Dumbass Diego again and feel a knot form in my chest.

Diego's cute and all—I'll give him that. He has these dark eyes, and his hair operates within its own gravitational pull that creates this effortless swoop effect. But at the end of the day, he's a loser. Never in class, always on some wannabe hoodrat gangsta shit even though he dresses like a fake skater.

I crumple up the empty bag of Sour Patch with the intention to hurl it at Diego's stupid head when Malachi softly grasps my forearm. I jerk my arm to brush him off, but he doesn't budge. He adds a bit of pressure to his grip. "He's not worth it, Rhea."

I let the trash bomb drop to the floor. "Fine."

Malachi nods and turns back toward the screen but doesn't move his hand from my arm. I wait a few seconds, and then a few more, and still, he doesn't move. My brain launches into rapid-fire panic: *Did he forget to move his hand? Should I move myself?* But then the slight warmness of the touch settles in, and it feels . . . nice. Really nice.

Do I want him to move?

I can't hear the movie anymore over the sound of my heart pounding in my chest. I slowly reach my free hand into the front pocket of my hoodie and cross my fingers.

Please don't move.

Prior to this moment, Malachi and I rarely touched. I can count on one hand the amount of times that we have, and they were always by accident. Such abstinence can be traced back to the dawn of our relationship: schoolyards and hand- ball courts. Boys over here, girls over there. As members of a rare co-ed friend group, Malachi and I came close to blurring some of those lines but never crossed them. On the bus, our crew would race to grab the seats in the way, way back. A speed bump would send all of the kids flying into one another.

Everyone would laugh, but Malachi and I were always the quickest to sit up straight, readjust our seats. While I'd shove, wrestle, hug, ride, and give rides on Zeke's back, I don't remember ever doing those things with Malachi.

I look over at Zeke and see that his eyes are still closed. Watching him groggily rub his Cheeto-crusted fingers across his eyelids beneath the faint glow of the projector in the park where we've spent every summer together makes my throat go dry. Zeke's family may just be the first of us to go, or maybe not. Maybe Malachi and I will still get to grow up here, even without Zeke, but either way: the feeling of knowing that we all may disappear from this place, slowly and silently, produces a certain type of preemptive loneliness.

I inhale sharply to prevent the glossy film forming over my eyes from devolving into a full-blown cry.

And then I feel it again: Malachi gives me a firm, yet comforting squeeze that loosens up a few tears. I glance over at him to make sure that this is actually happening. He meets my eyes for just long enough for me to see that his right eyebrow is quivering. He's nervous too. I become acutely aware of every single muscle and movement in my body, fixing myself to sit as still as humanly possible. I feel Malachi do the same.

"Paletaaaaaa! Paleta de cocoooooo!" A lady pushing an ice cream cart tattooed with stickers emerges from the crowd about fifteen feet away.

Zeke bolts awake from his nap. Malachi swoops his hand away from my arm with the *quickness*.

"Oh, I need one of those!" Zeke says, jumping to his feet from the sheer excitement of the prospect of dessert. "You guys want one?"

Malachi and I both ask for mango, and Zeke runs off to

flag down the paletero. I don't know what to say to Malachi, so I don't say anything at all.

Once Zeke's out of earshot, Malachi turns to me. "We should hang out sometime. Just the two of us."

Deep inside my brain, a fire alarm goes off and I am internally screaming. "Without Zeke?"

"Yeah. Just me and you."

I plunge my hands into the pocket of my hoodie and rub the spot of skin where Malachi's hand had been. "We hang out alone sometimes."

"Yeah, but I don't mean at my house or something. Like we could go out . . . to a place. Together."

"To 'a place'?"

He inches closer. "You know what I mean, Rhea."

I avoid his eyes. "We can't do that."

"Why not?" His eyebrows tilt upward ever so slightly in the center of his face to form a curious, innocent expression. I inhale shakily, like I always do when he makes one of these little gestures that makes it feel like I have nothing to hide.

Sure, I may or may not have had a crush on Malachi at different points in our friendship (once in fifth grade, then again at the start of eighth grade), but I've always been smart enough to not let it become a full-blown thing. Plus, last year, he spent a solid five months texting Ahmara—who is undoubtably the hottest girl in our class with like one million LykLuv followers—after they disappeared together on a field trip at the art museum. Everyone at school made a big fucking hoopla about how "cute" they were together. He had told Zeke that nothing happened, but I'm not so sure. I still see Ahmara's name pop up on his phone every now and then.

"We've been friends forever," I mumble to the floor.

"So?"

I look up again, and he's staring right at me. We make the kind of sincere, prolonged eye contact that's also historically been outside of our comfort zone.

Maybe he's being genuine?

Or maybe this is just his way of coping with the thought that he may be losing another one of his best friends in a few weeks.

"It'd just be different, okay?" I say, suddenly frustrated. The crew's already in danger of breaking up. Why can't he see that now is *not* the time?

"What if I like 'different'?" He leans closer to me.

My stomach churns in a way that's distinctly not unpleasant. But still, with everything going on with Zeke . . . "What if I *don't*?"

Right on cue, Zeke comes rushing back with three pastel-colored popsicles. "She gave me three for the price of one because I'm bien lindo." Zeke raises his shoulder to pose like a Barbie and flashes a cartoonish smile. Leave it to junk food to fully transform his attitude.

"C'mon, let's go see if we know anyone here," I say to Zeke, extending my arm toward him. He takes it, and I rush off, watching Malachi's face twist in the corner of my eye as I do.

We pass by a group of smart-looking, vaguely grungy twentysomethings waving flyers and looking distinctly out of place. There are more septum piercings and fine-line forearm tattoos than I can count. They're all dressed differently, but in an unnervingly cohesive, crunchy-liberal unofficial uniform. What's more distinct than their Urban Outfitters–esque attire is the energy that they're all giving off. They're smiling at everyone, but there's a distance there. Something feels a little forced—effortful, even.

I watch my neighbor hurry past the group and accidentally brush the arm of one of the girls. The chick flinches dramatically and grabs her purse.

Ah, yes. There it is.

Despite their best efforts to appear otherwise, they're uncomfortable here. Uncomfortable among *us*.

A white guy wearing a Karl Marx shirt and Yeezy sneakers breaks from the cluster to shove a paper in my hand before I can protest. Zeke reads the flyer from over my shoulder. "Eviction Defense Lawyers Guild."

The Marx guy mistakes our hesitation as interest. "We heard about the evictions, and we want to organize you all!" he chirps. "We can coordinate the meetings with your landlords, lead the discussion, and facilitate it all. We can get you justice."

"Oh, dope," Zeke says optimistically. "So, y'all live around here?"

The Marx guy shifts his stance. "Well, no, we don't, but—"

"Do any of you live around here?" I motion to the other hipsters in the cluster.

"I came here for a sneaker drop once," offers one of the other white guys. He's wearing a denim jacket decorated with political pins. They all smile apologetically.

"Bet." I drop the flyer on the ground and tug Zeke's arm. "Let's go."

"They're trying to help, Rhea," Zeke says as we walk away. "Their energy is off, but they're trying."

"Maybe we should go back," Malachi suggests. "What if

that's our best option? We can take the middle road. Set a meeting with Vic or whatever."

God, they can be so naive. "As if Vic will listen to us out of the kindness of his heart? Please."

"Maybe the volunteers can help with that?" Zeke suggests.

"I don't trust them." There were some weird savior dynamics at play there that need to be unpacked.

"Ah, yes, let's not break character here—you never trust anyone," Malachi says. His eyes cut to mine with a severity that summons the echo of our earlier conversation about hanging out one-on-one. He shrugs, offering a half-assed smile as if to say that he's only teasing, but it still stings. I ignore the double meaning of his words and press on.

"Look, if we want justice, we have to take matters into our own hands."

Zeke laughs. "You sound like an evil villain right now. All you need is a mask."

"Not a villain," I correct. "More like . . . a vigilante."

"Oooooh, like Batman?" Zeke asks.

Malachi grins. "Or Deadpool."

"Or the Bride in *Kill Bill*," I add. If only we could just kung-fu fever-dream our way out of this eviction crisis.

"You know what, Rhea?" Zeke says, smiling. "I think I can fuck with that."

Me too. *Vigilante* has a nice ring to it.

We try to cut between a gap in the line for some blackened shrimp po' boys, but we're distracted by a sudden, dramatic change in the music. The early 2000s Usher jams that have been playing for the past ten minutes give way to quirky chill-wave beats. At first, I'm skeptical—it sort of sounds like lo-fi,

Soundcloud stoner shit, but then I listen harder and hear that there's a lot of soul in the bass line. And whoever's singing is Black. I scan the crowd looking for who the hell requested this song.

Zeke points over at a boy and girl dancing (floating?) alone in front of the makeshift DJ station.

"Who are *they*?"

THREE

The boy is moving wildly—sort of on beat, sort of not—but his eyes are closed as if he's totally lost in the music, despite the fact that he's wearing massive wireless headphones that cover his ears. The girl moves alongside him, drawing arches in the air with her arms. She's wearing a long, printed tank top dress over a fitted white T-shirt paired with chunky black leather shoes with yellow stitching. And, well . . . not gonna lie, she's beautiful.

"Damn." Both Zeke and Malachi watch in awe at the bizarre duo twirling while completely ignorant of the weird stares that they're getting from everyone.

"They look about our age," Zeke says. "Should we go talk to them?"

"No!" Malachi and I both shout. I know why I don't want to meet them: those two seem like a lot, and we don't have time for a distraction like this. But Malachi . . . I don't know why he's so pressed not to go over.

"C'mon, Rhea, you're the one who said that we should go out and meet people," Zeke says as he nuzzles against my shoulder.

"Yeah, but you know I didn't mean that. I hate people."

"I know, sweetie." Zeke pats my arm. "Let's go!" He charges forward as Malachi and I drag behind him.

The girl stops dancing as she sees us approach, but the boy with the headphones continues twirling in his own world, eyes closed. Zeke's gaze is fixed on the boy, but he directs his words to the girl. "Hey, I'm Zeke."

"Hello, Zeke," the girl responds in a raspy, jazz-singer-like voice. She outstretches her hand to shake his, which forces him to let go of my arm. The air feels cold where Zeke and I had been hooked together. "And you two?" she asks with a warm smile.

"Rhea," I say, and she instantly repeats my name back to me.

"Mal—" He chokes on his spit and coughs. "Malachi. Sorry."

"Malachi," she says softly. The girl says all our names three times to herself while we wait uncomfortably. "I'm going to speak your names a lot until I remember them."

"That's cool, I've heard of that before," Zeke says politely, even though that's probably a lie.

Two seconds into this interaction and I'm already over it. I've always been a low-key proponent of #NoNewFriends, but now more than ever, I'm 1,000 percent not tryna get close with these randos. Today's news means that it's time for us to fortify our friend group, not open it up to strays. I'm about to wrap it up, but Malachi nearly pounces to cut me off and keep the conversation going.

"Soooo, what's your name?" he asks with an undignified amount of enthusiasm.

"Oh! Sorry! I'm Marley." We wait for her to introduce the guy still dancing behind her, but she just stands there, grinning with her fingers intertwined at her stomach.

"And this is . . . ?" Zeke asks cautiously, finally acknowledging the dancing boy that he hasn't taken his eyes off of since we walked up.

"Oh, yes!" Marley spins around and waves her hands wildly in front of the boy's face to get his attention, but he doesn't seem to notice.

"Do you want to try tapping him?" I suggest.

"Oh, no, he doesn't like being touched unexpectedly," she says matter-of-factly. "HELLO, HELLO, SPACEMAN." She tries once again.

"Spaceman?" I hear Zeke say aloud to himself with a hint of curiosity in his voice. Zeke quickly smooths the creases of his goofy T-shirt with Captain Picard's face on it.

At last, the boy opens his eyes, stops dancing, and pushes one headphone aside. He looks at all of us down the line, starting with Malachi and ending with Zeke.

"What did you think of the new series?" he asks without hesitation, gesturing toward Zeke's *Star Trek* shirt.

"Fun and nostalgic, cool effects, but didn't come close to *Next Gen*. I still cried at the end, though."

"Word. I'm Lou," he says without a trace of a smile.

"Zeke."

"How do you spell that?"

"Umm . . . Z-E-K-E." The slightest blush forms across his cheeks.

"Is that short for something?"

"Yeah. Ezequiel."

"And do you have a middle name? What's your full name?"

Zeke looks over at me to see if I think this is as weird as he thinks it is. I give him an affirming look. *It is.*

"Ezequiel Reynaldo Guevara Saravia."

"That's a nice name."

Zeke shoves his hands into his pockets and shifts uncomfortably. "Uh, thank you."

"You're welcome," Lou replies.

We all stand in silence for a moment until Marley puts us out of our misery. "Lou, this is Rhea and Malachi," she says, motioning toward us to keep the conversation flowing.

"Nice to meet you," Lou says, though he doesn't even bother moving his head to acknowledge us. His eyes remain fixed on Zeke.

Whatever wavy song that Marley and Lou had requested finally ends. "La Chona" comes on, which causes everyone around us to lose their goddamn minds and squeal in delight as they rush to the dance floor.

"Let's get out of their way," I suggest as a curvy couple starts partner-dancing and bumps me with their hips. The five of us scramble away and take over an empty spot of grass several feet beyond the official boundary of the block party.

"Are you two twins?" I ask as we plop down onto the ground.

"Irish twins!" Marley says gleefully.

"Y'all are Irish?" Malachi asks, confused. Marley and Lou both have rich brown skin and wild curls. They don't necessarily scream St. Patrick's Day vibes to me.

"No, no." Marley laughs. "That's just an expression. We're siblings but were born only eleven months apart. I'm fifteen, he's sixteen. Our mom had Lou, then didn't wait long to get knocked up immediately after."

Zeke, Malachi, and I laugh cautiously in that way that you do when you just met someone and don't really have a sense of their humor yet, so it's unclear whether they're joking or not.

"We moved here two weeks ago," Lou says to Zeke, though Zeke didn't ask anything.

"Nice. What street?" Zeke replies.

"We're up the hill on Rimpau."

"Ohhhhhhh, you're *up there*?" I reply. *Up there* is where the bougie Black people live. It's five minutes away by bike— only two minutes by car—but sometimes, it feels very far. Most of the houses are pretty big, like big enough where movie studios film there. Malachi's sister, Lacy, and her crew hang out over there, but we never do.

Marley chuckles. "Haha, yeah, I get that it's known for being pretentious, but there's more diversity around there than you'd think."

I cross my arms. "I didn't say it was pretentious."

"You didn't have to." Marley gives me an extremely kind smile, but that doesn't stop me from feeling sort of called out. I recline back onto my elbows, facing away from her.

This girl's bullshit "Good Vibes Only" personality is enough to put me off immediately, but as I glance at her and her brother from the corner of my eye, I get why Zeke and Malachi are so curious. I can't lie—they do look sort of cool.

Marley's aesthetic is that of the leading lady in an early-2000s high school indie movie, and Lou's dressed like an urban samurai with an airy, olive-green, kimono-like jacket layered over a soft white tank and black linen pants. He's wearing those funky hiking sandals that usually make every-one look nerdy, but he can pull them off. Zeke, Malachi, and I, on the other hand, all look basic as hell: Malachi's always in some variation of the unofficial Black kid uniform with his

Jordans, basketball shorts, and either a jersey or athletic-brand muscle tank. Zeke's really settled into the average nerd aesthetic, which consists of ill-fitting jeans and bizarre graphic tees that he finds at Goodwill. And me, well, I don't think I have a style at all. Whatever you'd call a fifteen-year-old girl caught between various iterations of androgynous, bland clothes that don't draw too much attention to her body is where I stay. Messy nails, messy eyebrows, messy bun. Oversize T-shirts to hide my flat chest, baggy jeans to hide everything else. No turning heads around here.

There was a brief period when I was younger where I felt pretty, and then there was a period when I didn't consider my looks at all. But recently, it's like I can't even begin to think about my body because I don't know what clothes make me feel good anymore. You get to high school and everyone is expected to have some sort of style or aesthetic all figured out, but there's no guidance on how to get there. Especially when you don't have a mom or big sister willing to help. The fact that I haven't been able to find anything on my own leaves me wondering if I'm dumb or just boring.

"So how long have all of you known each other?" Marley asks. Her voice is how I imagine that my own voice sounds in my head—soft, melodic, and mature—but in reality (as I know from watching Zeke's LykLuv stories), I sound like a squawking bird with allergies.

"We've been friends for all our lives," Malachi offers eagerly. "Just friends. I mean, *best friends*." He forces out an awkward laugh to cover that Freudian slip.

Just friends? An hour ago, I didn't think that things between us were as simple as that anymore.

"That's really nice." Marley nods politely then tries to

steer the conversation in another direction, but Malachi cuts her off.

"Aight, I don't wanna be rude, but I have to ask. What's up with the headphones?" Malachi motions at Lou.

"Oh, they're not on," Lou says flatly. We all wait for him to continue, but he doesn't.

"That's good to know. . . ." Malachi continues. "But like, why are you wearing headphones out with a bunch of people?"

"I don't like loud noises. I wear them and use the noise-canceling whenever I know I'll be somewhere with lots of chaos. I can still hear everyone, it's just at a lower, more manageable volume."

"Cool, cool, cool . . ." Malachi says, absentmindedly pulling blades of grass from the ground one by one. A long, awkward silence settles between us, but it feels like Zeke, Malachi, and I are the only ones who notice how cringey it is. Marley and Lou exude zen energy, seemingly unbothered by the overly long lapse in conversation. I guess they're used to people looking at them funny. In a way, they seem more like pretty, bizarre aliens pretending to be teenagers than actual teenagers.

"There you are," a voice calls out from the crowd dancing to "Suavemente." The sea of trotting couples parts and Lupe emerges, rolling toward us with little Stella and Kiké by her side. I wave while Stella and Kiké sprint ahead and immediately jump all over Zeke and Malachi. Stella accidentally knees Zeke where it hurts, and he visibly winces but hugs her anyway.

When Lupe reaches us, Zeke's surprise is apparent. "Ma, what are you doing here?"

"We come every year!" She beams, motioning to the crowd dancing merengue behind her.

Zeke lowers his voice to a whisper. "After today, I wasn't sure that you'd be, uhm, up to it?" Zeke casts Malachi a knowing look. Malachi catches the hint and starts distracting Stella and Kiké with a game of slide. Lupe sighs and moves close so that the little ones can't hear her.

She cradles Zeke's face in her tan hands. "My answer still stands, mijo. I'm devastated, but we're not gone yet. Let's focus on the present. This is our home. And no matter what happens at the end of the month"—she pauses to draw a shaky inhale—"we'll still come visit every year."

Zeke shifts away from the new kids to hide his face. He shuts his eyes as his cheeks turn red from grief or anger or both. Lupe and I subtly shield Zeke as he has his moment before she turns to me. "Cuida a tu amigo, ¿de acuerdo?"

I nod, knowing that I'd do anything to look out for my best friend. Lupe pats our heads before she turns to the others to say the sweetest words in the English language: "I made flan."

She whips out a big-ass Tupperware container from the canvas bag hanging on the back of her wheelchair, instantly uplifting the mood in classic Lupe fashion. "I'm so sorry, I didn't know that you made new friends, I would've brought more!" She hands me three spoons, each one individually wrapped in a napkin.

Lupe has been urging us to go out and "expand our circle" for years now, so I can tell from the buzzing grin on her face that she's pretty damn excited. Back in the day, she and Zeke's dad were high school sweethearts, notorious for throwing insane parties. Random adults at gas stations still talk about some of the wild nights that they spent with the young Saravias whenever they see Zeke.

"I can get more spoons!" Lupe suggests enthusiastically.

"Nah, Mom, we're good. Thank you, though." Zeke gives her a look, silently pleading for her to play it cool.

"Okay, okay." She sits with her hands in her lap as Stella and Kiké continue using Malachi as a living jungle gym. "Entonces . . ." she says at last, signaling to Zeke that she's waiting for a proper introduction.

"Right. Ma, this is Marley and, uhm, Lou," Zeke stammers.

The siblings wave politely at Lupe, and she continues grinning like one of those excessively chipper weather correspondents on the morning news. I watch her look at Lou for an extra second, then back at Zeke fidgeting with the lid of the flan container. She waits for her son to return her stare, but he deliberately avoids her eyes, remaining glued down below. This makes her smile even harder.

"Okay, we'll let you all keep hanging out, then. Stella and Kiké, let's go." The kids whine but quickly fall in line behind Lupe. They got a lot of energy, but they sure as hell know better than to make their mom ask them to do anything twice.

"She seems nice," Marley chirps once Zeke's family is gone.

"Lupe's the best," I say. I've always felt somewhat possessive over the adults in our metaphorical village, but the way that Marley watches Lupe leave, like she's so excited to get to know her better, kicks my internal intruder alert into high gear.

"Wait till you try this flan, though. It's fire." Malachi snatches the container from Zeke and rips it open, passing Marley a spoon for her to take the first bite—an act of chivalry that I have never in my life seen this dude extend to anyone. Normally, he's the kind of guy who when sharing takes both the first bite and the last. Marley thanks him like he's some hero or whatever before he runs off to steal a utensil from a food truck for himself. Zeke gives one of the remaining spoons to Lou, while he and I share the final one. We all moan in pleasure as the silky-sweet glob of joy melts in our mouths. If they serve dessert in heaven, swear to god it's flan.

Marley drops her spoon, and it lands right in a mound of wet dirt. "Here, take mine," Malachi offers.

"Oh, no, it's okay. I've had enough. You guys are already super nice for sharing it with us to begin with."

"No, no, I insist."

Deep in my mind, I hear a record scratch like in old TV shows. Hold up. *Nigga, you "insist"?* Shocked at these new-found manners, I give him a look, but his eyes are elsewhere.

"You're so sweet." Marley leans over and hugs him. It happens so easily, so naturally.

"Yeah, no problem," Malachi says with a sheepish smile.

I stare at his hand, lounging comfortably on her back for a few seconds longer than necessary. It took Malachi and me *years* to break the touch barrier, and now here he is getting close to a girl that he *literally* just met.

There's a feeling in the pit of my stomach that I don't like. I check to see if Zeke's seeing what I'm seeing, but he's also distracted. He and Lou are playfully tapping their spoons against one another, fake-fighting for the last bite.

With Malachi and Marley locking eyes to my right, and Zeke and Lou forming inside jokes to my left, I have nowhere to look but up. Maybe the gentrifiers aren't the only ones that I need to worry about breaking up my friends.

My sulking is rudely interrupted by several loud booms ripping through the air.

BANG-BANG-BANG.

Lou quickly shoves his headphones back over his ears

while Marley ducks dramatically like it's World War III. It takes a second before she realizes that they're the only ones spooked.

I can't help but laugh at her. There's something so satisfying about seeing the prissy new girl mess up her hair while dropping to the grass. "Girl, it's just fireworks. Not gunshots."

Marley straightens back up, completely unembarrassed. "Wow, but they were so loud! Those can't be legal."

"Trust me, they're not," Zeke says with a smirk.

"Looks like I'm not the only one who got confused." Marley points over at a group of four white thirtysomethings scrambling to pick up the strewn contents of one the girls' purses. She must have dropped it all in shock.

"Oh, they *definitely* thought it was gunshots," Lou says.

"No way," Zeke says. "If they knew that it was even a possibility that they'd hear real gunshots around here, there's no way in hell that they'd have moved to South LA, let alone be out here at night."

"Real talk. Can you imagine how quickly they'd pack up their shit and get the fuck outta here?" Malachi, Zeke, and Marley all laugh heartily.

Holy shit. *That's it.* I can picture it clearly: Duos of young white women with quirky bumblebee tattoos and pre-distressed denim jackets hear shots. They pack up their collection of succulents and stockpiled boxes of LaCroix faster than you can say "home-brew kombucha." They email their landlords as they flee to the Westside, stating that they will no longer continue renting in a neighborhood with so much . . . *action*.

I shoot forward to sit upright and grab on to Zeke's hand

in the grass next to me. My cheeks strain from the intensity of my smile. *"Oh my god."*

"What? What?!" Zeke asks frantically, searching my face for an answer.

"You're not moving!" I sing-shout.

"You're supposed to be moving?" Lou asks with a frown. Zeke notices the disappointment on Lou's face and blushes.

"Zeke, I know how we're going to keep your family in the neighborhood." I'm shouting now, but I don't give a fuck. I get up and run toward the tree at the end of the street. "Marley and Lou, nice meeting you, but we gotta go."

"What? Noooo," Zeke whines.

"We have to *go*!!!" I jog backward, frantically beckoning the guys to come on.

Zeke relents, waves the fake twins goodbye, and hurries his pace. Malachi follows slowly, irritated that I made him get up. I get the sense that he's trying to look cool in front of Marley and Lou. *Stupid.*

"Rhea, what the hell are you talking about?" Zeke leans against a tree, slightly out of breath. I start pacing as we wait for Malachi to catch up.

"Vic the Landlord said that he had an investor lined up to renovate the place and upcharge the rent for gentrifiers, but *what if*—" I clap my hands above my head and let them fall behind my neck like an Olympian sprinter who just snagged gold. "*What if* we make it so that nobody new would *want* to move here? What if we could get his investors to pull out?!" I'm talking so fast that it's hard to speak clearly.

"Okay . . . and how do you expect us to do that?" Malachi asks warily.

I shoot my hand in the air like a gun and pull the fake

trigger right as a round of fireworks cracks violently above our heads. Everyone at the block party keeps sipping their drinks and doing the Cupid Shuffle like it's nothing, but across the street, a white guy drops his CBD-infused latte.

"We make it so that any outsiders would be *afraid* to move in." The boys meet me with blank stares. More fireworks burst above us and in the background the DJ plays an NWA song. I pull them into a huddle to whisper the Hail Mary:

"We start a gang."

FOUR

"Fuck outtaaa here!" Malachi laughs so hard that he buckles over, gripping his knees for balance as if he's going to topple over and/or barf from the sheer stupidity of my idea.

"Rhea, I honestly can't tell if you're serious or not." Zeke searches my face with a worried expression. "You good?" He reaches his hand out to touch my forehead, but I smack it away.

"Yes, I am fine, and yes, I am dead-ass serious." I cross my arms and wait for them to get it together. I don't need their instant validation to know that I'm onto something.

"By starting a gang, you mean like, starting a *gang*? Like Rollin 30s, or Avenues, or Bloods-like gang?" Zeke asks cautiously.

"Yes and no."

"*Phew*. Wow, that *sent* me." Malachi continues cackling. "Rhea, you gotta warn a nigga before you pull some funny shit like this." He grabs the side of his abs. "Oof, stomach cramp. Can't stop laughing." I kick the back of his knee so that he tumbles onto the ground.

"Look, we don't actually start a gang, we create *the illusion* of a gang." From the concerned look on Zeke's face, I can tell that he thinks I'm batshit crazy, but he loves me so he's trying to be nice. "Y'all were *just now* joking about how scared the gentrifiers would be if they heard real gunshots."

Zeke shakes his head. "Yeah, but—"

"Well, what if we made it seem to the outsiders—the ones who've never bothered to really get to know this place or their neighbors—like there's a new gang around? There's no way in hell that Vic's investors would still give him money to renovate and jack up rent if new people didn't wanna move here anymore."

Honestly, I've seen *The Wolf of Wall Street*, like, three times, so they can trust me on this. Supply and demand, baby.

Zeke scratches his head. "How would we even do that, though?"

I pause to rack my brain for inspiration before it hits me. "Remember that documentary we watched about that crazy frat boy who tricked all those rich people and celebrities to pay millions of dollars to attend this fake music festival in the Caribbean or whatever?"

"Hahaha, yeah, the one where that guy said he was ready to suck dick for some water," Malachi chimes in. He's still messing around, but at least he's listening.

I nod. "Well, we pretty much do what he did."

"And how exactly do you expect us to pull that off? That dude had, like, billions of dollars behind him," Zeke says.

"It wouldn't be that hard, it's all about manipulating social media. We roll out a three-prong approach—"

"Of course, you got a whole executive strategy in the works already," Malachi sighs.

"Boy, bye." I hold up my palm to his face. "Part One is 'Hype': We launch a social media campaign across all platforms. We'll start conversations on Quipp to get people talking and post the pictures on LykLuv. Get the gang trending. Part Two is . . ." I hesitate, struggling to bullshit on the fly as Malachi crosses his arms. "Part Two is . . ."

"Branding?" Zeke offers cautiously. Malachi gives him a side-eye as if to warn him to not encourage me.

"What?" Zeke shrugs. "I took the improv elective last semester, I know how to follow a 'Yes, and' plug."

"Perfect!" I continue. "Branding. Malachi can design a tag and plaster it around the neighborhood." He's done throwies before, so he's good with a spray can.

"Oooh, yeah, we can graffiti some of these bougie new businesses—but not in the cool *Fresh Prince of Bel Air* way that they'd probably love, more like in a creepy, haphazard style," Zeke adds excitedly.

"Exactly. That lets them know that the 'gang' isn't messing around, and that they are operating in their territory."

"So, then what's Part Three?" Malachi asks, uncrossing his arms, but still looking at me like I'm possessed.

"Credibility." I'm on a roll now. The gears are all clicking into place with satisfying rhythm. "We'll make some official-looking Public Safety Announcement posters, warning people of gang activity in the neighborhood, telling them to 'stay vigilant' or some shit like that. Zeke will put 'em up all over, including in and around all the apartment buildings, so that hopefully the investors—and any potential renters—will see it and get spooked."

I pause for dramatic effect and am pleased to realize that nobody's laughing anymore. "Guys, people are so fucking dumb," I continue. "They're not gonna try to open another shitty rosé bar or move into an apartment that costs thousands of dollars a month if they think that a legit gang is active in the neighborhood."

Zeke rubs a hand through his thick hair. "I don't know, Rhea. I mean, wouldn't we get caught?"

"We pull the strings but stay behind the curtains. We don't put a face to the gang. It's all super shady and ghostlike."

Malachi props his head up on his chin. "What if people think it's real and somebody gets hurt?"

Malachi can be such a downer. Obviously, I don't want anyone to get hurt. If we're doing this to protect Zeke, to protect our block and all the other blocks like ours, we can't leave anyone worse off. And we won't. It's all just harmless mind games—we're playing chess, not *Call of Duty*. Plus, whatever we do, we'll be careful. More than careful, we'll be meticulous.

Nobody will get hurt.

I say it aloud, so that it feels even more true: "Nobody will get hurt. The OG neighbors will know better. They won't care about stuff circulating online if there aren't any real drive-bys or bodies. They were here when things were different, and lots still have former and current gang members in their lives. They won't be fooled by our games. But the gentrifiers? They don't know any better. They'll fall for it easily."

"So, a fake gang?" Zeke asks, less apprehensive than before.

"Yeah. A fake gang." Saying the plan out loud sounds insane, but this crew, their families, our block, means everything to me. *Without them, I* . . . My chest constricts at the thought of losing everyone, blurring my gaze despite my efforts to hold my expression strong.

Zeke's silent as he leans against a tree with Malachi

seated on the grass next to him. Malachi shakes his head. "I feel like this is mad disrespectful to Dante's legacy. He got killed because this shit isn't fake, it's real."

Dante.

We fall silent.

There are three of us now, but there used to be four. Dante died when we were in fifth grade, but we don't talk about him much. Too hard. He caught a stray bullet when a fight broke out at a track meet at the rec center down the street. We were all there eating Popeyes underneath a makeshift canopy tent, but Dante had stepped away with his big brother. They were buying some elote, and Dante wanted to make sure that the dude put extra mayo because that's how he liked it. Anyway, *pop pop pop*—folks scattered, running everywhere, knocking over trash bins and coolers. Zeke, Malachi, and I were all good—got swooped up by Lacy and her best friend, Camesha. The girls grabbed us and ran so fast that the beads on the ends of their braids whipped us in the face with each step. Dante's brother was okay in the end—took one to the thigh, but Dante was real short for his age. The second shot hit his spleen.

He didn't have a chance.

When we were little, it wasn't Malachi or Zeke who approached me first—it was Dante. My earliest memory in life was at that day care, sitting beneath the slide. I was pulling apart the rubber floor of the playground when Dante joined me. He asked why I was alone and I told him that I didn't know. He said that it was okay that I didn't know, but if I wanted, I could sit with him at lunch. He held my arm, just like Zeke and I do now, as he led me to the table where I'd meet the people who'd become my best friends for life. There was a moment after Dante died when I thought our group would fall apart, but somehow, we didn't. Malachi made sure of it. We lost Dante in a way that none of us could have prevented, but now with Zeke, we actually have a chance at fighting to keep us together. It's only right that we take it.

"When we were kids, this block—" Malachi continues.

"That was a long time ago." I clear my throat and force the memories back down to where they don't hurt so much. "Things have changed. LAPD has pushed most of the gang activity either out east or farther south. And the way that this neighborhood is going . . ." I look over at the sign advertising a $40 bottomless-mimosa Fourth of July brunch at the French Bistro café across the intersection. "We might not be killed literally, but this shit's designed to erase us, so that we can't live. Not here at least."

"And that's assuming that our new neighbors don't call the cops on us for walking home with Skittles and Snapple, killing us in other ways," Zeke says.

"That part." I nod solemnly.

We listen to a car whizz by, saying nothing for a little while.

Malachi drags his hands across his head as if washing his face with air. "Nobody gets hurt?"

"We keep things surface-level and we keep it in the shadows of social media. Nobody gets hurt," I promise.

Malachi looks over at Zeke, who's tapping his finger to the beat of the song in the distance. "What are you thinking, man?"

"I think it's crazy, but fuck, man, it might work." His words gain momentum with each sentence. "If we can get the investors to pull out, that would at the very least buy my mom some time to figure shit out. Vic would probably rather have us living in the apartment paying rent while he scrambles to find another cash source than have the building sitting empty for potentially months on end. It's nuts, but I think it can work. And if not, at least we tried."

I look over at Malachi on the scratchy, drought-resistant grass.

"So . . . ?" I try one last time. A visceral flashback of the sensation of his arm against mine flushes through my body. I brush aside those feelings and meet his eyes. "You in or you out?"

He rolls up onto his feet. "I think it's problematic on multiple levels, and for the record, I'm not even sure that it will work." He sighs. "But it's not like I have any other ideas. If this is our only shot to keep this loser around . . ." He slaps Zeke's hand and pulls him in for a one-armed hug. "I'm in."

"AYEEE!" I jump up and down and break into a celebratory twerk alongside Zeke.

"Y'all are too much," Malachi says with a laugh.

Zeke and I are throwing it back, chanting, "We-ain't-goin'-any-where!" "He-ain't-goin'-any-where!"

"This will be fun," Zeke says.

And he's right. Schemes like this are always fun.

At first.

FIVE

My house is the one that real estate agents always drive by and leave postcards in our mailbox asking if we're ready to sell because it doesn't look like anyone really lives here. Our lawn is consistently dry and the wooden railing leading up to the front door has been broken since before I was born. The curtains are always drawn since none of us are ever home during the day long enough to bother opening them. Inside, a brown pleather sofa with cracks in the cushions takes up 90 percent of the living room space. The only pictures on the wall are of my half siblings wearing brightly colored windbreakers back in the '90s. They're way older now—like, tax-paying-adults-with-small-children-and-corporate-jobs older. Plus, they live in Bakersfield, so it's mostly me at home solo. My mom's out with my stepdad all the time trying to make the best out of Marriage Round Two, so things are pretty empty over there.

It's always quiet when I wake up.

When it's finally a socially acceptable hour to meet up with the guys the next morning, I practically sprint out the door.

"Is climate change getting worse or is it just me?" Malachi fans himself with his hands as we reach the park entrance.

Zeke dives headfirst to claim a spot of shade beneath one of the few trees surviving the drought.

It's the day before the Fourth of July and it's hot as fuck. I'm talking 'bout that hell-on-Earth hot that you only get after several days of consecutive heat piling on top of one another. That kind of hot where it feels like the sun is slurping out all the moisture from your skin like a juice box.

"Maybe if you asked your mom for a reusable water bottle instead of wasting a ton of plastic with your Gatorade addiction, the planet wouldn't be trying to vaporize us," Zeke says, glancing up from his phone.

"Blaming individual actors for global warming is how governments and corporations get away with polluting Earth with no consequence," Malachi says.

Zeke sucks his teeth. "Man, you just heard that on some podcast."

"So? It's true. I drink Gatorade—that doesn't make me a terrorist."

"Fair." Zeke leans back to wiggle himself into a bizarre shape so that he can hide in the shade of the nonsymmetrical tree above us.

"Yo, watch my stuff." Malachi drops his space-themed backpack in my lap. He trots over to the basketball court to join the girls and guys picking teams. He's tall, so he's always picked first, but he's pretty uncoordinated. They start playing, and Malachi immediately misses his first shot.

"He looks like if Bambi tried to ball," Zeke comments.

"All legs, no power," I say, rolling over to find a cool spot of grass.

"Should we talk gang business?"

I laugh hard. "Dude, as much as I love hearing you say

'gang business,' we gotta think of a more low-key code name to use in public."

"I know, I know. I kind of wanna name it something cute. Like a reference that only we would get."

"Zeke, we're not naming it after anything related to *Star Trek*."

"Hear me out! It all makes sense. Think of all of the themes of colonialism in *Trek* and how gentrification—"

I roll my eyes. "Hard no."

"You're no fun," Zeke whines, sticking his tongue out at me. From the court, we hear the sound of everyone hollering as some girl jukes out Malachi.

"Aight, what if we go nerdy, but not *that* nerdy. A political reference, like . . . wait, who did you do your POC Power Project on?" The POC Power Project was a big multimonth extravaganza put on by our history teacher last year. She turned class into this elaborate experience focused on people of color who've used their power to make the world better. It sounds corny, but given that we had spent the previous two years only studying crusty colonial history, we got pretty into it.

"Wow, *yes*. I did James Baldwin. A queer icon." Zeke draws the sign of the cross across his chest. " 'The Jimmys' sounds like a sex thing, though, and 'the Baldwins' sounds like a bunch of retired country club pervs."

I take off my sweatshirt and plop it on top of my head in a futile effort to create shade. "Wait, what was the name of that woman who Ebony did hers on? The Sister Insider lady?"

Zeke laughs. "Sister *Outsider*, you mean?"

"Yeah! *'Your silence will not protect you.'* That's a good quote right there." I don't remember much about Ebony's presentation, but I remember the feeling that I had when she read a selection of the author's writing. It was like listening to a new song for the first time and instinctually knowing that it would become one of your favorites.

"How about 'SO-SI'? Like Sister Outsider–Sister Insider." I play with how the name feels in my mouth. "The Sosi?"

Zeke shakes his head. "Los Sosi?"

Probably better to keep it simple. "How about just SOSI?"

Malachi jogs toward us, dripping with sweat. "Any updates?"

"Official gang name: SOSI," Zeke reports.

"Does that mean anything?" Malachi asks.

Zeke and I shrug. "Sort of."

"Lit." Malachi's never been one to get lost in the details of things. He does his handshake with Zeke and jumps back up to return to his game. He jogs back to the court, but turns around right before he hits the asphalt. "Ay, yo, Rhea!"

I look up.

"Next shot I make is for the Mastermind." He points at me before tossing the ball, wildly. He completely misses and hits nothing but air. Everyone on the court falls out laughing, including Malachi. He pulls it together enough to plant his hands on his knees, look up at me, and shrug in a way that says, "Welp, I tried." Malachi can be such a fool, but that's surely one thing I could never knock him for—the boy does try.

Zeke clears his throat. "Hey, have you ever thought about—"

I cut him off. "Back to planning." I don't know where he was going with that thought, but I don't want to find out. Zeke frowns, but I keep it pushing. "Now we just have to figure out the Hype part, and how to get the attention of the people who have influence. 'Cause once they post about SOSI, *boom.* We're solid," I say.

"Fine. But how can we do that without revealing who we are?" Zeke asks. "It's not like any of us have a lot of followers, and we can't ask Lacy and her friends to 'spread the news' or whatever."

Fair point. I bite my lip and lean back. I let the challenge sink in for a second before the ultimate idea strikes. "We should make a promo video!"

"Rhea, I don't know if that tracks well for, like, a gang."

"No, no, it's perfect." I scramble up onto my knees. "Remember how for that fake music festival they got all these models to appear in that insane clip to announce the event? We should do that. Something to put SOSI on the map." My mind starts racing on some Neo-in-*The-Matrix*-level shit. "The Fourth of July is tomorrow, so we do it then. Cop some fireworks, stage clips that look and sound like shots being fired, people running, whatever. We get that video circulating, and *that's* how we get SOSI trending."

"Yooo, that's brilliant." Zeke beams. "We can find fireworks at the Cookout tomorrow, but we'll need to have the tag ready, which means we should probably buy spray paint today."

"Bet." I pull out my phone and text Lacy for a ride. "She's down the street, so she'll be here in a few minutes," I report back. I glance over at the court and tune in to Malachi's game. "Wanna tell him it's time to go?"

"Nah, let him finish losing first." Zeke runs his hand through his long, dark hair, which he's been growing out all year in order to look more "mysterious."

"What'd you think of Marley and Lou last night?" he asks out of nowhere.

"Lou seems chill," I offer, sensing exactly why he's asking.

"Yeah, I thought so too. A little strange, but I don't know. . . ." Zeke tugs at a frayed piece of string hanging from his jeans that are way too heavy to be wearing in this weather. "He kind of has a Spock-like sex appeal to him. Serious, but clever. I'm into it."

"Jesus Christ, Zeke," I groan. "Promise me you won't ever tell him that."

He makes two "Live long and prosper" signs before smashing his hands together like they're scissoring. I nudge his shoulder and he topples over, cackling at his own horny joke. He pulls it together to ask, "And Marley?"

"Seems fine," I lie. I replayed in my head her lingering hug with Malachi at least forty times before bed last night.

"She and Malachi seemed to vibe," Zeke continues. I can feel him looking at me, but I pull out my phone to check my texts, even though I don't have any new ones.

Zeke catches the hint. "Lacy should be here any minute, we should get going." He calls out to Malachi right as he airballs.

Malachi jogs over wearing a corny smile so big, it's as if he didn't just completely bomb out there on the court. The blazing sun pours straight into his dark brown skin, giving him the glow of an onyx statue. He pulls up his shirt to wipe the sweat from his forehead. The gesture pulls my eyes to his abs, where they linger for a second. His request from the other night flashes back into my mind: *We should hang out, just the two of us.* . . . The breath in my chest flutters before a car horn yanks me back to reality. *Gotta stay focused*, I remind myself for the second time this week.

We reach the park entrance as Lacy pulls up in her Ford Taurus SE from the '80s with the extra seat in the front row between the driver and shotgun. "What happened? Is everyone okay?!" She searches our faces frantically as we hop in.

"We need a ride to the art store," I say as we slip into the back seat.

"Girl, you said it was an emergency!" Lacy puts on her hazard lights and turns around to flick me in the head.

"Thank-you-I-love-you-you're-my-favorite-fake-sister-ever-please-love-me-tooooo." Zeke and I blow a series of kisses at Lacy until she gives in to laughter.

Lacy is tall and lean, just like Malachi, just like their father. Sometimes, she looks so much like Malachi, it's freaky. Wide smiles, outstandingly clear skin, long lashes, and kind eyes. They'd look even more like twins if it weren't for the crooked purple scar that cuts through her left eyebrow. But even that scar—given how she got it—is yet another way that she and Malachi are bound together.

Malachi opens the door to shotgun, but Lacy pulls it shut. "Nuh-uh, you're riding in the back. I'm picking up Camesha."

"C'moooon," Malachi whines. "I need the legroom more than her."

"Be grateful I'm not making you walk."

Malachi gives up and folds into the backseat with me and Zeke. Lacy whips around fast, music blasting, while taking her turns a little too hard for someone with a car as ancient as hers. When we pull up in front of the Kernshaw Mall, I hear Camesha before I see her.

"Field triiiip!" Camesha claps excitedly as she trots toward the car. She runs a vlog called *BFT 4 U & Me*, which is about Black feminist theory and personal finances. Today, she's wearing one of the skintight baby tees with her brand's logo that she sells to her 300K+ followers. "The babes are all here!"

Given that Camesha and Lacy have been best friends since before Malachi and I were even born, she's been yet another pseudo-big sister to me since Day One. If Lacy is a warm mug of chamomile tea, then Camesha is an IV of Red Bull straight to your veins. She's loud, funny, and never without a story.

"Long time no see," I say once she buckles in, reaching forward to squeeze her shoulders as a substitute for a hug. "New bae?"

"You know me. *Always* a new bae." Camesha flashes a mischievous smile and rubs the fingers on one hand together. "This one wouldn't know about that life, though," she says, playfully nudging Lacy's shoulder.

Camesha's a year older than Lacy, so she already graduated from Bayrex Charter High, but chose an untraditional job. From what me and the boys gathered from eavesdropping, Camesha dates rich dudes for a living. One time, we overheard Lacy ask why she does it and Camesha's answer was crystal clear: "I've been dating goofy-ass niggas ever since I was fourteen, and I was doing that shit for *free*. At least now I'm being properly compensated for my time by men who see my value."

And from all the luxury vacation videos in Bali that I've seen on LykLuv recently, it looks like her value is expensive as fuck.

When we finally pull into the art store parking lot, the girls wait in the car to passionately debrief last night's episode of *Real Housewives of Atlanta* while we head inside. The store is one of those multilevel IKEA-esque shopping hellscapes where you have to walk down every aisle to get to where you want. An apathetic college-aged cashier gives us a half-assed greeting, but we ignore him. Better to not draw too much attention to ourselves.

"Here it is!" Zeke slides into the aisle. The soles of his shoes are so worn down that he glides across the linoleum floor, which makes the sneakerhead in Malachi cringe. He checks the bottom of his immaculate Jordans to remind himself that they're still in mint condition.

"Whoa, why is it locked?" Six shelves of spray paint tease us from behind a black metal cage.

"*California Penal Code 594.1 provides that no aerosol paint containers be sold to persons under eighteen years of age,*" I read aloud. I rattle the cage, but there's no use. "This is ridiculous. What's the worst that can happen if you let everyone buy spray paint?"

"Maybe a group of ambitious yet desperate young people will use it to graffiti the city as part of some crazy scheme to start a gang . . ." Malachi mumbles.

I roll my eyes and ignore him. I'm an expert at tuning out the haters when I'm focused. "Camesha is eighteen, isn't she?" I say to Zeke.

"Yes!" Zeke shuffles out of the aisle and returns a minute later with the girls by his side. They stop by the front desk to ask for assistance, but when the cashier guy sees me and Malachi waiting at the cage, he frowns.

"I'm going to have to check *everyone's* ID cards, you know that, right?"

"Why?" I bite.

"It's the law."

"C'mon. Don't be such a narc," Malachi begs.

"Yeah, dude, this big-ass company? They don't care about *you*," Camesha says. "You don't need to go all Justice League to protect their products." She leans in, riling herself up. "Like, do they pay you overtime? Do you get paid family leave? Do they even give you a 401(k) match?!"

The guy stares at her blankly and confirms that he, like the rest of us, has no idea what Camesha is talking about. "Look, I'm just not trying to get fired today," he says flatly. He backs away, keys jangling from the belt loop of his cargo pants.

Lacy turns to us. "I don't know what y'all are up to, but you're not getting arrested on my watch."

"It's nothing sketchy—" Malachi begins.

"Great. So, you'll give up, then?" Lacy has always tried to keep me and the guys out of trouble, *way* more so than anyone that I'm related to by blood. When she goes all Responsible Pseudo Guardian like this, it always reminds me of the track meet years ago. It's hard to know exactly how much danger we were in that day when the shots popped off, but I like to think that Lacy saved my life. She could've only swooped up her brother that day, but nah—she grabbed me too. I'll always owe her for that. So, when she furrows her brow at me, I hold my hands up in surrender. The last person that I want to worry is her. She props the door open for us as we head out, single file.

"What now?" Zeke asks when we're back in the parking lot.

"We have other options." I pull out my phone and search

How to Make Your Own Spray Paint. Everyone gathers around my shoulders and I press play on a video that promises to be easy. We all watch eagerly for a minute before it becomes abundantly clear that this, in fact, looks hard as hell.

"I don't know how a DIY video that involves a glue gun, a saw, and a pressure valve can be considered 'easy,'" Malachi groans. He reaches over to pause the video.

"Why do you need spray paint so bad?" Lacy asks.

"It's for a Fourth of July project," Zeke lies.

"Well, then ask Mom or Dad to get it for you," Lacy suggests to her brother.

Malachi grits his teeth. "It's not . . . that kind of project."

Lacy raises an eyebrow. "I thought it wasn't sketchy?"

"Wait—" I open the search engine again and type in something else. "Give me a minute."

Camesha and Lacy return to the air-conditioned refuge of the car while I walk across the row of empty spots next to us. Malachi peeks over my shoulder and lets out a choke-laugh-gasp. "You can't be serious!"

"Watch me." I finish the video with the sound on mute, shielding it from Zeke.

"What's happening?" Zeke jumps around trying to catch a glimpse of the screen.

Malachi shakes his head. "You know the government can, like, track this shit, right? You're probably on some *list* now."

"Let me see!" Zeke rips the phone from my hands. *"'How to Steal'?"* His mouth fully hangs open as I grab it back. "RHEAAAAAAAAA!"

"Hear me out." I point at the Walmart across the street. "Spray paint costs, like, four dollars max. This is a big-ass chain store, they make gazillions of dollars a year. I'm not going to hurt anybody. It's a victimless crime."

"It's *a crime*," Zeke corrects.

I sigh. "Yes, but it's worth it." I lean in. "*You're* worth it."

"Okay, butterflies aside from you professing your *obvious* undying love for me," Zeke begins. I can't help but laugh. "You're waaaay too amped about this, girl. Let's just ask Camesha to go across the street for us."

Valid point. I shrug off the little tinge of embarrassment and try to head back to the car, but I don't get far.

"Hey, Ms. Vigilante," Zeke says, plopping his hands onto my shoulders. "Ground Rules: I'm down for SOSI so long as it's *fake*. The minute the gang becomes real and we start breaking the law in a real way, we shut this shit down. Aight?"

I nod. He's being overly paranoid. I *got* this.

"I'm going to need a verbal response from you, ma'am."

"Fiiiine, yes. I understand."

"And you too," Zeke says, turning to Malachi. "Got it?"

"Chocolate Boy Scout's Honor," Malachi replies with a salute.

We walk back toward the car, the heat from the asphalt seeping through the soles of our shoes with each step. I hand Camesha $5 and she buys the spray paint across the street without a problem.

"Yo, can you drop us off on Rimpau?" Malachi asks Lacy once she starts the car.

Rimpau?

Malachi responds as if reading my mind. "Marley and Lou have a pool." His words are casual, but he avoids my glare like he's bracing for my reaction. "I told them we'd come over."

So, they're already texting each other. Great. "How'd you even get her number?"

"We followed each other on LykLuv. Then we got to talking—"

I grit my teeth. "Who messaged who first?" All eyes dart to me and I'm instantly mortified. "Actually, don't answer that. It doesn't matter." I pretend to not see the smirk on Lacy's face in the rearview window. "Why don't we go to your house? It's closer anyway."

Zeke shakes my shoulders. "Rhea, did you hear the man? They have a *pool*."

"So that's all it takes, huh?" I grumble.

"What do you mean?" Zeke asks.

I roll my eyes at how blind these guys can be. "All Marley and Lou have to do is flex their fancy house and they've practically bought you two. They're low-key just like the other people buying up the neighborhood."

"C'mon, it's not like that," Zeke says, exasperated.

"What makes them so different then, huh?"

"They're *trying*, Rhea," Malachi cuts in. "They're getting to know us. They're inviting us into their home. They're putting in effort. It's different, okay?"

The strained look on Zeke's face—and the sweat gathering on his forehead—makes it clear that he's not on my side.

"Look," Zeke pleads. "We got what we need today. We launch tonight. We stop by Marley and Lou's. A quick pit stop."

I don't see how our plan to keep our crew together involves opening it up to invasion by weird newcomers; however, I can't say no to Zeke. Not with everything he's going through and definitely not with that blindingly optimistic, cinnamon-roll smile that he's using on me right now. I swear, sometimes Zeke is so freaking cute, I could punch him in the face.

I bite my lip. "Fine."

Zeke erupts into cheers.

Off we go to the rich girl's mansion.

SIX

"Aight, losers, have fun," Lacy says as she lets us out. Her car is old as hell and can't handle the steep incline, so she drops us at the bottom of Marley and Lou's street. Before Malachi can fully jump out, Lacy grabs a handful of his shirt and pulls him close enough that she can plant a kiss on his cheek. He grimaces as he smears the Vaseline from his skin, but there's the faint trace of a smile underneath it all.

When the guys and I pull up to the house, we're gasping and out of breath from walking up the massive hill. "I wouldn't wanna live up here and have to climb a goddamn mountain every day to get home," I complain.

"If you could afford to live here, you'd have a car that can handle the hills, dumbass," Malachi says breathlessly as he rings the door.

"*Hellloooooooooo!*" a tall woman with a silver-streaked afro sings at us as she opens the door. "Zeke, Malachi, and Rhea!"

"Good guess," Zeke jokes, still panting.

"I was adequately prepared for your arrival," she says with a wink. "I'm Mom, known in some circles as Jennifer. Or Ms. Allen. Call me whatever you'd like."

I honestly hate it when adults do that—like either tell me

you want to be called by your first name (like Lupe) or make it clear that you want to go by your last (like Mr. and Mrs. Reed). Don't leave me here in the middle so that I'll feel compelled to not call you anything at all or just refer to you in relationship to your kids (like Marley and Lou's mom).

"They're out back in the pool house," Jennifer/Ms. Allen/ Marley and Lou's mom tells us as she hands us each a glass of ice-cold water.

Malachi and Zeke gulp it down dramatically as if they haven't drunk anything in years.

"Is there, like . . . cucumber in this?" Zeke asks, surprised, but intrigued.

"There sure is," she replies.

"Classy." Malachi smiles, impressed. Ms. Allen laughs— that same jazz-singer, raspy trill as Marley—and refills our cups.

The house is big, but not as big as I had imagined. I was expecting marble sculptures and fountains and gadgets every- where, but it actually looks like Malachi's house: Alvin Ailey posters, some African American art that I recognize from the Sunday street vendor in Leimert, and well-worn furni- ture that they clearly brought over from their old house. It's a bummer that it's all so . . . familiar. It would've been easier for the guys to understand that the fake twins aren't one of us if the house was more over-the-top. There will be other clues, though, I'm sure. Time will tell.

As we make our way into the backyard to the pool house, I feel both Malachi and Zeke straighten up next to me. I catch Malachi sniff his armpits to make sure he doesn't reek from playing ball earlier.

Zeke slides open the doors, and we're greeted by Marley

sitting on the floor with Lou crouched over, painting her nails. His are already done: neon green on one hand and a glittery black on the other.

"Hey! We're so happy that you made it." Marley beams a huge, pageant-queen smile. She tilts her neck, signaling for me to shut the door behind me. Cool AC settles around us.

Zeke and Malachi watch Lou delicately sprinkle each of Marley's fingers with what looks like fairy dust. "Do you guys want next?" she asks warmly.

"Nah," Malachi says, stifling a laugh.

"Um . . . no, thank you," Zeke responds. "Well, just not today."

Lou glances up from his craft to cast Zeke a crooked smile. I hadn't noticed his dimples last night. He looks different without the headphones too. He has a chiseled jawline and tiny freckles that run across his insanely symmetrical nose. His looks remind me of those international runway models—not at all soft like the boy bands that everyone's into these days, but strong with structural features that make you look twice and linger. I can see more clearly now why Zeke's oozing nervous energy.

"What are you watching?" Malachi asks as he makes himself comfortable on the couch in front of the television. Zeke and I take the two beanbags on the ground.

"It's a documentary about archaeology," Marley chirps.

"She's a real nerd about it. I suggest that you don't engage with her, or else we'll be here for hours," Lou says. He's noticeably more vocal today now that he's on his own turf at home.

"Oh, like Ancient Aliens?" I say.

"Sort of, but the Ancient Aliens theory is racist. Just

because white people couldn't build it, that doesn't mean that everyone else couldn't."

Zeke nudges my shoulder and whispers, "Sounds like some shit that you would say, huh?" I reposition myself farther away from him.

"Hm, I never thought of that," Malachi replies to Marley from the couch. "You're really smart, huh?"

The sexist undertones of his comment make me cringe. I feel like I'm watching a completely different version of him. It's like when your friend answers the phone and you witness how their voice completely changes for strangers. The disconnect here is real.

"I like to think so," Marley says with a grin.

My blood starts to pump so hard that I feel it in my ears. Sure, Malachi and Marley may have shared a dance floor meet-cute and a little-spoon moment last night, but I didn't expect for them to be out here charming each other in broad fucking daylight. I press down deeper into the beanbag, wishing that it could swallow me whole.

"So, what are your signs?" Marley asks with a disgustingly earnest smile.

It takes all my inner strength not to roll my eyes. Of course, this girl is one of those *OMG, what's your star sign?* chicks. Predictable.

"I think I'm a Cancer?" Zeke offers.

"Oooh, I love Cancers! I'm a Virgo. We're going to be very good friends."

Zeke crooks his head and smiles like he doesn't really know how to respond to such a forward declaration.

"Lou's a Scorpio, you know, which is interesting," Marley adds.

"What's interesting about that?" Malachi asks.

"Cancers and Scorpios are both water signs. Highly compatible."

"Easy, Marley," Lou warns his sister.

"Okay, okay!" She innocently puts her hands up in the air. "What about you, Malachi?"

"I don't know. My birthday's January third."

"Ah, a Capricorn! Fellow earth sign. You're very good at sticking to your promises."

"Also interesting, highly compatible . . ." Lou mumbles under his breath. Marley sort of twitches and keeps chatting immediately, seemingly trying to cover up Lou's comment.

"Rhea? What about you?"

"Aquarius," I say reluctantly, not excited to hear whatever she's about to say.

"Hmm, that makes sense." Marley makes eye contact with me for way longer than I'm comfortable with until I turn away.

"Your mom's real nice," Zeke says, shifting the conversation. "Is your dad home too?"

"Nope, just Mom." Marley raises her hands to the light to examine her new manicure.

"Our dad's the reason why we left Michigan," Lou says flatly.

"Oh. I'm sorry?" Zeke offers.

"I'm not." Lou screws the cap back onto the polish. "You guys hungry?" The way that Lou steers the conversation away from the personal is so slick, I can't help but feel a hint of respect. Over the years I've gotten real good at shutting down family questions too.

"I'm starving, I haven't eaten in a minute," I reply, just as eager to keep the conversation surface-level.

"How could you be starving if you ate a minute ago?" Lou asks earnestly.

"It's just an expression," Marley explains. "Sometimes when people say 'a minute,' they mean 'a long time.'"

Lou exhales. "That one doesn't make any sense at all," he mumbles, and pulls out his phone. From over his shoulder, I watch him add *"I haven't done X in a minute"* to an extremely long list of common phrases in his Notes app. "I'm autistic, so sometimes I miss figures of speech the first time around, but it's amusing to keep track of them. Most sayings are really weird if you think about it."

Across the room, Zeke catches Lou's eyes with a smile and nods.

"We can go to that new place? The one that does Taco Thursday?" Marley suggests as Lou finishes typing his note.

"What happened to Taco *Tuesday*?" Zeke asks.

Malachi laughs. "Yo, you know how on Tuesdays everyone goes to the birria truck or Taco Kell? So, that desperate new spot next to Genie Theatre that we tried that one time—the one where the fried fish joint used to be—is tryna do Taco Thursdays to get people to show up."

"I think they're trying to be ironic," Marley adds, as if this makes it sound any less obnoxious.

"White frat boys are *always* trying to be ironic," I groan. We've seen the owners of the new Mexican food restaurant around a lot since their grand opening this summer. It's hard to miss the duo of white guys walking down Kernshaw Blvd. wearing Mexican sarapes over salmon-colored shorts like they're straight out of both the pueblo and the Ivy League.

"I don't know, we're kinda broke," I point out.

"Everything is one dollar: tacos, chips, drinks, whatever," Marley says.

They should be giving it out for free. . . .

"I'm down," Lou says.

"Yes, me too. Yes." I can practically see the hearts in Zeke's eyes from here.

"Great!" Marley beams. "I'll go ask Mom if she can drop us off."

"What happened to getting in the pool . . . ?" I mumble under my breath to Zeke.

"Let's just try something new, okay?" He casts his eyes over toward Lou.

I ungracefully climb out of the death trap that is this bean-bag and follow everyone into Ms. Allen's car, where I get the treat of watching Malachi hold the door open for Marley. I take the way-back row of the SUV that's not even a real row because I'm squeezed in so tightly that I have no choice but to sit all scrunched up like a shriveled-up hobbit. Lou takes shotgun while Zeke, Malachi, and Marley pile into the middle row, laughing like they've been best friends on a TV sitcom for at least six seasons.

When we get dropped off, everyone jumps out, but they forget to pull the lever to free me from the prison of the backseat.

"Helloooo," I call out after them.

"Shit, sorry, Rhea! Forgot you were there." Zeke rushes back to release me while Malachi's laughing at something that Marley said that wasn't funny at all. By the time I clamber out from the back of the clown car, I'm absolutely over this shit.

The sight of the restaurant's new sign sets me over the

edge. "Colony Cantina" is spelled in large, iron letters against a dark wood backdrop that looks exactly like every other "elevated fast casual cuisine" (read: overpriced and underspiced) restaurant sprouting up around the city.

"Zeke, we really should go." I readjust the cluster of curls that had gotten caught on the car door during my ungraceful exit. "We still have to think of the tag design, print out the posters, get the firecrackers—"

"Sis, relax. We'll work on that stuff later."

"Later?" The Fourth of July is tomorrow, and that'll be our one shot to make the promo video without sounding any alarms. "It's not like we have a lot of time, dude."

"I know," Zeke says in a serious tone. "But I also need to make time for other stuff too." Several feet away, Lou sits down to reserve a table for us overlooking the street corner where we stand. "Thirty minutes, okay?"

"Fine." I roll my eyes and settle into my bad attitude.

We climb the stairs to Colony Cantina and open the door, our vaguely sweaty bodies welcoming the sweet sensation of chilled air. The temperature is so goddamn comfortable—the complete opposite of the dry, desert hellscape outside—I want to crumble facedown onto the tile floor to feel the coolness against my skin. I almost feel less pissed about the decision to come here, until I hear a nasally voice coming our way.

"Be-un-ven-eedo!" The dopey, ginger-blond dude who co-owns the restaurant barrels toward us. He's wearing a black baseball cap that says "Colony Cantina" in an arc with a tiny sombrero underneath it. He runs his hands up and over his head in the shape of a rainbow in a demented SpongeBob impersonation.

"I thought the internet decided that white dudes wearing sombreros isn't cool," Zeke says, glaring at the hat.

"It's not a sombrero, it's a picture of a sombrero."

"Ese pinche pendejo—" Zeke murmurs.

"Ceci n'est pas une pipe," I say.

"Wow, where did *you* learn that? So crazy!" The white dude beams at me with wide, condescending eyes like I'm a prize-winning poodle at the Westminster Dog Show. What kind of backwards-ass compliment was that supposed to be?

Malachi makes a contorted face like he caught a whiff of rotten eggs. "Aight, my guy, we're gunna order now." He pushes forward to the cash register and pulls out two dollar bills.

"Sure, sure. Hell yeah, brother." The white boy shuffles back behind the counter to take our order. I notice his name on the brass tag above his shirt pocket: Troy.

"I'll have chips and a horchata," Malachi orders. Troy rings up the total and says it's $2.29 with tax. "Fuck consumer tax, honestly." Malachi digs into his pocket to pull out two quarters. He pays and turns to join Lou at the table, but Troy calls him back.

"Don't forget your salsa, bro!" Troy flashes a giddy thumbs-up before sliding him a tiny bowl of soggy, unseasoned diced tomatoes and onions. Malachi looks back at us over his shoulder and shudders. I bite my lip to stifle a laugh.

When Zeke goes up to order next, Troy gives him a "special" greeting. "What can I get you, *compa*?" He leans in to overly emphasize his pathetic attempt at Spanish slang.

Zeke gazes back at the guy with a bored, blank expression. "You know what, *compa*," he says with some bite, "I'm good."

Zeke, Marley, Malachi, and I slide into the booth while

Lou sits in a chair that he pulled up on the edge. I try to make room for him, but he explains that the sensation of being accidentally brushed against makes him want to punch a hole in a wall. Probably best to not mess with that.

"White boy needs to chill the fuck out," Malachi says as he settles in.

"Dude, I don't think he can. I think he's just like that. A hardo to his core," Zeke says.

"Bruh, look at this dude." Malachi points his chin back toward the cash register, where Troy's leaning over the counter, head balanced on his chin like some bullshit philosophy major, tryna spit game at some girl way out of his league.

"This is legitimately too painful to watch." Zeke grabs Malachi's drink to take a sip. He immediately spits it right back into the cup.

"What the hell?!" Malachi shouts through uncontrollable laughter.

"Dude, that's straight-up *MILK*. Not even rice milk, just *milk*." Zeke's seething, but the rest of us can't stop laughing. Zeke uses a spoon to fish an ice cube out of my drink to wash out the taste of the "horchata." He bites the edge of a tortilla chip. "At least they didn't fuck these up." He sprinkles salt over the basket and tosses a few more in his mouth. A trashy country pop song about chugging margaritas plays over the speaker.

"I just can't believe it," Zeke says.

"Can't believe what?" Lou asks.

"This." Zeke waves his hands wildly over his head. A young blond woman sporting cornrows walks in with a stroller containing a small dog. Troy rushes around the counter to tuck a tiny Mexican flag napkin into its camouflage collar. They giggle as Troy takes a photo, probably for LykLuv. "My family is getting pushed out of our home . . . for this."

"Oh, I didn't realize—" Lou begins.

"Not for long," I interject. I grab Malachi's backpack and unzip the front pocket to pull out the Sharpie. I scratch "SOSI" onto the table and take a picture. I flash a smile at Zeke. "We start today."

"Start what?" Marley chirps in.

"Nothing," I bite.

In the corner of my eye, a graceful figure with long legs floats down the walkway right outside of the restaurant. Malachi sees her too, and leans over to bang on the window, startling the woman. She sees us and waves. I point to the front entrance and she nods. I jump out of the booth and run to meet her at the door.

"Hiiiii." I rush forward to give Auntie Inga a hug. "Where have you been? I haven't seen you in weeks." I squeeze her thin frame.

"Baby, I got promoted! You're looking at the new head nurse for the ICU department at UCLA Medical." Auntie spins around to model her dark blue scrubs embroidered with her name and new title right above the top left breast pocket where she sports her Black Trans Lives Matter button. At six foot three, she's the tallest woman I know, but also the most elegant, even in her hospital uniform.

"Ayyeeeee!!" I give her a high five.

"It's been a busy adjustment so far, but it'll calm down," Auntie says. "I'll have y'all over the next weekend I'm free."

"What are you doin' around here?" Malachi asks. He joins the circle to give Auntie a hug. "The food here *sucks.*"

"Y'all know I got no business in a place like this." Auntie

laughs. "I'm on my way back to the parking lot. I just dropped a new friend off at the clinic on the corner for therapy, but I wanted to walk them in since it's their first session. A neighbor connected us." Accompanying anyone who needs help to whatever service they might need is very on-brand for Auntie. I know she'd do the same for me.

Right as I'm enjoying catching up, Marley jumps in out of nowhere.

"Hey, sweetie," Auntie greets Marley, extending a hand, though Marley goes straight in for a hug. "Are you a friend of Rhea's?"

I open my mouth to say not really, but Marley speaks first. "Oh yes! We met yesterday, and she's been so nice. My brother and I just moved here from Michigan."

Ugh.

"You're kidding! I was born in Michigan," Auntie says excitedly, which I didn't know because, well, I never think to ask adults about whatever life they may have had before I knew them.

"That's wonderful. And whose aunt are you?" Marley chirps.

"All of theirs," she says fondly, waving her hands around the room. Zeke waves wildly from his spot at the table with Lou, and Auntie Inga blows him a kiss.

We pull Auntie over to our table, begging her to stay for a minute. She reaches out to shake hands with Lou, but he declines. "I'm sorry, it's great to meet you, but I don't like handshakes."

Malachi and I exchange a confused look, but Auntie's totally unfazed. "It's a beautiful thing to know your boundaries." She flashes Lou an understanding smile. He returns her grin, one bigger and less inhibited than I've ever seen on him before.

Auntie launches into a sort of Welcome Presentation for the fake twins. The only thing she's missing is a PowerPoint. She explains that she lives in the apartment complex right next door to Zeke's. "Anyone is welcome in my home anytime, at any hour, no questions asked," she assures.

"She really does mean that," Malachi adds. He doesn't say so, but he's referring to Camesha. I don't know the full details, but what I do know is that about eight years ago, something very bad happened to Camesha's mother, and Camesha was no longer allowed to live with her. At first, the foster agency dropped Camesha off with some creepy family out in the Valley, but that didn't last long. She went to two other homes after that, each for less than six months, before eventually ending up in a house right back in the neighborhood.

Her foster dad was very old and very absent, which Camesha didn't mind because by that point, Auntie had already unofficially taken her in. For years, Camesha would go over to her foster dad's house when she knew her case manager was coming for a visit, but almost exclusively lived in the spare bedroom of Auntie's apartment. Now that she's aged out of the system, she still lives with Auntie.

"I'm over there all the time too," Zeke pitches in. Zeke's lucky to have a great family, so he hangs out with Auntie for other reasons. Auntie's couch is always host to kids who need a safe place to crash. Some stay for just a night or two, while others stay for several months, but they all show up for the same reason: they came out to their families . . . but it didn't go well. Auntie lovingly refers to her open-door policy as carrying the torch of the trans women of color before her like Sylvia

Rivera and Marsha P. Johnson, who did something similar back in the '70s. She makes sure that we, and everyone who steps foot in her house, know this history of found family and community care. Anyway, it's almost as though Auntie knew Zeke was queer before he did; she had been giving him extra attention for as long as I can remember. She even made it a point to build trust with Lupe early on, somehow knowing that one day, Lupe would turn to her to have a hard conversation about letting go of the expectations she had for her oldest son.

"Well, it sounds like the community is lucky to have you," Marley says, her voice annoyingly sincere.

"Agreed," Lou adds.

Blegh. I can't stand their whole perfectly polite bit.

"Isn't this place cute? I love the decor," Marley says in an attempt to keep the conversation going.

Of course, she loves it in this tacky-ass gentrification hellhole. I can't stop myself from crouching over in sheer frustration. "You can't be serious—" But before I can fully lean into my hissy fit, I knock over my lemonade, accidentally sending the cup flying at Zeke and drenching his shirt.

"Shit!" I jump up to grab some napkins, even though there's no use. When the stain dries, it'll still be sticky and gross. Zeke glares at me with less patience than usual. I try to convey my innocence through my eyes, but he doesn't buy it. Everyone wipes the juice off the tabletop and trays. "I'm sorry. . . . It was an accident."

"I know, baby. It's all good," Auntie says in her signature comforting tone.

There aren't any napkins left, so I'm just sitting here, like an asshole, doing absolutely nothing.

"I should get home and change," Zeke announces as he

stands to wring out the bottom of his shirt. Auntie goes to bring the car around front while Lou asks the front register for wet paper towels.

"Zeke—" I begin. I bet he thinks I did this on purpose to create an exit.

"We're going home, okay? You win. We're leaving." The last time that I heard this much frustration in his voice directed toward me was when I spoiled the end of *Attack on Titan* for him. This time, though, feels worse. I fall back to give him some space.

Malachi immediately strolls up next to me. "You're being rude to Marley," he says quietly. "Tone it down."

My face heats up. The only thing that pisses me off more than Malachi being all chivalrous with Marley is Malachi having the nerve to complain that *I'm* not holding open doors for her to parade into my world. "Well, you're being thirsty," I clap back. "You can tone it down too."

"Rhea, c'mon, I—"

I ignore him and stomp down the stairs like a brat, but whatever. I start picking at the leaves of plants lining the walkway as we wait for Auntie's silver Ford Exhibition to roll up. I feel Marley approaching me from behind, but I don't turn around.

"I know it was an accident," she says softly. I stay facing the wall, pulling apart a tiny flower to examine the seams. "I'm really clumsy too, you know. Just wait, you'll see me make a huge mess soon."

As if waltzing into my goddamn friend group isn't already showing the signs of a clear mess ahead.

Auntie honks her horn, so I brush past Marley without a word.

This time, I claim shotgun and let Marley and Malachi squeeze into the way-back row so that Zeke and Lou can sit in the middle row with some space. At least Marley isn't back there alone, so nobody will forget to let her out.

When Auntie pulls into the shared driveway between her and Zeke's apartment buildings, Malachi, Zeke, and I climb out, but Marley and Lou stay back.

"What? You're not coming?" Zeke asks, the disappointment in his voice apparent.

"We should head home," Marley says.

"I'll see you tomorrow, though, right?" Lou asks, leaning out the backseat window.

Zeke blushes a bit and runs his fingers through his hair. "Yeah, tomorrow. Definitely." Lou points at Zeke's phone and motions for him to come closer. Zeke passes the phone and Lou enters his number. Lou smiles, then Auntie turns back on the engine. They drive off, turn the corner, and disappear.

Zeke looks at his phone and laughs.

"What's so funny?" I come up behind his shoulder to peek.

In his contact, Lou put his name, followed by every single flower emoji. Zeke digs into his pocket and pulls out a little cluster of flowers tied together at the stems to show me and Malachi. I recognize them from the bushes back at the restaurant. Zeke chuckles to himself and returns the bundle to his pocket. "Aight, let me get outta this gross shirt and we'll get to work."

We start walking down the driveway to Zeke's apartment door, adorned with a cross that his mother made in a pottery class with her book club when we hear him.

"We're going to make a l-o-o-o-o-o-t of money, my friend! Call me!" We whip around and watch Vic the Landlord wave

his sunburned-pink hand in the air at a Tesla driving away from Auntie's apartment.

"Looks like somebody's desperate," Malachi teases.

Vic notices us and rolls his eyes. "I don't need this from you today."

"Who was that?" Zeke asks.

"A business associate," Vic says, looking down to send a text.

"You hear about the new gang on the block?" I say with a smirk. "I don't think y'all can trick a bunch of latte lovers to move here once they catch wind of how shit's popping off."

"What the hell do you mean by that?" Vic growls, furrowing his sweaty brow. We shrug and turn back toward Zeke's door. "You better not be up to anything, I swear to fucking god. . . ." Vic trembles with anger like he's about to blow up right as a young-ish white couple pushing a baby stroller comes walking down the sidewalk.

Perfect timing.

I place both of my hands over my heart and channel my inner Hollywood. "As a landlord, it is your duty to protect your residents from the troubling increase in gang-related violent activity on this block. If one of your tenants gets killed by a stray bullet because you didn't want to increase your security measures, blood will be on *your* hands!" I shout in my most tragic, damsel-in-distress voice. The couple with the stroller hears us and picks up their pace to a near sprint. Vic waves at them, but they don't wave back.

"I don't know what you're talking about, but you better keep that shit to yourself," Vic threatens in a low voice.

"If you haven't heard yet, you'll hear about it sooooon," Malachi sings.

Zeke fiddles with the keys and we hear Vic grumbling into his phone as he stomps away. "Hello? What do you know about this new gang in the neighborhood? . . . Yes, I said gang. Find out everything you can and let's move our meeting up to tomorrow. . . . Okay fine, enjoy the Fourth with your family, whatever. Let's meet Monday, though. . . ."

"Well, there's no turning back now," Zeke says. He uses one arm to hook with mine and the other to do his handshake with Malachi. I glance at Malachi, but we don't really acknowledge each other.

At least something went right: SOSI is officially in motion.

SEVEN

I push open the door to Malachi's bedroom and see him in his natural element: crouched over his desk decorated with empty bags of jalapeño chips and inky-black fountain pens. The Fourth of July Cookout has already started, but we still have SOSI prep to do before heading out.

My phone vibrates with a text from Zeke: *Runnin' some errands. Be there in 10.*

I hit him with a thumbs-up, but wish he'd get here sooner. Malachi's working on the SOSI tag, but we haven't been alone together since the block party, and well, I don't know what to do with him. We've gotten on each other's nerves before, but this is different. Even the air feels awkward.

Malachi rips out a sheet from his sketch pad. "What do you think of this?" He holds up a drawing of tic-tac-toe with S-O-S running on a diagonal and a line through it.

I tilt my head sideways. "Is the line supposed to be the 'I'?"

"Yup. It's a stretch, but the graphic is recognizable and super easy to throw up."

It's not perfect, but I see his point. "It will do."

Malachi reaches out for a high five, which I reluctantly

return. "Let me add this onto the PSA posters and we're good." Malachi takes a picture and sends it to his laptop. He cuts and pastes the tag into a square beside the warning: *"Please be aware of the following symbol, which is the emblem of the SOSI gang."*

"We should list a phone number for people to call in tips and stuff," I say in an attempt to fill the silence more so than to be helpful. "People will be paranoid if they know that there's a hotline to feed their anxiety."

"Cops can trace numbers," he replies without looking up from his laptop. "I already told Zeke to stop by the library to make a burner email on his way over. Better to do that stuff on public computers, you know?" He adds the email address to the flyer.

I spot a tiny pile of half-drawn birthday cards in the recycling bin by his desk. It was Zeke's birthday last month, so these must've been the draft cards that didn't make the cut. Ever since we were kids, Malachi has always made Zeke and me handmade cards for every birthday. One year he drew this incredible zombie apocalypse scene for Zeke. Another year for me, he drew the desert landscape from one of my favorite books, *Dune*. The movie hadn't come out yet, so Malachi read the book to figure out how to imagine the details just right. I know he makes cards for both me and Zeke, but I can't help but notice that the ones he makes for me seem particularly intricate. I almost crack a smile before it occurs to me that he'll probably be making one for Marley now too.

Malachi puts the finishing details on the flyer and clicks print. Five copies slowly *put-put-put* out of the machine before he breaks the silence. "You okay?"

I avoid his eyes, pretending to study the *Boondocks* poster on his wall that I've seen a million times. "Yeah, why?" I shoot back, a little too spastically.

"Just checking in, I guess." He twirls a pen between his fingers and waits for me to respond.

I don't.

He presses again. "So, there's nothing you want to, uhm, talk about?"

"No," I lie. There's a certain kind of loneliness when you're in a room with someone you care for but cannot communicate with, even if it's self-imposed. "Is there something *you* want to talk about?" I cross my arms and stare him down, trying to intimidate him, though I don't know why.

This is my chance. Malachi is sitting here, *trying to clear the air*, but rather than feeling grateful for this newfound sense of maturity in him, I just feel—I don't know—pissed, to be honest. One minute he's suggesting to make everything messy with me, then the next he's all over the new girl. Plus, he has the nerve to pull this shit when what we really need to focus on is SOSI. I give him a sarcastic shrug that borders on rude and turn my back to him, closing the door on whatever conversation could have taken place.

"Aight, cool . . ." he mumbles, tapping the pen against his desk.

"Cool," I huff.

We both check our phones. No messages on my end, but Malachi smiles at his screen. He starts to type something, erases it, then tries again. He sends off this carefully constructed message, and I don't even have to guess who it's for.

Eventually, the doorbell rings. I hang back and let him

answer it. I listen to the voices move down the hallway as I wait on the edge of his bed, unable to get comfortable.

"Thank god," I mumble as Zeke enters wearing a bright peach shirt with a yellow star on it. It's one of his favorites—a treasured cosplay item for when he dresses up as Steven Universe at costume parties and nerd conventions.

"*Happy Fourth of July, my fellow Americans!*" He bows to Malachi's messy bedroom with his arms outstretched. Malachi and I stare at him blankly. "Just kidding, ya filthy animals. Fuck the founding fathers! Black lives matter! Chinga la migra!"

"That's what's up." Malachi gives Zeke dap before pulling one of the flyers out from the printer. "What do ya think of these?"

"I . . ." Zeke holds both ends of the paper and brings it very close to his face. "Love it!" He throws the page into the air, spins, and plops down on the bed.

"Someone's real peppy today." I nudge him to make room for me to lie down with him.

"What can I say? I'm in a good mood." Zeke raises his arms to stretch in place. He's like an old man, always proclaiming that he needs to stretch out his back.

Malachi tosses one of the crinkled chip bags at Zeke's chest. "So, what were these mysterious errands that you were running this morning?"

"Ah yes, check this out." Zeke shoots up to grab his drawstring backpack from the floor. He reaches in and pulls out a tiny white box.

"Yo, is that *Apple*?" Malachi asks in total disbelief. Everyone and their mama may have snagged an iPhone during a Boost Mobile holiday sale, but having a MacBook or any additional Mac products or accessories—that's some next-level shit.

"Noise-canceling earbuds," Zeke says proudly.

"Bruh, if you can afford these then we don't need to be trying so hard to keep you in the neighborhood. You're gucci." Malachi snatches the box from Zeke's hand to get a closer look.

"My cousin at the mall got the hookup. He still owed me from last month when I stayed up talking to our abuela for like three hours to distract her while he snuck out to go mess around with that chick on student council. I went by the food court to see if anyone's hiring for a summer gig, but everyone told me to come back next year when I'm sixteen. Decided to cash in on the favor from mi primo while I was there."

"Aren't you more of a speakers guy, though?" I ask.

"I am, but these aren't for me." Zeke wrestles the box away from Malachi. "They're for Lou."

Lou? I look over at Malachi and see that he's also putting on an unnaturally broad smile.

Here's the thing about Zeke: when he has a crush, he tends to come on a bit . . . strong. For anyone this would be an embarrassing habit, but for Zeke, there's an added layer. Like back in sixth grade, he was really into this guy Theo Benton (*everyone* was into Theo Benton). It wasn't like Zeke was expecting anything to happen, but in English class he wrote a poem that was obviously about Theo (he was the only boy with dimples, braces, and "shimmers of blond within his thick, brown curls"). The teacher thought it was so goddamn magical that she read it aloud, anonymously, but at the end, accidentally put it right back on Zeke's desk, so everyone knew that he had written it.

As you can imagine, this didn't really make the rest of sixth grade easy for Zeke.

Malachi's signaling me to say something, but I'm not tryna be the bad guy today. I jerk my head. This time is on him.

In a total punk-ass move, Malachi sits back down in his chair and literally spins around to avoid responsibility. I sigh and ask Zeke if I can see the box, which he passes me gladly.

I tread carefully. "This is a big gift for a new friend. You don't think it's a little—"

"Forward?" Zeke fills in.

"I mean, yeah, but also intense?" I wince a little when the words come out, hoping that I'm not going to be the one to hurt his feelings.

"I don't think so. We've been texting nonstop since yesterday."

"Yeah, that's great, but do you know for sure that he's . . . Damn, I don't know. Are you sure it's not a friend vibe?"

Zeke sighs. "Rhea, he paints his nails."

"Yeah, and so does Diego and like every e-boy on the internet."

"I know that we haven't known him long, but I'm sure he likes me." The sight of Zeke standing there in his pink shirt all excited holding this expensive gift for a boy who he just met is simultaneously the cutest and most nerve-racking thing I've ever seen. I've always envied Zeke's emotional vulnerability, but I also see it as my job as the practical friend to remind him to protect his heart.

"Malachi?" I force him to swivel around in his chair.

"Well . . ." he begins in a real serious voice, but then Zeke smiles this optimistic smile filled with so much sunshine that it hurts to see. "If Zeke wants to shoot his shot, then fuck it—go for it, man."

I massage the sides of my head and give Malachi a dirty look as he high-fives Zeke. Malachi mouths an apology, and I give up.

"Great, let's go!" Zeke spins and leads the way out the door.

Malachi grabs his galaxy JanSport and swings it over his back, flipping off the light switch before I have time to finish putting on my shoes.

"Hey! Still in here," I call out.

With Zeke still heading outside, Malachi doubles back to his room and peeks his head through the door. "Sorry," he says mischievously.

"No, you're not," I huff, tucking the extra length of my shoelaces up and over the sides.

"You're right. I'm not." He teases his finger over the light switch, flips it on and off again, then runs to catch up with Zeke. It's a playful moment, but I frown anyway. Why can't I stop acting weird and just move on like him?

By the time I meet the guys out front, Malachi is already back after having run around the corner to tag the SOSI symbol all over the alley. I decide that Malachi will be the first to post. It's on the back of his house, so there's a non-suspicious explanation for him noticing it. He records a simple video of him zooming in and out of the logo. Caption: *"Y'all seen this SOSI shit? Ppl really out here tryna bang smh."* Send.

Zeke smacks a couple of flyers against the jagged wood of the power line post on the street corner. I pull off a strip of duct tape and sandwich the flyers together so that they surround the pole: *"PSA: Beware of Rise in Gang Activity in the Neighborhood. Report tips to and share concerns at: antigangtaskforce@community.com."*

Zeke does a little chef's kiss in the air. "This is art."

EIGHT

There's no need to wonder about finding the Cookout; we can already hear and smell it from several blocks away. A wave of pulsating energy hits—that feeling when you know that people are dancing nearby—and my pace quickens. We turn a corner and end up on a street lined with art vendors and food stalls. The sound of African drums reverberates through the air and mixes with the smell of curry, empanadas, and baked sweet potatoes. Most of the shops are adorned with kente cloths or flags from island countries in the Caribbean between tiny swatches of red, white, and blue. Within a single city block, there are more intricate styles of braids woven through melanin-rich women's heads than there are stars in our flag. And it's all so beautiful.

"Yo, what do you think they're up to?" Zeke points at a cluster of three people handing out flyers in front of the kids' face-painting station. I recognize one of the women from the grocery store, but I can't quite place the other two.

Malachi bends down to swipe up one of the discarded flyers from the floor. "It's for a community meeting," he reads. "About the evictions."

Zeke grabs the flyer from Malachi to take a closer look.

"The address is for the building next door to mine. Auntie must be hosting it."

"Makes sense." I'd honestly be surprised if Auntie Inga wasn't trying to help the people in Zeke's building out. Auntie lets us care for her when she needs it, like when she twisted her ankle and we coordinated round-the-clock food drop-offs, but she's typically *too* good at lending a hand to others. For her birthday every year, the neighbors have to form James Bond–level espionage and top secret planning committees just to successfully surprise her so that she can actually receive all the love from us without offering to help with this or that.

"Think they have a shot?" Malachi asks.

"I don't know about them, but I know we do." I grab Zeke's arm and give him a wink. "Once we cop these firecrackers tonight, it's game over for Vic."

A short woman with a fire-red wig calls Malachi's name, so he spins off to say hello while Zeke and I begin an ocular pat-down of the food situation.

"Ohmigod, Mean Oxtail Lady is here!" Zeke squeals.

Ah, yes—the elusive owner of Ackee Rainbow. The Jamaican restaurant is literally never open, and when it is, the owner has the biggest attitude when she takes your order, like *you're* the one interrupting *her* day. But goddamn, does she make the best jerk sauce in the city. "What an honor it will be to receive her shade on this national holiday," I say, praise hands raised high. We attempt to hop in line but are instantly intercepted.

"Hey, nena, looking cute today." Dumbass Diego winks at me and licks his lips like the creepy dudes who hang out in the 7-Eleven parking lot.

My skin crawls. "Don't call me that."

Diego smirks as he leans on his skateboard like a cane. He's wearing a large black tee with a logo of some metal band that he probably doesn't even listen to layered over a striped long-sleeved shirt. His dark hair artfully swoops out from underneath a beanie despite the fact that it's eighty-five degrees. I can't believe that this was my "type" for all of last year.

"I see your boyfriend here, but where's his boyfriend?" He points his chin at Zeke and scans the crowd behind us.

"Diego, just . . . shut up," I say. I hate it when I can't think of a comeback. Zeke's pretending that his attention is occupied by something off in the distance, but I know that he heard Diego and that it stung.

"Yo, sorry, I ran into my mom's friend Leena and you know how it goes once she starts—" Malachi reappears at Zeke's side and his face falls.

"'Sup, man?" Diego places the silver chain around his neck between his teeth and smiles condescendingly at Malachi.

"'Sup." Malachi's voice is completely flat. He's not even trying to play nice.

"What are y'all getting into tonight? You're not going to keep Rhea here all to yourselves, will you?"

"I'm a human being. Not some toy, asshole," I say with spite.

"Not a toy, but it's about time that you and I play with each other again, isn't it?"

Zeke steps in front of me, strengthening his hold on my arm to prevent me from launching at Diego and beating his ass.

Diego's laughter brims with smugness. "C'mon, nena, you'll be back for more eventually. Might as well dump these losers and make me your summer fling."

This time, it's Malachi who takes a step forward. It's been a while since I've seen the two of them stand anywhere near one another, which makes me realize how much taller Malachi has gotten in the past few months. He now towers over Diego. I'm not sure who would win in a fight. Either way, I don't want to find out.

"Bruh, are you and your wannabe K-pop hair done?" Malachi barks.

"With her, no. But I got something to talk to you about." Diego looks Malachi up and down. "Take a walk with me."

Malachi rolls his eyes. "And why the hell would I do that?"

"Because maybe I got something important to share." An unsettling smirk unrolls across Diego's face like a red carpet lining the path to hell. "And maybe you want to find out."

Zeke and I exchange a worried look. Malachi's always been curious. Maybe too much so.

Malachi turns to me with a question behind his eyes, hesitating to see if I'll stop him. But from the way he's leaning toward Diego, it looks to me like he's already made up his mind. Fraternizing with the enemy. *Classic.* What else would I expect from him after the way he's been cozying up to the fake twins all week?

I cross my arms. "Whatever, dude. You do you."

Malachi frowns. He follows Diego behind one of the food stalls. "I'll be right back," he says as he tucks into the shadows.

"What the fuck is that about?" Zeke asks me once they're gone.

"I have absolutely no idea."

Zeke lets go of my arm and turns to face me, grabbing both of my hands in his. "Can I ask you something?"

"Of course." The corners of his eyes crinkle and I worry that this is about to turn into a Sentimental Zeke Moment. I bite my lip in preparation. If his googly eyes start watering, there's no way in hell that I'm not crying too.

He swallows before he goes on. "If I'm not here to hold you back from clawing out some high school dude's eyes, will you let Malachi do it?"

"Zeke!" I drop my hands. "You're not going anywhere."

"But if I do. Will you let Malachi help make sure that these guys don't mess with you?"

"I can fend for myself." I love Zeke to death, but he can be such a dad sometimes. I step back to demonstrate the right-hand hook that Auntie taught me.

"I know, girl, but—"

"Look, Diego's an exception. I don't think I'll have to worry about guys bothering me like this. It's not like I'm anyone's top pick."

"You may think that, but swear to god—and don't hit me when I say this—you're getting prettier and prettier every day, girl. You've always been beautiful. You already got those naturally pouty lips that other girls would pay thousands on injects to achieve, and now with those hips coming in to match? I don't want anyone thinking they can cross any lines with you until you're ready."

"Zeke!!!" I rush to cover his mouth with my hands to stop this moment from continuing any longer. It's bad enough that I have to fumble through high school in this body; the fact that even Zeke is noticing the changes makes me feel as though I'm a mannequin trapped in some tacky shopping-center display case against my will.

He pries my hands off his face and laughs. "It will make

me feel better to know that you'll let Malachi help ward off the creeps."

I want to vent to Zeke about all of these new dynamics with Malachi, but I can't. As a trio, we're all equally close, but that's not to say that there aren't different, unspoken laws shaping the ways that we relate to each other. One-on-one, Zeke and I have epic sessions spilling the tea on everyone and everything. He knows all my secrets, and I know all of his. It's no surprise that Malachi and I, on the other hand, never get into those kinds of conversations together. Like touching, it's always been one of those things that we've silently, mutually agreed is out of bounds for us. The idea of confiding in Zeke about how at the block party Malachi suggested we hang out alone and how shit's been weird ever since . . . it just feels messy. I can't risk screwing up the vibe of our crew. Not ever, but especially not now.

"Well? Will you?" Zeke asks, pulling me back to reality.

"The burden shouldn't be on girls to fight off assholes, but if it will get you to shut up about it, then yes. I will let Malachi hold my earrings if I ever decide to deck someone."

"Thank you," Zeke says, leaning his moppy head of hair onto my shoulder.

When Malachi and Diego reemerge from the back of the food stall, they look shady as fuck.

"Aight, man." Diego gives Malachi dap before turning to walk away. "Text me, nena!" he shouts at me as he shuffles away in his black ripped jeans. I flip him off. He raises a backward peace sign to his mouth and sloppily shoves his tongue between his fingers. Classy.

"What'd he want?" Zeke asks right away.

Malachi frowns. "Nothing."

"That didn't look like nothing," I say.

"Just some classic Diego bullshit. Don't worry about it." Malachi awkwardly fiddles with the straps of his space-themed backpack while we stare him down. "Seriously, it was nothing." Malachi laughs at the end of his sentence, but it sounds forced to me.

"Whatever he wants, you know that Diego is an asshole and that—" I say.

"*I know*," he shoots back.

Excuse me? I hate his rude-ass tone right now. And why so defensive?

"Okay, then," I confirm.

"*Okay.*" Malachi takes the wave brush from the back pocket of his jeans and rubs it across his head ten times real fast.

The epicenter of the Cookout is in the little park with the fountain, which has been converted into a makeshift arena for the local artists and Soundcloud rappers to perform. Marley and Lou are already there waiting for us. Zeke breaks into a half jog to meet Lou, who's wearing his headphones while perched on the edge of the fountain like a bird. Next to him, Marley is balancing on the ledge, cross-legged in a way that I can't imagine is comfortable. They look like sculptures of happy people frozen in time at a suburban mall.

"Helloooooooo!" Marley jumps up and gives Malachi a long hug. She moves on to Zeke next, but I duck down to pretend to tie my shoe to avoid her. I'm messing around with my shoelaces to wait her out, but I can feel her standing there, waiting patiently for me to finish so that we can hug. Honestly, who the hell does that?

I stifle a groan and give up, standing back up to receive

an excessively eager squeeze. Her hair smells like lavender, which is a pleasant surprise for a split second until I remember that I don't like her.

"So nice to see you!" she says to me.

What I want to say is, *Bitch, we saw each other yesterday, calm down*. But in reality, all I say is "Okay."

Over Marley's shoulder, I see Zeke spin his drawstring backpack around so that it's resting on his stomach. He pulls out the tiny white box, fumbling with it a bit. "I thought you might like these," he says shakily.

I had been hoping that Zeke would wait until they were alone to do it. But then again, that's never been his style.

Lou turns the box over in his hands a few times while Zeke stands there, shoving his hands so far deep into his pockets that for a second I'm worried that he might end up accidentally pantsing himself.

"Are these . . . earphones?" Lou asks at last, the confusion in his voice obvious.

"Yeah, it's no big deal. I have a cousin who works at the Apple store, so I got 'em for free. They're noise canceling." Zeke's words hang in the air. Malachi, Marley, and I all shift uncomfortably, unsure whether or not to intervene. "I figured that you may like them because on hot days like today, your headphones might not be as comfortable. . . ." Zeke's voice trails off with each word. Lou just stares at the box in his hands.

"Thank you," he says at last. Lou moves to remove his bulky headphones and a small smile of relief spreads across Zeke's face. But only for a second. Lou abruptly brings his hands back down and crams the bright white box into his back pocket. He's not going to wear them.

I can feel Marley frown a little bit, as if whatever outcome she was hoping for didn't come true either. "Are y'all ready to walk around?" she says in a borderline inappropriately chipper voice for the immediate aftermath of such a painfully awkward moment. We're all grateful to move on, though, so we start browsing the street of art vendors.

I stride ahead of the group, but feel Marley hastily catch up to me.

"So, Rhea, what kinds of things do you like to do for fun?"

I keep looking straight ahead to make my disinterest clear. "I don't know, read, I guess."

"Cool! Me too!" *God, she's relentless.* "What kinds of books?"

"Anything." I speed up a little bit, but she's quick to match my pace.

"Great—that's great. I read this wild book recently by this woman Octavia Butler. Have you heard of her?"

"No." *Does she ever quit?*

"Okay, well, I think you'd love her. So, the book is—"

I stop dead in my tracks. "You know what? I'm gonna go buy some water." Before she can even open her pretty little mouth, I veer left and jump between a crowd of adults hovering around a stall selling black soap and incense. Once I'm on the other side and know for sure that I wasn't followed, I let out an audible sigh.

Aight, I'm fully aware of how wild I'm looking right now, but here's the thing: Zeke and Malachi are all that I have. I can't just let some new girl walk in and fundamentally restructure our friend group. We have more important shit to deal with than her and her brother. And if Marley wants to make herself a priority and fuck up what Zeke, Malachi, and

I have going? Well, she can stage a coup if she wants, but I'm not going to make it easy for her.

I let go of my compulsive anti-Marley thoughts for long enough to pay the vendor for a bottle of water. It's overpriced, but I don't mind; it's at that perfect point where the outermost layer closest to the plastic has frozen a little, so when you squeeze the bottle, flakes of ice float around.

A few feet away, I notice two white teenagers, probably Lacy and Camesha's age, walking through the crowd. From what I can tell, they're the only non-Black or brown people here. They smile and laugh as they walk around with food that they bought from the Ethiopian stand. *If only everyone who moved here would come to our events like this, rather than just walk their dogs while avoiding eye contact with us and only waving at people who look like them.*

For a second, I almost feel a little guilty for judging them and literally conspiring to prevent more of them from moving here, but then . . . one of the teens takes out his phone to record a video. The other starts flashing gang signs that he probably looked up online and hooting like a monkey behind my neighbor Mr. Laita's back. The duo cackles in gross delight.

Mr. Laita is one of those giant men, probably a former linebacker or army guy, and is sweating profusely. Beads of moisture—so big that you can hear them drop—roll down his bald head. I want to go up and say something to the white kids, but the level of entitlement underneath their fake-ass Ray-Bans and overrated Carhartt tees is impenetrable. Instead, I go out of my way to get close enough to shoot them a dirty look before saying hello to Mr. Laita and returning to the main strip of the Cookout.

When I finally spot the crew again, Zeke's standing weirdly

far away. By the way that he's staring at Lou, who's not staring back at him, I'm guessing that they still haven't recovered from the Apple fail. Malachi's also looking salty, pouting like when he loses to me in *FIFA*. Marley's fidgeting with her hands as Dumbass Diego circles back to introduce himself. He and his friend gesticulate at her, copying the mannerisms of their wack older brothers who they're still too young and ignorant to realize don't have any game either. Diego and Malachi have their backs partially turned to me, but I can still gather from their body language that Diego's making some progress with Marley, and Malachi isn't happy about it.

What is it with this girl that attracts so much attention?

While still desperately spitting game at Marley, Diego drapes his arm around Malachi's back, and I think that I see him slip something into the front pocket of Malachi's JanSport. Diego pats the fabric of the backpack and pulls away. He points at Marley, likely delivering one last corny line, and skates away.

I wait until Diego and his friend are at a safe distance before I come forward. "Malachi, did Diego just put—"

Marley cuts me off, clearly waiting for my take on Diego. "He seems . . . nice? Right?" I get where she's coming from: being the new girl in the neighborhood, she wants to lean on her "new friends" to determine whether to tolerate some hot but potentially creepy dude's bullshit. Not knowing where the social lines stand, it's a delicate balance to play.

But that's her problem, not mine.

"He's great," I say in the most convincing voice that I can muster. Zeke raises his eyebrows at me, but I ignore him. Marley's a big girl—she can figure these things out on her own.

Eager to change topics, I point at the buff guy holding a snow cone several feet away. "Yo, that's Dep!"

"Damn." Both Zeke and Malachi bite their fists once they see the girl next to him. She has one of those insane Fashion Nova hourglass bodies and is wearing a lethal pair of skin-tight, high-waisted jeans that are so thoroughly ripped up the sides that they're practically see-through.

"You're into that?" Lou asks, confused.

"A man doesn't have to be straight to appreciate a thick ass," Zeke says, holding his hands in the prayer position. This makes everyone, including Lou, fall out laughing. The tension starts to melt away.

"Yo, he might still be selling fireworks, let's go over," I suggest. If we're going to record the SOSI promo video tonight, we're gonna need a lot of fireworks, and they're going to have to be the illegal kind that makes a serious bang—not the backyard packs that you can buy at the grocery store. If anyone has or knows where to get some of the big illegal stuff, it's Dep.

"Yooooo! Long time no see, lil friends." Dep pulls each of us into a sweaty embrace, his dreads whipping against my back as he does. "And Malachi! Damn, you're getting tall." Malachi steps forward and gives him a cautious one-armed hug. Dep introduces us to the girl by his side, who is somehow even hotter up close. He leans back to readjust his stance so that he can put his weight on his good leg. "What are y'all getting into today?"

"Nothing much, just chillin'," Zeke says casually, catching glimpses of Dep's girl out of the corner of his eye.

"How's school been? Malachi, you still tryna ball?"

Malachi shrugs and rolls around a rock on the cement

beneath his shoe. Dep's the nicest guy in the world and always has been, but I don't think that Malachi has ever learned to look at him and not see Dante. It's hard not to—even when we were little, the brothers looked exactly alike. Dep's older than us, but somewhere in the way that his eyes crinkle when he smiles, you can still see the traces of Dante, or rather what Dante would have looked like had he been able to make it to twenty-one.

"Actually, Dep, could you hook us up with some fireworks?" I ask. I'm no good at small talk—better to get right to the point.

"You're not tryna do some hoodrat shit and set 'em off in someone's backyard and set a tree on fire, right?"

I smirk. "Close, but not quite."

Dep lets out a hearty laugh. "Aight, in that case, come with me."

We tell Marley and Lou to wait there while we follow Dep. He hands his girl the snow cone and leads us away from the crowd to where some cars are parked on a neighboring street. We pull up on two dudes wearing all black lounging against a silver Camry. "Can you hook these lil guys up with some fireworks, my G?"

"Fa sho." One of the guys walks around to the back of the car and pops the trunk, revealing a mountain of fireworks of all sizes in the back.

"Whoa," we mutter in awe, parsing through the brightly colored tubes and canisters decorated with warnings that read: "Peligro Extremo."

"We're looking for something loud. Doesn't have to be that big, explosion in the sky like at Dodger Stadium, but it should be sharp and loud. Like, uhm . . ."

"Shots?" the firework guy says.

Malachi and I look at each other and shrug. Fuck it, might as well be explicit with what we need. We turn back to the guy and nod.

"Y'all tryna pull a prank on someone, huh?"

"Sort of, yeah," I mumble.

"I got the perfect shit for that." The guy opens up the backseat of the car and pulls out one of those plastic bags with "Thank You" written a dozen times on top of one another. "This will scare the shit out of anyone, trust."

He hands me the bag, and it's heavier than I had imagined. There are about twenty bundles of firecrackers, each one consisting of three bright red tubes tied together.

"You light these muthafuckas up, and they'll pop one after another—a straight line of evenly spaced *bang-bang-bangs*." The guy holds his hand up as if he's holding a gun, cocked to the side as he mimics the noise. "That'll sound much more like shots than the hectic *ba-bang, ba-ba-ba-ba-bang* of regular firecrackers that you'll see other niggas selling."

It sounds perfect. "How much?"

"Fifty."

"Fifty?!" Malachi and I holler. We huddle together with Zeke and pull out all of the money between us. We're at $18.

"Can we just give you what we have and take some of it?" Malachi asks.

"Sorry, mane, but I gotta move this all at once. It'd be too hard to sell the rest. This one's an all-or-nothing deal."

Dammit. It's a miracle that we even scraped eighteen bucks together, I don't know how we're gunna get thirty-two more.

"Can you hold on to this for us, and we'll get back to you

ASAP? And if we're not back within an hour, sell it to whoever you want?" Malachi begs.

"Please?" I tack on to the end, trying to use the last shreds of our youthful innocence to guilt this guy into helping us out.

The guy looks over at his friend still leaning against the hood, then over at Dep. "Are they good for it, my G?"

"No doubt," Dep says with confidence.

"*One* hour," the guy says while shaking Malachi's hand. I click the side of my phone to note the time and take off into a jog with Zeke and Malachi by my side.

"You think the rich kids got cash?" I ask the boys.

"Marley and Lou? They live up there and stuff, but I don't know. I feel like they're not stacked like how I thought they'd be," Malachi says.

"Yeah, like Lou made a weird joke over text about repo people taking their shit back in Michigan," Zeke adds. "It took me a second to realize it might not have been a joke."

To be honest, I don't care about the backstory of the siblings, I just wanna know if they can help us or not. "It's worth a shot asking, though, right?" I push.

"We'd probably have to tell them what we really need the money for," Malachi mumbles.

"Says who? We use their cash and say it's for fireworks, but SOSI stays between us. We literally *just met them.* Do you seriously think that we can trust these strangers?"

Malachi and Zeke both rub the backs of their necks and mutter noncommittal phrases.

"Great, so it's settled." I turn the corner back to where we had left Marley and Lou on the edge of the Cookout.

Marley straightens up when she sees me approaching. "Hey! How was—"

"You got any money?" I blurt out.

"What do you mean?" she says, laughing melodically.

I roll my eyes. "M-O-N-E-Y. Cash. You two got any on you?"

"Oh, uhm . . ." She reaches into her back pocket and glances over at Malachi, who offers her an apologetic half smile. "I have five dollars. Lou?"

Lou quietly searches through his pockets and pulls out another $6.

"That's it?" I huff.

"Rhea. Chill." Zeke steps forward to put himself between me and the fake twins.

"Y'all live in that big-ass house and you don't have money when you go out?" Frustration builds in my chest. If we can't get those firecrackers, then the whole thing falls apart. Our bootleg posters and graffiti aren't enough—we *need* to make a video and get it trending if we want people to believe that SOSI exists. Nobody will take us seriously unless they hear shots.

"I told you, things are complicated in our house," Marley says defensively.

"I'm sure they are," I quip back. They got a nice house, nice clothes, and a nice mom who's actually around; I doubt things are nearly half as "complicated" in their house as in mine.

Zeke raises his voice. *"Rhea."*

I see the impatient way that they're all looking at me and roll my eyes. I turn back to Marley. "Sorry, whatever. It's important, okay?"

"I don't know why you need money so bad, but is there any other way that we can help?" Lou asks.

"Yeah, do you have a gun?" I ask sarcastically.

Lou flinches. "What?!"

"She's joking! She's joking," Zeke says with his arms out-stretched, trying to defuse the situation. "Lay off, Rhea," he whispers underneath his breath.

"Would anyone's parents give you the money you need?" Marley asks.

Malachi, Zeke, and I are quiet for a second before we bust out laughing.

"Maaaaaaann, my mama *giving* me money?! She'd be like, *'Boy, I put a roof over your head, and you have the nerve to turn and ask me for money without doing any work? Please!'*" Malachi cackles.

Zeke wipes his forehead. "I asked my mom for an allow-ance once and she said she didn't understand me. I tried asking her again in Spanish and she dead-ass told me that *allowance* isn't a word in our culture." The cash that we do have was earned over the course of weeks mowing neighbors' lawns, cleaning out people's garages, and babysitting. Not some magic allowance.

I wipe away one last tear and gather myself. "Real talk, though, how are we gonna get the rest of this cash?"

Just then, the voice of God (if God was a middle-aged Black dude) interrupts the music blaring on the speaker. "All right, all right, all right. Now who's ready for"—a corny drumroll noise plays—"the dance contest! Whoop-whoop!"

Oh god. There are few things in the world that make me more uncomfortable than watching people who can sorta dance get in front of a large group of people and give max effort like they're some pre-problematic Chris Brown.

"First prize wins forty dollars cash, baby!"

The five of us spin around to look at each other. I can't

dance for shit, Malachi moves like one of those inflatable guys at car washes, and Zeke has absolutely no rhythm. We start bickering about who has to do it, but the argument doesn't last long.

"Hold this for me."

Lou hands his tote bag to Marley and walks straight for the makeshift dance floor, his bright white headphones glistening beneath the fading sun.

NINE

"No way," I mutter in disbelief as Lou struts toward the DJ to sign up. I have a brief flashback to the moment that we first met Lou and remember the chaotic, bizarre way that he swayed to the spacy music that he and Marley had requested. There are many ways to describe Lou's dancing, but "good" isn't one of them.

"Oh my god, is he serious?" Malachi asks in disbelief.

"Of course he is. You guys need the money, Lou can dance, so why not?" Marley says, completely even-toned and confident.

"But can he, though?" Malachi whispers to me under his breath. We laugh.

We're too old to do this shit badly but still get points for being cute. And that's not to mention the massive headphones drawing particular attention to Lou. Whoever watches Lou bomb will have ammunition to drag him for at least six months, maybe even a whole year. I may not like Marley, but Lou's all right, and even I don't want to see him embarrass himself.

Zeke starts pleading with Marley to get her to bring Lou back. "We'll find another way to get the money, he doesn't have to do this."

Marley just waves her hand at us as if we're all crazy. "He'll be fine! Dancing is his special interest."

"Special interest?" Zeke asks.

"Yeah, it's like the thing that he's really passionate and knows a ton of facts about. It's great. Much cooler than his last special interest."

"And what was that?" I ask.

"Collecting gel pens."

"Oh." Zeke swallows and grips his hair.

"Look, he's coming back!" Malachi shouts.

Lou approaches us and we all sigh in relief.

"Can you hold these?" Lou removes his headphones and hands them to Zeke before sliding the Apple earbuds out from his back pocket. "They're noise canceling, right?"

Zeke nods and Lou places each of the earbuds into his ears, which I now notice are pierced. A sly smile spreads across his lips as he mouths something privately to Zeke, who immediately blushes and starts fidgeting with the seam of his shirt, grinning at the floor. With a wink, Lou strolls back toward the dance floor to join the five other contestants.

The DJ explains the rules. During the first song, all contestants will freestyle one by one. After everyone goes, audience applause will determine who's out until there are only two dancers left. The final song will be a dance battle between the last two standing. Winner takes all.

A sizable crowd of mostly high schoolers has formed by the time that we manage to push our way to the front. The other contestants represent a mixed bag. There's a kid who looks not too much younger than us, but still has a sweet face and no doubt will score points for being adorable. A hot guy with an immaculately maintained fade, maybe a junior in high school, flashes a cocky smile. The oldest one in the group is this long and lean girl who looks like she grew up in the Black dance academy down the street. Under different circumstances, she'd probably have the advantage, but here at the Cookout, people don't necessarily wanna see technique—they wanna see chaos. Hence, I'm guessing that the biggest competition will come from the two girls wearing matching rompers that no doubt were made *specifically* for throwing it back. And then there's Lou—looking off into the distance, standing there all serious in his white T-shirt and charcoal cargo pants.

The first song is a bass-heavy banger by a local rapper who recently made it big—a crowd favorite. One by one, the DJ highlights each dancer down the line and every single one is *fire*. The youngest kid moves quick and hits every beat drop with a dab. The older guy is smooth as hell and gets everyone in the crowd chanting "Aye!" when he whips out some insane footwork. The girl who looks like she's been formally trained busts out a very Shakira-esque freestyle, her hips locking and isolating in ways that I didn't even know was possible. The romper girls don't disappoint either: the crowd loses their mind as they twerk in tandem with so much vigor that it would make even Cardi B shed a tear. The people on the front line of the crowd reach out to fan them down when they finish.

At last, it's Lou's turn. By my side, Zeke tenses up so hard that I'm not entirely sure that he's still breathing. I want to tell him that Lou will be fine, but after seeing everyone else absolutely kill it, I don't have the heart to lie to him. Malachi covers his eyes like he's about to watch a lamb get slaughtered.

The DJ points to Lou. "Let's hear it for our final contestant! Show us what you got!"

Lou steps forward and motions for the crowd to step back and give him more space. Zeke cringes as the sea of bodies yell in curiosity, "Okay, man! Give this nigga some space!" "Fall back, y'all!" Once Lou has the area cleared to himself, he begins.

With outstretched arms, he fans his hands from one side of his body to the other, drawing sharp lines through the sky as he hops to every beat. He gains momentum and hurls himself into a series of spins so fast and precise that the crowd starts to chatter. As he twirls like a top, he brings his outstretched arms in and out like a ballerina before sending them outward on a tilt so that he looks like a firedancer, or maybe an airbender, shooting wind into space. He whirls wildly, getting faster and faster, bringing the energy of the crowd up with him.

He drops to the floor to flash a dramatic fallen-maiden-like pose before shooting back up like lightning, perched on his toes to start voguing. He's dancing to the same song as everyone else, but watching Lou move feels like witnessing something else entirely. The crowd loses it as Lou whips into a series of pirouettes and kicks between skillful death drops to the floor and the occasional dab. When he hits his final move—a vogue trot that turns into a cartwheel culminating in a backbreaking pose—the crowd goes *wild*.

Zeke's jaw hangs open like an old-school cartoon. Malachi had given in to the performance after the first gravity-defying move; his hands are still stretched above his head as he hollers along with the rest of the crowd. Marley jumps in place, clapping giddily.

The DJ asks the dancers to stand in a line and he moves his hand over each of their heads for the crowd to cheer for their favorites. Everyone gets a decent response, but the finalists are clear: when the DJ hovers over Lou and the romper girls, the screams are so loud that you can probably hear us all the way from the beach.

Zeke pulls himself together and turns to Marley. "How the hell did he learn to dance like that?"

Marley smiles knowingly. "Last summer, he got really into the teen ball culture community."

Ahhhh. This explains the dance moves, but to be honest, I hadn't really imagined Lou having his own friends separate from Marley. Much less a whole secret life. I feel like an asshole for underestimating him. I watch Marley zealously cheer on her brother and wonder if maybe, just *maybe*, I've made some unfair assumptions about her too.

The romper girls start working the crowd, getting everyone to clap as the DJ cues up the final-battle song. Lou stands as far away as possible from the circle of humans around him and maintains his signature resting pensive face.

I'm honestly getting hype myself, believing that Lou may be able to pull this shit off and win the money for us. But then, the music starts.

The second song is what I had feared: the fast-paced twerk bop that everyone has been blasting nonstop all summer. The crowd surges into an uproar. The romper girls smile cockily and brush the hair from their shoulders. They start revving up their thighs, ready to destroy.

The girls go first and don't hold back. They clap their asses like thunder, sending the crowd into mayhem. One of the girls plants her hands on the ground and kicks her feet up into the palms of her partner, who holds her ankles as she twerks upside down. They both go so hard that you can see the sweat forming on their edges. A rogue hoop earring—unable to keep up—is sent flying into the crowd.

When the DJ motions at Lou for him to take his turn, the tension is palpable. Lou had whipped out some crazy unexpected shit during the first round, but he can't just do that again. I wonder what else he got. Lou outstretches his hands to crack his knuckles, puts his hands on his knees, and shows us.

What happens next is the stuff of legends. One by one, Lou rolls through every single one of the romper girls' moves, pulling up his shirt so that we can all watch him throw it back better than any chick I've seen. When he gets to the point where the girl had twerked on her hands with the help of her friend, Lou turns into a freestanding handstand with his legs in a V, shaking without anyone's help at all. Everyone has their phones out, gassing him up. Lou seals the deal by falling from the headstand straight into the splits, which sends everyone and their mama screaming like they all just saw Queen Megan Thee Stallion herself grace us with her glory. Everyone behind us is jumping, clamoring, and climbing over one another in awe and sheer excitement as Lou dusts off his pants to collect the grand prize from the DJ.

We rush over to Lou and usher him out of the crowd toward a quiet side street away from the main strip of the festival. Marley stands close to swat away all the hands that try to shake Lou in congratulations. When we're finally by ourselves, Lou takes the wad of bills and spreads them out on the ground in front of us.

"Lou, that was *amazing*." Malachi's pacing back and forth, recounting the spectacle as if we all didn't literally just witness it together. "You were all like, whoaaaa, and then you went all Super Saiyan and everyone was like AYEEE!!"

Zeke takes a seat on the cement parking lot divider next to Lou. "You really blew us all away back there."

"Thanks," Lou says with a smile, wiping the faint trace of sweat from his brow. "These were a big help, really." He points to the earphones.

"You don't have to wear them for me, it's really okay," Zeke says gently.

"It's not that I didn't like them. It takes me a second to get used to new stuff sometimes. I was worried that they'd feel too light without the pressure of the headphones, but it actually was way more comfortable, and less sweaty, than the bulky ones."

Zeke starts cheesing like a Kardashian on TMZ.

"And now, my gift for you." Lou brings the wad of bills together and hands it to Zeke. "For whatever you need this cash for so badly."

Zeke reaches out to hug Lou but catches himself. "Sorry," he says. "I'd give you a hug, but I know that's not really your thing."

"Who says it's not my thing?" Lou replies.

"I thought you said that you don't like being touched?"

"I don't like *gentle* touches. Like handshakes or strokes on the back make my skin crawl, but I don't mind firm hugs." His eyes flick toward Zeke, then back down. "Deep pressure can feel really good for me."

"Oh," Zeke says, turning bright red. He swallows and nervously runs his hand through his hair.

"We're gonna go get some kettle corn with the extra money," I announce to Zeke and Lou, lightly tugging Malachi and Marley to come with me. The three of us walk back toward the Cookout to give the boys some space. Right before we turn the corner, I peek over my shoulder and see Zeke gripping Lou's biceps, hard. He leans in for what I know will be his first kiss. I turn back around and smile knowing that no matter what happens, Zeke got to reach this milestone here at home.

Malachi, Marley, and I follow the smell of kettle corn to reach the stand where for $4, you can get a massive bag the size of a body pillow. The line is long as hell, so we almost jump ship until we hear someone calling Marley's name from the front of the line.

"Mom?" Marley responds, startled to see her here.

Ms. Allen waves us over, and we walk over cautiously with our hands up, making sure that everyone knows that we're not tryna cut.

"You kids having fun today?" Ms. Allen asks eagerly. Malachi and I smile and nod in that sort of awkward, polite way you do when you don't really know someone's mom that well yet. "Hey, where's your brother?"

"He's waiting in the shade. Taking a break from the crowd to cool off," Marley replies without skipping a beat. The man that had been standing in line beside Ms. Allen leans into our conversation. He theatrically places his hand on the small of her back like some corny daytime television suitor. I hadn't even realized that they were here together.

"Why are you here with *him*?" Marley says with some bite in her voice. I'm intrigued by the deviation from her typical la-dee-da sunshine tone.

"Marley, you remember my new friend, Mr. Staples." Staples is tall, maybe six-four or six-five, but that's about all he has going for him. He has the look of a washed-up, light-skinned playboy desperate to seem relevant. He's wearing goofy trousers and a loud, printed shirt that's trying way too hard with cheap black glasses from the checkout line at the sporting goods store.

Staples extends a hand to Marley. "Nice to see you again, girlie. Pretty, like her mom," he says with a wink.

We all cringe. I'm surprised (maybe even impressed) when Marley looks him dead in the face and simply says, "Ew."

"Hey, hey, be nice," Ms. Allen says with a laugh to try to lighten the mood. She touches Staples's arm gently to console him. "Rhea and Malachi, you two go to Bayrex Charter High School, right? Well, Mr. Staples here is the CEO of the organization that runs the Bayrex Charter network."

It's not like I needed one more reason to dislike Marley and her family, but this certainly is the icing on the goddamn cake.

For the past four years, the boys and I have attended Bayrex Charter. It's a shoddy school in East LA fashioned out of an old, abandoned church building. The place eerily resembles a dungeon. Only three of the fourteen classrooms contain real windows that open. The lights are that creepy, bright white kind that reminds you of that classic scene in horror movies when the power cuts off for a second in a police interrogation room then comes back on just as the incarcerated serial killer bangs on the two-way glass. It looks nothing like the sleek Silicon Beach public schools on the Westside.

Half the teachers at Bayrex Charter are fresh college graduates from fancy schools in the Northeast here to teach us for charity for a year or two before going to medical school or whatever. They're more afraid of us than we are of them.

The other half drink tea from thermoses every morning so that their throats are well hydrated enough to spend the day screaming at us. A few care, but they burn out quickly. I don't blame them.

"Ah, some of my young students!" Staples booms. "How do you love Bayrex?"

Malachi clears his throat. "One time, the only water fountain in the entire building broke, so for seven weeks, none of us were able to get anything to drink except the room-temperature milk that they serve in the lunchroom. Some people who work for a tech start-up came to volunteer for the day, but they mostly just took pictures of us and handed out reusable water bottles with their company's name on it. We didn't have any water to put in them, though, so we threw them away."

A deeply uncomfortable silence fills the air, seemingly choking Marley and her mom out of any ability to respond.

It warms my heart.

"Oh, that's, uhm . . ." Ms. Allen searches for words while Marley glares at Staples. It feels good to see them squirm. If you move into a house in the bougie part of the neighborhood and then date the jerk who runs our shitty schools, some heat is well warranted. It's things like this that make Marley and Lou sus to me—they may be Black, but they're still outsiders. Who's to say that they're even capable of grasping what's going on in the neighborhood? Let alone what we're doing with SOSI and why it's so necessary to protect our home?

"Bayrex Charter is a high-quality alternative to LAUSD public schools," Staples says in the rehearsed voice of a politician. "You're too young to see it now, but we're doing you a favor."

"Be careful with the fireworks tonight, kids!" Ms. Allen claps her hands, deftly changing the conversation. Whatever she sees in Staples, she's not blind enough to not notice that his ass was about to get roasted if he kept mouthing off.

Staples rubs his chin, looking nostalgic. "You know, back when I was your age, this neighborhood would be wild on the Fourth. So many people would fire shots into the air, it wasn't safe to go out. You're lucky to be young here now that things are much cleaner."

Malachi laughs nervously.

"Right," I respond, offended by his use of *cleaner*, but not wanting to sound off any alarms about our plans for tonight.

"Well, Ms. Allen and I have some exciting plans of our own tonight," Staples brags, completely unprompted. "I got a new electric car recently—automated driving, deluxe white-on-white interiors, the whole thing." He nudges Malachi's arm and whispers, "Take it from me, kid. The ladies love a fast car."

For the first time since I've met her, Marley looks like she could literally wither away and die of embarrassment. If only that's all it took to make her disappear.

"We're leaving *now*!" She grabs Malachi and me by the wrists to drag us away.

Staples waves at us and shouts the single most annoying thing that old people tell kids who they don't know: "Don't do anything that I wouldn't do!" There's something about this saying that makes my skin crawl—it makes me feel like life is scripted and we're all just bound to follow in the dull footsteps of the adults in front of us.

I wait for Marley to pick up the conversation as we walk away, but she stays quiet. She's stomping more so than walking, even though she doesn't know where we're going. When she really starts leading us in the opposite direction of the cars, Malachi breaks the silence.

"Hey, it's this way actually," he says, pointing toward the side street where Dep's friend is waiting with the fireworks.

"*Great*, then why didn't you say anything before I led us all the way over here?" Marley shoots back. Malachi looks at her with some hurt in his eyes. Seeing that dude with her mom must have really set her off. Marley sighs and gathers herself. "Hey, I'm sorry. I didn't mean to be rude. It's just . . . I'm sorry."

"It's okay," Malachi says while trying to get her eyes to meet him for a smile. She doesn't.

Marley shakes out her shoulders and exhales. "Ugh! Okay, it's whatever. I'm fine. Let's go."

Malachi steers us through the crowd back to the silver Camry filled with fireworks. We hand the guy the cash and he passes us the grocery bag full of explosives, which Malachi immediately stuffs into his JanSport.

When Marley asks what we need all of it for, I can hear the nervousness in her voice.

"Don't worry about it," I say coldly.

—

I stomp loudly as we return to where we left Zeke and Lou in case they need a bit of a warning that they're no longer alone. The sun has finally begun to set, the air gradually cooling around us.

"We got the stuff," Malachi announces. He turns around so that Zeke can see the weight of the firecrackers shift his backpack as he jumps in place.

"So, what is this mysterious *stuff*?" Lou asks. He and Zeke are still sharing the cement block on the floor, positioned as close to one another as possible without touching.

I pull out my phone to check the time. "Don't worry about—"

"Yeah, you already said that, you know." Marley cuts me off before I can finish. I glare at her, but she doesn't shy away.

"Oh, c'mon, can't you tell us? Hate to pull this card, but I *did* win you guys this money, so . . ." Lou turns over his hand with the palm facing up. Without hesitation, Zeke grabs it and squeezes.

When Zeke opens his mouth, I can tell he's about to let them in, so I do the responsible thing: I shout over him.

"Don't you have to be home to watch Stella and Kiké now? You're late, Lupe's gunna kill you." I look Zeke dead in the eyes, begging him to not ruin our plan. I'm happy for Zeke, but nothing's stable enough yet for us to let more people in on SOSI. *We're* not stable enough. I quietly mouth my desperation. *Please.*

He looks at me like I'm fucking up his life rather than trying to save it, and I pray he doesn't mean it.

"She's right," he says at last. "I should get going."

Malachi frowns and Marley frowns even harder. Lou looks disappointed too, but not as much as Zeke.

I don't want to be the bad guy here, but if I have to, I will.

Malachi, Zeke, and I drift in silence away from the Cookout. The encroaching darkness of the postsunset sky charms the streetlights to turn on. I usher us all to the back alley behind the old church several blocks away. The church, as well as the surrounding businesses, are all closed for the holiday, so we can make some real noise here without anyone freaking out.

Zeke breaks the silence. "We could have told them."

"Their mom is a *lawyer*," I remind him. "And she's dating the scumbag who runs our school. It's a bad idea."

"C'mon, don't act like this isn't personal," Malachi huffs. "Just admit that you don't like them."

"It's not that I don't like them." I step up to Malachi. "We don't know anything about them, and they don't know anything about us. There's no history there. No trust."

"Well, you're the one making it hard for us to build trust in the first place," Malachi bites back.

Zeke has already fallen for Lou, and Malachi seems real keen to keep Marley close, so then where will that leave me? *Alone* to pull off the entire SOSI stunt while they're running around, trying to hook up with the new kids? Heat builds in my face, and I kick a trash can off to the side. "For god's sake, Malachi, the girl took us to that bullshit Colony restaurant and *loved* it."

"Jesus, Rhea, it's only a restaurant!" Malachi's voice is strained. "And she was just making conversation."

"She could rat us out immediately, then the plan falls apart and then Zeke's gone. Is that what you want?" I push.

Zeke attempts to mediate. "Guys, I know we're all under a lot of stress with this—"

"Look. The three of us? *This*—" I draw a circle around us. "*This* is what we're trying to protect." I back away from Malachi and turn to Zeke. "I'm happy to see you and Lou catch feelings for one another. I really am." I smile at him sincerely, and he smiles back. "But that has to stay separate."

"I don't know," Zeke says, shaking his head. "We don't *have* to do this alone. Some new ideas, some more hands." An optimistic grin brightens his face. "New people could be nice."

"The onslaught of *new people* is what got us here in the first place." My voice cracks a little, which catches me off guard. I break away from Zeke and grab the backpack. "Here." I toss Malachi the spray paint and motion toward the concrete wall. I avoid his eyes even though I can feel them searching to meet mine.

I crouch on the floor to pull myself together. I don't know why I've been getting like this recently. I want to fight *for* Zeke, *for* our crew—not against them. Zeke hovers beside me for a moment before pressing a hand against my back. I dab the beginning of a tear away from my eye. "I'm sorry," I whisper. "I'm just . . . angry. Not at you, but at, like, the whole thing."

"I get it," Zeke says. He squeezes my shoulder. "Let's make the promo, okay?"

Zeke pulls out two all-black sweatshirts from his bag, carefully selected as the generic swap-meet kind without any identifying marks. He and Malachi put on the sweatshirts and get ready. I turn off the automatic Cloud synchronization functions and put my phone into airplane mode so that my location won't be tracked. I start filming.

We make a series of vague, confusing, and threatening videos: in one, firecracker "shots" go off in the background while the camera zooms in on the SOSI symbol and Malachi uses the voice distorter app on his phone to shout, "SOSI! GANGGANGGANG WE RUN THIS SHIT!" In another, Zeke sets off the firecrackers in the background while I shoot videos from my own perspective like I'm running away from the "gunfire," screaming that somebody's strapped. We shoot a ton of videos like these—some anonymous, some from our own perspectives as if we were caught in the wrong place at the wrong time.

I decide that the best course of action is for me to post the video running away from the "gunfire" first, then have the boys share it. Afterward, Malachi will share our videos on Quipp in the same thread as the post that he had made earlier with his spotting the SOSI tag by his house. Between the three of us, we can be sure to spread it around to the sophomores we know with the hashtags #SOSI, #gang, and #StaySafe. And from there, well, it'll just be a matter of time before the juniors and seniors see it too and it really starts spreading.

I turn off airplane mode and look at Zeke. "You ready?" My hands tremble as I clutch my phone in its matte-black case.

"Yes." Huddled together in a circle, we all wait quietly as we watch the little circle spin as our phones upload our propaganda. A tiny vibration surges through my hands once the videos go live.

SOSI takes its first breath.

TEN

Within forty-eight hours, SOSI is trending locally on every single social media platform known to (hu)man. I knew it'd get going eventually, but *damn*. Even I didn't expect for it to go viral so quickly. Every day of the week is hectic.

MONDAY

There are few places for teens of color to dissociate from the bullshit of the outside world. Genie—the janky, but lovely, Black-owned, discount movie theater—is one of them. Zeke, Malachi, and I have plans to sneak into some trashy R-rated horror movie. Marley and Lou crash because Zeke "invited" them or whatever. We sit in the way, way back, where all the other underage friend groups hide out. In the lightwash of tiny cell phone screens, face after face lights up, stops scrolling, and watches a video of what they all believe is a new gang on the block. At one point, a girl with her hair in pompoms spins around in her seat and shoves the phone right up to our faces: "Have y'all seen this shit?!"

Marley leans in to get a better look, her face concerned. "Oh no."

"What is it?" Lou asks.

"Something about a gang. I didn't know that was . . ." She chooses her words with care. ". . . a dynamic around here."

"It hasn't been for a long time, but apparently a new group is staging a comeback," I say casually.

"Well, hopefully the people involved will find the opportunities that they need without things getting violent," Marley says to the girl. "I don't want anyone to get hurt."

"With this shit?" Pom-Pom Girl says soberly. "Someone always will."

TUESDAY

Zeke and I are walking to CVS to pick up some Arizonas and hot chips when we pass by a group of four very concerned-looking white people. They're all huddled around a light post. Through a gap between their pale limbs, I see what they see: our PSA signs for the "Community Anti-Gang Task Force."

When Malachi opens the burner email we set up to see if anyone has reached out, the inbox already has seventy-six messages. Ninety percent are from freaked-out Bethanys, Sharons, and Brents, while the remaining 10 percent are from longtime locals either ranting about how LAPD's gang enforcement strategy has been racist since Day One or expressing skepticism over whether the appearance of some janky graffiti really means that anyone is any less safe in our community now than they were a few weeks ago.

One rando (username: UrNeighbor323) creates a sub-zeggit about SOSI. They post a grainy photo of the Anti-Gang Task Force flyer and the comments section gets tense.

u/UrNeighbor323: THIS is what we need to be talking about here. Gang activity has returned to the block. They'll be pushing drugs soon and god knows what else. Maybe gentrification isn't the worst thing in the world if it means keeping our kids safe.

u/KofaParkStanAcct responds: We can have community-led investment without displacement.

u/Dem4Justice jumps in: You can't have your cake and eat it too.

u/PplOvrProfits: Who says?

I open a fresh tab and create an anonymous ghost account. I try to stir the pot under my new alias, ConcernedCitizn:

u/ConcernedCitizn: My partner and I just bought a home in the neighborhood last year, and I have to say ... SOSI doesn't make us feel confident in our investment ...

u/UrNeighbor323: Exactly. I've lived here my whole life. There's nothing wrong with wanting to see an increase in my home value.

u/PplOverProfits: Traitor.

WEDNESDAY

I'm biking over to Malachi's when I catch a glimpse of some kids tagging the parking lot behind IHOP. Normally, I'd mind my business and keep going, but there's something about the graffiti that makes me roll backward to get another look. When I'm able to see what was going on, I snap a picture and pedal off, fast.

When I get to Malachi's house, I wheel my bike into the backyard. Before going inside, I take out my phone to get a better look at the picture. I have to make sure. . . .

There were three guys in the parking lot and I didn't recognize any of them. In white-and-black bubble letters with a neon green border, they painted on the wall: "SOSI."

I hear Lacy call my name from the other side of the screen door followed by footsteps.

Zeke made it clear in the parking lot of the art store that the minute the gang becomes real, we shut it down. The thing is, though, I don't know where that boundary is—what makes something real or not. Where does strangers claiming our sign fall on the spectrum?

Wherever it is, I know that it's a close call.

When I hear the screen door slide open, I delete the photo.

TODAY

It's Thursday now, five days after SOSI went live, and the day has all the potential to be the best one in a minute. The fake twins are out of town melting away in Palm Springs on a day trip with their mom, so it's just the original crew once again. How it should be.

When I turn the corner to pull up to Zeke's, I pause when I see Malachi a few feet ahead. He's standing outside the apartment building, but not going inside. His eyes are glued to his phone. He's waiting for something.

Someone?

Dumbass Diego skates right up to Malachi. I wait for Malachi to blow up at him, but instead, the two of them walk into the alley between Zeke's and Auntie's buildings. When they emerge moments later, Diego throws down his board and skates away. The entire interaction lasts less than a minute.

"You ready to go in?" Malachi asks when he notices me waiting.

"So, you and Diego are now best buddies or some shit?"

"Chill out. He's letting me borrow *Assassin's Creed* for a few days." He holds up a PS5 game box before tucking it into his backpack. "I still hate the guy, just can't afford to buy the game new."

Zeke must've heard us because he opens the window, immediately launching into a fiery soapbox speech about the gaming industry and the glories of free-to-play cross-platform games. The guys start laughing and the moment passes, but still. I can't shake the suspicion that nothing involving Diego can be so innocent.

Inside, Malachi, Zeke, and I sprawl out on the beige carpet of Zeke's living room. Lupe is over in the kitchen making camarones al mojo de ajo for everyone, so you know it's about to be lit. I take in the smell of garlic being pushed around the room by the standing fan and revel in the empty space of Marley and Lou's absence.

Zeke rolls over to stick his phone charger into the nearest outlet and is met with a spark. "Dammit."

"You good?" I ask.

"Yeah, that shit sparked me, though."

"Language, mijo," Lupe calls out without taking her eyes off the sauté pan.

"Sorry, that *thing* sparked me."

"We have to tell Mr. Vic about that," Lupe says.

"Ma, do you really think that dude's gonna fix it? He's doing everything in his power to get us out of here. No way in hell he's gonna prevent us from being electrocuted."

"Maybe not, but the man might care about a fire hazard that could burn this entire building to the ground." On the other side of the door, we hear the footsteps of what sounds like men wearing expensive, hard-sole shoes. "Perfect timing, that sounds like Mr. Vic right there. Why don't you go ask him yourself right now?"

"Maaaaaaaaa," Zeke whines, lying back all dramatic onto the floor. He grabs a pillow from the couch to cover his face.

"Ezequiel Reynaldo Guevara, do not make me ask you twice." Lupe gives us all that look that you know means she ain't messin' around with us. Plus, you know that when your mom pulls out your first *and* middle names, she don't got no time for your foolishness. Zeke stands up reluctantly and sulks. From their bedroom, Stella and Kiké "ooooooooooooooh" in unison at the sound of their brother being chastised.

"Have fun, my G!" Malachi waves at Zeke from the comfort of the carpet floor.

"Bruh, I'm not tryna go out there alone. Get up." He kicks Malachi in the leg.

"Nah, man, you're a big boy—you got this!"

"Malachi Samuel Reed . . ." Lupe mumbles in a low, frustrated voice from the kitchen.

Malachi bites his lip and gets up real quick. "Yes, ma'am."

I'm tryna cop a plate of that shrimp, so I don't wait for Lupe to pull out my full name. I get up and notice how the coolness of the cement hallway seeps through my socks as we meet Vic and his henchmen.

Vic's standing there stroking his chin as if he's listening

real hard to the important-looking men talking to him, even though that dense head of his is probably empty. Beside him is a blond woman, probably in her late twenties, dressed in a smart blouse with well-tailored pants and a leather hand-bag. She looks like the go-getter young protagonist of an early 2000s' workplace romcom.

"So, you see, if we open up this wall here, we can add a hallway window to let more light in and make the entry more appealing," Important-Looking Guy One says. To his right, Important-Looking Guy Two rolls out a big poster of architec-tural blueprints. Guy One turns to point at the plans to show Vic the "vision for the space."

"If y'all are gunna put up windows, gotta make sure there are bars on that shit," Malachi says casually while reclined against the wall. "Otherwise, Vic will be replacing broken glass every other night."

"That or pay extra to make the windows bulletproof. That'd be easier honestly," I add.

The architects raise their eyebrows and turn to Vic. "You didn't mention any . . . security considerations that we need to take into account," Guy One says cautiously.

"Don't mind them, they're just messing with me," Vic says in a forcedly lighthearted voice. "Young jokesters, they are—aren't cha?" Vic smiles at us like an aged, murderous clown. The young woman clocks his deranged attempt at being polite and winces.

"I don't know, man, with the new gang in the neighbor-hood, I would def make some *adjustments* to your plans," Malachi says to Guy One.

"Gang?" asks Guy Two, who quickly rolls back up the blue-prints and stands at attention.

"Yeah, didn't you see the graffiti out back? This place is SOSI territory," Malachi says casually while picking a piece of lint off his shoulder.

"Vic, does our supervisor know about this . . . *concern* in the neighborhood?" Guy One asks as he takes a step backward from Malachi and clutches the car keys in his pocket.

"Well, sir. If I may—" the woman begins, but Vic cuts her off.

"There is *nothing* for your boss to know!" Vic shouts, flustered. "Kids, can you get the hell out of here and stop screwing up my meeting?" The woman subtly elbows Vic, but maintains a forced, tight-lipped smile for the architects. If she's trying to save Vic from making a fool of himself, she's failing hard.

"Sure thing," Zeke says. "But first: I know that you said that you don't care if everyone in here dies, but my mom wanted me to ask if you could fix the outlet in our living room that keeps sparking. I know that unlike other landlords, you don't 'do' repairs, but she's worried that my little siblings will get hurt and she won't be able to save us all, given that she's in a wheelchair and all. . . ."

The architects cast Vic a look of extreme disgust. Guy One curls his lip. "If these renovations do go forward, we can help make the space beautiful, but to maintain it requires—"

"I *do* maintain my buildings." Vic wipes a thick layer of sweat from his forehead and flings it at me and Zeke. I feel some moisture hit my arm and almost vomit in my mouth.

"Please mind your temper," the woman whispers.

"Thank you for such an . . . informative meeting today. We'll speak to our supervisor and get back to you with updated plans, including the changes that we discussed." Guy One shakes Vic's hand, then the woman's.

Guy Two follows him, moving quickly, as if he's damn near ready to sprint away. He's been watching Malachi fearfully out of the corner of his eye throughout this entire conversation. The look on his face makes it seem as though he's doing the math to calculate how much of a head start he'd need to outrun this young criminal.

Vic pleads with the men. "Look, there's really no need to hurry out on account of these young people. And your supervisor and the investment team really doesn't need to know that—"

"We do need to get going," Guy Two contributes in a clear effort to wrap things up so that he can get the hell out of here. Vic nods and forces a polite smile. He shakes the men's hands once more and they exit the building much more quickly than how we heard them enter.

"You three!" Vic points a beefy finger at each of us one by one and starts to quake with anger.

The woman grabs Vic's shirt collar. "Can't you keep it professional for *one meeting*?" She lets go and storms out the building.

He opens his mouth to start yelling, but then closes his eyes. He inhales, casts the three of us one last glare, then barrels away down the hall after the woman without another word.

"What about the outlet?" Zeke calls out to Vic's back. Vic raises a middle finger at us over his shoulder and slams the door on his way out.

"Good work." I give Zeke and Malachi high fives. When we're back in Zeke's apartment, Lupe asks us how it went.

"You know how Mr. Vic is," Zeke says coyly.

Lupe calls Stella and Kiké into the room and sets out the giant bowl of cooked shrimp. "It was on sale at Vallarta. Seventy-five percent off regular price! Can you believe it?"

And believe it we do, devouring the decadent seafood meal to the very last bite.

We spend the rest of the afternoon liking, boosting, and forwarding every post about SOSI. We watch the number of reactions climb and climb, the comments section getting more and more lit.

Around 5:00 p.m., Malachi announces that he's hungry . . . again.

"Nigga, didn't you *just* eat like thirty shrimp?" The guys have always had a big appetite, but honestly, over the past few months, they've started taking things to another level.

"I'm a growing man, Rhea," Malachi says with a shrug. Lupe was nice enough to feed us lunch, but we know that even on sale that meal wasn't cheap. Malachi points out that it's Taco Thursday at Colony Cantina.

"Bruh, whyyy do you wanna go back there?" Zeke asks.

"I don't feel like sitting in El Pollo Loco with their shitty interrogation-room lighting, and don't feel like going any-where where we'll be stuck talking to our neighbors for hours." This is a valid point. There are plenty of dope restau-rants around us, but the odds of getting entangled in a boring conversation telling one of your mom's friends what you've been up to in school, hearing about what their kids have been up to, blah blah—it can be a whole thing.

We give in and head to Colony Cantina, where we're greeted by Troy's co-owner, Lance. He's super tall and wears a baseball cap in an attempt to hide the fact that he's balding. Thankfully, unlike Troy, he doesn't bother us much. He lets us order our chips and water without any awkward "compas" or "brothers." The restaurant's a ghost town, so we have the place to ourselves. We take over the same corner booth from last week.

"So, are y'all ready for the party tomorrow night?" Malachi says once we're settled. Zeke and I fidget with the napkins on the table between us. "I know, it's different than our usual weekends, but we're ready. It will be fun!"

There he goes with this whole *different* thing again.

Our crew is well-liked enough, but we're never really invited to parties. Like, yeah, sometimes we'd show up at a random classmates' birthday barbecue, but that's pretty much it. I guess people don't look at the three of us playing board games from the library at lunch and see "rager" energy. Fair enough.

Growing up, though, we'd always hear from Camesha and Lacy about all the wild house parties that happen up in the hills by Marley and Lou's place. Booze, weed, whining, and grinding. Even when she was much younger than we are today, Lacy was always cool enough to be invited. Tomorrow will be our first proper high school turnup thanks to the fake twins, who somehow—after only a month in LA—were able to snag an invite. They asked us to come with, and Malachi said yes on all of our behalf before Zeke and I even had the time to overthink it.

"I feel like it's going to be . . . a lot," Zeke says while attempting to bend and tie the straw of his water cup into a knot.

"And the dude's house who's throwing it—his parents will be out of town? Like they're trusting him to stay in that big-ass house alone?" This is the craziest part to me. If I ever had a ton of money, a pool, and a high school–aged offspring, I would *never* leave them solo on a Friday night. I guess in theory if you have enough money to replace anything that breaks, might as well let your asshole kid have some fun. But still . . .

"Yes, his parents won't be there, so yes, it will be a lot, but we *got* this, guys. It's time for a new chapter. We gotta start checking some firsts off our list," Malachi says animatedly, like a washed-up high school football coach giving his team of underdogs a pep talk.

"I can name at least one first that you're tryna check off with Marleyyy." Zeke winks and throws a crumpled-up napkin at Malachi, who flares his nostrils and huffs back at him.

"Man, shut up." Malachi shifts his gaze out the street-facing window to stare down the cars driving by. Hanging out just the three of us all day had put me in such a good mood that I had momentarily forgotten about Marley. Zeke keeps teasing—asking if he thinks that him and Marley will have decorative M&M's for "Malachi & Marley" at their wedding—and now I'm the one pretending to focus on what's happening out the window.

When Zeke finally lays off the jokes, he brings up the idea that we've been playing with for the past two days ever since we first heard about the party. He leans in over the table and speaks quietly. "Y'all are still game for the stunt, right?"

"Definitely. It will be the best SOSI exposure yet," I chime in, relieved that the conversation has shifted away from Marley. "If all of those people post about SOSI at once, shit will go crazy—it may even make the local news."

"Who's gonna do it, though?" Malachi asks, though I can hear in his voice that he doesn't want to be the one.

"I will," I volunteer without hesitation.

"And I'll help." Zeke leans his head against my shoulder and smiles.

"Dope. And I'll just . . . ?" Malachi waits for me to fill in the blank.

"Make sure that we get everyone's attention. Keep your phone on and text us when it's time."

Malachi claps his hands together. "It's a plan, then."

"What's a plan? The three of y'all are finally gunna smash?" Dumbass Diego's voice cuts. It's silent around the table except for the sound of Justin Bieber rapping in Spanglish over the restaurant speakers.

"Can't you tell when nobody wants you around?" I groan in his direction.

"Nena, we don't have to play these games, I *know* you want me, anytime, anywhere." Diego winks at me and my skin crawls. I tell him to fuck off, but he's already talking to Malachi now. Malachi leans away and looks at Diego with disgust, but still: he's listening to him. I don't like this new level of vague tolerance between them at all.

"Y'all hear about SOSI?" Diego asks while he makes himself comfortable, sliding into the booth next to Malachi. He drops his skateboard on the floor, blocking the walkway beside us.

"Yeah, crazy, right?" Malachi replies as he tries to shove Diego out the booth.

Diego catches himself and laughs before pulling himself right back up. "Do you think they're Black or Latino?"

"Does it matter?" Zeke asks.

"To some people, yeah." Diego helps himself to our basket of chips.

"That sucks," Zeke says.

Diego shrugs. "That's exactly how they want us. Against each other." There's a callous casualness in his voice that makes me want to protest, but the depth of his observation catches me off guard. "I'm tryna get in on that shit either way, though," he continues, a jagged smirk fixed across his face. "Better to be in than out, you feel me?"

"IDK, man, that life is complicated. Plus, I hear SOSI's super underground, nobody's ever really seen them," Malachi says, quite convincingly.

"I've seen 'em," Diego declares as he dumps salt on our chips without asking. Malachi, Zeke, and I instinctively avoid eye contact with one another. "Saw a bunch of dudes tagging some shit the other day. Check this out." Diego whips out his phone and leans over to show Malachi his screen. I watch Malachi's face turn from nerves, to confusion, to fear.

"Wow," Malachi says. "I've *never seen* that one before." He puts just enough emphasis on his words to tip off Zeke and me that something's wrong. Diego passes the phone across the table, so that we can take a look. It's the same tag that I had seen the other day. I tense up and slide the phone across the table back to Diego.

"You two can cover your ears if you want, but I got some grown-folk business to talk about with Malachi," Diego says after single-handedly finishing off the last of our food.

"Hah hah, very funny," Zeke says sarcastically.

"Suit yourself but remember . . . snitches get stitches!" Diego slams his hands on the table, making both Zeke and me jump. Diego laughs hysterically. I kick his shin under the table.

"Aight, enough, man. Let's go outside," Malachi suggests.

What's the need for privacy?

"Nah, now I'm comfortable. Let's talk here." Diego flashes a capsule of pills from the pocket of his hoodie. "I've asked around and from what I can tell, SOSI isn't pushing anything yet. That's gonna be my way in. I have a supply for candy— mi abuelo and abuelita are both real sick, so . . ." His voice catches. For a second, he actually looks . . . sad. He readjusts his beanie and clears his throat. "Anyway, it's whatever. It just means I have access to pills, and I could use the money. But I need someone with green. You sure your sister can't put us on?"

"*Us?*" I search Malachi's face for signs of lying.

Malachi rubs the space between his eyebrows. "There's no *us*," he says firmly. Usually when Malachi lies, he scratches the back of his neck, not his face. I don't know how to read him right now.

"Better get in early before I blow up. I'll be runnin' this block one day," Diego snickers. "Think about it, aight?" Diego winks as he slides out of the booth and grabs his board. He gives me one last gross look and jogs out the door. "This play-list sucks!" he shouts as he jumps to smack a sticker onto the archway of the restaurant door on his way out.

Zeke watches Diego leave, shaking his head. "He's a lot."

"I fucking hate that guy." Malachi scratches between his eyebrows once again. "He makes an interesting point, though," he says cautiously. I notice the vein on his neck twitch underneath his deep brown skin. He's clenching his jaw.

"What do you mean, *interesting*?" I watch his face for any clues as to what's going on in his head.

"SOSI isn't pushing any drugs, and everyone knows it. But maybe if they were, they'd earn some street cred." Malachi tries to take a sip of his water, but the cup's empty, all ice.

I look at him hard to make sure that I'm hearing him right. "Are you suggesting that we start *dealing*?"

"It might not be a bad idea. It's money in the bank, and it adds to the whole SOSI vibe."

"Too dangerous, man. SOSI's supposed to be a shadow and that's it," Zeke says sternly. "Once we add faces and products to the mix, the line between real and fake gets real fucking blurry."

"Also, think of Lacy," I add. "How pissed would she be if she found out that you started messing with that shit after what went down with you two last summer?"

He doesn't like to talk about it, but Lacy didn't get that scar of hers playing jump rope. Malachi had been walking home one afternoon when a car pulled up on him. The guy in the passenger's seat leaned out the window and told Malachi that if he walked a paper bag over to a car parked around the corner for him, and if he didn't peek inside, then he'd give Malachi $200. He flashed the cash right in front of him. Malachi didn't necessarily need the money, but he was feeling reckless, so he agreed. He took the cash, but Lacy had seen the interaction. She snatched the bag from Malachi's hands and ran over to tell the guys to fuck off, but they flipped out. Lacy stepped in front of Malachi just in time to catch the glass bottle hurtling toward his head.

"You can leave Lacy the fuck out of this," he bites back.

"Chill, man. Jesus. Rhea's right," Zeke says.

Malachi sighs. "But think about it: What if SOSI as it is

now isn't enough? We got the tags and the posters and the social sort of, but what if it doesn't have enough bite to really get the investors and developers to pull out? At least if I start dealing, we'd be able to earn enough money to buy Zeke some time. Plus, I feel like—"

"*Malachi.*" I can't listen to this shit any longer.

"Everything, uh, okay over there?" Lance asks from the other end of the dining room.

It's easy to forget to keep my voice down with this place so empty. "Yeah, we're good," I reply.

Lance nods and goes back to staring out the window, dreaming of better customers who'll spend more than $3 here.

Zeke leans into Malachi and whispers. "Bruh, we already talked about this, even before SOSI. I get that you're trying to help, but drugs? That ain't it."

A heavy, awkward quiet settles between us.

"Great, now y'all think I'm stupid," Malachi says angrily after several moments of silence.

"We don't think that," I say, and I mean it. I reach across the table to softly grab his forearm. He's startled for a hot second, in part because I've been cold to him all week, but also probably because this is the first time that I've initiated any touch between us. Ever. I watch the embarrassment on his face morph into something else. He doesn't move from my grasp.

"Promise us that you won't get into anything with Diego?" Zeke pleads gently.

Malachi gives Zeke a small smile and nods. I remove my hand from Malachi's arm so that I can lean back in the booth, and for a split second, I think that I catch him frown as I do.

"HEY-OOO!" Before my back can even hit the cool fabric of the seat, Corny Troy suddenly marches straight to our table. "Can I take a pic of y'all for the LykLuv page? I gotta show everyone that this is the place to *be*, nah mean? Colony Cantina turnup—woot woot!" Troy fist-pumps the air on the "woot-woot." He's kind of like the sun—it hurts to look directly at him, but even when you move somewhere else, you can still feel his oppressively cringey energy all around.

"Nah, man, we're straight," Malachi says.

"Your hair looks awesome, did you buy it online?" Troy leans forward to pet my hair. I shrink away from him into the far corner of the booth.

Malachi stands up, half-ready to throw hands when Lance jogs over. "Sorry about that," Lance says to us through a wince, passing us some shitty coupons that we'll never use as he glares at Troy. Troy responds by holding up both hands like we have him at gunpoint. He trots away, spastically spinning around once on his way back to the register.

We all groan.

"That asshole still took a picture of us, didn't he?" Malachi asks as we all watch Troy stare at his phone, smiling.

I sigh, exhausted from being made to feel like an animal on display at a zoo. "Let's get out of here."

"Okay, but, Rhea, we have to do one thing tonight," Zeke says, hooking his arm with mine. "I want to tell them."

I roll my eyes. We can't even go a day without talking about Marley and Lou anymore. "We talked about this. It doesn't concern them—"

"But it concerns me. This is *my* life that's about to be uprooted. I should get to decide who gets to be in the know."

Yeah, obviously, the eviction is happening to him, but the loss . . . it would affect all of us. "Zeke—" I plead.

"I get to tell Lou or—"

I scoff. "Or what?"

His brown eyes pour into mine, the softness of his face hardening. "Or I'm out."

ELEVEN

Lou and Marley meet us at night once they come home from their road trip. We gather in the parking lot behind the old liquor bank like we're in some low-budget mafia movie.

All the kids around here used to use this lot as a shortcut to get to the park, but the new building developers put up a fence with a big "No Trespassing" sign. There's a surefire way to tell if a new owner is local or not: look to see whether or not they put up a fence, and if so, notice who they're trying to keep out.

I hang back while the guys rush to greet Lou and Marley. I note the way that Malachi's looking at Marley, and how Zeke's looking at Lou, and feel utterly pissed that their hormones are driving a decision as huge as letting people who we barely even know in on our plan.

I cross my arms and claim a vacant cement stump as a seat.

"So, you're probably wondering why we're here," Malachi begins, like a reality TV show host.

"No," Lou says flatly.

"It's about your secret, right?" Marley adds.

"Hm. Good guess," Malachi says, visibly a little disappointed by his reveal being spoiled. He shakes it off and launches into his spiel. He tells them about how we've all lived here forever, and how Zeke's family has lived in that apartment for his whole life. (In fact, his mom first moved there with Zeke's dad back in 1999 and have stayed there ever since because the location's perfect and rent control kept it cheap as the city got more and more expensive.) He tells them about Vic the Landlord, and how he's jacking up rent and evicting everyone so that he can renovate the place and rent it to a bunch of Chads and Karens. Zeke pops in at the end to explain SOSI and the stunt that we plan on pulling at the party tomorrow night.

"So you guys are behind what everyone's posting about . . ." Marley murmurs.

"You've got many layers to you, sir," Lou says. He gently tugs on Zeke's shirt collar and Zeke practically melts.

Marley glares at her brother. "Just to make sure that I understand: y'all are starting a gang to scare away investors and potential gentrifiers, so that Zeke *may or may not* be able to stay in the neighborhood, *even though* his landlord is racing to max out his profits by the end of the month. Is that right?"

"Yup!" Zeke chirps.

"That's crazy." Marley shakes her head in disbelief. "What about the other gangs in the area? Like the actual gangs? Won't that cause problems?"

"Nah, there isn't really one group active on this block right now, and there hasn't been for several years. We're gonna keep things super tight to this corner of the neighborhood," Malachi explains.

"All we're doing is tagging some buildings and getting some posts to go viral—we won't fuck with any activity that might make any real crews want to dig into us. Nobody who's real will take us seriously because we'll have no real footprint," I add.

"I don't see how this possibly could work," Marley says in a low voice. "Even if you don't piss off any locals in the process, I don't think that gentrifiers would be stupid enough to fall for the trick."

"Maybe they will." Lou clears his throat. "When Alexander the Great and his troops arrived in India, they entered the jungle and came across a bunch of monkeys. The troops spent days rounding up all the monkeys, tying them to trees, and interrogating them because they thought that they were people."

For the second time this weekend, Lou leaves me speechless.

Marley sighs. "Okay, cool story, but what the hell is the point of that?"

"Even the most successful colonizers in world history wasted time and were made into fools by their own biases." Lou stands up to shake out his legs. "Those looking to 'conquer' new lands are extremely gullible."

"But didn't Alexander the Great ultimately win the Battle of the Hydaspes?" Marley asks as she crosses her arms.

"Alexander and his troops were in parts of the northwest, but he never conquered the subcontinent. There were Indo-Greek kingdoms established around modern-day Pakistan, but that's pretty much where his troops were like, 'Okay, we're over it,' and gave up. Plus, thousands of years later, India's a free country that has managed to retain so much of its rich cultures despite various other colonial periods. Who's to say that they didn't win the war?"

Marley glares at her brother. "You're really stepping into my lane here with the ancient history stuff."

"Don't blame me for knowing how to win you over."

"Who said you won me over?" Marley pipes back.

"You did as soon as you uncrossed your arms and stopped twitching your eyebrow." Lou smirks at Marley as she rolls her eyes. "C'mon, let's help them out. It's a good plan."

She doesn't look sold yet, so I pile it on thick. The only thing worse than letting Marley in on SOSI would be her knowing our plan but not being complicit. "We're doing this for Zeke, but we're also doing it for the whole neighborhood. The place where *you* live now too," I say, resisting the urge to add: *Whether I like it or not.* "This plan is for everyone that we've grown up alongside, for everyone before us who hustled to make the hood so special, and for—"

"For kids like Stella and Kiké," Zeke adds. "The little ones deserve to grow up in a community with deep roots to nourish them."

Marley scans our faces and sighs. "And here I was, just wanting to make some friends and have a normal summer. . . ." Marley walks over to Zeke with her hands on her hips, eyes fixed in a disapproving-mom stare. When she reaches him, she lets her arms fall and goes in for a hug. "Where do we start?"

The guys clap as Marley loosens up.

Whoop-dee-fucking-doo.

I'm not sure how useful she'll be, but at least if her hands are dirty too, she can't rat us out.

Lupe has her book club (aka wine club) with Mrs. Reed and their friends tonight, so Zeke has to get home and watch his little brother and sister. My mom used to be in the book club too, but she stopped showing up after my older siblings went off to college when I hit second grade. I've tried to convince her to hang out with Lupe and Mrs. Reed again, but she never hears me. It's like she stopped putting effort into all aspects of her old life after my siblings left—her friends, the house . . . even me. Every now and then I get sort of mad about it, but at the end of the day, my mom's not a bad person. She's just tired.

I try not to think about it too much.

Sometimes I keep Zeke company while he babysits, but as much as I love Kiké and Stella, I don't feel like watching a sing-along tonight. Plus, he invites Lou to come with him, and I imagine that they might want some alone time after the kids go to sleep. Marley yawns and says she's still recovering from heat exhaustion after being out in the desert all day, so she bikes home. Zeke waves goodbye and splits off with Lou, leaving Malachi and me alone together.

Part of me wants to make an excuse to leave as well, but we both know that I don't got shit to do. I walk with Malachi on autopilot to his house and don't say much. When we get to the door, he holds it open. "You're coming in, right?"

I shrug and step into the home that I know better than my own. I start to relax when I hear Lacy and Camesha squealing down the hall. At least with the girls here, I don't have to stress so much about filling the gaps in conversation with Malachi that seem to get bigger and bigger with each failed attempt at pretending that things are normal between us.

"Girl, do that shit one more time, I swear to god." Lacy's wielding a wooden spoon as a sword, and she points it at Camesha, who's deviously grinning from the breakfast nook beside the refrigerator, threateningly holding a Froot Loop between her neon-green fingernails. The girls stare each other down and Camesha sends the cereal flying, hitting Lacy right on the eyebrow next to her scar. Camesha laughs wildly and sprints past us in the doorway to hide in the living room. Lacy shouts at Camesha that she's gunna beat her ass, but just keeps on laughing, cracking an egg into the bowl of box brownie mix.

"Oof, that girl kills me sometimes," Lacy says to me and Malachi.

"You know you love me!" Camesha yells from the other room. Lacy lovingly rolls her eyes and adds the vegetable oil to her mix.

"Did you get the good kind?" Malachi steps forward to swipe a finger in the bowl, stealing a lick of the shiny brown batter.

"Ghirardelli all the way, babyyyyy!! You know I'm too nice for Betty Crocker," Lacy says proudly.

"Ayyeee!" Malachi dusts off Lacy's shoulders, and she tosses her hair and flexes. I've always liked witnessing these little moments between them where I can catch a glimpse of Malachi in Brother Mode as opposed to just my friend. But it's also sort of bittersweet. Both Zeke and Malachi have siblings, so whenever they go home, their houses are always rowdy.

There's always someone else there. Zeke and Malachi care about our friendship, of course, but they also have their own families. But for me, their families *are* my only family—just without the blood relation or the guarantee that they'll always be there. That's what sets me apart from the guys, though I'd never try to explain it to them. Some things are too desperate, too pathetic, to admit out loud.

"Rhea, can you grab the chocolate chips for me, love?" Lacy points to the cabinet above the microwave. I climb up on my toes to reach the bag and toss it her way. She rips it open with her teeth and unleashes a waterfall of chocolate into the mix. "Where's Zeke?"

"Watching Stella and Kiké," Malachi says. "Dad's not home, right?"

Lacy says no, so Malachi jumps to sit on top of the table as part of his recent bit to sit on anything but a chair. He's always been a Good Kid (he's only brave enough to break house rules when his dad's not home), but he's been leaning more into these subtle acts of subversion recently. Like at the end of last year, I needed to borrow a pencil, so I took his backpack and found several crumpled-up pages of homework assignments, all completed, that he had told our teacher he didn't do. I assumed this was all just a part of us getting further into high school, him wanting to act out and all. But now with the whole sudden interest in dealing . . . I know it sounds silly, but somehow, the table sitting feels related.

"You know I love Zeke, but it's nice to see the two of you spending time together," Lacy says as she pours the brownie batter into a greased pan.

"Rhea's always here," Malachi says dismissively.

"Yeah, but . . . Y'all don't really know this yet, but a lot of shit changes when you start tenth grade, so it's important to—"

"Okay, *Mom*," Malachi says in a fake whiny voice as he slides off the table and walks past me into the living room. Lacy shakes her head like how she always does when Malachi's being hardheaded. I dip out of the kitchen and follow him, even though I really do want to hear what she has to say.

Camesha's sitting in the knockoff La-Z-Boy chair in the corner reclined so far back that she's practically lying down. Her posture mimics the photo on her T-shirt of Rihanna lounging on a beach surrounded by money.

Malachi's on the couch flipping through channels. I plop on the opposite side, as far away as possible without it seeming weird. His mom is addicted to local news, so his parents are some of the last people in Los Angeles still paying for cable TV. Weirdly, though, I fuck with the local news too. Nothing makes me feel more connected to the city than moments like last month when we all gathered around to watch a live car chase on the 110 freeway for a solid forty minutes. There's something about the changing landscapes as they speed across neighborhoods and the "Fuck the Police" vibe that gets us all rooting for the driver even when it's totally his fault. It reminds me how much I love this outrageous, messy city.

"Oh, this is about to be fire," Malachi says, tossing the remote onto the coffee table as a nature documentary takes over the screen. "If anyone ever makes a movie about my life, I want it to be animated and I want this muthafucka to voice me."

Camesha spills her Froot Loops as we cackle at the thought of the middle-aged, white British narrator of the show playing Malachi Reed, average neighborhood Black kid from South LA.

"Dude, you're trippin'," I say.

"What? Swear to god, in my mind, my voice sounds classy as fuck, like this."

"ArE youuu SuREEE?" Camesha says, cracking her voice with every syllable.

"Yo, in two years, Imma be on some Black James Bond shit, just wait."

"Nigga, puberty ain't gon make you *British*!" Camesha cries.

"Y'all wait and see." Malachi leans back confidently and starts laughing along with us.

"This is a new one," I say once we all calm down. For the past two years, Malachi and I have been super into nature documentaries. It didn't really start for any particular reason, but it's become the default thing that we always end up watching when it's just me and him around.

"Do you think that mountain lion there could fuck up a puma?" he asks.

"Wait, aren't those two like the same animal?" I reply.

Malachi shakes his head. "No way."

"Look it up," I challenge him.

Malachi turns to me, narrowing his eyes. "I bet you a party-size bag of Takis that you're wrong and I'm right."

I furrow my brow to match his intensity. "Deal."

He looks it up and, as expected, I'm right. I take a little bow and blow my nails to flex 'cuz I'm full of useless facts like this. "One day Imma go on *Jeopardy!* and destroy *everyone*."

"Hah, you *thought*." Malachi throws a pillow at me and we

start clowning back and forth, arguing about who's smarter and would become a TV-game-show fan favorite. Camesha joins in, and it starts to feel like the awkward energy curse has been lifted. Suddenly, we're back to the chill, pre-Marley space where we had been for our entire lives.

"We should add this park to the list," I declare.

"Yo, so true," he says excitedly, pulling out his phone. "What's the name again? Grand Tet?"

"Grand Teton National Park," I correct. Malachi types into his phone, sending the buzz of a notification to my own pocket. *Malachi has added a location onto your shared list: Travel Bucket List.*

"This place isn't far from Yellowstone, so we can stop there on the way," he says matter-of-factly, even though neither of us can drive, or have ever even left the state before. There are already forty-seven other locations on our list—Angkor Wat in Cambodia, Tsingy de Bemaraha National Park in Madagascar, etc.—that we say we're gonna visit together once we get to college and snag some of that sweet scholarship money. It's not like we really know much about these places or even have the faintest idea of what it's like to be out in nature like that, but we share this fantasy of becoming these Black explorers. Pretty much all the hosts on National Geographic are white, but hey, maybe we'll be the first. And until then, we'll just keep sipping ice water to stay cool from the comfort of his parents' black pleather couch, growing our list one by one.

"I'm tryna get my sugar daddy to take me somewhere pretty like this." Camesha points at the aquamarine lake on the TV. "But he's so boring sometimes."

"What do you expect from some landlord–real estate developer? They aren't known to be the most interesting people,"

Lacy says as she joins us, taking a seat between Malachi and me.

"I know, but he's really irritating me these days." Camesha sighs and shoves a handful of cereal into her mouth. "I feel like I deserve a vacation. Like he keeps asking me again and again to meet some friend of his, but I'm not taking referrals right now. Between his boring ass and my blog, I'm maxed out on time."

"Why does he want you to meet his friend so bad?" I ask.

"He says he's some hotshot that would be a 'strategic' client for me to have. He says it, though, as if I'm not already strategic as fuck. Ya girl is only eleven months away from having saved up enough to not only move out of Auntie Inga's place, but to *buy* my own house." She mimes making it rain dollar bills.

"Shit, you make money like that? Watch me grow up and get a fake job like you too, then," Malachi jokes.

Camesha flicks a Froot Loop at his head. "Hey, watch yourself, boy. My work *is* real work."

"Just be safe, okay?" Lacy says in a concerned tone.

"I will text you if and when I meet this friend of his." Camesha blows Lacy a kiss. Her phone rings and she excuses herself to the porch to go talk to her client.

While the brownies bake, Malachi, Lacy, and I finish the nature doc before switching to play *Super Smash Bros.* Lacy snags Kirby and completely serves us. We stand no chance against her alone, so Malachi and I join forces to try to beat her, but she still demolishes us time after time.

"Imma take a break so one of you two losers can experience winning for once." She tosses the controller and bounces into the kitchen. When she's gone, I move fast to swoop up

Kirby for myself, but Malachi doesn't even try to beat me. He makes a bunch of rookie mistakes and I win, easily.

"You good?" I ask after I kill him twice in a row.

"Yeah, I've just . . ." He aimlessly draws circles with the little white glove on the screen from his controller. "I've missed you."

I know what he means, but instead of being real, I find myself playing the immature communication games that I normally hate. "But you see me every day."

"Yeah, but you've been low-key angry at me since the block party. I can feel it."

Great. So, he's noticed—*really* noticed. The crazy thing about being mad at someone is that you can simultaneously want them to know how upset you are—to really feel the ice that you're sending their way—but also desire them to be totally oblivious, so that you can continue holding on to your bad feelings and never have to confront the ways that you're hurting one another.

I take a deep breath, then lie to my best friend. "That's not true, Malachi."

"Rhea, after over ten years of friendship, you don't think I can tell that you're pissed?"

"Maybe you're the one acting weird." There's a sick comfort in keeping your true feelings locked up inside.

"Me?!" He looks aghast at first, like I've accused him of some heinous crime, but then takes a controlled breath. "Okay, fine. I'll own up to my part. I should've course-corrected earlier when I first felt things were off. But what about you?"

Another chance. He's giving me another chance to be honest. The words are right there on the tip of my tongue, but there's a dam blocking any truth from coming out. I want to talk to him for real, I really do, but I can't stop picturing Marley's stupid Doc Martens in my head. Or worse, I can't stop picturing *Malachi picturing* them.

I avoid his eyes. "It's all in your head. Everything is fine."

He drops the controller and presses his palms to his forehead in frustration. "*Why* are you gaslighting me?" There's genuine confusion in his eyes paired with an uninhibited sense of desperation that makes my heart whimper. It doesn't feel good to stoke this messiness between us, but I can't stop. Miscommunication is a tornado that can hurl you around and around until you can't tell which way is up. And now here I am—drowning in all the things that I can't bring myself to say to him.

"This was fun. I'll see you at the party," I say, abruptly getting up and putting on my shoes. Camesha and Lacy rush in and beg me to stay, trying to use the brownies still in the oven as leverage.

"Rhea, please." Malachi's brown eyes offer me one final olive branch.

But I don't take it.

"I'll see everyone later. Have a good night." I slip my heels into the back of my sandals and rush out the door.

I start fast-walking home and feel my pocket buzz.

I pull out my phone and see a text from Malachi, which I ignore. Another buzz. Then another. I give in and click the button to show the notifications on my lock screen.

There are three texts from Malachi, then a notice from an app. The hazy light of my phone illuminates the alert. *Malachi has added a location onto your shared list: Travel Bucket List.* I unlock my phone to see what he put. When I read it, I quicken my pace into a full-on run.

Right below Grand Teton, I see his most recent entry: "Where We Can Be Us Again."

When I reach my front porch, I wipe away my tears even though I know that when I open the door, like always, I will be the only one home.

TWELVE

A girl in tight-fitted white jeans walks by as the headlights of a car on the street behind us illuminate the tiny flecks of blue lint on her ass—remnants of when she undoubtedly was grinding on some dude whose jeans left their mark. The thunderous roll of "Ayyye!" breaks out on the other side of the window of the house, where it looks like someone is dancing on a table. Everyone looks so cool, so carefree, so . . . comfortable.

I don't realize that my hands are shaking until Zeke grabs them.

"You ready?" he asks.

I was expecting Zeke to be nervous too, but he looks just as excited as he did two years ago when we went to Six Flags for Malachi's birthday. I try to steady my breath, but the smell of weed makes it hard to stay calm. "This will be fun," Zeke says assuringly.

He lets go of my hand and offers me his arm to walk in together. I grab hold of him and feel more grateful than ever for Zeke's subtle self-confidence.

"My first LA party!" Marley squeals as she runs over to grab Zeke's other arm.

I fight the urge to literally shoo her away. Marley's hair is pulled back in a giant, low ponytail poof with ample extensions in a way that shows off her large forehead. She looks like a cross between a 1960s civil rights leader and an Ethiopian runway model. She's gorgeous.

"Let's go in!" Marley shrieks in excitement. A boy walks by and gives her a super-grody up-down, then a nod. She recoils a bit but shakes it off before anyone else notices.

"Shouldn't we wait for Malachi?" Lou asks. His text said that he's on his way with Lacy and Camesha, so he should be here any minute.

Lou's standing a few steps away from the three of us, but the energy between him and Zeke is so magnetic, even I can feel that they're tethered together. Lou's wearing these Harajuku-style pleated black pants and a simple muscle shirt that shows off his arms. On anyone else, it'd look ridiculous, but there's something about Lou's somewhat-detached, indie-kid demeanor that makes it work. Normally I forget that he's only a year older than us, but tonight, it shows—he looks much closer to a man than a teenager.

Zeke had texted me photos of several outfits splayed out on his bed before we met up in an attempt to elevate his wardrobe to keep up with Lou's style. I was able to talk him out of wearing one of his bizarre graphic tees and into a flannel jacket with jeans that actually fit. He put some effort into his hair, and it's looking much more '90s surfer than overgrown bowl cut gone wrong.

Everyone looks the part tonight, like they really belong here, except for me. I tried to pick out something nice but got sort of panicky and freaked out. I settled on the same oversize sweatshirt that I always wear—the only thing that I did to shake it up was wear the hoops that Lacy got me for my birthday and clean my Air Force 1s. But not everyone can be cool, right?

Right as I'm about to ask Zeke to help me find the bathroom so that I can attempt to do something, *anything*, with my hair, Lacy, Camesha, and Malachi pile out from the backseat of some car that I don't recognize. They stand up and laugh hysterically at something that the driver says to them. Malachi sees us and waves so eagerly that he knocks his Dodgers hat right off his head.

"Wowww, look at him all cleaned up," Zeke muses as we watch Malachi wobble toward us. Next to the girls, he looks giant tonight, taller than I had ever really noticed before. I ignore the little flutter in my chest that likes what it sees.

"Yooooooo!" His voice is much louder than necessary, even with the music in the background. He leans in to hug me, and Zeke backs away, just as thrown as I am.

"Oh my god, are you *high*?" I whisper.

"Psshhh! Nah!" He leans away and swats at the sky before wrapping himself around Zeke.

"Bro, yes you are!" Zeke says in shock.

"Don't worry, he didn't have any," Lacy whispers to me slowly, her voice like molasses.

"We did hotbox the shed in the backyard before we came, though," Camesha says while adjusting her cleavage. Both of the girls look ready to slay tonight. A group of chicks walk by looking salty as hell and curl their lips.

"Yo, those girls stay looking for trouble," Lacy says in a voice that's meant to be threatening but ends up sounding self-conscious when she moves her arms to cover her abs under her crop top.

Camesha rubs some Carmex onto her lips and kisses Lacy on the cheek. "Bitch, ignore them. They're just jealous. They haven't evolved enough yet to know that real queens support queens, ya feel me?"

For a split second, I feel Marley look at me, though her eyes have already retreated by the time I try to catch her.

Malachi gives Lou a nod and Marley a high five before facing the front door. "To boldly go where no man has gone before!"

"HAH! I knew you secretly like it when we watch *Trek*!" Zeke yells at Malachi's back. Then he whispers in my ear, "Let's wait and see what else slips out from his subconscious tonight now that he's secondhand stoned."

An intriguing prospect.

Even at parties, there's a role for shy girls, I think. Or at least that's what I tell myself as we make our way through the living room, passing the kitchen counter littered with plastic handles of vodka and Henny stolen from someone's parents. With Zeke and Malachi, I've always felt comfortable (for the most part). They get me, so when I make a joke, they laugh. But even then, I've never fooled myself into believing that I'm not shy. At school, vibing with other people doesn't come easily to me. It always takes me a second to warm up to people, but here with everyone running around, saying hi and bye so quickly, there's not enough time for me to settle in with anyone. If it weren't for Zeke by my side, I'd probably shrink into my crewneck until I could effectively disappear.

I can't tell if we're the youngest people at the party, or if all the boys my age have grown and all the girls have learned to put on makeup, so that they look three years older. I let out a sigh of relief when we see the first people we know,

Jamal and Jabron. We've all gone to school together since kindergarten, so I walk over to them, maybe too eagerly. It's comforting to see another familiar face, even if we aren't that close.

"Yooooo." Jamal gives Malachi and Zeke dap, then Jabron quietly does the same. They're twins—both tall and fit with shoulder-length locs, big bronze eyes, and dimples to match—but Jamal does all the talking.

"Rhea!" Jamal pulls me into a hug, which is more friendly than usual for us, but the party vibe is making everyone feel a bit more loose. He smells good, like oak and sage or something. "Looking comfortable in the crewneck, as always," he teases after we let go. I nudge his shoulder and he flashes me a bright smile, full of post-braces confidence.

We all stand around making small talk about nothing with everyone (except for Lou) seemingly putting in various degrees of effort to appear comfortable in this new environment. Some next-level-gorgeous girl who I've never seen before waves at Marley. *Literally how does she already have so many friends??* I turn back to the guys and try to focus on appearing to have fun.

"Is this your first time at one of these Lenway parties?" I ask Jamal when there's a lull in the conversation.

For a second, he looks like he's going to laugh at the suggestion, but then he takes a swig from his red cup and visibly winces. He swallows before he speaks. "Actually, yeah, it is. You?"

"What do you think?" I ask.

He narrows his eyes to study my face as if it's a hard guess. "A fellow virgin," he announces at last. "Party virgin, I mean," he adds frantically. We all bust out laughing. "Aight, aight,

aight, speaking of first times—do you think the SOSI guys are gunna make a debut tonight?"

"Wh-what do you mean?" Zeke asks, choking on his drink.

"You know, a debut. Like finally come out tonight and show people who they are, maybe flex a bit. They've been real low-key since they came onto the scene."

"Maybe they run things differently. Maybe they'll never show who they are," Lou says in a voice equal parts cool and mysterious. Even in low-lighting, I can see stars dance across Zeke's eyes as he watches Lou speak.

"Maybe," Jamal says. "That'd be a cool, real-life hood version of some Anonymous hacker-vibe shit."

This makes Zeke smile triumphantly. He has a *V for Vendetta* mask hanging on the wall of his bedroom. The conversation shifts back to mindless chatter as Marley impresses everyone with her ability to rap the lyrics to every single song that comes on. Several guys walk by to say hi to Jamal and talk about how they're gonna dominate the football season this fall. I knew that Jamal's leaving Bayrex Charter to start Morsey High School because their football program is legit, but I hadn't realized how big of a deal it is that he'll be the only sophomore on varsity there.

Meanwhile, Zeke and Lou hold hands and flirt like there's no tomorrow. That is until, suddenly, Zeke lets go of Lou and takes a step back from our circle.

His face falls. "Shit."

The sliding door of the house opens, and a crew of guys walk into the yard. I've seen these dudes before at the park a few blocks south of our neighborhood. They all got their colors on.

"Wonder if they got beef with SOSI yet," Jamal whispers.

"Now that the block's active again, I'm sure they got something to say." He takes another sip of his drink but doesn't wince this time. I wonder what happens first: Do you get used to the taste of alcohol, or do you just get real good at hiding your innocence?

Lou and Marley exchange a worried look that Jabron, the silent observer, definitely sees.

"I'm gonna go get some water," I announce.

"Water?" Jamal teases.

"Yes, *water*," I clap back.

He smirks as I roll through potential comebacks in my mind, but then he says something that surprises me. "I like that. You stick to water and you own it."

I don't quite know what to say, so I sort of smile and move a strand of hair away from my eyes like how I've seen girls in movies do for my whole goddamn life. This makes Jamal smile even more. I guess art does imitate life.

When I turn to walk away, Zeke flashes me a nosy look that says that he wants to talk about this little moment later. Malachi doesn't look at me, or at Jamal, but he does glare at Zeke, who's mouthing, *YAS, girl!*

Inside, half the people are whispering about the guys who just showed up, while the other half are constructing conspiracy theories about SOSI. One guy says that he thinks SOSI is bullshit, but a girl quickly jumps in to correct him, asserting with confidence that he's wrong and she knows it because her friend gave a SOSI guy head last weekend.

I fill my cup with water from the sink and throw back one glass, then another, to buy myself time to eavesdrop. When I go back outside, Jamal notices me first, almost as if he had been watching the door, waiting for me. The thought of the star football player checking for me is so ridiculous, I can't help but laugh as I slide the door closed and dodge a coven of drunk girls stumbling in front of me.

Back in the circle, the conversation has split into two: Jamal and Malachi are arguing over Marvel versus DC with Jabron nodding soberly on one side, while Marley and Zeke are speaking to each other in hushed voices on the other. Lou's not around. I couldn't care less about superheroes in spandex, so I opt to join Zeke and Marley.

"All I'm saying is that you need to be careful. Nuance and body language can be hard for him, which makes dating tricky. Plus, hanging out with people all day can take a ton of effort," Marley explains to Zeke, who looks more annoyed at her than I've ever seen.

"Look, Marley, you don't give him enough credit. Lou and I have talked about autism. We have our own boundaries. I know not to make any assumptions. And he knows how to check in when he feels like he's pushing himself too much socially," Zeke asserts.

Marley frowns and begins again. "I just don't want either of you to get hurt—"

"Are you talking about me, Lil Sis?" Lou says coolly as he walks up cradling three drinks. He passes one to Marley and one to Zeke. He waits patiently for Marley to respond, his direct attitude and perfect posture making him seem much more mature than us all. Marley opens her mouth, but Lou speaks first. "Zeke and I are solid. I'm careful about how I spend my cognitive energy, and he's who I choose to spend it with."

"But—" Marley begins.

"Enough." Lou's voice comes out stern. "I've come a long

way, and remember, *I'm* the older sibling here. Not you." Lou grabs Zeke's hand and leads him away straight toward the empty bench in the corner of the lawn. They sit and immediately start making out heavily.

The look on Marley's face is a strange combination of frustration, hope, and fear. I've seen other women in my life make this face when watching the people they love take risks with their hearts. If she weren't so annoying, I'd maybe feel some sympathy for her.

"Looks like they've really settled into a groove," Malachi says, merging our separate conversations back into one.

"I know, isn't it great?" Marley stretches her lips into a smile that doesn't quite reach her eyes.

"Are you, um, interested in anyone like that?" Malachi stammers. Maybe it's the secondhand high lowering his inhibitions, but never in my life have I ever seen Malachi be so bold. I have to remind myself to close my mouth once I realize that it's literally hanging open in shock.

"Um," Marley begins awkwardly. "Uh. Wow, the music is so loud! Hah! I can't hear *anyone*." She grabs my shoulder. "Rhea, can you show me where the bathroom is?"

Me?

"I don't know where it is," I say curtly.

"Well, can you help me find it?" she asks, raising her eyebrows at me urgently.

The fact that I'm out of water and don't feel like standing anywhere near Malachi is the only reason why I give in and follow her into the house, leaving the guys outside.

"Well, Malachi's pretty faded," Marley says, followed by a forced laugh once we find the line of people in tight shorts waiting for the bathroom.

"Yeah, he always gets like this," I lie.

"Really?" Marley crinkles her nose. "That's . . . well, surprising, I guess."

"What, you're not into stoners?" I know for a fact that Malachi's never smoked a blunt in his life, but I see my window of opportunity and am not going to let it slide away.

"Um, not really," she says to the floor.

A few places ahead of us in line, a person wearing neon-pink biker shorts and a matching crop top with an ombré buzz cut bangs on the bathroom door. They put their ear to the wood and groan. "Shit, this motherfucker's in here throwin' up. We 'bout to be here for a minute."

Marley shifts her weight from one foot to another and crosses her legs. I figured she was just looking for an out from the conversation with Malachi, not that she legit needs to pee. "There's no way this is the only bathroom in this humongous house," she complains.

She's right. This place is easily three stories with no less than five bedrooms. The host had roped off the staircase to prevent anyone from going upstairs, but I'm pretty sure that we can sneak up there if we try. I tell Marley to come on and we relinquish our spot in line, heading for the curvy staircase in the entryway.

I look around to make sure that everyone is sufficiently distracted, which is easy because there's an extremely hot couple, both with glowing skin, captivating the room's attention with a contest to see who can blow the perfect smoke rings from the bong. I motion Marley forward, and we slip between the duct tape barrier up the steps. The first door to our left is a sparkling-clean bathroom. She thanks me and sprints inside, shutting the door behind her.

I've never really had girl friends (not that Marley's a *friend* per se), but still, I don't know what I'm supposed to do now. Do I wait for her awkwardly outside the door where I can hear her stream? Do I go to the bottom of the stairs and hang out there until we go back outside together? Can I dip and let her find her own way back? I flip through my vague knowledge of Girl Code that I've gathered from watching TV, Lacy, and Camesha over the years.

I decide to dip, but before I go, a familiar voice catches my attention. Light peeks through from behind a cracked door down the hall. The nosy bitch in me brightens up and I can't stop myself from tiptoeing a few steps closer to hear what's going on up here, so separate from the party downstairs.

"I got Oxy and Percs for now, but tryna expand, you know," the familiar voice says. I hear the sound of a zipper pull away and the other voices in the room let out one of those collectively learned, masculine-TV-show-esque gasps.

"Damn, son, you're stacked," one guy says.

"I got a hookup for weed coming in soon too. Next weekend, hit me up."

I hear someone counting dollar bills and money exchanging hands. I know for a fact that Malachi is downstairs, but there's something about the way that these guys laugh together so easily—the subtle confidence that they won't get caught—that makes it a little too easy for me to imagine him right there with them. I worry if the memory of Lacy's scar is still enough to keep Malachi away from all of this. I *hope* it's enough. The Malachi I've known my whole life would never lie to us. Never lie to me. But there's been so much change between us this summer, so much change within himself, that

I'm not so sure anymore. In the absence of total confidence, hope is all I can hold on to.

I don't catch the next few sentences over the sound of the bass on the speakers. But I do hear my cue to hide. "Don't carry so much shit on you at once," the second guy says as he and the others approach the door where I'm crouching.

I dart into the nearest closet and wait for the footsteps to pass before coming out. I may be nosy, but I'm not stupid. Better to not know who's doing and buying what—knowing too much is an easy way to get into real trouble. I hold my breath and hope that Marley takes her time.

The footsteps carry down the hall and ultimately to the bottom of the stairs. When the coast is clear, I climb out of the closet and brush a strand of curls from my crewneck. The door to the room where the guys had been talking is wide open, the yellow light now fully illuminating the hallway. Then everything goes dark.

Someone flips the switch in the room. I try to jump back into the closet, but there's not enough time.

"Aw, were you looking for me?" the familiar voice says, his tone coming through much more clearly than a minute ago. He takes a few steps forward and I see his face. Of course it was him.

"Hey, Diego," I say, rolling my eyes.

"You're not supposed to be up here," he says, half-flirting, half-threatening.

"I'm waiting for Marley."

"The new girl?" Sparks of interest flash across his eyes.

I nod.

"Nice," he says, licking his lips.

Marley flings the bathroom door open, "You know what I

think about Malachi?" she starts before realizing that we're not alone. "Oh, sorry." She looks at Diego a bit embarrassed and smiles sheepishly in a way that's annoyingly endearing.

"You two have met, right?" I say boredly, even though I know that they have.

"Briefly," Marley says.

"Too brief," Diego adds smoothly. "Can I get you a drink, hermosa?"

Hermosa? I didn't even know it was within Diego's vocabulary to step up from skeezy to romantic. Marley casts me a questioning glance, clearly asking whether or not this is a good move. I have a brief flashback to the way that Diego treated me last year and all the shit that I went through after the fact. I look at him run a hand through his impeccable hair in the same way that he lured me in before he kissed me. I see the effect that it has on Marley as she can't help but grin.

I could warn her to not fall for his crap. I really could, and it'd be so easy. Instead, though, while Diego bats his deep brown eyes at her and offers up the best rendition of his crooked, hot bad-boy smile, I flash her two enthusiastic thumbs-up.

Go for it, I mouth.

THIRTEEN

For the first few minutes, it feels good. I run into Jamal in the kitchen filling his Solo cup with water. I crack a joke that actually makes him laugh.

But it doesn't take long for the guilt to settle in.

I know Dumbass Diego well enough to know that he hasn't grown much in the past year and that Marley doesn't know the shitshow that she's getting herself into with him. Jamal's looking at me differently than I've seen him (or anyone) look at me before, though, and it feels . . . nice. We're leaning against the sink and he moves a little bit closer. I get excited, but then I think of Malachi, and when I think of Malachi, I have no choice but to think of Marley.

Shit.

"I'll be right back," I say to Jamal, touching his shoulder lightly before I go. It's crazy how over the course of one night, it's come to my attention that there may be someone for me in between the two extremes: Malachi, my best friend, and Diego, my enemy.

I make my way from the kitchen to the living room to the dining room to the game room, and still no sign of Marley and Diego. Maybe I'm wrong. Maybe Diego can be nice to girls (just not me). I try not to let this bother me and remind myself to do the right thing and find Marley. I even go outside to look for her, but still, she's nowhere to be found.

I slip back up the stairs for one last look in case she forgot her phone or something. It's sort of a last-resort effort—the option that I didn't think would turn into anything but would at least make me feel like "I did all that I could"—so I'm taken aback when I hear a nervous voice coming from the next room over. There's no doubt in my mind that it's her. My pace quickens from a lazy walk to a run.

I open the door without knocking and see Marley pressed against the wall with her arm extended, pushing Diego away. I don't waste any time trying to put the pieces together.

"Nope. Nuh-uh. Fuck this. Diego, get out," I bark.

"It's not what it looks like," he slurs.

"Don't care. Get out."

He clicks his tongue. "Don't be jealous—"

"Leave her alone." I hurl my phone at his head, but he ducks. My phone hits the wall, shattering its screen. Diego glares up at me with his signature condescending expression—slightly startled, slightly impressed—before his eyes glaze over. Looks like he sampled whatever he was selling earlier.

Marley's standing there frozen, amber-brown eyes unblinking. She clenches her fist but doesn't move, casting me an uncertain look as Diego crouches by her feet. Opposite her, I throw a punch in the air and mouth, *Do it!*

There's no need to tell her twice. She winds her leg back and kicks Diego in the shin, unleashing a feral yelp from his throat. He scrambles to his feet, cradling his soon-to-be-bruised leg, and slams the door on his way out. I turn to congratulate Marley on landing such a skilled hit. But then—

Very slowly, then all at once, she slides down the wall, hits the floor, and starts to cry.

Fuck.

I rush over to her. "Are you, um, okay?" I ask, which is a stupid question given the obvious tears, but I don't know where to start.

Her eyes are bright red and puffy. I'm surprised that she's not a pretty crier like the girls in movies—she's got snot everywhere and her lips are pushed out in a way that's not at all graceful. I instantly feel shitty that even right now, I'm trying to find ways to put this girl down. *Why am I like this?*

I take a seat on the floor next to her and try again. "Did Diego try to do something?"

The sniffles turn into a full-out sob. She leans over against my shoulder and I stroke her head, my heart breaking for her.

I could have prevented this.

But I didn't.

"He was nice at first," she says at last, her voice and hands both shaking like hell. "But then he kept trying to grab my waist, then other things, and I wasn't into it at all."

With me and Diego, the kiss was consensual—it was the lies that followed that weren't. It's horrific, I know, but I thought that would be more or less what would go down with him and Marley too. A kiss-and-tell, not . . . this. I kick myself for being so cruel, and so naive. I should've known that by this point he'd have graduated to attempting to force himself onto girls. I watch the tears fall onto Marley's jeans as she fiddles with her ponytail.

"Did he, um . . . ?" I search my brain to find the right

words. Nobody really prepares you for the first time that you talk to a girl that's been hurt like this.

"No. But I could tell that he was going to try before you came in."

A rage wells in my chest that makes it hard for me to breathe. I blink back my own tears because me crying too won't help. "I'm sorry that I let you go off with him. You don't deserve to be left with bad guys."

"I'm no stranger to bad guys, Rhea." She stops crying and her voice goes cold. "Why'd you think we uprooted our family and moved from Michigan in the middle of high school? Didn't you ever wonder about my dad?"

To be honest, no. I hadn't. From the jump, I've been so focused on Marley as this disruptive character in my life, it hasn't really occurred to me she's, like, *a person* in and of herself. "What happened to your dad?"

"He 'happened' to my mom. He 'happened' to her a few times when we were little, but around three years ago, he started losing it, coming home in fits of anger and 'happening' to her twice a week." She uses the bottom seam of her shirt to wipe her face. "My bedroom was next to theirs, so I'd hear every minute of it."

I don't know what to say, so I wrap my arm around her, pulling her close. "I'm sorry that all of you went through that." I lean into her and we stay like this, quietly intertwined, for longer than I've ever held someone before. It's her who ultimately pulls away, not me.

"Look, Rhea, I know you like Malachi." The change in conversation is so abrupt, I freeze. "You don't have to confirm or deny it or whatever, I know that you two are best friends, so there's probably a lot of shit there. But I need you to know that I'm *not* interested in him. I'm not interested in guys much at all—I only went with Diego tonight because it seemed like you were vibing with Jamal, but I didn't want to be around Malachi and give you the wrong idea since it seems like he's really confused and trying to use me to make you jealous."

To make me jealous? I shake my head at the idea.

"No way, he likes you. He's not into me at all," I say firmly. "At least not anymore."

Marley's self-deprecating act is sweet, but unnecessary. I know that I blew it with Malachi weeks ago.

"Rhea." Marley looks at me with a sisterly look that reminds me of Lacy. "You can't be that blind, can you? Every time he says something to me, he immediately looks at you to gauge your reaction." I think back on the past week and wonder if this is true. "Lou and I thought it was so obvious, girl."

I wonder if Zeke noticed too. Since I haven't opened up to him about Malachi, I've been navigating this whole dynamic by myself, totally in the dark. Marley must catch the confusion on my face because she continues to lay things out for me.

"Rhea, from Day One, I have been trying to be *your* friend. Zeke's a sweetie and Malachi's chill and all, but in my mind, being cool with them is just a means to an end to be friends with you. Yeah, you've been pretty territorial, but you're funny and smart, and the way you've orchestrated this SOSI shit to keep your block together is so dope."

My cheeks burn. An instinctual denial of Marley's kind words competes with a tiny part of me that's glowing, yearning for this moment to be true. The fact that Marley sees how hard I'm working and gets it feels like a gift too big for my hardheaded self to receive.

Marley continues. "I get that it was probably a shock for me and Lou to enter the friend group that you've had for your whole life—especially with Malachi being super weird—but I knew you weren't this harsh person. And I have a feeling that we could be really close, if you let us start fresh."

I think she's right. I *know* that she's right. "I'm sorry for being cold. And for not warning you about Diego."

She puts her hands up as if to say no apologies necessary, though the mention of his name starts her trembling all over again. The gut punch of guilt returns. I don't think it'll ever go away.

"It's whatever. Nothing really happened," she says quietly.

"Just because things didn't escalate, that doesn't mean that nothing happened."

She pauses, seemingly considering my words, before nodding.

"I don't understand why you'd forgive me, Marley."

"I like you enough to commit to the process of forgiving you." Marley shakes out her legs, then laces her arm with mine. "God, he's such an idiot. I can't wait to, like, hex him or something."

I cackle at the thought of Marley standing over a cauldron, and she joins in. "For what it's worth, everyone calls him Dumbass Diego."

Her honey-smooth laughter warms the space between us. "Dumbass Diego, Dirtbag Diego, Diego the Douchebag . . . I think we can get creative with that." We rattle off new nicknames until a voice yells at us to get the fuck back downstairs. We jog down and apologize to the super-tall, angry sophomore dude waiting for us at the bottom of the stairs with his arms crossed like a bouncer. We slip past him and crack up at the ridiculous look on his face—homeboy needs to *chill out*.

It's easier to make our way back outside than it was a half hour ago. Clusters of people break off and head out. Marley leans over a table and asks a random girl where everyone's going. "After-party at another house. They got a pool."

"If we're gunna do the plan tonight, we have to do it now," Marley whispers to me.

She's right. Zeke and Lou are exactly where they've been for the past hour, lips locked underneath the wall of ivy, legs and arms intertwined on the iron bench in a way that can't possibly be comfortable. To watch them fall in love so publicly— it's stressful to observe while also being the most compelling thing that I've ever seen.

I clear my throat, but they don't seem to notice.

"*A-hem,*" I say louder. No response. "Zeke!!" I poke his forearm wrapped around Lou's neck. When he looks up, he seems truly shocked to see me, as if he had been so lost in his kiss that he had forgotten that other humans exist. "Show-time, dude."

With his fingers still tightly gripping the back of Lou's neck, he looks at me bitterly like I'm the Grinch here to ruin Christmas. "Five more minutes?"

"Nah, we gotta do it now, people are leaving."

Zeke looks around and notices that the backyard is much less crowded than it was before with the same bewilderment of when he first saw me.

"Looks like we can wait five more minutes," he declares. Lou lets out a soft moan as Zeke shifts some of his weight up onto his lap.

Marley and I roll our eyes in unison and march over to Malachi.

"So then he was like, 'Whoahhh!' and I was like, 'Ayeeeeeee!!'" Malachi leans groggily as he talks while the guys around him laugh in slow motion at whatever vapid story he's telling.

"Malachi, we need to talk," I interrupt. All the guys break into corny "Ooooohs" like I'm the principal calling him into the office.

Malachi stumbles toward Marley and me, and drapes his arms around our shoulders. Marley glances at me with a raised eyebrow and I search Malachi's face for any signs that maybe there's some truth to her theory. His touch here is way too casual to feel natural for us, but then again, he's faded. Of course, he picks tonight of all nights to make himself even harder to read than usual.

I brush his arm away and Marley does too. "We gotta pull the stunt now. Zeke's 'busy,' so you have to help me."

Malachi looks over at Lou and Zeke, laughing. "At least one of us is starting sophomore year off right."

"Nigga, are you going to help her or not?" Marley asks impatiently. I'm once again surprised by how much I suddenly fuck with this girl and kick myself for being such a bitch up until now.

Malachi raises his hands in mock defense. "Chill ouuuuuuutt."

"Am I the only one taking this shit seriously? Do you and Zeke not care if he's sent away to the goddamn Inland Empire and the crew falls apart?"

"Rhea—" Malachi steps forward. I step back.

"No, I'm over it." If I have to do this without the guys, so be it. "Marley, can you help?"

She nods. "Yeah, girl, I got you."

"Great." I snatch Malachi's JanSport from his back before he can protest.

Marley and I go to the edge of the yard with an insane view of the Los Angeles skyline. We pause for a second to take in the lights before hopping the fence. We slip into the mess of dry brush and dirt on the uneven stretch of land separating the party house from its neighbor.

Marley uses the flashlight on her phone to guide us to the perfect spot. Once we're sure that we're hidden from all angles, but still close enough to the party house, I unzip the bag and pull out the firecrackers. "Two lines should be enough."

Marley steps her foot right into the patch of dirt where I'm about to lay out the fireworks. I look up and see that her eyebrows are pressed together, her mouth strained into a tight pout.

"Don't get mad," she pleads, wrapping her arms around her waist to fight off the dry desert night windchill.

I should have known that she'd have second thoughts. I swallow my frustration and meet her concerned glare. "What's up?"

She bites her lip and frowns. "Is this, like, going too far? I mean, I'm down to help, but if I were on the other side of that fence—"

"You're not."

"I know, I know. But with all the wild shit in the news with disturbed kids coming to schools—"

"Parties around here used to get shot up all the time."

"Yeah, *used to*. But have you ever been to a party that got lit up?"

As much as I'd like to shut her down, I can't lie. I let go of the fireworks and shake my head.

"Neither have I," she continues. "The videos were clever and all, but this is like, next-level shit. People are going to be scared. *Really* scared. And not only the gentrifiers, but *our* classmates, *our* friends, *our* neighbors."

I press my fingertips to my forehead. "Look, none of this is real, Marley. The fireworks, SOSI—it's all an illusion."

"The fear *is* real, though." She pauses and brings her hand to stroke her throat. "We just need to remember that, okay?"

She looks at me with a soft gaze that reminds me of our conversation back upstairs. I guess if anyone knows what it's like to feel unsafe at home, it's her.

I offer my palm, which she stares at blankly until I finish the gesture and take her hand into mine. "I hear you," I say, watching the tsunami of guilt well up behind her chestnut-brown eyes. Her guilt is contagious, but my drive to keep our crew together is stronger. "I'll take care of everything, aight? You just make sure that nobody gets hurt when people start running."

Marley sighs. "I'm sorry. I'm not trying to stop you or make you feel bad. I want to help because I get it; if Lou and I were ever going to be separated, I'd do anything—"

"I know," I say softly. In the distance, I hear the DJ change to a slow R&B song, which means that the crowd must be dwindling. It's now or never.

I look at Marley once more. "Thank you for, uhm—" I pause, struggling to find the right words to match her compassion. "For being here."

After all that I put her through, I can't say that I'd still be standing here if I were her.

Marley lets go of my hand to plug her ears. She takes one big step back and gives me a sober nod, followed by the glint of a smile.

I flick out the lighter and set off one end.

We break into a sprint back toward the house and make it over the fence as the flame hits the first explosive.

BAM!

At first, there's confusion—bodies are still huddled against one another and everyone flinches reflexively. A few people look up at the sky. I try to yell to get the chaos started, but nobody can hear me over the sound of the music.

But then they hear Marley.

Her bloodcurdling wail cuts through the air. "HE GOT A GUN!"

FOURTEEN

Nobody tries to hang around to figure out who the hell "he" might be. Chaos rips through the crowd, and each consecutive bang of the firecrackers sends people flying to the door. I'm talking like *Lion King*, Mufasa dying–level stampede. Chairs are knocked over, drinks are spilled, girls are grabbed by their boyfriends and tucked under their arms for cover. I don't know who said it first, but I know that our plan worked because I hear several people blaming SOSI from the jump. One of the guys in colors looks around to see who's behind it, but the crowd is too thick for him to make out anything. Eventually, he follows everyone else through the sliding door, back into the house, and out the front door.

When Marley and I emerge, Lacy grabs my wrist and pulls us away, transporting me back to the track meet five years ago. We run up the hill, joining the others who are waiting for us on a front lawn two houses up. We jog until we reach the end of the block and then walk for what feels like a mile down the windy, hilly streets of well-maintained houses. Once the adrenaline subsides, we sit on a street corner with a light pole to catch our breath.

"Yo, it's been a minute since one of these parties been shot up," Camesha says as she wipes the sweat from her forehead.

"Did y'all see who started it?" Lacy asks, patting her edges.

"No, but I heard it was SOSI," Lou says naturally. His flat tone makes him the most convincing liar of us all.

"Check this out," Zeke says as the glow of his phone illuminates his face. He holds the screen up for us to see his Quipp feed. *"Party in the hills shot up by SOSI. Smh. #SosiShooting."*

"Damn," Malachi says, taking out his phone now too. He pulls up LykLuv and randomly clicks on a few notable cool kids' stories. "They got videos of everyone running. #SOSI is all over LykLuv too."

It's genuinely hard to contain my excitement and keep my post-near-death-experience poker face on. "This is so fucked," I say solemnly. I join Camesha on the little patch of grass and sneak Marley a fist bump on my way.

"Looks like Jamal and his brother got away quickly," Zeke says while scrolling through his feed, but I know that comment is specifically directed at me. I give him a look to chill out and he smiles mischievously.

"Be careful with this new shit, y'all. Real talk," Lacy says in her authoritarian, big-sister voice. "I don't want any of y'all getting hurt. Whoever these SOSI guys are, don't fuck with them, you hear me?" We all nod. "Now, how the hell are we gunna get home?" The original plan was for us to ride back with Lacy's friend, but he's long gone, lost in the chaos.

"We're not far from our house. I'll call my mom, she'd be super happy to give you all a ride," Marley offers. She whips out her phone and walks a few steps away, pressing her phone up to her ear so that she can hear over the sound of the ghetto bird (aka a police helicopter) circling above our heads.

Marley tries her mom three times, and Lou calls her twice too. "Still no answer," Lou announces after one last try.

"That's so weird, she's literally always on her phone, especially when she's waiting up for us to come home at night. . . . She's never not answered before," Marley says. I sense the hint of concern in her tone.

"Maybe she fell asleep." Lacy starts typing on her phone. "No worries, though, I got enough on my debit card for a Lyft." She taps the screen a few more times. "Carlos will be here in six minutes."

"That's quick," Zeke says, though his voice is more disappointed than pleasantly surprised.

"Six minutes is plenty of time," Lou says, grabbing Zeke's hand with a wink.

Zeke smiles shyly. "We'll be right back." The boys walk over to the massive tree two houses over whose trunk is conveniently just wide enough for them to lean against and not be seen. The older I got, the more I realized how much of our environment was low-key built for making out.

"Ugh, they're all over each other," Marley mutters. "Almost as gross as my mom with her giant boyfriend."

"Maybe PDA is contagious," I tease as she joins me on the grass. She gives me a look that conveys some of the guilt that she's still holding, but there's also a smile there—a wild one fueled by adrenaline. I can feel the Bad Bitch energy radiating from her too. The firecracker scheme couldn't have gone any better.

Malachi comes over to us, sulking and souring the vibe. "Sorry I wasn't helpful."

Is that all you have to say? If Marley was right about the whole him-using-her-to-make-me-jealous thing . . . it may have worked, but not in the way that he planned. Whatever jealousy-induced anger that I had at Marley has now morphed into plain ol' anger at his dumb ass.

"No apologies necessary. Rhea was great," Marley says. She stands up and announces that she's going to pull Lou away from Zeke. "We're close enough to walk, so we better get going. I'll text you tomorrow, though, so we can hang?"

Malachi opens his mouth to respond, but when I tell Marley that sounds great and give her a hug, he quickly realizes that she wasn't talking to him. He takes out his wave brush and runs it through his hair vigorously to shake off the moment.

Our Lyft driver pulls up and Lacy takes shotgun, while me and the boys pile into the back. Camesha closes the door behind us and waves.

I lean out the window. "You're not coming with us?"

"Nah, love, my sugar daddy's sending me a car. Gunna go spend some time with him tonight. He says he has something special planned." She rubs her fingers together and adds, *"Cha-ching!"* A nondescript town car with tinted windows pulls up behind us, and she jumps in.

"All set?" Carlos the Lyft driver asks.

"Yeah, three drop-offs, but we're all close by," Lacy confirms.

I had texted my mom and told her that the party got shot up. After I sent my message, I watched the little gray bubble of ellipsis dots pop up, so I knew she saw my message and had started typing. But then they disappeared. She never replied.

That was twenty minutes ago now.

I check my phone once more, even though I know that there aren't any new notifications. "No answer?" Malachi asks when I shove my phone into my pocket. I shrug, and he nods. "You can crash with us tonight."

I don't feel like going home to an empty house tonight, so I set aside my frustration with him. "Yeah, that'd be nice."

Lacy listens to the exchange then updates our route. "Still three stops, but I changed one," she tells Carlos.

Zeke pulls out his phone and texts the group chat with me, him, and Malachi: *Rhea, you really did it. Social is going off.*

I follow his message with a little heart.

Zeke adds another text: *Thank you.*

We stare out the windows in silence, passing by the turquoise Liquor Bank before turning up Kernshaw Blvd., the central lifeline of our neighborhood. I close my eyes for a minute but am awakened by the glow of neon lights as the car stops. The Lyft driver takes a turn into the Krispy Kreme Donuts drive-through.

"Is this the right address that you put in?" he asks Lacy, noticeably irritated.

"Yes, okay, don't be mad, I'll buy you a donut and leave a big tip, I swear."

"Miss . . ." he groans.

This poor man's out here working late and here we are, a bunch of teens pressuring him to let us get donuts at midnight. "Please," she says, batting her eyes. Luckily the driver is youngish and clearly into Lacy's vibe.

"The 'Hot Donuts Now' sign is on! You can't pass up on the 'Hot Donuts Now' sign," Zeke pleads. This is fact and the driver knows it. He shakes his head and pulls up to the little speaker for us to place our order. We all applaud.

Lacy pays for an assorted dozen, which is way more than we can throw back right now, but we'll appreciate the leftovers in the morning for breakfast. The hot glaze almost burns my fingertips as I shove the sugary dough into my mouth. Lacy thanks the driver and gratuitously licks her fingers clean as he watches, which I guess is another type of thank-you for him.

The sprinkles on the donut stick to Zeke's face and accentuate how bright red his lips are from all the making-out tonight. I'll tease him about this later, but for now, I let him be. We drop Zeke off in front of his house, but he doesn't go straight in. "Yo, that donut made me realize how starving I am. Imma get some food, but y'all go home."

"Dude it's *late*, get the fuck inside," I shout out the window.

"Don't worry about it! Just some fast food. I'll text y'all when I'm home."

I'm about to protest, but Malachi tells me to lay off. "He's fine, there's, like, three spots right on the corner." I know that we're technically the ones behind the biggest "threat" to neighborhood safety right now, but still. I don't love the idea of Zeke going around by himself at night.

"Don't get kidnapped!" Malachi shouts at the top of his lungs.

"I'm too mature to be 'kidnapped.' If anything, I'd be *abducted*," Zeke replies between laughs.

"Jesus Christ, don't forget to text, okay?"

He blows me a kiss and walks away as our driver pulls off to drop us at the Reeds' house.

———

Once inside, Malachi throws an armful of blankets and pillows onto the coffee table. I grab one and claim the La-Z-Boy recliner for the night. Malachi takes the lumpy couch, even though I remind him that he doesn't have to sleep out here in the living room with me. We used to have sleepovers spread out here in front of the TV growing up, but now that we're older, I figure it may be time for us to stop sleeping in the same room. And to stop calling them "sleepovers," I guess.

"Nah, I'm good out here. It's hot as hell in my room anyway," he says while kicking off his shoes. I watch him walk over to his room and return wearing just basketball shorts. He took off his shirt, like he always does, and as he walks into the living room, I can see the faint outline of muscles across his tight chest. He has serious abs now too, and I wonder how long they've been there. Malachi's always been cute, but right now, he looks *hot*. I grab another blanket to hide the fact that I suddenly don't know what to do with my hands.

"So, how was your first high?" I ask, more so to get my mind off his biceps than out of genuine interest.

"Yeah. I was"—he pauses to reposition himself—"faking it. I wasn't high."

Silence falls for a few seconds until I say the only thing that I can think of: "Oh."

"Don't you want to know why I was faking it?"

Of course I want to know, but the new effect of his voice in a half whisper as we lie down alone in the low light of this familiar room is really throwing me off. Everything is the same, yet I feel different. *He* feels different. My head is spinning. "Why were you faking it?"

"You only see me as the guy that you've been friends with for your whole life, which is great, you know, that we got mad history together. But I can be other things to you too." He looks in my general direction, but his eyes graze past me as he draws a shaky inhale. After another deep breath, he focuses on me at last, but I feel the tremendous effort behind the gesture. He's blushing, fighting the impulse to turn away. It's then that the full context of his movements finally registers to me: this is Malachi being brave. I tighten my grip on the recliner as he continues. "I figured maybe if I acted differently, you'd feel like you saw a different side of me and maybe . . ." His voice lowers to a hush. "Well, maybe you'd like it."

I bundle myself deeper into the blanket. "You thought I'd be into you acting like a fool?" I joke.

"C'mon, Rhea," Malachi pleads softly. The gravity of the look in his eyes sends a gentle buzz of anticipation down my spine.

"Okay, okay . . ."

He brushes his hand over his lips in a way that leaves me momentarily breathless, stunned by the thought of the softness of his mouth.

My voice comes out in a whisper. "I know that there are different sides to you, Malachi."

"Well, you don't act like you do. You keep me in this box, but random Jamal who's been around forever, he takes like one sip of alcohol and suddenly you're all interested in what he has to say."

"Jamal was just being nice to me." I sit up to face Malachi. "Nicer than you've been, anyway."

"You haven't given me the chance to show you that I can be nice to you like that."

"Yeah, maybe, but then you were *real quick* to move on to somebody else, huh?" Even I'm taken aback by how angrily the words spill out of me. I don't have to say Marley's name, we both know exactly who I'm referring to. "At the block party you went from talking about how you 'like different' with me then were all over her within a span of, like, thirty minutes."

"Rhea, you literally shut me down. What was I supposed to do? Wait another year again watching you get close to other guys and just silently take it? I figured if you couldn't see me as more than a friend, but if Marley did, that might push the needle."

"Wait, what do you mean another year?"

"Oh, c'mon," he says, annoyed. "You know what I mean."

My heart vibrates in my chest. "I don't, I swear."

"Do you not remember that day you kissed Diego last year?" Hearing Malachi acknowledge the event out loud for the first time makes me recoil. "We were at the skate park—you, me, and Zeke—and I had asked Zeke to give us a minute so that I could tell you that I liked you. Zeke walked away, and I left you alone for, like, five minutes to go splash some water on my face over at the fountain to get my shit together, and when I came back, you were walking away with Diego."

As Malachi talks, the lighting and colors of my memory of that day shift. The spotlight has always been on Diego, but as I mentally rewind, I notice for the first time other moments. Zeke and Diego fade while Malachi is turned up to Technicolor. The volume on the yellow and purple of his lucky Kobe jersey glows. I remember him acting weird all day, fidgeting a bunch, being real defensive when I teased him. I remember him sending Zeke off and being mildly confused when he ran over to the water fountain. And I remember the look on his face when I waved over my shoulder at him as I walked away with Diego. I hadn't understood his facial expression at the time, but I can see it clearly now in high definition. It was disappointment.

"I didn't realize . . ." I stammer.

"I'm not trippin' about that anymore, I get it." He massages his temples and the light from outside catches his cheekbones. "All I'm saying is that I'm not tryna blow it again. I like you."

The churning in my stomach ramps up to a full-blown somersault. My mouth goes dry.

I like you too. You know I do. But . . .

"It'd be safer if we kept things the same as they've always been." The words jump from my mouth seemingly on their own.

"Maybe. But that's assuming that these feelings will just go away with time." He exhales profoundly. "They won't for me, Rhea. The feelings, I mean. They won't go away."

His words turn my core inside out as our eyes lock.

We've looked at each other before, thousands of times over the course of our friendship. I know every line, every contour, of his face, so nothing in this stare should be new to me. But in this moment, there's a combination of rare elements—a cautious smile tugging at the corner of his mouth, a slight blush bringing out the auburn undertones in his skin. I can feel my own eyebrows raised, my teeth softly biting my bottom lip, praying for him to keep going, begging myself not to tear away.

We've looked at each other thousands of times before.

But never like this.

"How does this not scare you?" I ask softly, incredulously.

"It does, a little bit." He shrugs. "But not enough to make me want to ignore it forever."

I pause, overwhelmed by the honesty, by the willful

fracture in our barrier of the things we've always left unsaid.

"It . . . it does, for me. I mean—" My inhale is unsteady. I want to sit still, but I can't stop wrapping and unwrapping my sweatshirt's drawstring around my pinky, so tightly that the skin momentarily loses its color. I gulp. "This does scare me."

When I look up, I expect to see the traces of disappointment, embarrassment, or frustration, but instead, I see his smile. Warm and relaxed as it's ever been. The same one that got me through the confusion of elementary school, the anxiety of middle school, the pressure of starting high school. That face, and the glow behind it, that has gotten me through it all.

Deep in my chest, I let out a little silent cry of frustration. *Why can't I let us grow?*

"I'm not in a rush," he says as if reading my mind.

I say okay and he says okay too, and we both turn to look up at the ceiling fan as it lazily pushes hot air around the room above us. I'm not usually up this late, but the dull quietness of the hour makes me fall in love with the night.

"Do you think that we're gonna save Zeke?" I ask earnestly.

Malachi hesitates, but responds in a serious, sincere voice. "To be honest, before tonight, I wasn't convinced. But now? SOSI's all over social media, they're on the cops' radar, but they have no leads. It'll definitely be on the news tomorrow. There's no way in hell the investors are still gonna dump millions of dollars into the renovation with all this bad press about the block."

I play with the fringe of my hair at the base of my neck. "You don't think we overdid it?"

"No way. We're exactly where we want to be."

Exactly where we want to be . . .

I look over at Malachi and realize how much I want to kiss him right now.

But I don't.

. . . Not quite, but almost.

I check my phone to see if I have any messages from my mom or Zeke. Still nothing.

"Zeke is fine," Malachi says, noting the concern on my face. "He probably forgot to text us after he tore through his midnight burrito and passed out." This would be very on-brand.

"Don't worry, Rhea. Everything went perfectly tonight." He waits for me to make eye contact with him before adding one last bit for emphasis: *"Even this."*

In the middle of the night, I wake up to the sound of sirens ripping down the block. I look over at Malachi, but he's still fast asleep, forearm draped over his eyes, shielding them from the blue and red lights coming in from the window.

I check the time and it's nearly 1:45 a.m.

The last thought that I remember before drifting back to sleep is that I hope that nobody got hurt.

I am wrong.

Holy shit, I am wrong.

PART TWO

For the master's tools will never dismantle the master's house.
They may allow us temporarily to beat him at his own game,
but they will never enable us to bring about genuine change.
—AUDRE LORDE

FIFTEEN

I'm sitting on the couch next to Malachi, and we're both sweating because he has his hand dangerously close to my knee and he's leaving it there and I'm looking at his hand, then at his face, then back at his hand, and trying to figure out what I want to happen, when Zeke busts through the screen door, all panting and out of breath.

Thank god Malachi's parents aren't home because Zeke is practically shouting. "Yo, someone died and they're blaming it on us!"

"Us?" Malachi clears his throat and rises to attention. "Like *us* us?!"

"Shhhhhh! Keep your damn voices down," I say, glancing out the open window to make sure that nobody's hanging around outside.

"Nah, obviously not *us* us," Zeke continues. "They're blaming it on SOSI."

"Shit," Malachi replies.

Yeah, *shit*. I wait for him to continue, but he just crosses his arms and leans back into the couch. Is that really the best response that this fool can think of right now?

"Do the cops know anything?" I ask Zeke.

He lets out a groan fit for an elderly man five times his age before flopping onto the floor. "So, around like 1:30 a.m. last night, Jamal and Jabron were walking back from the party in the alley behind the El Pollo Loco—you know the one where you can get extra tortillas for free when the cash register guy is high?" Zeke rambles. I nod impatiently. "That one. And they found a body."

They ran, obviously, because it's not a good look for two fifteen-year-old Black guys to be seen standing over a dead white dude. Soon after that, the El Pollo Loco stoner went to hit his bootleg Pax pen during his break, and he saw the body too. He didn't run, though. Partly because he was high as hell, and partly because he had been at work and had an alibi, so he knew he'd be cool. He called it in, police arrived and taped the whole area off. Gunshot wounds, but nobody heard the shots.

The cops questioned everyone working in the restaurant that night and were met with a bunch of blank stares and the sassy frown of the manager, who was probably thinking that she don't get paid enough to deal with this bullshit. The security cameras were conveniently pointed about five feet *away* from the crime scene. Nobody saw what happened.

The detectives went to the neighboring houses, but nobody knew anything there either. All the young white couples were freaked out and real quick to welcome the officers into their living rooms. They made sure to mention that they've been worried about the rise of "dangerous activity" in the neighborhood and that they had noticed a bunch of kids "hanging around" late at night, but at the end of the day, they didn't know shit. Meanwhile, the Black and brown folks talked to the cops through the peepholes. Time and experience had taught them not to open their doors to pigs. Plus, it's not like they had anything to hide. And even if they did, old habits die hard: snitches get stitches.

Zeke's apartment was one that got a visit from the detectives. Lupe hit 'em with the classic—pretending that she didn't speak a word of English. "Lo siento, cuidate, buena suerte." Shut, lock, fasten the dead bolt. "It's their fault for canvassing our neighborhood without a single cop who speaks Spanish. South LA ain't all white yet," she had said.

"Lupe don't play." Malachi laughs.

"They got any suspects yet?" I ask Zeke once we're all caught up.

"I don't think so. From what I hear, they're just floundering."

"Lit, so we got nothing to worry about." Malachi kicks his feet up onto the coffee table, even though his father would be pissed if he caught him *disrespecting his house like that*.

"Nuh-uh, it's not that simple." It never is. "It was one thing when SOSI was known as this untraceable 'gang' that breaks some stuff and fires off 'shots' every now and then; it's another thing entirely for the gang to now have a *murder* on its name. We've been careful, but once the cops start really digging into SOSI, it might lead back to us, and if they don't have any other suspects by then . . . we're totally fucked."

"We're *maybe* fucked," Malachi corrects.

I scoff. "A white person was killed. Do you seriously think that they'd hesitate to arrest some frizzy teens from the old neighborhood?" Zeke and Malachi exchange a cautious look between them. "We're all a part of this case now, whether we like it or not."

"So, what's the plan?" Zeke asks.

"Let the gang take the rap. Cops can pretend that they 'dissolved' SOSI, all this shit blows over, and we can go back to living our normal lives," Malachi says.

"Have you forgotten *why* we even started this in the first place?" I glare at Malachi, then motion toward Zeke, who's staring at the outdated carpet. Malachi offers a nod as an apology. Zeke tips his head back.

"Any other ideas, then, Queen Bee?" Malachi asks me.

"*Duh.* You know I already got a plan." Sort of.

"We're listening," Zeke says, even though their short attention spans have already left them both low-key watching *Rick and Morty* on the TV from the corners of their eyes.

"We have to solve the case before the cops do, obviously."

Malachi tosses a pillow at me and breaks out laughing. "You watch *one* HBO series and suddenly you think your Black ass is the new Nancy Drew!"

I grab the pillow and throw it back twice as hard, hitting Malachi right in the face. The way I see it, we have two options: we can do nothing, leave our fate to the police department, and give up on stopping the eviction; or we get ahead of things, regain control over the SOSI narrative, and save ourselves a potential trip to juvie. My choice is clear. I swipe my iPhone from the charger and make my way to the front door.

Malachi groans. "C'mon, where are you even going? You're walking with a lotta purpose for someone who doesn't even know anything."

"It's not necessarily a bad thing that people think SOSI

is capable of something like this—for better or worse, that means our plan is working. We just need to make sure that it keeps working *without* getting any of us implicated. Think of it as damage control," I say while tying my shoes.

Malachi laughs incredulously. "Do you know how crazy you sound right now?"

"Look, we've worked too hard to let everything fall apart right now. The OG neighborhood is counting on us to not fuck this up. We're in deep. Inaction isn't an option anymore." I pause for the pushback, but he's silent. I grab the remote and turn off the TV. "Get your stuff, let's go."

I ignore their frustrated sighs and continue straight outside to the front steps, where I wait. As expected, before I can even finish humming the chorus to the twerk anthem of the summer, Zeke and Malachi are by my side.

They may be idiots, but they're loyal.

We start walking toward the El Pollo Loco, and Zeke and Malachi break into an argument about quality of life in Wakanda versus Bikini Bottom when we're stopped. The *whoop-whoop* of the cop car cuts through the music playing from the huddle of Android speakerphones gathered at the bus stop.

Everyone who looks like us stops to make sure we're okay.

Everyone who doesn't keeps walking.

"Can I talk to you three?" asks a short cop with a buzz cut through a thick mustache visibly soaked in sweat. It's not like we have a choice.

"Don't say shit," I whisper to the guys.

"How long have you lived here?" the cop asks. I catch my reflection in the shine of his badge and note the number.

"All our lives," Zeke says with pride.

"Great, great . . ." The cop glances around, noting all of the watchful eyes protecting us. "In that case, can you tell me a little about the neighborhood?"

Can I tell this stranger about my neighborhood? For damn sure I can. I can tell him about all of the freaks, and the saints, and the aunties, and the turnups, and the local rap scene, and the people who drive by and say we're all *too much*. I could tell him what it really means to live here, to have lived here, and to be a part of this community in South LA.

But now isn't the right time for any of that.

I get ready to lie but am interrupted by a raspy voice on his walkie-talkie. "We've got eyes on the suspect, copy. Latino, male, fifteen years old. Shoulder-length hair. Suspected affiliate of SOSI—" The sweaty cop cuts off the radio.

What happened to "They don't have any suspects"? I raise my brows at Zeke. He gives me his signature flustered shrug that sends beads of perspiration flying from his sheepdog haircut.

The cop turns back toward his car and glances at us over his shoulder. "You be safe now, you hear?"

Malachi gives him a sarcastic ay-ay-Captain salute as we keep walking. We only make it about half a block before we're stopped again. This time, though, it's Zeke.

He's standing there all stressed, Vans frozen to the sidewalk.

"What now?" Malachi sighs.

"I have to tell you guys something." Zeke shoves his hands as far down into his jean pockets as they can go. "But you have to promise that you won't get mad."

"You know how I feel about making promises that I can't keep," Malachi chimes back. I shove his shoulder.

"You can tell us anything," I reply in the most sincere voice that I can muster, glancing at Malachi at the end to make sure he's taking notes on how a normal friend responds.

Zeke's entire body is shaking, hard. I open my mouth to speak, but he cuts me off. "Wait—not here." He grabs my wrist and pulls me into the alley behind the smoke shop with Malachi following closely behind. Zeke kicks a damp cardboard box out of the way and glances over his shoulder twice. We watch a tiny squad of cockroaches pass by.

Finally, Zeke spits it out. "I saw the body." He winces. "I was . . . fuck, dude, I was there. When I got out the Lyft to get something to eat last night. I saw him on the floor on my way out with my burrito."

My heartbeat quickens, but I stay chill for Zeke's sake. We're all quiet for a few moments. Until—

"*Why* didn't you lead with that shit when you first came over?!" Malachi clenches his hands into fists and punches the air.

"Because I didn't do it!"

I fight the urge to point out the obviousness of Zeke's statement, epitomized by the fact that he's wearing a coral-pink shirt right now that says "Make Empanadas, Not War."

Zeke runs his hands through his waves. "I got there *after* he had died. And then something bad happened." Zeke pokes his sneaker at an unreasonably high glob of dried gum caked to the concrete.

"Something worse than seeing a dead body?" Malachi deadpans.

"Yeah, worse. I started to run away, but then I realized that I wasn't alone. Someone else was there, but I couldn't tell who it was." He pauses and grabs ahold of his elbows. "Someone saw me standing over the body."

The voice of the police radio rings in my head: *Latino, male, fifteen years old. Shoulder-length hair.*

Holy shit.

They're looking for Zeke.

SIXTEEN

Zeke is doubled over his knees, trying not to barf. Malachi's hands hang from his neck as he shakes his head at the sheer fuckery of the situation. "This is bad," he announces.

"No shit, Sherlock." I take out my phone and run a quick search to see how much press the murder is getting.

Zeke glances up from his crouched position. "Is it everywhere?"

He looks so stressed that I consider lying, but there's no use. "It's all over the news, all over social." I keep scrolling. "SOSI's either explicitly mentioned or referenced in every source."

"What do we do?" Zeke asks.

The sun is coming down hard, making it difficult to look at the boys without squinting. I wanted to go by El Pollo Loco and have Zeke walk us through what he saw, but given that he's probably a suspect now, poking around the scene of the crime is out of the question.

"Zeke, let's go to your place and see what the local news coverage is looking like. Maybe something in the report will give us a clue on where to start." It's not the greatest plan, but it's all I got. And from the pessimistic looks on the guys' faces, it's also the only idea on the table right now. We walk in silence for the two blocks to Zeke's apartment.

When we arrive, there's a police car in the driveway.

"No fucking way." Malachi instinctively moves in front of Zeke to shield him from whatever lies ahead. Zeke is way wider than Malachi's thin torso, but it's the thought that counts. I move to Zeke's side with my arms outstretched, ready to create a distraction for him to get away if need be. My heart pounds so furiously that I can feel my pulse ringing in my head. Coupled with the heat, it feels like I'll either pass out or burst at any minute. Maintaining our huddle formation, we back away, hoping not to draw the attention of the officer lounging against the hood of his car.

"Wait, do you hear that?" I whisper. From down the street, an ambulance hurls toward us. It screeches into the driveway, double-parking behind the police. Two medics jump out with a stretcher, their equipment's wheels crunching the fallen leaves on the sidewalk. Zeke's weight shifts, and I grab his waist right before he collapses.

His voice comes out as a hoarse whisper. "Ma?"

Malachi sprints ahead while I half stumble, half carry Zeke. The bright lights of the ambulance against the beige stucco building exterior accentuate how dingy the place is— the paint's chipping in various places and the grass (dead, as always) is mostly dirt.

"Ma!" Zeke yells once we enter the hallway and see the stretcher in front of the door to his unit. Stella and Kiké peek their heads out first before we finally see Lupe's face. She sees us running and pulls open the door for us. Zeke's crying by the time we reach her, but a wave of relief washes through my body. She's okay.

A medic shakes Lupe's hand, then slips into the unit next door.

"Dios mio, Ma. Pensé que . . ."

"I know, I know. I saw the terror on your face, cariño. They're not here for me."

"Wh-what happened?" Malachi asks, completely out of breath.

"You know the old woman next door?" We nod. "Well, when she saw the news this morning about the gang murder nearby, she fainted." Lupe draws the sign of the cross on her chest. "It must've brought up some difficult memories for her."

The tsunami of feelings in my chest overwhelms me. On one hand, even though we had nothing to do with whatever the hell happened last night, I feel extremely guilty that the idea of SOSI scared this woman so much. There's reason for the rest of us to be freaked out too: cops plus a dead body equals way more pressure. But on the other hand, there's a tiny, dark glimmer of pride at the thought that everyone is taking SOSI so seriously. If our plan continues to infiltrate the psyche of the city and people respond accordingly, we really *can* save Zeke.

"Can someone tell us what's going on here?" Down the hallway, Important-Looking Architect Guys One and Two from a couple weeks ago stand frozen, clutching their briefcases as cops and EMTs jog up and down the corridor. Everyone ignores them until Guy Two tries again. "We have a meeting with the owner of this building."

This catches a cop's attention. "Do you mind stepping outside with me?" the officer asks casually. The architects nod and walk out with the cop, who begins to explain: "So, the recent uptick in gang activity . . ."

I don't hear the rest of the conversation, but a minute later, I watch the architects from the window. They frantically make a phone call, jump into their Mercedes-Benz, and speed off like *Fast & Furious*. Between the shuffling of footsteps and buzz of radios, I catch the officer's final words to his partner as he returns to the hallway: "Not sure I'd still go through with renovating this place if I were them."

It's working, I mouth to Malachi. An electrified wave of adrenaline rushes through my veins and I'm unable to hold back a smile. Those fools are *terrified*. I can't believe my plan is *actually* working.

Lupe's voice brings me back to the gravity of the moment. "Let's give the medics some space," she says while wheeling back into the apartment.

Right. Sometimes my tunnel vision is so strong, it's easy to forget my surroundings, which in this case is a murder down the street and a medical emergency next door. Now's not the time to be out here grinning like a psycho. Does being this amped make me a bad person?

I shut the door behind us as Malachi turns up the television. He plops onto the couch and I sit next to him, rather than in the farthest seat possible, for the first time in what feels like a while. It's a serious moment, but I feel him smile a bit when our arms brush. Still, I instinctively shrink away.

The breaking-news theme music that sounds like a *Law & Order* spoof plays alongside generic photos of palm trees and the beach.

"A murder investigation is under way in the Kofa Park neighborhood of South Los Angeles. Around 1:30 a.m. last night, a beloved fifty-seven-year-old landlord, real estate developer, and local restaurant investor was slain in the

parking lot behind a fast-food establishment near one of the apartment properties that he owned. The innocent victim had been walking alone when he was shot to death by the killer. While there were no eyewitnesses, police have identified a violent new gang in the area, known as 'SOSI,' as the culprit in this unprovoked, malicious tragedy."

Wait. What?

"Yo," Malachi begins. "Doesn't the victim description sound like . . . ?"

"Vic?!" I shout. "Zeke, the dead white guy is *Vic?*"

"*Whatthefuck*," Zeke wheezes. The cops' sudden interest in the architects makes way more sense now. "Ohmigod, he was facedown when I saw him, so I wasn't sure, but like, I thought he looked familiar."

"I'm surprised you couldn't smell him. That man's B.O. was hard to miss," Malachi says.

I elbow him. Vic sucked, but now's no time to joke. This changes everything. The fact that we personally knew the victim and that Vic and Zeke are directly linked through the eviction brings the police's theory about SOSI way closer to home. Too close.

"Did you hear any gunshots? Any arguing before you saw him?" I ask Zeke.

He shakes his head frantically. "*Nothing.* When I walked by the parking lot on my way inside to order? No dead body. When I walked out? Dead body."

"The killer must've used a silencer," Malachi says.

Maybe. But do those things even work *that* well?

The newscast switches to an interview with a blond woman who looks distraught. An overly tan reporter adjusts the buttons on her blazer and shoves the mic at the lady's face. *"Here, we have the victim's daughter, Amelia Reagan. Tell us a little bit about your father. You two worked together at his company, Becker Real Estate. What possibly could have led to such a tragedy?"*

"Wow. Vic was so gross, it's honestly kind of wild that he has a daughter," Zeke muses.

"I guess that proves he got laid at least once in his life," Malachi adds.

"Wait," I say. "We met that woman—Vic's daughter. Here at the apartment, remember?" She was trying to do damage control for Vic after he totally blew it with those architects.

On-screen, Amelia dabs a crumpled tissue against her hazel eyes. "My father was a good man," she chokes out. "He cared about this neighborhood and his tenants; I don't know why he'd be targeted by the gang." Amelia tilts her head in a way that makes it seem like she's searching for her light, trying to make sure that the camera hits her best angles.

"A landlord who cares about a neighborhood that he doesn't live in and tenants who he's trying to push out? Yeah, right," Lupe murmurs. I look at her, impressed by the hot take. She catches my raised eyebrows. "Bless his soul, whatever," she adds.

The corny breaking-news jingle chimes again, and the screen switches to a shaky camera focused on a house where two police officers lead someone in handcuffs. They blurred out the face of the person being arrested, but I recognize those black ripped jeans instantly.

Diego.

"Yo, is that—" Zeke begins.

Latino, male, fifteen years old, shoulder-length hair, suspected affiliate of SOSI.

"Yes." I manage to sound calm even though it's not how I feel.

"This is probably his dream come true. Diego's been tryna get street cred for years, now he got it," Malachi says coldly. "Let him take the fall. Problem solved."

I'm probably the one who hates Diego the most here, especially after that shit he pulled with Marley, but still, Malachi's reaction rubs me the wrong way. I wait for Lupe to roll into her bedroom before I speak up. "Not only is it fucked up to let an innocent person take the fall for something he didn't do, but once the cops realize he doesn't know shit about SOSI, they're gonna realize they made a mistake and let him go."

"Assuming that he wasn't sloppy enough to be carrying when he was arrested," Zeke says as he flicks a clump of lint from the arm of the sofa.

Malachi tenses up. "He's stupid, but not *that* stupid." There's a hint of anxiety in his voice that I can't quite trace. "Why do you assume that he's innocent, anyway?"

I guess I don't really know whether or not Diego did it. I've always thought of him as a mostly harmless idiot, but after having graduated to forcing himself onto girls like Marley, who's to say what else he might be capable of?

I pull out my phone and open up a blank Note.

Suspects: Dumbass Diego. It's short, but it's a start.

"Should we text Marley and Lou?" I ask.

"They're already on their way over," Zeke replies.

"Awesome," I say, sincerely relieved. I may like calling the shots most of the time, but this is beyond me—we're going to need help to figure this shit out, and the now endearingly-known-as-fake twins are smart as hell.

"Since when are you so excited for them to join us?" Malachi asks.

"Since last night." It's bad enough that Zeke and Malachi have watched me be rude to Marley ever since we met—they don't need to know about my bullshit setting her up with Diego. Plus, that's her story to tell, not mine.

Zeke squeezes my arm. "Does this mean we can finally be one big happy family?"

"If joining forces to solve a murder before the cops come knocking counts as 'one big happy family,' then yes."

Zeke claps excitedly, then changes the channel. "I know Vic had a name and all, but it's probably not a good look for anyone to overhear us talking about him too much. Can we give him a code name? Like . . . DWG?"

"DWG?" I ask.

"Yeah, Dead White Guy."

It's pretty callous, but given how the news always refers to kids like us as *that Black/brown kid who got killed by a cop*, it seems reasonable.

"Good idea." When Malachi stands up from the couch next to me, I frown, which he notices. "I'll be right back," he says to me, and me only.

"Okay," I say, trying to sound indifferent.

He smiles and turns toward the bathroom door. "Okay."

"Okay," Zeke mimics in a breathy voice. I punch him in the shoulder, but it's too late. He's in full-on chisme mode now. "I'm sorry, but *what* was that little moment?!"

"Nothing," I hiss.

"Nothing?! Bishh, don't make bed eyes at our friend then tell me it's *nothing*!" Jesus Christ, Zeke really does see everything. "Did something happen after I left last night?"

I'm genuinely not sure how to answer. Like, sure, something happened in the sense that we talked—like *really* talked—but what followed wasn't anything like what I've seen in movies. There was no dramatic meeting of the eyes and fireworks signaling that everything's different now. No kiss. To be honest, I choked. The idea of trying anything on top of everything else going on felt like too much of a risk. He owned up to his feelings, I neither confirmed nor denied mine, then we went to sleep. It was all very PG.

I'm not sure that's really much of a story to brag about.

There's a knock at the door. "You're safe for now, but I want details later." Zeke ignores the dirty look that I give him as he lets in Marley and Lou.

I get up and hug Marley. She squeezes me back, and there's a genuine warmth there—none of the bitterness that I would have had if I were her.

Lou and Zeke exchange a steamy kiss. "It's a little early for tongue, isn't it?" Marley says as she takes a seat cross-legged on the carpeted floor. Lou waves her off.

"Do you think Diego did it?" she asks me right away. Zeke must've texted them the news of the arrest while they were on their way over.

"I'm not sure," I admit. "I mean, we know he's an idiot, we know he wanted to make a name for himself—"

"And we know that he's capable of violence," she says.

I get a brief flashback of Marley's face, streaked with tears last night in the upstairs bedroom as she fumbled with her ponytail. "Right."

Marley clears her throat as Malachi reenters the room. I catch Zeke peel away from Lou to give him a knowing look that makes it clear that the two of them have discussed

Malachi and me before. I blush. *Why does it feel like I'm constantly the last person to find out everything about my own life?*

Malachi returns to the couch, pretending that he doesn't notice everyone staring. The rest of us circle the glass coffee table so that Zeke can fill in Marley and Lou. He tells them what he saw last night, but when he gets to the part about the cop's radio and how the tip led them to Diego . . .

"I'm sorry, *what*?!" Lou's expression contorts into a horrified grimace. He starts rapidly tapping his index finger against the table.

"Don't worry, they're not going to catch me," Zeke says. "While they're wasting their time with Diego, we have a head start on the investigation."

Lou seems to consider this and calms down a bit. "So then we're coming clean about SOSI in the meantime, right? Admitting that it was fake?"

Zeke dodges Lou's eyes. "Well, no . . ."

A fresh wave of shock hits Lou's face. "What do you mean *no*?"

I cut in. "SOSI is working. People think it's real. Now's not the time to give up."

Lou casts me a crazed look as if I'm speaking Elvish. "Rhea, now is *exactly* the time to give up. So long as the cops think SOSI is real, Zeke can get in real trouble. We can pick it up again *after* we know for sure that Zeke is in the clear."

Marley's eyes are fixed on her brother's shaking hand. She says his name softly, but he ignores her.

"There's not enough time for that." The eviction is still scheduled for only two weeks from now. The architects' fear earlier was promising, but we don't know for sure what they're up to yet. "I admit that the SOSI narrative slipped out of our control a bit, but—" I hold my hands up before Lou can jump back in. "We just have to get ahead of everything. We can clear Zeke's name *and* keep the heat on the evictions."

He shoots me a dirty look as if this is all my fault, which feels unfair. It's not like I called up Captain Capitalism and told him to fuck up our community in the first place. "Oh, c'mon, what's *your* plan? We give up on SOSI, then where does that leave us? We get fourteen days with Zeke before we never see him again? That's what you want?"

Lou glares at me, finger-tapping accelerating into overdrive, but doesn't respond. Instead, he turns to Zeke. "Babe, you can't be serious about this."

Babe? Blegh. This is exactly why I didn't want him getting involved in the first place. People catch feelings and then suddenly everything gets all complicated.

"Lou, this plan *has* to work," Zeke says. "I don't want to leave. This block is my family. And you—" He steadies Lou's vibrating hand. "You and me are just getting started."

Zeke's eyes crinkle as he pulls Lou to his feet, suggesting that the two of them go for a walk to cool off. When they leave, I don't love the awkward glances that I get from Marley and Malachi. They have to understand that I'm just as scared as Lou. I'm *terrified* that this plan won't work. Maybe Zeke would be safer in the short term if we come clean, but taking the gas out of SOSI before the evictions, right as we're finally seeing the results that can keep him—keep everyone in our neighborhood—here for good? No way.

I start weaving together an admittedly far-fetched theory about the stoner who works the cash register when Malachi's phone vibrates. He's getting a phone call. "Weird," he says. "It's Lacy."

Lacy? Malachi's face moves quickly from confusion to panic as he listens to his sister's voice.

"Are you sure?" he asks into the phone. "Shit. Shit. Okay, calm down. Just breathe." Marley and I exchange worried looks. "Yeah, we're at Zeke's. We'll go over right now. I'll see you soon. Bye." He almost hangs up but catches himself. He jerks his phone back and adds, "Love you."

Malachi's phone thuds as it hits the table. He doesn't look us in the eyes.

"What the hell was that?" Marley asks.

"We have to go to Auntie's right now," he says.

My lungs constrict in my chest. "Why?"

He sighs as a misty layer forms over his eyes. "Camesha is missing."

SEVENTEEN

"Missing?! Like *missing* missing?" Marley frantically runs her hands over her curls.

"She's gone. Disappeared. Nobody knows where she is, and her phone is off."

"Who was the last person to see her?" I ask.

"Us." Malachi sinks against the nearest telephone pole, gripping the back of his head. "When she got in that car sent by her client last night."

Malachi's mom's voice rings in my head, reminding us to always stick together and make sure everyone gets home safely at the end of the night.

We let Zeke walk by himself, and he ended up seeing a dead body.

We let Camesha go home alone, and now she's missing.

It really sucks when parents give good advice.

We fill in Zeke and Lou and run next door to Auntie Inga's apartment. We take two steps at a time, bounding up to Auntie's unit on the second floor. She opens the door before I have the chance to knock. "Come in, sweet ones."

There are already five glasses of ginger lemonade waiting for us on the dining table. She knew that we'd be coming.

Malachi practically knocks over a chair in his rush to fold Lacy into his arms. She burrows her head into her little brother's chest, smearing the mascara running down her cheeks onto his clean shirt. Normally Malachi would wince at the stain, but today, he simply bunches up the fabric and uses it to further wipe Lacy's face.

Across the room, Zeke is the first to give Auntie a long, heavy hug. "How are you holding up?"

"I have faith that she's okay, but right next to the faith is a pit in my stomach the size of Africa." Her voice cracks as she repositions a rogue wave from her long, pale orange wig. Her Amy Winehouse–esque wingtip eyeliner frames her eyes, streaked red with the residue of sleeplessness.

"What do you know about that sugar daddy guy she's been seeing?" I ask.

"Not much more than what you and anyone else with access to the local news knows," she says.

"Camesha's on the news?" Lou asks.

"No, of course not. The stations don't give a fuck about a missing Black girl," Lacy says.

I pause, perplexed. "So, then . . . the guy is on the news?"

"Haven't you heard?" Auntie scans our faces for recognition, but we're all lost. "They found the creep dead in the parking lot behind El Pollo Loco late last night."

This is the part where the world starts spinning. "Camesha was dating *Vic*?!"

"I just threw up in my mouth a little bit," Zeke winces.

"Wait, wait, wait, how did they even meet?!" Malachi blurts out.

Auntie sighs. "He owns this building, you know, so he'd come by occasionally. Maybe two years ago, I remember taking Camesha to go back-to-school shopping. When I finished locking the door, I turned around and saw him staring at her. I had a bad feeling about him from that moment. He asked for her name, and I made a point to say that we're shopping for her *high school* supplies," she groans. "I added Camesha to my lease once she turned eighteen, so I guess he got the memo that she was finally legal."

"Barely legal," Lacy huffs.

"Exactly. But he didn't care. He asked her out a few times, and she refused, obviously. I don't want to 'yuck' anyone's 'yum,' but he wasn't necessarily 'in his prime,'" she says with a shudder. "Eventually, though, he started leaving gifts at the house, and at some point, I guess he offered to pay her to spend time with him. Camesha was so set on this plan to make enough money to buy a place of her own, so she decided to let him treat her."

"And now he's been found dead on the same day that Camesha has gone missing," Lou says point-blank.

Auntie presses her fingers to her temple and lets out a pained exhale. "Yes."

Lou continues. "And Camesha was last seen getting into a car that he sent for her. . . ."

Auntie and Lacy nod.

I try to imagine Camesha killing someone, but it doesn't stick. Yeah, I've seen Camesha whoop some ass on occasion when girls try to mess with Lacy, but still, she's not murderer material.

"You know, I respect Camesha's choices about how she lives her life as an adult, but still . . . I can't say that I haven't hoped that this man would die and leave my baby alone. I didn't think that it'd happen like this." Auntie lights cedar-scented incense that fills the room with a warm, earthy scent. "Be careful what you wish for, I guess."

"I'm sure that Cam's okay," I say softly, touching the back of Auntie's hand. She gives me a forced, tight-lipped smile.

"God, if only I had stopped him last night," Auntie says, her voice strained as she takes a shallow sip of lemonade.

"Last night?" My eyebrows shoot up my forehead.

"I saw Vic at the gas station," she sighs. "I can't stop thinking about our interaction. Maybe it was something that I said in that moment, or didn't say, that led to Camesha's disappearance."

"How'd he seem?" Malachi asks. "Was anything off?"

"Just his usual, smug self. We didn't talk for long—it was late and I was by myself so I didn't want to linger. Plus, I was rushing to drive by the party and make sure y'all were okay after I heard it got shot up. But still. I can't stop thinking that had I done something . . ."

"How could you have known? This isn't your fault," Lacy says. I hope she knows that her best friend missing isn't her fault either.

"What's this about?" Marley asks, reaching over to grab a flyer from the coffee table.

"Oh, yeah," Auntie hums. She sniffles a bit and my heart breaks. "I'm working with some neighbors to organize folks against gentrification." I take a closer look and see that it's the same handout from the Cookout.

"How's it been going so far?" Zeke asks, his voice hopeful.

"Word is spreading, but we've hit a setback. We had a couple of allies—young people, new to the neighborhood—that were helping us out, but I think news of the shootings last night may have scared 'em off."

The fact that SOSI successfully creeped out some new-comers is badass, but I wipe the smug grin off my face when I see a wave of disappointment wash over Zeke. I get where he's coming from. Having a little faith in Auntie's movement might feel better than putting all his eggs in the SOSI basket, but still. I can't see Auntie's plan yielding the results we need as quickly as we need them. It's a bummer that the volunteers were scared off, but also . . . not surprising. If anything, it proves that we're really onto something with SOSI. Putting faith in outsiders to help "save" us won't get our block the security that we need.

"You must be exhausted," Malachi says to Auntie, reading the room. Auntie would never kick us out, but I also get the feeling that she needs some time alone.

On my way out the front door, though, something sucks the breath right out of my lungs. It hits like a wave, taking me underwater and tossing me to shore—choked, bruised, and disoriented. A crumpled-up eviction notice sits in the trash can by her door. Just like the ones at Zeke's building.

Auntie's not helping organize only to lend a hand to others.

She and Camesha are being evicted too.

My vision goes hazy and I fumble against the stairway banister, desperately clinging to the searing-hot metal for balance.

Zeke, Lupe, Stella, Kiké, Auntie, Camesha . . .

"You good, girl?" Marley asks.

"Vic owned this building too," I mumble, head still spin-ning. "It's happening to everyone."

Half of my family.

These evictions could wipe out *half of my family* here. . . .

I look at Malachi, then at Zeke a few stairs down. Malachi's eyes widen with understanding and he kicks the railing, hard.

. . . And that'd just be the start.

Zeke watches us from below and grips his elbows. He grits his teeth. "Let's go."

We descend the stairs slowly and stay quiet until we reach the park on the corner. The eviction crisis is more widespread than we thought. This is bigger than us.

We have to stop the evictions, now more so than ever.

Lou gets right to it. "Do you think Camesha did it? Could she be hiding out somewhere?"

I know he's scared for Zeke and bitter about being out-voted on SOSI, but he's a little too eager to pin the murder on someone else. "Way to breeze over the gravity that she's missing," I say.

"Sorry," Lou says to us all, but mostly to Zeke. "Do you, though?"

"No," Zeke says firmly. Across the circle, Malachi's eyes search mine, pleading that Camesha's safe and innocent.

"But technically, she's still a suspect, right?" Lou pushes. He crosses his arms and raises an eyebrow at me.

I liked Lou better when he talked less. But . . . he's right. I roll my eyes and pull out my phone to add Camesha's name to the list alongside Diego. A knot forms in my stomach as I type. Camesha's like a sister to me. Including her in the lineup feels like a betrayal.

"Don't forget to add Auntie Inga too," Lou says.

"Auntie?" I whip around. "Why the hell would I add her?"

"Were you not listening? She was the last person to see him alive. She was alone, so she doesn't have an alibi. Plus, she seemed unhappy with Vic creeping on Camesha. She's fiercely protective. Could be a motive." Lou picks at a dandelion growing underneath his knee.

Malachi shakes his head, offended. "Auntie's literally the nicest person on the planet. She would never." As I watch Malachi and Lou get heated going back and forth about Auntie, I remember my conversation with Marley back at the party about how the fear that SOSI creates is real. It dawns on me that the suspicion—and the hurt that comes with it—is real too.

"It's better to be thorough and explore all options," Lou says to Malachi. Zeke's staring off into space, so Lou squeezes his thigh to bring him back down to Earth with the rest of us. "I don't think Diego did it, and I think the cops will realize that quickly too. And when they release him, I don't want them looking at Diego's circle for any other *Latino, male, fifteen-year-olds.*"

"We should hit up Jamal and Jabron," I suggest. They were there too, last night. "See if they know anything."

"Good idea." Lou nods, serious and businesslike.

I try to catch Zeke's eyes and smile—let him know that we're going to do everything we can to protect him, but he seems to have already floated back into space. I hope that I'll be able to catch him before he drifts too far.

EIGHTEEN

After an animated argument about whether their food is so bad that it's practically a hate crime, we decide to meet Jamal and Jabron at Colony Cantina to avoid heatstroke. Not my first choice, but I guess if Colony Cantina is gonna exploit our neighborhood, we can at least exploit their AC. We're all low on cash, so I use Apple Pay on my phone to order the only safe option on the menu (tortilla chips) and claim the same booth in the back.

"Yo wassap, my nigga!" Jamal approaches us in the signature Black-boy jog-shuffle so that his Nike slides don't come off. Behind him, Jabron follows like a shadow. The guys give each other dap.

"How extra is that dude at the counter, though?" Jamal comments. He plants his hand on the tabletop, hunching over in laughter.

"Man, I can't even," Malachi says, leaning back against the window.

"Incoming . . ." Marley mumbles.

Troy skips over and hovers at the edge of our table for several seconds, smiling and bobbing his head at all of us. Nobody says a word, but Troy doesn't seem to mind our irritated expressions.

Jamal breaks the silence at last. "Bruh, can I help you?"

Troy points up at the speaker on the ceiling. "Pac! A true LA legend. I bet you all are too young to know about him."

Let me remind you: five of us here are locals all born and raised in the heart of South LA. *Of course we know who Tupac is.* I stare at Troy in disbelief.

"You should check out his Essentials Playlist on Spotify. It's a bop!" Troy's not that old—probably only twenty-six or something—but his attempts at slang make my skin crawl. "Gangsta rap was *it* back in the day. I'm from Connecticut, but I've heard what it used to be like over here. Have you seen *Boyz n the Hood*? It was filmed nearby, you know."

Never in my life would I have imagined myself in this situation: facing a white man boldly and unsolicitedly mansplaining Black culture to a group of melanated teenagers while wearing a baseball cap with a sombrero on it, serving people wet tacos with a side of ketchup.

Eventually, we're saved by Troy's co-owner. He's been attempting to sweep up a mess in the corner, but his awkward movements make it clear that although he runs this spot, homeboy has never worked in the service industry before in his life. "Hey dude, can you man the front?" he calls over to Troy.

"Right on, Lance!" Troy shouts back. Lance frowns at the room, looking for a busboy to take over and clean up the mess for him.

"Peace, brothers." Troy gives each of the boys an excruciating fist bump—except for Lou, who just stares blankly—and walks away, smiling like a doofus.

"Like . . . who was that *for*? Did he think that was for us, or for him?" Zeke shakes his head, floored.

"They love talking about how much they listen to Pac almost as much as they love playing Christopher Columbus, pretending that they're the first people to 'discover' us," I say, snapping off the end of a pointy chip.

"I bet he wouldn't be so quick to bump all this gangsta rap and reminisce all nostalgically if shit was still poppin' off here. Like could you imagine that guy ever setting foot in this neighborhood back in our parents' day? Hell, even back when we were little?" Jamal cackles. "He'd be scared to death."

"Couldn't have said it better myself," I reply, hiding a grin.

"I mean, it wasn't perfect then either," Malachi mumbles. I can tell from the way that he bites the inside of his cheek that he's thinking of Dante. It takes significant effort for me to inhale deeply enough to calm the rush of static stars that flood my brain. Zeke clears his throat and fiddles with the saltshaker. We all have our own tells—quiet versions of some visceral reaction to whenever Dante is referenced.

"Perfect, nah, but nothing's ever perfect," Jamal says. I catch Malachi's eyes and we fall silent, watching an old man in an emerald-green car with hydraulics drive by the window. Dante's favorite color.

"You said you have a question for us," Jabron says to me, his raspy voice so low it's nearly a whisper. Marley and Lou both flinch and I remember that this must be the first time they've ever heard the quiet twin speak.

"Last night when you guys saw . . . you know . . . any chance you noticed Camesha nearby? Malachi's sister's best friend?"

"The hot one with the blog?" Jamal asks.

Marley chuckles. "Yeah, her."

"Nah. Didn't see her. She okay?"

I shrug. "We don't know. Nobody's seen her since the party last night."

Jamal lowers his voice to a whisper. "You think she murked that dude?"

"No, no. We're just worried about her with everything going on, that's all," Malachi rushes to reply.

"Did you hear any gunshots? Before you saw him, I mean?" I ask.

Jamal shakes his head. "Not one."

Zeke, Jamal, and Jabron all stumbled upon the body, and not one of them heard any gunshots. Neither did anyone working in the El Pollo Loco just ten feet away from the crime scene. Feels sus to me.

"Did you see anyone else at the scene?"

"I remember a dog barking. It didn't sound too close to us, but someone had to be walking it. And I saw one of those white space cars parked at the end of the alley. Some super-tall bald head ducked into the driver's seat as we walked out, but he didn't drive away immediately. Then, literally right when we saw the body, an *airplane* flew over us." Jamal pauses for dramatic effect like that was some big reveal.

I shut my eyes. "Jamal, our neighborhood is only a few miles from LAX. Planes fly over us all the time."

"Yeah, but like, the timing was crazy."

These two couldn't be less helpful.

"I know we don't have any answers, but you should ask Auntie Inga about what she told the cops. They were questioning her for hours, apparently," Jamal offers.

"Yeah, she mentioned that she ran into Vic last night and that the two of them chatted," I explain.

Jamal lets out an uncomfortable cough. "Uh, I heard a different version of the story."

I exchange a nervous look with Zeke and Malachi. Could Auntie be hiding something from us?

"Anyway, we gotta run. Enjoy your nasty drinks," Jamal says. He turns to leave while Jabron gives the table a solemn nod.

Across the restaurant, Lance disappears into the kitchen. Soon after, Troy shuffles back to our table. He's scratching his neck now and looks flushed, his skin an inflamed pink that makes his strawberry-blond hair seem only brighter.

"Hey, *brother*." He addresses Malachi. "I meant to ask you—where's your friend, *yo*?"

"What friend?" Malachi asks.

"You know, the emo one?" Troy waits for our blank expressions to turn into something more helpful to him, but we stay stoic, genuinely confused. "Dammit, you know who I'm talking about. Not emo, what do you kids call them now? The 'e-boy' or whatever? Vaguely skater vibe?"

God, he's old.

"Oh, Diego?" Zeke offers a little too excitedly, as if he solved a puzzle on a game show. I shove him underneath the table to remind him that there's no prize here.

"Yeah, him!" Troy clenches his fist triumphantly, having successfully communicated with us.

"He's not around," Lou says mysteriously.

"Well, how about you?" Troy points to Malachi, who then points at himself.

"*Me?*"

"Yeah, do you have any of his *stuff* on you?" Troy leans in. The whites of his eyes are a throbbing bright red. "I got cash."

Malachi stiffens. "I don't know what you're talking about."

Troy rolls his eyes and looks at Malachi as if to say *C'mon, man, give me a break.* "Well, can you hook me up with a SOSI plug, then? I want to buy local, *nah mean?*" He sounds like Will Ferrell imitating Michael Scott imitating Eminem.

"Why do you assume he's into that shit? You think that all of us deal?" Zeke scolds.

Dumbass Diego must be out in the streets spreading rumors he's pushing for SOSI.

Idiot.

I make a mental note to deal with this later.

"Chill out, bro. Meant no disrespect. I figured because . . ." Troy sees Lance walking toward our table and grumbles, "Well, my mistake. Enjoy your meal."

Every time we've been here, Troy has bothered us and reduced us all to characters in his fucked-up fantasy of running a restaurant in a community of color and being all chummy with his customers. But this time, he went too far. It's one thing to be seen as a token for someone's LykLuv, it's another thing entirely to be an assumed drug dealer. Malachi's face is hard to read right now—he looks more embarrassed than angry, which is surprising since I half expected him to cuss Troy out. But then again, after getting to know Marley, I'm realizing that maybe I'm not as good as I thought at guessing what the people around me are thinking.

I wait for Malachi to look up and catch my eyes, but he doesn't. He just keeps swirling the straw in his shitty agua fresca around and around.

"Was he bothering you? I'm sorry. I know he's a lot, but he means well." Lance towers over our table, his Colony Cantina baseball cap tipped back at such an angle that we can see his receding hairline.

"Whatever. We're good," Marley says with some bite in her voice.

"He's weird but harmless. You know how trust-fund kids are," Lance says.

"And you're not?" I ask. "You didn't get any help from Mom and Dad to purchase this fine dining establishment?" I lazily swirl a hand over my head, broadly gesturing at the tacky framed posters of spring breakers in Cabo decorating the walls.

Lance's face turns the color of those crusty strawberry shortcake ice cream pops that are always at concession stands even though I've never actually seen someone buy one. "Having a little bit of help is very different than having enough money to not have to care about anything," he says defensively.

It's funny how he can call what was probably thousands of dollars just "a little bit of help." That's the craziest part about people with money—they can make any amount sound big or small based off their mood.

"Speaking of help," Zeke says. "Are y'all hiring?"

All of us, including Lance, stare at Zeke with varying levels of shock. Never in my life have I seen this boy clean up after himself without being asked. And now he wants to clean up other people's stuff? No way. Plus, he hates this place.

"Seriously?" Lance asks.

Zeke nods enthusiastically.

"Our busboy just quit. . . ."

"Zeke, c'mon, man," Malachi says, shaking his head in disbelief.

"No, I want to do it. I'm serious."

I point to the Sriracha on the table and pretend to gag, but Zeke ignores me. He turns to Lance. "When can I start?"

"Tomorrow? We need help in the mornings." All the spots at the mall said that Zeke was too young, but this fool didn't even ask his age. I know I'm not one to talk about following the rules, but c'mon. Whatever happened to due diligence or whatever?

"Perfect, see you tomorrow, then." He repositions his hair to show more of his eyes than usual. "I'm Zeke, by the way."

Lance shakes Zeke's hand and that's it: the deal is done. Zeke's going to work at the very establishment that's part of the movement to push him out of the neighborhood in the first place. What kills me more than the irony of the situation is that it's a total time suck. Lou has already taken up a good bit of Zeke's time, and now with a summer gig . . . Even if he stays, I'm wondering how much I'll get to see Zeke at all.

Once Lance retreats to the counter, Lou excuses himself and storms off to the bathroom. Maybe he's just as frustrated about Zeke taking on another time commitment as I am. Or maybe he knows something that I don't. Marley scooches out of the booth to follow him.

Zeke clears his throat. "Before you two say anything, you should know that I have two motivations for working here." When he sees that I'm not trying to interrupt him, he continues. "One is money, obviously, but the other is information. The news report said that Vic—"

"Shhh!" I nudge Zeke. "Code name, remember?"

"Right. The news report said that the DWG was a local

restaurant investor too. Given his goal to skyrocket rent around here, I'm guessing that he might have invested in places like this."

"Maybe not even *places like this*, maybe literally Colony Cantina," I say, catching on.

"Exactly. And if that's true, then maybe Lance and Troy know something."

I high-five Zeke, but Malachi still looks pissed. "I don't trust these guys," he says.

"I don't have to *trust* them to eavesdrop and take their money," Zeke says with a smirk. "I'm all in on your plan, Rhea. We gotta do everything we can to clear SOSI's name and find the real killer. There's no other way."

Marley comes back to the table and says that Lou's had enough of this place. "We should probably call it a day."

"Is Lou okay?" Zeke asks nervously.

"He's fine, just frustrated." She holds out her arm, revealing a cracked iPhone. "You left this at the counter, Rhea." She runs a finger down the fractured surface. "We gotta get this screen fixed, girl."

"With what money?!" I reply. It's easier to laugh off the busted screen as a financial thing than admit that maybe I want to keep it this way for a while. It's become a necessary reminder of how I broke it at the party . . . and how guilty I still feel. I pocket my phone and scoot out of the booth.

Malachi dumps the remaining tortilla chips into his hand and heads outside. Troy and Lance are both standing at the front register, waving goodbye as we leave. Zeke waves back, Malachi gives them the finger, and the rest of us just keep walking.

NINETEEN

On our walk back from the restaurant, I let everyone drift ahead of me. I keep thinking about what Camesha said before she stepped into that car last night. How her client had something "special" planned.

We left the party around 11:45 p.m., so our Lyft must have been called sometime around midnight. The DWG called Camesha's car around the same time, though we have no idea where he called it from. Zeke walked to the restaurant, ate, then didn't see the body until his way out around 1 a.m.

It's a short window, but a lot can happen in an hour.

I grab my phone to pull up the subzeggit about SOSI. I've kept the app front and center on the home page, but I've been too busy to check it recently. The original post—a grainy photo of the Anti-Gang Task Force flyer—is still pinned at the top, but there are dozens more comments since the last time I logged in. Shit's popped off since the news this morning.

UrNeighbor323 posted a link to the news segment about the murder, which mentions SOSI as the alleged culprit.

> **u/UrNeighbor323:** You see? This is EXACTLY what I said before. SOSI's out here killing innocent people.

u/KofaParkStanAcct: I heard that "landlord" was more of a slumlord. Don't know how "innocent" the man was.

u/ButFirstCoffee: When I moved here, the relator assured me that this neighborhood was on the upswing, not the decline.

u/NiceGuyRy: Looks like it's time to pack 😅

u/PplOvrProfits: We didn't want y'all here in the first place anyway. Don't let the door hit you on the way out 👋

Everyone on here seems pretty plugged into neighborhood gossip, for better or for worse. Maybe it's worth mining these people for information?

I make sure that I'm still logged into my ghost account, ConcernedCitizn, and return to the main forum to see what info I can get.

u/ConcernedCitizn: I don't know if SOSI's behind the shooting. What was their motive? It doesn't add up. Anybody else feel that way?

That feels vague enough, right? I don't wanna tip off LAPD and outright ask for any leads, but maybe people will have reactions? I'm about to slip my phone back into my pocket when a notification vibration surges through my palm. I've already gotten my first response.

u/SemiCharmed87: SOSI 10000% killed that guy. We know it, the police know it. Don't go stirring up shit. The gang is BAD NEWS.

"Bad news"? I laugh at the G-rated word choice. I reply:

u/ConcernedCitizn: You sound pretty certain??

The three "typing" dots appear and then . . .

u/SemiCharmed87: SOSI is guilty. I'd watch my back if I were you, bitch.

Damn. I know the internet's full of trolls, but that felt a little much. You'd think I personally attacked SemiCharmed87's mama by the way they're coming for me right now. Before I can reply, I see that my comment casting doubt on SOSI has been flagged and deleted. When my screen refreshes, I get a fresh notification: *You have been removed from this forum for violating community guidelines.*

"The fuck?" I groan.

"You good?" Marley falls back from the boys when she sees me trailing behind.

"Yeah, some asshole got me kicked off the SOSI subzeggit." I try not to let this bother me too much. We should be focused on building out our suspect list anyway.

"What do you think of all of this?" Marley asks me after a beat.

A few steps ahead, the boys take turns burping. It's funny, but also so absurd. Like honestly, *fuck this*. We're so young that we can still buy student tickets at the movie theater, yet here we are, trying to save our goddamn neighborhood. I want to tell Marley that I think all of this is complete and total bullshit. But I know that isn't what she was asking about.

I ignore the strained feeling in my chest and explain to her my thoughts about the DWG. "I think it's weird that neither the twins or Zeke heard gunshots, but the news report said that Vic was shot in that parking lot. And I think that based on what Auntie told us about how he creeped on Camesha, he seems like the kind of guy who probably had a bunch of other sketchy stuff going on in his life."

"Agreed. If he was paying for a girlfriend, who knows who else he was paying, and for what." Our footsteps slap through a puddle of water pooling around a broken fire hydrant.

"How are you feeling today?" I don't know whether to bring up the Diego incident from last night.

"Not gonna lie, it was satisfying for a second to get the news that he was arrested." Marley smiles weakly. "But only for a second."

She doesn't think that Diego did it either. The burping in the background stops as Malachi and Lou suddenly take off into a sprint as we reach the tunneled underpass that leads to the strip mall. Malachi wins by half a step and does a touchdown dance while Lou catches his breath. Zeke's halfway between us and the boys, laughing hysterically while applauding above his head.

"How'd the rest of your night go?" Marley points her chin toward Malachi up ahead. I'm grateful for the tunnel's shadows to hide the cheesy grin on my face.

I tell Marley about my conversation with Malachi, and she hangs on every word, sprinkling in the occasional supportive "Yass!" and "I told you!" She's one of those people who listens, like *really listens*, when you talk, so much so that by the time I finish telling her the story, I feel 80 percent more interesting than I was five minutes ago.

"That's great!" she exclaims before asking the golden question: "But what now?"

"I don't know. I messed it up in the end." I shrug. "The moment was perfect, but I couldn't bring myself to say that I liked him back. So, I don't know." This is the part where I was hoping she could fill in the blanks as my new certified Feminine Friend.

"Well, what do you *want* to happen now?"

My honest answer is somewhere between everything and nothing. We're not in middle school anymore, so I don't want to be all *I like you, hehe!* then do absolutely nothing to act on those feelings. But at the same time, I kind of want everything to stay the same. This shit with Zeke and the DWG is enough stress; I don't know if I can handle dating on top of it all.

I try to think of something to actually tell Marley, but end up hitting her with the anxious, gritted-teeth emoji face.

"Rhea," Marley begins in an oddly maternal voice that I don't hate. "Don't get me wrong, Malachi's cute and all, but are you sure that you even *really* like him? Like him, specifically?"

"That I'm sure of." I slow my pace and Marley does the same to create even more distance between us and the guys ahead.

"Okay, but why him and not any other person?"

I could tell Marley about how I like the way Malachi's dimples only show when he smiles super hard, and how he hums made-up opera versions of old R&B songs whenever he exchanges the books in his locker, and that he sketches these really cool, imaginative dreamscapes that are way different than what anyone would expect from him.

But instead, I tell her about the first Sunday after Back-to-School night in fifth grade.

A "homegoing." A return to the Lord, or to the homeland, or to wherever it is where Black people don't have to suffer anymore. That's what the family called his funeral.

Dante's homegoing.

I played sick that morning. I've always had the capability to be extra, but on that day, it was my best work yet. The night before, I planted the seeds: I spent the day fake-coughing all over the house, placing little mountains of tissue on the top layer of every trash can. I made sure to wheeze extra loudly when my mom was on the phone with Lupe to coordinate who should ride with who. So, on the morning of the big day, when my mom came in to tell me to get dressed, I told her that I couldn't because I had the flu. I pointed to the evidence strewn about the house. My case was rock solid.

My mom sighed. "You sure you want to handle it like this?"

"I'm sick. I can't help it." Cough, cough, wheeze, cough.

Mom walked straight to my closet and pulled out the black dress that she bought from the clearance rack at Ross and placed it on my bed. It had puffy sleeves and polka dots, which I hated, but it was the only age-appropriate option on sale, so I didn't have another choice.

"Don't forget the headband," she said as she retreated to her own room to get ready. "The Reeds will be here soon."

I didn't move.

I was buried in a bundle of blankets at the foot of my bed when Malachi knocked on my door. He didn't announce himself, but I knew his footsteps.

"Your mom says you're not coming to the funeral," he said from the doorway.

I kept quiet, pretending to be asleep.

"I know you're awake, Rhea."

I ignored him. I would not break character.

I listened to Malachi's footsteps enter and move toward the pale gray butterfly chair in the corner of my room. My ears pricked up as I heard him grab the copy of *Ready Player One* that I had been reading. He paused, then I heard the flutter of hundreds of pages being fanned open like a deck of cards in the hands of a poker dealer.

"No!" I pushed off the covers and grimaced as my laminated Naruto bookmark hit the floor. There are few things more distressing to me than losing a page. Malachi knew this.

"Faker," he said flatly. I pushed back the covers and emerged from my cocoon. He shoved his bony wrists into his pockets, which caused the shoulders of his suit jacket to tent upward. I sat there quietly, wrapping the extra length of the drawstring of my plaid pajama pants around my pinky until it started to lose feeling.

"Rhea—"

"We'll never be the same," I interrupted. "Me, you, and Zeke. It's different now." I still remember the feeling: like I was part of this smooth-riding machine that suddenly lost a wheel and threw us all off-balance. I felt as though I was thrown particularly far from the others.

"It's different, but it'll be okay," Malachi said, breathing shakily by my side, no doubt trying to live up to the toxic curse of Black Boys Don't Cry.

I stared at the popcorn ceiling to avoid his eyes. "I don't think we should be friends anymore," I said.

Malachi removed his hands from his pockets and rubbed his palms over his freshly cut head. "Why not?" I was expecting anger, but his voice merely indicated curiosity.

"Dante was the glue. And when the glue is gone, the rest of us have to fall apart." It was just like my mom's first husband—after he passed away, my siblings and mom drifted, so now it's time for the same to happen to my friends. Alone before Dante, alone after him.

Malachi cleared his throat, but Mrs. Reed knocked on my door. "You kids ready to go?"

My mom answered her before we could. "Rhea's being difficult. She doesn't want to go. You should head out without us."

"And you're just . . . going to let her not go?" Mrs. Reed's voice lowered to a whisper. *"They're ten years old, girl. C'mon."*

"I don't have it in me to fight her today," my mom said at a volume much less inhibited.

The concern in Mrs. Reed's voice made sense to me. Even I knew that this wasn't exactly the kind of stunt that my mom should let me win. The adults disappeared down the hall as Mrs. Reed went to tell Lacy to turn off the car radio so the battery won't die.

"Look, she left." I nodded in the general direction of my mom's room. "Now it's your turn."

"I'm not leaving you here alone, dummy. Not today." Malachi paused. "Not ever." He stood up to grab the black dress on my bed and tossed it on my lap. "Get dressed."

There was something about his voice that made me feel like I'd regret it if I didn't go with him. I went to the bathroom down the hall to change.

When I came back to my room, he was fiddling with the purple ribbon of the stuffed animal on my bed. As he looked up, I caught this raw, surprised expression on his face.

There was a trace of a smile. "You look—" he began. I waited. He sighed. "Your mom told me to tell you to not forget this." He stepped forward and held out the black headband lined with flowers made of soft fabric. He was shaking a little and I didn't understand why. "Nothing's ever gunna change between you and me, okay?"

I was ready to protest, but when he looked me in the eyes, there was something heavy in his stare that caught me off guard. I forgot how to push him away.

When I took the headband in my hand, he practically bolted out of the room. There was something about how frazzled he seemed that made the moment sort of funny to me. Funny enough to keep going. I followed him out the door and into the car. We rode to the funeral in the backseat, in silence.

At the homegoing, Zeke, Malachi, and I sat together in the front row next to Dante's parents and his brother, Dep. I was a little bit surprised by our placement at first, but when I thought about how much time the four of us spent together in life—burning grass stains onto the knees of our jeans, wearing out the springs in pogo sticks, building intricate universes in *Minecraft*—it made sense why we'd be among those closest to Dante in death.

The ceremony was a blur . . . until the slideshow started. A giant projector creaked from the church ceiling and began to play photos. Pictures of Dante running, Dante laughing, Dante scoring the winning touchdown during his Pop Warner game. They put up one that I took of Dante doing that gross thing where he'd twist his tongue up to pick his nostril and everyone laughed nostalgically.

This was when I ran.

I found shelter in the dusty, peach-colored collection of stalls on the far end of the church. Everyone else was glued to the slideshow, so I had the girls' restroom to myself.

There was a familiar knock at the outer door. "Are you okay?" Zeke's zany voice was so high-pitched that it used to make even our fifth-grade teacher Ms. Flores giggle, but it sounded different that day. His words came out low, soft, and controlled.

Malachi pressed open the swinging door before I could respond.

"You can't be in here," I said, nose sniffling.

"Stop doing this," Malachi said. "Come out. Please."

I nudged open the door to the stall. I noted the moisture forming over Malachi's brown eyes, big and round like his cheekbones, even when he frowns. Zeke had already melted into full-blown tears. His tie was too long, extending below his belt. He grabbed the end and used it to wipe the snot from his nose. Then he hugged me.

Zeke applied just enough pressure to loosen the tears that were too scared to fall. Malachi came in next, draping his arms around each of us, resting his chin in the space between our foreheads. We stood there for what felt like forever. A huddle of limbs in clothes that our parents picked out, holding together what remained of our little universe.

A gasp pulled our attention to the bathroom entrance. "You can't be in here," an older lady scolded, glaring down Zeke and Malachi. We uncurled from one another.

"Oh, leave them alone, they're just kids," the slightly-less-old woman accompanying her said.

The older lady sighed. "Honey, their friend was killed. They're not *just kids* anymore."

She pointed to the door and we left, avoiding her eye contact on the way out.

We returned to our seats just in time for the boys to walk alongside Dante's father, brother, and uncles to serve as pallbearers as they brought Dante's casket, and his body within, down the church aisle and out into the hearse. I watched Zeke and Malachi carefully as they clenched their jaws and breathed through their noses, trying to be tough for someone. For who exactly, I still don't know.

Although they were much shorter than all the other men, I had this little daydream of Zeke and Malachi as grown-ups. Somehow, even when I came back to reality, the boys continued to remind me more of the men than of the boys that their bodies were still stuck in. Maybe that's what loss does to you— makes you older than you are without changing a thing about how you actually look. It's an energy shift, something subtle, but something that cannot be undone. I felt a sharp jab of pain in my chest, a rush of cold down my spine. I missed them. Zeke and Malachi were only thirty feet away, but still, I missed them, and who they've been until now.

We're not just kids anymore.

"And now here we are," I finish, almost forgetting why I chose to tell Marley this story in the first place. The cocktail of grief and intimacy from that day always leaves me disoriented. "It was the worst day of my life, but had Malachi not been there to bring me to the service and hold me—hold us all—together until it was over, I don't think that I ever would have forgiven myself." I pause, unsure how to explain what's about to come out my mouth next. "Weirdly, I remember thinking from that day onward that I'd fall in love with Malachi when we were older."

"And now here you are," Marley says, smiling softly, despite the sadness in her eyes. "Older."

I nod.

Marley grabs my hand. "Let's make it happen, then."

I crinkle my brow. "Make what happen?"

"Tell the damn boy how you feel."

TWENTY

I spend the following morning reorganizing all the unused spices in our kitchen cabinet, first by name, then by color. I keep checking my phone out of habit, though there aren't any new messages. It's hard to not feel restless. I don't think I've gone more than a day without seeing either Zeke or Malachi in at least seven years.

Zeke's working his first shift at Colony Cantina while Marley and Lou are at the African Marketplace with their mom and Staples. Meanwhile, Malachi has been busy comforting Lacy all day. Given that I'm the only one who doesn't have anything else to do, anywhere else to be, or anyone else to be with this morning, I decide to do some solo investigating.

The fact that Jamal heard a different interpretation of whatever went down between Auntie and Vic the other night seems worth digging into further. I'm not convinced Auntie has anything to do with the murder, but maybe her fear about having said the wrong thing to Vic is right. I'm hoping that someone saw their conversation and can help me paint a fuller picture of Vic's behavior that night.

I run a search of the gas stations in the area. There are

seven total, but three are significantly more expensive than the other four, so I doubt Auntie would go to those. My mom usually gets cheap gas from the "Four Corners": aka the intersection on Slauson and La Brea, where there's a Sinclair, an Exxon, a Shell, and a Chevron on the four corners. It's just a few blocks from the Lenway party house. I bet that if Auntie stopped to get gas on her way to check on us, she'd go to one of those.

I grab a Pop-Tart and text my mom that I'm leaving. The little blue message floats at the end of a long line of other little blue bubbles sent by me—an entirely one-way conversation consisting of mostly "Heading out" or "Home" texts that are eventually given a lazy thumbs-up or (if I'm lucky) a little heart by my mom. She's home now—asleep in the other room with my stepdad—but we haven't crossed paths in at least three days.

When I get to the Four Corners, I start at the Sinclair. I like its dinosaur logo, so I have a feeling that this place might be lucky. I ask the bearded man behind the bulletproof glass surrounding the counter if police have stopped by to ask questions about the man on the news who was killed or the tall woman who he was seen with. No luck.

I try Exxon next. The skinny teen cutting lotto tickets for an impatient motorcyclist says he has no idea what I'm talking about before his uncle commands him to go sort the Gatorades.

Shell's the same story. "No cops, no dead guy, no tall woman, none of your damn business," the lady in charge bellows at me. But in the reflection of the mirror above the cash register, a young woman in the corner catches my attention. She's unpacking a box of sunflower seeds, but clearly eavesdropping. She looks interested, to say the least. However, I get the feeling that if she were to speak up, her employer wouldn't be happy.

The Boss Lady points me to the door. I do as I'm told, but as I head out, I catch the young employee's gaze. She stares back for a second too long before her eyes flit away. She *must* know something.

I half crouch, half scurry over to an empty gas pump and click the "Call Attendant for Assistance" button. I hide behind the trash bin so that the manager won't see me. I press it again as another car pulls up into the pump in front of me, and the eavesdropping employee comes out at last.

The woman is young, late twenties maybe, with pink streaks rippling through her cascading ponytail. She laughs when she sees me squatting on the pavement. "Why d'you wanna know about the man who was here last night so bad?"

I *knew* that she must've seen something.

I stand and dust off my hands against my jeans. "My friend is missing, and she knew him. Now that guy's dead, so I'm trying to figure out what happened." Better to keep things vague.

The woman gives me a long up-down, as if she's sizing me up to see if I'm worth her time. "I don't go round giving out information for free, you know," she says at last.

Right. I check my pockets for cash, even though I know that I don't have any. Who carries cash anymore? The woman pulls out her phone and mindlessly scrolls through LykLuv while she waits for me to get it together.

I give up. "Look, I don't have any cash—"

"I take Venmo," she replies.

Seriously? I suck my teeth. "I don't have Venmo."

"You got Cash App, then?" She bugs her eyes and shrugs at me.

I roll my eyes. "Aight, fine. What's your handle?"

The woman smiles and shows me where to send the money. I only have $18 on my debit card, so I send her $5, hoping that's enough, but I have no sense how much is appropriate for a situation like this.

Her phone chirps and she guffaws. "Did you literally put 'bribe' as the description?"

I blush. It's not like I do this all the time! I panicked. "Look, can I just ask you a question now?"

The woman offers a sly grin. "Shoot."

Her eyes remain fixed on her phone, but I guess that's my cue to start talking. "What did you see last night when the guy came in?"

She flips a strand of pink hair behind her ear. "So, what had happened was, old guy came in. Bought a Super Size cup of Dr Pepper, two cans of Red Bull, and a three-pound bag of cheese puffs. Filled up a full tank of gas, talked to this tall lady in scrubs, then bounced. Cops said he was dead, like, an hour later. Wild."

No doubt that the woman in scrubs is Auntie. "And the tall lady—how did she seem?"

"That sounds like a whole new question, if you ask me." She rubs her thumb and pointer finger together.

I sigh, pulling out my phone to send another $5. This time though, I search for a more discreet payment description. I pick the little cartoon detective emoji and send the payment.

The informant checks the confirmation and smirks. "Cute."

"So, about the woman—" I continue.

"Right, right." She leans in. "Off the record, I'll tell you what I didn't tell the police. She and that man? They were arguing. Like, for real for real. Yellin' and cussin' and shit. For a second, I thought I'd have to call security, but the lady up and left, midfight. Hectic."

Auntie made it seem that she and Vic just talked—not *fought*.

"I wonder what they were arguing about," I muse aloud, hoping to avoid the question fee.

"I don't know, but it looked serious."

"Why didn't you tell the cops about the fight?" The woman flashes a smile again and I sense another Cash App request that I can't afford coming. "C'mon, can I get a buy-two-questions-get-one-free deal? Please?"

The woman snickers. "Fine. When the lady came in, she was so sweet. She paid for her gas, bought some sweet tea, then tipped me ten dollars. She *tipped*. At a *gas station*. Meanwhile, that gremlin of a man practically spat in my face when I didn't give him his change fast enough." The woman's lightly condescending sneer toward me morphs into a genuine smile while remembering Auntie. "She seemed like a good woman. When I heard that white guy died, I didn't wanna give police any more reason to press her. If she was guilty, the police would find her, but I didn't need to help them. We gotta look after our own." The young woman pulls up the collar of her work shirt to reveal the new LGBTQ+ flag with the trans pride stripes incorporated.

My mouth forms the beginning of a *Thank you*, but the woman's eyes dart back to the interior of the gas station. Inside, her boss is frantically searching for her.

"Thanks for supporting my Happy Hour fund, kid," she says while backpedaling away. "Good luck finding your friend."

The sides of my head pulse with the surge of fresh questions. The news reporters said that Vic was walking alone when he was shot. If he'd planned on spending the night strolling around, then why load up on gas and snacks? What the hell were he and Auntie arguing about? And more importantly: Why did Auntie lie?

TWENTY-ONE

After Zeke gets off work, he and I meet up with Malachi to spend the afternoon calling cab companies, trying (unsuccessfully) to track down the town car that picked up Camesha. Later, we head to Marley and Lou's house, so that I can fill everyone in on what I learned at the gas station.

"What do you think of Auntie as a suspect?" Marley asks me when I finish. "She fought with Vic, then she was just driving around for the rest of the night?"

"No alibi," Lou points out.

"No alibi," I confirm. "Still seems unlikely, though." Even though she and Vic were arguing, that could have been about anything: the evictions, the broken water heater—who knows. It's sketchy that she lied, but she probably didn't want to distract our attention from looking for Camesha.

"If the DWG had been messing with Camesha, that's another story, but it sounds like things were okay between them. Right? Gross, but fine?" Zeke presses.

"Agreed." Auntie may resent the man who hired Camesha, but she's made it clear over the years that she's not one to hate on working girls or mess with their incomes.

"Let's keep her on the list for now," Lou says. "There's still so much we don't know."

The five of us make our way toward the pool house but pause in the living room to catch a glimpse of the news coverage of the DWG murder. Ms. Allen is watching from the couch, her giant boyfriend's arm draped around her shoulder.

"Nice to see you kids again." Staples greets us with his used-car-salesman-esque smile. Marley gives him a stank-eye so funky that I have to cup my mouth to keep a laugh from escaping. I guess he's been around a lot recently because when Ms. Allen isn't looking, Lou mouths a generous *Fuck you* at him, to which Staples replies with a silent *Shut up.*

Even though Staples works with schools, he sure as hell hates teenagers.

"It's a small world and it keeps getting smaller," Ms. Allen says, shaking her head as the news channel shows a slideshow of photos of the DWG.

"Did you know him?" Lou asks, taking a seat on the arm of the couch. I watch Staples try to flick Lou, but Ms. Allen's lying against him in a way that keeps him centimeters out of reach.

"Unfortunately, yes. Besides Auntie Keisha, that man was the only other person I knew in this entire city."

Marley perks up. "Then how come we never met him?"

"I said that I *knew* him, not that I *liked* him." Ms. Allen lets out a forced laugh, followed by a forced cough. "Believe it or not, that man introduced me to your father."

Marley drops her canvas tote bag and moves to sit on the floor, leaning against her mom's shins. Her mouth hangs open, but it's almost as if she can't actually put any words together until she's physically touching her mom. "But . . . we all grew up in Michigan. That doesn't make sense."

"Well, you know Auntie Keisha and I have been friends forever. She went to college out here, so I came to visit once. That man who got killed was a classmate of hers. At a party one night, she told him that I lived in Michigan, so he introduced me to your father because he was from Chicago. He was one of those obnoxious 'Coastal Elite' California people who assumed that all of the Midwest is one state, but your father was cute, so I didn't mind."

Ms. Allen tells her story casually, but Marley visibly winces at the mention of her father's looks.

"And now they're both dead," Lou says, his voice sharp yet unemotional.

They're both dead?

"That guy and your aunt, you mean?" Zeke asks cautiously.

Lou looks over at him. "No, that guy and our father."

Okay. I know that I'm not the best listener in the world, but the fact that Marley and Lou's dad is dead seems like some pretty new information to casually lay out there. I check Malachi's and Zeke's faces: they're both equally shook. I knew that their dad was shitty, but I figured he was just . . . elsewhere. Not dead.

"And can you believe that man had the nerve to call me when your father passed away?" Ms. Allen tsk-tsks. "It's not good to speak ill of the dead, but honestly, good riddance." Maybe it's just the surprise of the moment playing tricks on me, but for a split second, I swear that I see the ghost of a grin flit across Ms. Allen's face. Staples plants a kiss on Ms. Allen's cheek so wet that I can hear it. "May they both rest in peace."

"And to think he was killed so close to home. Good thing we were out across town in Marina del Rey for date night—right, darling?" She touches Staples's arm, and he lets out a grunt in agreement.

On the news, the daughter of the DWG, Amelia, wraps up an interview with the aggressively spray-tanned reporter.

"I was his only child, so now it's on me to step up to manage his affairs. He owned an extensive real estate portfolio with the Becker Real Estate Group that included several apartment complexes as well as investments in various new, local businesses."

The daughter's doing that weird half-cry, pat-her-makeup routine again. The orange-tinted reporter asks her whether she'll miss working with her father.

"Oh, definitely. Everything I know, I learned from him. But now it's time for me to honor my father's legacy and chart a new future for the company—one that really centers serving the communities that we work in. I've volunteered with various organizations over the years that help at-need families reach their full potential, and I'm excited to bring that perspective to our vision."

"Somebody get her an Oscar, amiright?" Malachi cackles. The joke falls flat on the room still recovering from the prior conversation.

"We're going to the pool house," Marley announces, snatching her tote bag and storming out the glass door before it can get even more awkward.

"Don't forget that you and your brother are coming to brunch with us tomorrow! Bonding time!" Ms. Allen calls after us with a wave.

I cringe and follow the crew out to the backyard.

Marley and I plop into the green beanbags while Malachi and Lou take the couch. Zeke stands off to the side, lingering by the door. Marley picks up the remote and starts scrolling.

"Since when does Staples hate you two so much?" I ask. There were some real icy glares fired between the three of them.

"We told Mom that we think he's cheating on her," Lou says flatly.

"He's always whispering into his phone and sneaking out in the middle of the night just to slide back into her bed." Marley sticks out her tongue in disgust. "Mom confronted Staples with our theory, but you can guess how that went."

"She believed him instead?" Malachi asks.

"Exactly. He won, but now we're enemies, or whatever," Lou says, bored.

He and Marley turn their attention back to the television before Zeke blurts out, "I didn't know that your dad died."

There's a darkness in his voice that surprises Lou and Marley. They've never seen this side of Zeke before.

Lou sighs. "It honestly did not occur to me to tell you."

"That's absolutely insane." Zeke stares at him, stunned. "When I told you about how my dad died would have been a *perfectly reasonable* time to bring it up." Zeke stands up from the couch and moves toward the back wall, his arms hugging his own chest.

Zeke's dad passed away during a tricky time—it was right after Stella and Kiké were born, and not long before Dante died. It was a car crash on the 405 freeway, a freak accident— three-car pileup, no survivors. Losing a parent would suck for anyone at any time, but for Zeke, it was made worse by the fact that him and his dad were tight as hell, like a model father-son duo: always sporting matching Dodgers jerseys, playing *FIFA* together on weeknights, going to watch the low-rider show in East LA on weekends.

So, for about half of third grade, Zeke would spend recess in the bathroom stall farthest from the door, sobbing. Malachi and Dante would bring scratch paper and markers to draw quietly as they sat on the floor, backs against Zeke's stall, keeping him company and standing guard to give dirty looks to whoever dared to even consider making fun of Zeke.

After a couple of months, we got Zeke to leave the bathroom and join us in the corner of the yard, where the four of us camped out for the rest of the school year. I don't think I've ever heard Zeke mention his dad out loud since then, so the fact that he talked to Lou about it is no small deal.

Lou stands to face Zeke. "Well, when you told me about your dad, we were talking about you, not me, so I didn't think to say anything."

"You can't listen to a person open up about their personal shit and then just completely withhold something that huge on your end. It's a total violation of trust to, like, confide in someone and then . . . Ugh." Zeke runs a hand back and forth over his hair. "That's not what a normal person would do."

As his words slip out, Marley, Malachi, and I wince. I look over at Lou and see that his fists are clenched so tightly that he's trembling.

Not normal.

The words seem to endlessly ring in the air.

"I thought that you were okay with *not normal*," Lou spits, staring at Marley's commemorative tote bag from last year's Neurodiversity Now walk-a-thon.

Zeke's brain finally catches up with his own words. "Wait,

I didn't mean—" But Lou's already out the door. Zeke takes a few steps after him, but Marley gently warns him to hang back. Zeke kicks the wall once, then again and again. "You guys know that I didn't mean that." His voice cracks.

"This is what I was afraid would happen," Marley says, patting the couch beside her for Zeke to take a seat.

Zeke hesitates, but then curls up on the couch and buries his face into the nook of his elbow. "I fucked up."

"Yeah, you did." Marley closes her eyes and lets her head roll back so that she's staring at the ceiling. "What's interesting, though, is that this is exactly how I imagined you hurting him, but it's also different."

Zeke speaks into his arm, so his voice comes out muffled. "Different how?"

"Because you're clearly in love with him."

Zeke doesn't say anything, but I can see the tips of his ears turn red.

"I've read the poems, Zeke," Marley explains.

I flashback to sixth grade: Theo Benton. *Of course* Zeke's sentimental ass never grew out of his poetry phase.

A distressed groan climbs out of Zeke's little burrow, which makes Marley chuckle. "No, no, don't be embarrassed. They're sweet. I never thought that anyone else besides me and my mom would *really see him*. But you do." Marley places her hand on Zeke's head and strokes his hair gently. "I've messed up too. I didn't trust him when he said he was ready to start dating, but I don't have any right to police his independence. If anything, I've been condescending and—" She pauses to choke down the emotion building in her throat. "I think both of us have some apologies to make to Lou."

I play with the frayed edge of a rug as we all listen quietly to the television's Netflix preview run on repeat. The ad is for some cheap true-crime drama, heavy on the blood and reenactments. Eventually, Malachi clicks play to free us from the endless trailer loop.

"So, how *did* your pops die?" Malachi asks Marley, shattering the silence and every social cue in the universe along with it.

"Oh my god, Malachi, read the room," I grumble.

"It's okay," Marley says, looking at Zeke pitifully. "He was shot."

"By a stranger?" Malachi asks.

"Not really." She laces her fingers through Zeke's hair, although it seems like she's not doing so just to comfort Zeke, but herself too. "My mom shot him."

Ms. Allen looks like your classic middle-class, middle-aged, professional Black woman who plays the responsible, though vaguely whimsical, mother in an NBC sitcom. I would *never* peg her to have earned a teardrop tattoo.

Malachi gasps. "Okay. Not trying to be an asshole, but like, how is she not in jail?" His face looks as shocked and confused as when Lacy first explained to us that blow jobs don't actually involve any blowing.

"Chill out," I warn Malachi. It's been less than forty-eight hours since Marley opened up to me about her family. It doesn't feel right to crack open this shit so soon. I look over at Marley to gauge how she's feeling, but her face is cold—devoid of any of her usual warmth.

She nudges Zeke to scoot over and gets up to retrieve a white box from the cabinet. She ruffles through loose papers and photos until she finds what she's looking for. She turns back around and hands me a newspaper clipping, slightly faded but protected by one of those slips of three-ring binder plastic that litter the Back to School section in Target every fall.

At first, I skim the article so quickly that I don't digest any of the information. I force myself to start again and read slowly. Malachi appears over my shoulder as I take in the headline: "Domestic Violence Turned Lethal."

The tone of the article is sensationalist, but it does make one thing clear: it was self-defense. The neighbors all knew that the twins' father had been mistreating their mother for a while, so there was no question as to what happened. Even their grandma on their dad's side testified on behalf of Ms. Allen because she knew her son was a piece of shit. Plus, it helped that their mom's a lawyer, and knew a bunch of people who were able to help her out. The article ends with the mention of the "two young children" in the house.

That's a whole lot of trauma for such a peppy girl to carry.

"Were you, uh, there when it happened?" I ask carefully.

"God, no." Marley shakes her head and sits back onto the couch to continue playing with Zeke's hair. I pass Zeke the article. "But that's why we ended up moving out here. After that whole shitshow, my mom needed a fresh start. So, uhm, if you don't mind—it's not like, a secret or anything, but she needs to make some new friends and people make assumptions, so if you wouldn't mind not telling your parents—"

"Say less." Zeke places the article facedown on the arm of the couch.

The true-crime drama on the TV shows an interview with a woman explaining how she relocated to an open-carry state so that she could keep a gun on her at all times. Marley points at the screen and smirks. "Smart woman. My mom kept her gun too. *Just in case.*"

That last part's a joke, but that's some dark humor to wrap my mind around. Malachi and I force out strained half laughs.

"I'm going to check on Lou," she announces, untangling her fingers from Zeke's hair and slipping out the door back to the main house. Once she's out of earshot, I turn to Malachi, whose brown eyes are as wide as I've ever seen them.

"Ms. Allen killed her husband," Malachi whispers.

"Ms. Allen knew, and hated, the DWG," I shoot back.

Zeke sits up. "The DWG introduced Ms. Allen to her husband. The DWG called Ms. Allen after she killed her husband. Ms. Allen didn't pick up her phone the night of the party. Ms. Allen still has a gun. . . ."

"And the DWG was shot," I finish. Marley and Lou have already gone through hell, so if this is true . . .

I wince as I take out my phone and type another name onto the suspect list. I add an asterisk next to her name:

*Ms. Allen**

TWENTY-TWO

The sun has begun its descent behind the hills, painting the sky a hazy gradient of desert oranges and pinks. The view is interrupted only by the shadows of rail-thin palm trees, tipped over ever so slightly in that subtle gangsta lean that makes the LA skyline look blissfully tipsy.

"Rhea, just let me try again," Malachi begs.

"I don't want to keep having this argument," I say to him over my shoulder.

"But you're not even listening to me," he complains.

"It's not that deep."

He presses his palm against his forehead, exasperated. "I just feel like I should still be able to use the staple gun."

"No way." When it was Malachi's turn to hang the posters for Camesha, he wasted at least nine staples per flyer. I blast two efficient clicks of the staple gun against the light post, fixing up another poster. "You liked it way too much." I hold out my hand for Malachi to pass me another flyer. He sighs and passes me the next one in the stack.

After we'd left the fake twins' house, Zeke left to draft a million apology texts to Lou. Neither Malachi nor I felt like going home, so we decided to put our restlessness to good use.

I try not to look at the posters for long. It's too depressing. "MISSING" is written in red above Camesha's high school graduation picture. She's smiling through bold purple lipstick with that signature mischievous glint in her eyes. . . .

My phone buzzes once. I ignore it at first, but then it keeps on going. I'm greeted by twenty notifications from the Zeggit app. I'm half expecting the alerts to be update reminders, but they're all messages. From SemiCharmed87. Aka the jerk that got me kicked out of the community safety forum on SOSI yesterday.

> I'd drop the conspiracy theories if I were you.
>
> SOSI did it.
>
> Leave the investigation to the police.
>
> Smart girls mind their own business.

Blah, blah, blah. I stop reading after the first few lines. I hit the block button with the swiftness of a caffeinated gamer on a killstreak. People who send strangers dozens of messages have too much free time. Niggas gotta get a hobby, jeez.

"All okay?" Malachi asks.

I tuck my phone away. "Yeah, it's nothing." There's only a few posters left in the stack. "Let's put the last ones up over there."

We cross the street and walk up to the half-abandoned church. The building looks the same as always—dark and scary with stained glass that'll leave you feeling more creeped out than "spiritually lifted." Except today, there's a janky wire fence blocking off the front lawn. And a "No Trespassing" sign.

"You think they're finally going to knock down this place?" Malachi asks.

As much as I'd like to see this eyesore go, the idea of a luxury pet spa potentially being erected in its place makes me defensive. "Sure as hell hope not."

"Wait, there's another sign on this end." Malachi points out from the corner of the lot. "Future site for Bayrex Charter Middle School No. 2."

I join him near the intersection and see the bright blue banner flapping in the wind. In the bottom corner, there's a logo that seems familiar: Becker Real Estate Group.

"Oh my god," Malachi says. I whip around and see him standing there, horrified, with his hands over his mouth like he just saw the ghost of Donald Trump. "Becker Real Estate. Isn't that the name of the dead white guy's company?"

Shit, he's right. I remember on the news: his daughter, Amelia, made sure to say the company's name at least five times between her fake cries. Even then, it seemed more like an advertisement than an interview to me.

"Staples is the charter school developer. This second campus must be his creation," Malachi says.

"So?" I ask.

"So, we were all over at Marley and Lou's house when their mom and Staples were watching the news broadcast about the murder. Ms. Allen told us all that stuff about how Vic knew their dad or whatever, but Staples just sat there and acted like he didn't know the guy," Malachi says.

"He didn't say that he *didn't* know him," I offer.

"Yeah, but don't you think it's weird that he didn't mention that he knew him at all? Like that's weird, right?"

I guess it is odd, but I'm not sure what to make of it. "That conversation was pretty heavy. Maybe he just didn't think it'd be appropriate." If I were him, I don't know if I'd bring up in front of a group of teenagers the fact that I worked with the guy who introduced my current girlfriend to her abusive ex-husband who she ultimately killed.

"I think we should look into this," Malachi declares. "We saw Vic talking to someone in a Tesla before he died. And remember at the block party how Staples bragged about buying a fancy new car with automated driving?"

Oh my god, yes. I'll never forget how mortified Marley was in that interaction. "I admit that this detail piques my interest." The only problem is that Staples hates Marley and Lou. "How do you expect we get close enough to Staples to investigate him?" I ask.

Malachi strokes his head. "He and Ms. Allen said they were together the night of the murder, right? Date night in the Marina or whatever? Maybe we should see if their alibi is legit." Malachi smiles this proud little smile that's so earnest it makes me want to believe in this as much as he does.

"Look whose Black ass is Nancy Drew now," I say with a smirk.

"Nah, you're Nancy Drew. I'm Sherlock Holmes. The old-school one, though, not the *Iron Man* actor." He hits me with a wink that makes my face burn. "I don't know how we can prove where they were that night, though."

"That part, I can figure out." I text Marley and ask her to send me the address of where she and her family are having brunch with Staples tomorrow. There's clearly a very easy way to test Staples's (and Ms. Allen's) alibi for the night of the murder:

We'll just break into his car.

TWENTY-THREE

Malachi and I ride our bikes to Shaw Supreme—a sliding-scale brunch spot with cajun shrimp and grits that has earned the cosign from the neighborhood. I text Marley that we're here and hover beside the entrance. I had told her that we want to investigate Staples because of his connection to Vic's company; I left out the part about how checking his "date night" alibi will also tell us whether her mom is really a suspect too.

Marley darts outside, shiny black key fob in hand. "You have five minutes before Staples freaks out."

"Dang, how'd you swipe his keys so fast?" Malachi asks.

"I didn't *swipe* them. I said I left my tampons in the car. He practically choked on his grits and threw the keys at my head."

I high-five Marley. Using the old man's internalized misogyny buys us at least a few extra minutes—he'll feel too awkward to look for her right away.

"Now, go!" She shoos us off. "Look for the white Tesla."

Malachi and I take off into the parking lot decorated with murals of Snoop Dogg. Staples's brand-new car stands out in the sea of used Hondas, Fords, and Toyotas. I slide into the driver's seat and try to figure out how to turn on the touch screen. "Stand guard, all right?" I tell Malachi.

"Why you always got me standin' guard while you do all the shady shit?"

"Because you don't have the balls to do the shady shit yourself," I mumble.

"You underestimate me, Rhea."

"Let me focus." These cars use Google Maps, which saves the locations that the driver visits. It's one of those default settings that most people don't bother, or don't know how, to turn off. I doubt a single guy Staples's age without any tech-savvy kids knows how to dig through his settings to deactivate it. I click around and, as expected, Staples's location history has been running in the background. Never thought I'd be thanking Big Brother for tracking our every move, but today, I'm sending him flowers.

Today's history floods the screen: his house, Ms. Allen's spot, the restaurant. Nothing crazy. Yesterday, he went to their house again, Massage Envy, some office downtown, and a supercharging station. I scroll back to the day of the murder, anticipation flooding my fingers, but when the page should be loading, nothing happens.

I click back to yesterday and try again, but still the page doesn't load.

What the hell?

I go back even further to last month and all the locations come right up. Realization rushes in. It's not that the page isn't working; the data from the night of the murder must have been manually deleted. *He* must've deleted it. Or maybe Ms. Allen? They were together, so it could have been either one.

But why?

"Rhea!!"

I drop Staples's keys beneath the steering wheel. When I shoot back up, Malachi is dragging me out the driver's seat. My eyes dart over his shoulders to see Marley standing across the parking lot looking *stressed*. Staples emerges by her side seconds later.

Staples holds out his hand to Marley and she pretends to pat down her pockets. He shakes his head and starts striding straight toward us like a shark pursuing blood.

Malachi and I duck. I shut the car door, but there's nowhere to hide—let alone return the keys to Marley without being seen. The parking lot is surrounded by a gate, and Staples's car is in the corner. We're screwed.

Then Malachi points to the next car over, but I shake my head. Staples is too tall; if we try to just hide behind a car, he'll see us. Malachi points again, and I roll my eyes. I whisper-shout, "He'll see us!"

But Malachi doesn't listen. He grabs my hand and pulls me toward the cement floor. Before I can fully process what's happening, we're scooting underneath the body of an early 2000s Ford Exhibition. Pebbles and twigs cut into my skin as I shimmy underneath the metal pipes of the car, still warm from the engine. I tuck my left foot out of sight milliseconds before Staples stomps over.

"You must've left the keys in the car," he huffs. Staples flings open the door and starts palming the leather interior. Marley's yellow boots emerge a moment later.

Beneath the underbelly of the Ford, Malachi and I lie frozen together, our limbs glued to our bodies like corpses in a coffin. I turn my head and find Malachi's face inches away from mine. His breath is wavering, laced with the same adrenaline coursing through my own body.

"If this is some prank, I swear to god . . ." Staples kneels, preparing to look for the keys on the floor.

I bury my face into Malachi's shoulder. We hold our breath as if that'll save us from getting caught.

"Wait!" Marley shouts. "I dropped my purse over there earlier. Maybe the keys fell out?"

Staples groans and stands back up. "Disorganized. Just like your mother."

We listen to their footsteps travel past the front of Staples's car. I crane my neck to see if we can make a run for it. Marley sees me, and her eyebrows shoot up her forehead so high that they practically merge with her hairline. I slide out a hand and count off to three before tossing the keys into the empty space in front of the next car over.

Marley coughs to cover up the sound of the brass scraping the pavement. "Found 'em!"

Staples abandons the pothole where he had been searching and snatches the keys from her hand. "Thanks a lot, now my food's probably cold." His complaints gradually grow quieter as he barrels back toward the restaurant.

Malachi and I linger under the car until we're sure that they're back inside before we escape. My hands are still sweating, mind still buzzing, from the close call. When we stand, Malachi hovers close to me—the typical space between us made ever so slightly smaller by the forced proximity of our hiding spot. He looks at me playfully and I detect a hint of a question in his eyes. He leans in but doesn't get far.

His phone buzzes, and I silently curse Steve Jobs for inventing such disruptive devices. When he checks his texts, his eyes grow wide, then mist over.

A giant smile bursts through his full lips.

"Camesha is back."

TWENTY–FOUR

It's incredible to hear that Camesha is safe, but her reappearance doesn't necessarily make the situation any less messy. She, Staples, and Ms. Allen still top the suspect list. If any of our current theories about who clocked the DWG are right, somebody's life is about to get way worse.

When we get to Malachi's house, Mr. and Mrs. Reed are making pancakes in the kitchen while Lacy and Camesha are whispering on the couch.

"Welcome home," I say to Camesha, embracing her. "I know you love drama, but you really put everyone through it this time."

"Ugh, I know, I'm so sorry. Auntie is so pissed at me." She rubs the tattoo of an ankh on her wrist.

"So, what the hell happened?" Lacy asks.

"Well, after I got in that car leaving the party, I got a call from my client—well, *ex*-client now, I guess—and we had a disagreement."

First Auntie, now Camesha. *Two people* fought with Vic on the night of his murder. This isn't looking good for anyone. "What did you fight about?"

"It wasn't a *fight*," Camesha says defensively. "A disagreement. He wanted me to meet a friend of his, but I said no. I told Vic off and things got heated. He overstepped, so I had to put him in his place. He started apologizing all dramatic, but I was ice cold, completely freezing him out. Vic knew he was a troll of a man and that he'd never do better than me, so he was desperate. He said that he'd pay the driver to take me wherever I wanted to go, and that he'd book a hotel too. A mini vacation, is what he called it."

One "disagreement," then suddenly she's running off on a vacation?

"Where'd you go so late at night?" I ask.

"Vegas."

"You just casually went to *Vegas*?!" Malachi says. "But you're not even twenty-one yet, you can't do anything there."

"Who needs to 'do anything' when you got a fancy-ass hotel room with an en suite hot tub?" She smooths a crease of her shirt, a silhouette image of a Megan Thee Stallion album cover. "Sometimes I just want to be a pretty girl alone in a city where nobody knows my name."

"But what happened to your phone? We tried calling you a million times." Lacy crosses her arms in a way that makes it seem like even though she's relieved to have her girl home safe, she's still reeling from the stress that Camesha put her through.

"I dropped it in the lobby, and it broke, but I wasn't pressed about it. Vic was supposed to meet me there, but he never showed up. I figured he was giving me some space, like I wanted. So, I thought I'd spend a couple days out there, enjoy being unplugged from technology, and fix my phone later. I had no clue all this shit was going down back home."

Ah, that explains why the woman at the gas station saw Vic loading up on snacks. It's almost a five-hour drive to Vegas, so if he planned on meeting Camesha there, I'm sure he'd want to stuff his face along the way.

I want to believe what Camesha is saying, but it all feels too simple. I don't think she's telling us everything that really happened that night.

"Camesha, I don't know if you should keep working with guys like this," Lacy says.

"I know there are risks involved, but I like what I do, and I get a lot of joy out of it," Camesha asserts. "Like, I'm about to become a *homeowner*. Do you have any idea what having my own space—having *privacy*—after all these years would mean to me?"

"But your client is dead. Maybe it's time to switch things up?"

Mrs. Reed walks in the room balancing a high stack of pancakes. "You're looking for a new job?" She doesn't do the best job to mask the optimism in her voice. "How about you look into a position at the new charter school? As you're a Bayrex alum, I'm sure they'd love to have you. They're opening up two new Bayrex campuses this fall, both a middle and a high school."

That explains the construction site Malachi and I saw.

"Our schools suck, our teachers are exhausted, and they're already making more? How the hell did they get the money to expand?" Lacy asks.

"Yo, the people who run that shit—not like the principal or whatever, but the people in the office downtown—they're stacked," Malachi says, slathering a pancake with an unreal amount of butter. I find myself wondering about Staples again. He's pretty high up at the company and has a nice car but doesn't strike me as rich.

"Watch your language, boy," Mrs. Reed says, bopping Malachi on the head with the spatula.

"What—it's true! Our principal is complaining about how we don't have money for this or that and how our test scores suck and we're all 'underserved youth' or whatever, but then the suit people are out here making bank. It's fucked up if you think about it." Malachi earns himself a second bop on the head from his mom that makes him drop his fork.

"You'll be surprised to learn how much money people at the top make. It's complicated, but you'll understand when you're older," Mr. Reed says.

Except I understand it now, I want to say.

Capitalism is a bitch.

—

I spend the rest of the afternoon with the Reed family, eating too many pancakes and wondering if anyone has noticed that Malachi and I have been sitting closer together than usual. There hasn't been much movement on the crush front since the night of the party, so I was starting to worry that since I still haven't taken any steps on my end, he changed his mind. But then when everyone is distracted, Malachi leans over and brings his lips to my ear. The smell of brown sugar and cinnamon on his breath from breakfast mixes with the body spray that he's recently started wearing that I used to hate, but now inhale gladly.

I can feel his heart beating (or is it mine?) when he whispers, "I'm happy you're here."

My spine tingles. It takes every ounce of strength not to inch away from him—not because I don't want this, but because I've wanted it for so long that now that it's happening, it's a little overwhelming. It's sort of like I've been waiting to see this movie for years and now I'm finally watching it, but the brightness and volume are turned up extremely loud—I instinctively shield my eyes, even though I want nothing more than to watch what happens next.

Words feel too difficult to form right now, so I just inch my hand near his so that our knuckles brush against one another. A little spark jumps straight from our skin into my chest. I draw a sharp inhale, and he does too.

I smile, only pulling away when Zeke texts the group: *Done with work. Roller Planet?*

Roller Planet is the roller-skating rink to end all roller-skating rinks. There's no cheesy '70s music and disco balls—just trap music and old-school R&B. The place has been around for so long, we've all had a birthday party there over the years, as have our parents back in the day. It's the closest thing to a club that you can get at our age: there's dancing, talking, occasionally fighting, and even a slow song for couples' skate every hour. Malachi's an incredible skater, able to go backward, spin, and roll-bounce as good as all the super-legit regulars there. Girls always whizz by and hold out their hands for Malachi to grab, but he normally just gives them a smile and a wave.

Maybe today, though, he'll feel like skating with a partner. . . . I imagine the dim lights and music as we use the scene as an excuse to put our hands on each other and keep them there. "I'm down if you are."

Malachi meets my eyes with a mischievous grin, and I wonder if he was thinking about the same thing as me. He replies to Zeke's message: *Rhea and I are in. Meet there in 30?*

Marley sends an elaborate string of emojis including the thumbs-up, twinkle stars, unicorn, roller skates, and heart eyes smiley.

"I'm assuming that's a yes from her too," I say.

We can debrief the Tesla situation there, she adds. My throat tightens, unsure how or whether to bring up what I found—or rather didn't find—in the car, and my suspicions about her mom.

"Are you going to skate with me?" Malachi asks, bringing my attention back to the moment. Still holding my phone, I type out a chain of the most colorful emojis available and send it directly to him. He glances at his phone and smiles. "I'm not going to assume that's a yes, but I hope to soon receive your active and enthusiastic consent," he says, quoting Camesha's blog.

I blush. "Great."

He smiles. "Excellent."

I laugh. "Cool."

He beams. "Dope."

My mind floods with the prospect of us—the same, but different.

TWENTY—FIVE

Malachi recruits Lacy and Camesha to come with (mostly so that Lacy can give us a ride). When we pull up, Marley's already there wearing a pastel romper with her hair in two giant pom-poms. She couldn't be dressed any more different than Lou, who's in all black, sulking against the railing at the entrance.

"I haven't gone skating in years!" Marley squeals, literally buzzing with excitement. "This is such a great idea. Take our minds off things, have a little break."

"What do y'all need to take your minds off of so badly?" Lacy asks, raising a brow.

"The never-ending horror of this teenage existence," Lou says. He doesn't mean it as a joke, but we all laugh anyway. Lou even smiles a bit too, until Lupe's car rolls up and Zeke jumps out.

With his skates tied together at the shoelaces and hanging around his neck like a scarf, Zeke walks up to Lou, who sharply turns down the ramp to enter the rink. Marley gives Zeke a sympathetic shrug and follows her brother inside.

It's high school skate hour, so everyone inside is our age. The lights are dimmed enough that I forget it's daytime. The sound of dozens of wheels whizzing across polished wood merges with the R-rated lyrics booming from the sound system. Malachi and Zeke go straight to the graffiti-tagged lockers to put away their shoes while Marley and I get in line to rent.

"You aren't skating?" I ask Lou. He stands underneath a fluorescent blacklight, examining the filthy carpet as he places his headphones over his ears. Looks like he didn't feel like wearing the earbuds from Zeke today.

"God no. I didn't want to come in the first place."

A few feet away, Zeke hears this and frowns.

"But you're here and you promised to put away your bad attitude," Marley says through the gritted teeth of a forced smile.

"I'm here for the arcade games, and for the games only." Lou slips on his headphones and heads to the coin machine, where he inserts a $10 bill. "Let me know when you're ready to leave," he says grimly, then stomps away toward the Guitar Hero machine.

"He's still pissed at Zeke, huh?" I ask Marley as we inch forward in the skate rental line. Zeke and Lou are my only real-world example of what it looks like to date within the friend group, and they're not really making it look easy.

"Yeah, but he still came. Normally, he'd lock himself in his room for days when he gets upset like this. The fact that he's here shows that he really does like Zeke," she says, tapping a swirl of baby hair to her forehead.

I nod. "I like your outfit," I say earnestly, admiring how much thigh she's comfortable showing. My legs are covered in scars from playing AYSO growing up, which didn't used to bother me, but recently have become the only thing that I see when I look in the mirror.

"Thank you! It's super breathable. I can show you where I ordered it online—it'd look so cute on you too."

I scoff. "Marley, I haven't worn shorts in two years." There's no way in hell I can pull off something like that. When it comes to style, I'm much more of a chameleon than a peacock. Or not even a chameleon—more like one of those weird beige fish that blends into the sand so that nobody will see it. Hidden in plain sight.

We reach the front of the line and order two pairs of the generic tan-colored skates with bright orange laces. Marley takes a second to examine my outfit: an oversize hoodie and baggy jeans that cuff at the ankle like sweatpants. "I assumed that this whole giant clothing thing was an intentional vibe. Do you not feel good in other stuff? Because you're gorgeous, you know." I instinctively shush Marley. She rolls her eyes. "Oh my god, girl, *please*. Put on some Lizzo and be nice to yourself."

"Easier said than done." We plop down on one of the cracked, shiny couches to tie up our skates.

"No doubt about that but tell you what: better learn to love yourself before anyone else—it makes the road ahead a smoother ride." Marley winks, then leans in. "Speaking of . . ."

"Ready?" Malachi says as he and Zeke cross the carpeted floor of the lobby. He glides effortlessly in his skates, which for some reason is kinda hot. It's like how in fifth grade all the girls in our class liked Justin Lyons because he could run really fast; even before we have the words for it, we learn to link attraction to the way that a person's body moves.

Malachi reaches out his hand to help me up from the couch. I grab on and he pulls me toward him, though the skates provide some unexpected momentum. I crash into him and we end up pressed against each other. Zeke and Marley politely turn away, which makes my cheeks burn.

Malachi doesn't shy up, though. He leans forward and slowly traces my jawline with his thumb. The music fades away and all I can hear is the belt buckle on his jeans clanging softly against my phone in the front pocket of my hoodie. When I meet his eyes, all of the air leaves the room.

"So?" he asks. I watch his lips slide into a smirk.

Why can't I just let the words come out?

Before I can get it together, he's already backing away from me to let a group of squawking girls pass. He hits me with a destabilizing, flirty smile. I'm grateful for Marley, who's conveniently there at my side to discreetly grab my waist before I melt to the ground.

She gives my side a squeeze. "He's ready when you are."

Out in the rink, Marley and I awkwardly try to groove and look cute or whatever while Zeke and Malachi literally skate circles around us. Marley at one point gets bold and tries to go backward, which ends with her splayed out on the floor, pom-poms disheveled, laughing so hard that she cries. We retreat to the little island in the center with the rest of the losers who can't skate but were brought here by their more coordinated friends.

Seated on the refuge of benches, Marley's profile is so distinctive—a massive forehead and high, round cheekbones. She looks just like her mom. I remember Ms. Allen's smirk in the living room and get chills.

"You all right?" Marley interrupts my train of thought.

Does she suspect her mom? Maybe even a little bit?

I consider asking her, but that seems like a surefire way to destroy our new connection, which is the last thing I want to do. Nobody ever told me what I was missing by never having real girlfriends. Sure, gender is fluid and a social construct, but still: it's nice to share space with her in a way that feels different from being with Zeke or Malachi.

But god, does she look like her mom right now. . . .

"What's on your mind?" she asks again.

The fact that your mother may be a serial killer.

I watch two boys behind her hype themselves up then wobble toward us. Marley simply holds up her hand before they can even open their mouths, "Thank you, but no thank you." Her voice is so commanding that the boys immediately turn right around and sit with quiet defeat. "You were about to say something?"

If the theory is true, it would crush you.

I don't even know if Ms. Allen would count as a serial killer since her first murder was self-defense. That one would be a freebie, right? And the serial killer count wouldn't start until her next victim, so that would mean Ms. Allen is just a regular killer, then?

"Earth to Rhea . . ."

"What's your mom like?" I blurt out at last.

"You've met her. You know what she's like."

"Nah, but what's, like, *your* experience of her like?"

A warm smile spreads across Marley's face. "She's strong. And funny, you know, like once you get to know her? She eats a baguette with brie and guava jam every Sunday." Marley pauses, memories wafting across her eyes. "Every Christmas, me, her, and Lou watch Bruce Lee movies together while we do tarot card readings and eat Indian food takeout. She's dynamic."

The gentleness with which Marley talks about her mom

isn't only insanely on-brand for Marley, it's also convincing. Ms. Allen seems like a good person, not a killer.

"So, are you going to tell me what you found in Staples's car?"

"It was a dead end." I don't think an empty navigation system is enough to implicate anyone just yet.

Marley shrugs. "Well, at least you tried." She adjusts the scrunchies in her hair. "What about *your* mom?"

"What about her?"

"Oh, c'mon, I painted you a whole portrait of my mom." Marley laughs. "Give me a little more. What's her energy like? What's her sun sign? Oh, and her moon and rising too!"

"I don't know her sign, so—"

"Rhea." Marley hits me with her annoying empath eyes, and I cave.

I take a second to search for a word. "She's distant."

Marley leans toward me, resting her elbows on her knees. "Has she always been like that?"

"Not always. It sort of started when my half siblings left for college, but it wasn't until maybe second grade when she wholesale checked out. She used to hang out with Lupe and Mrs. Reed." I can't help but smile when I remember the boys and me literally running circles around our chattering moms' legs and Lupe's wheelchair as they whispered about how fine our teacher was. "She was older than the other moms in our class, but she liked them. Eventually though, she dropped out of the carpool and playdate rotation." My face dips back into neutral. "That's when the four of us in the crew really solidified."

"Four?" Marley asks.

"Dante."

"Right." She nods in a way that reminds me that she's no stranger to loss herself.

"Want to hear a funny story, though?" I offer to shift the mood.

"Always," Marley says with a smile.

"So, like, the summer before sixth grade, I was hanging out with Zeke and Malachi, right? Dante had already, uhm . . ." I look for the words, but Marley nods me forward.

"Yes," she says, her voice soothing.

"Exactly. So anyway, we're hanging out at Malachi's house playing *Scythe*—"

"Wait, what's *Scythe*?"

"It's a steampunk board game."

"Sounds nerdy," Marley teases. "Love that for baby you. Continue."

"Well, technically, we still do *Scythe* Sundays." Marley's eyes light up with the glimmer of a tangent, but I cut her off before we stray. "*Anyway*, so we're all chillin' and then Mrs. Reed tells me that I'll be staying the night at theirs because my mom has to go out of town. I used to sleep over Malachi's all the time, so I didn't really think about it."

"Isn't it funny how you and Malachi used to have sleepovers as kids, but like, soon you two are probably gunna—"

"Marleyyy," I whine. "Do you want to hear the story or not?"

"Sorry. Continue."

"So, when my mom comes to pick me up the next morning, I'm watching Mrs. Reed from my spot on the couch as she opens the door and her eyes go wide when she sees my mom. I can't see what's happening, but I hear Mrs. Reed go, 'Oh. Ohhh. OH!'"

Marley leans in more.

"So, I walk to the door and see that my mom's wearing a veil. Like, a tacky-ass wedding veil. And she's smiling big for the first time I had seen in a while, and when she sees me she just says, 'We're not going to be alone anymore.'"

"Fuuuckkk," Marley sighs. "Your stepdad?"

"Yup. I had met him before, but like, I didn't even make the cut for my own mom's wedding list," I say, forcing out a laugh.

"Do you like him?"

"He's whatever. Keeps to himself. They've been married for four years now and still every time we cross paths in the house he says, 'Oops! Don't mind me.' And just sort of grabs something from the fridge and slips out of the room."

For several seconds, Marley doesn't say anything at all. "Do you really think that's a funny story, Rhea?"

I roll my eyes. *"Why so serious?"* I respond in my most convincing impression of Heath Ledger as the Joker. Marley smiles at me weakly, and I feel immature.

We settle into the lapse in conversation, the silence between us drowned out by the ambient noise of skates on polished wood circling around us.

"Why do you think your mom . . . wilted away from you?" Marley asks finally.

Her question catches me off guard. Nobody's really asked me this before. Zeke and Malachi have been here to see this all happen in real time, so there hasn't really been anyone else to tell until now. I look at Marley and her eyes are fixed on mine, waiting intently for an earnest response.

I sigh. "She was grieving the loss of her first husband, grieving the fact that she had me with a dude who didn't stick around, grieving the aftermath of my siblings, aka the children born from the original love of her life, moving away. And there I was—literally six years old when it was just the two of us left—and she had to look at me every day like, 'Damn, I gotta do this shit *all* over again, and this time, I gotta do it alone.'" I rub a piece of lint from my sweatshirt. "I don't blame her really. It was overwhelming. She was alone and I was six. I get it."

"Yeah, Rhea, but you were *six*," Marley says. "And she wasn't alone. You were there too."

The muscles in my neck stiffen as I clench my jaw. The wound-up pressure ushers in a familiar sensation: a woozy almost headache that signals that I've gone beyond my comfort zone, I've opened myself up too much. I hit my emotional limit for the day. "I don't need to get into this right now," I snap. I forget we're on skates and stand up too quickly so that I almost eat shit, but Marley catches my hips before I completely bite it.

"Change is hard . . ." Marley says, cautiously rising up on her wobbly skates beside me. "But that doesn't mean you can give up on your family."

I scoff. "Change is bullshit."

Right then, Malachi skates by mouthing the words to the sentimental neo-soul hit that's been featured in every romcom and prom-posal this year. He looks directly at me while he and everyone around us sings along to the chorus.

Marley smirks. "Y'all have all this built-up tension, but we're not trapped in a Victorian novel. It's time to *release*. Everything isn't going to come crumbling down if you go from friends to something more."

"I've tried to tell him that I like him too, but the words

won't come out. I'm, like, *right there*, and then get paralyzed with fear. Like a possum."

"First off, you're way cuter than a possum. Second, if you can't find the words, you can always use body language." She gives me a sexy wink that I'd have to practice in the mirror for weeks to pull off half as well as her.

The idea of being the one to initiate crossing that line with Malachi makes my stomach plummet. "I am *not* going to kiss him first."

"Oh my god, why not? It's not like you both haven't hooked up with other people before. And he's probably just as nervous as you."

"Yeah, but like, he's . . ." Ugh. I don't even have a good excuse. "Can't we just flip a coin and decide who's gonna be the one to make The Move? Like shouldn't there be an app that automatically decides who's gonna initiate and when it's going to happen, so that the whole thing seems less intense?"

Marley laughs wildly, her curly pom-poms shaking in the air. "C'mon, that would be so unromantic. And he already shared his corny lil teenage dream with you! Now it's your turn."

Another sappy song plays and Zeke skates by, blowing us a kiss, but in a way that feels a little performative. Before he flits away, I catch him glance up at the arcade balcony, most likely hoping that Lou is jealously watching him have fun. He's not.

"Why don't we all go to the beach tomorrow?" Marley suggests. "Lou and I haven't been yet. You and Malachi can walk around the boardwalk or whatever. You'll have your pick of places to make out. And you need a break from SOSI stuff."

How did we jump straight to full-on semipublic make-out? Panic seizes some muscles in my chest that I didn't even know existed. I lean over, placing my head between my knees to catch my breath.

"You'll be fiiiine," Marley says, stroking my back. "You've been friends for your entire life."

That's exactly why I'm so nervous. There's so much to lose.

"Uh-oh." Marley's hand freezes in the middle of my spine. She puts some pressure into her palm, almost as if to hold me down.

I push back against her resistance. "What's going on?"

On the opposite end of the rink, Zeke's holding the handrail mounted to the wall. There are three guys around him, all seemingly a few years older than us. They give him dab at first, but one of the dudes hangs back, clearly sizing him up. He looks sort of familiar, but I can't place him from here. Zeke's fumbling with the seam of his brightly colored Adventure Time T-shirt, which stands in absurd contrast to the tattoos and white ribbed tanks of the taller, more muscular guys around him.

This doesn't look good.

As Marley and I scramble to gather enough momentum to check on Zeke, we see Malachi pick up speed across the rink. His hard frown sticks out from the sea of skaters baby-twerking. The guys around Zeke inch closer, the tone of their conversation clearly shifting. Then, suddenly, they have him pressed against the wall.

"Zeke!" Malachi shouts, but there's a cluster of people in his way. The guy that had previously been standing on the fringe reaches for something in his back pocket. Suddenly, his face snaps into place in my mind as a memory rushes back to me: he's the guy from the house party who hung back during the firecracker stunt, looking for someone. Looking for SOSI.

It's too loud to hear what's happening, but people are staring now, slowing to watch whatever's about to go down. A girl in cherry-red booty shorts takes out her phone and points it at Zeke as he struggles to keep his balance on the skates, the older guys' grip on him tightening.

It all escalates so quickly that I hardly see it happen: the security guard shouts, and Zeke is being whisked away up the ramp back to the lobby by someone in all black. Marley and I catch up to Malachi and run-skate-tumble up to the balcony, where we find who grabbed Zeke: it's Lou. Thank god, it's Lou. He kneels in front of a slightly disheveled Zeke with stone-cold determination, fingers moving fast as lightning to untie Zeke's skates for him.

Zeke's eyes are wide as he sits on the edge of the bench, stuttering. "W-w-we gotta go *now*."

The rest of us kick off our skates and grab our shoes from the locker, but there's no time to put them on. With our socks sliding against the floor littered with crumbs and fallen earrings, we run.

TWENTY-SIX

Fifteen years old. Latino. Shoulder-length hair. Known affiliate of SOSI.

Leave it to some hood dudes to track Zeke down before the cops. Under different circumstances, I'd been impressed to see the streets outsmarting the Man once again. But the fact that word has gotten around that Zeke might be both *that guy* who started the SOSI "shooting" at the house party and *that guy* seen standing over the DWG's body is nothing to celebrate.

Yesterday, Marley's beach idea seemed like a fun little excursion, but today, it's become a necessity. With Zeke's name out in the streets, we can't have him walking around until we get things under control. Whether people think that he bangs with SOSI or that he just has intel on the gang doesn't matter—it's not a good look for him to be around right now.

Even though we all live less than twenty minutes away from the beach, we rarely go. As broke-ass nobodys without cars and money for parking, it's a brutal haul to make it out there. Malachi asked Lacy to drive us, but she and Camesha are "busy," though they wouldn't tell us what they're up to. So that means we're stuck on the musty, deeply unreliable public transportation system.

We plan on meeting Zeke at Colony Cantina in the afternoon when he gets off his restaurant shift. Even though it's out of the way for him, Malachi insists on walking over together. Coincidentally, this morning is one of those rare occasions where my mother and I are in the same room. When Malachi's silhouette approaches our front door, it's open except for the security screen so that we can let some air flow in. "He's getting really cute," she says. "I told you he'd grow up nicely."

My mom does this occasionally—preface her opinion as "I told you," even though the reality is that she doesn't tell me much of anything at all. Referencing conversations that we've never had is her weird way of pretending like we have a normal relationship. It's a bizarre, vacant ritual that I've come to just shake off.

"Yeah, Mom. You told me." I say goodbye. She doesn't ask where I'm going or when I'll be back.

"Yellow," Malachi says when I open the door.

"I think you mean *Hello*?"

"Right, yes, that too, but damn. You look, uhm, very nice. I don't think I've seen you in yellow before."

My usual palette is strictly blacks, grays, and earth tones, but last night, Marley had her mom drive her over to drop off outfit choices. She pushed this flowy, oversize yellow shirt-dress, claiming vehemently that Black women created the color. She rattled off a list of yellow inspiration (*Beyoncé in the "Hold Up" video, Angela Bassett at the* Black Panther *premiere, Zendaya on the red carpet—Rhea, it's literally science),* and who am I to argue with Beyoncé?

"Trying something new," I say, attempting to sound casual.

"I said it before and I'll say it again—" Malachi brings his hand up to his neck, biceps flexing underneath his pale gray T-shirt. "I like new."

We walk together, occasionally brushing hands, all the way to Colony Cantina. When we finally make it within view of the restaurant, I stop dead in my tracks. "Oh. My. God."

In the distance, Zeke is spinning a sign like one of those Statue of Liberty people in the spring for tax season. He's soaked in sweat, putting on a pathetic show for an audience of pigeons. The sign twirls, smacks the side of his head before tumbling to the ground. He sort of catches it with his foot and attempts to kick it back upward, but just ends up sending the whole thing flying into the bushes. It's almost too embarrassing to watch.

We pull up on him as he finishes his battle with the shrub. "They're not making enough riches off their soggy tacos?" Malachi jokes.

"Apparently sixty percent of restaurants fail within the first year, even when they're backed by corporate bros," Zeke says, picking a leaf from his hair. "They're desperate for customers."

I smile at the thought of Colony Cantina shuttering before the end of the year.

"Is that Auntie Inga inside?" I ask, pointing through the glass door into the restaurant.

"Yeah, go say hi while I wrap up. I got six minutes and twenty-two seconds left in my shift."

I salute Zeke before we skip inside to meet Auntie. She's at the cash register, talking to the restaurant owners.

"Hey! Didn't expect to see you here," Malachi says, nearly tackling her in a hug.

"Hey, babies," Auntie says in her velvety voice. My heart warms instinctively by Auntie's presence but knowing that she lied about her conversation with Vic makes me keep a slight distance. If Auntie notices my coldness, she doesn't comment on it.

"Why, if it isn't our favorite customers!" Troy beams.

I roll my eyes. "We're just here waiting for Zeke."

"You don't want to buy a burrito?" Troy offers.

"No."

"What about some chips?"

"No."

"An artisan, small-batch, probiotic elderberry sparkling water?"

A disdainful groan gurgles from my throat as I debate whether to claw out my eyes or his.

Lance watches our exchange uncomfortably before turning back to Auntie. "Should we, uhm, talk later?"

"No, it's okay," Auntie says, brushing the bangs from her eyes. "Rhea and Malachi are friends of Zeke and residents of the neighborhood. This concerns them too."

Lance gives Auntie a weak smile. "Right, yeah."

Auntie continues the conversation that we interrupted. "What I was saying is that I know you two are new to the neighborhood, but being in business here means being part of the community. And as a community, we gotta look out for one another, and now's the time to do it. We need your support. We can't just sit by and let these dirtbags push us out of our homes."

"Forsuuuuure," Troy says. "I'm all about fighting the Man. But what can we do?"

"We're planning a protest. We could really benefit from the support of local businesses. You can donate supplies and attend as a display of solidarity. You could also—"

Auntie is interrupted once again by a flurry of commotion outside—commotion apart from Zeke's horrific sign twirling, I mean. In front of the restaurant, a blond lady adjusts her hair as a reporter and cameraperson set up for a shoot. I haven't seen her in person since that time with the architects at Zeke's apartment, but I recognize her immediately from all the recent news coverage: it's Vic's daughter.

"Ameliaaaa, hiii!" Troy brushes past Auntie. *Rude.*

"Excuse us, one moment," Lance says to Auntie, noting her raised eyebrow at Troy's impolite exit. Auntie follows the owners with a determined rhythm in her step that signals trouble. I toss Malachi a curious look and we rush to follow.

"You can set the equipment up right there," Amelia says to the cameraperson.

"May I ask what's going on here?" Auntie asks.

"Press conference. We want to show the restaurant as part of my father's legacy as a local investor," she says, fluffing her hair.

"Legacy? Great! In that case, should we talk about the evictions? And how you're following in Vic's footsteps to displace dozens of families that have lived here for decades, if not generations?"

The reporter and cameraperson shift awkwardly.

Amelia chuckles politely. "Hah! Ms. Inga. So charming, so *direct*, as always." She smiles affably at the news team. "We love to see constructive dialogue, don't we? Such an important part of investing in an up-and-coming community."

"Dialogue?" Auntie huffs. "Like how you aren't return-ing any of your tenants' phone calls, right?" Auntie crosses her arms, venom oozing from her strong stance. Yet Amelia stands calmly, an unbothered grin painted across her face.

"Thanks a bunch for stopping by, Ms. Inga," Lance says to defuse the situation. "We'll see you at the protest, and I'll get back to you about making a donation." He gingerly motions us all out of the news crew's shot.

From the sidelines, I can still hear Amelia: "Can you get a shot of the Latinx kid and the sign? How cute!"

"Nope," Zeke says, dropping the giant arrow and sprinting inside. "Shift's over! Gotta clock out!"

Malachi and I stand with Auntie as we wait for Zeke. I try not to pay too much attention to the press conference on Vic's "legacy" unfolding behind us.

Auntie sighs. "It sounds terrible, but when Vic was found dead the other day, I thought that maybe we'd all catch a break, you know. Like, maybe his daughter would be more humane and she'd inherit his property, but not enforce the rent spike. Unfortunately, though, she now counts as the 'new owner' and was able to jack the prices up even more."

Malachi grimaces. "And the way she was talking about *'investing in the community'* but completely dodged your questions about the evictions? Horrible."

"It's horrible, but it can be stopped," Auntie says force-fully. "I already spoke to my neighbors in my building to see if they'd be willing to participate in a protest. Lupe went around knocking on doors to connect with everyone in hers, too, and the people are down. We can get a permit and hold the event three days from now. If our buildings organize together and we get support from the wider community as well, we have enough people to make some noise—really shame our new Inheritance Baby Landlord, Amelia."

Personally, I have my doubts. We don't have enough time to change hearts and minds to get people to think that we matter. SOSI may be messy, but at least we can move quicker in the shadows.

"Are you working with those law students from the block party? The Eviction Defense Guild Coalition Co-op Whatever?" I ask. The strange power dynamic with that group—and the image of the volunteer clutching her purse—creeps back to me.

"They'll be supporting in the background as legal observers for the protest to help keep us safe, but we made it very clear that us tenants are leading all angles of the fight," Auntie says. "We're the ones in control of our own liberation."

I want to press more on this, but Malachi interrupts me first. "Damn! So you and Lupe are just gunna put your middle fingers up and tell the landlords to fuck off?" he asks. His eyes are practically sparkling with wonder like an anime character witnessing someone's superpowers for the first time.

"Something like that," Auntie says with a laugh. "Sort of like what y'all are up to."

I choke on my own spit. "What do you mean?"

Auntie leans over to whisper, "SOSI has a nice ring to it. I'd love to hear the origin story behind the name one day."

My jaw drops, and she promptly uses her finger to press my chin right back up. She draws her fingers across her lips like a zipper and pretends to lock her mouth shut and throw away the key.

"Anyway, my dears. I need a hashtag for the protest. Any ideas? I was considering #GentrificationIsBad?"

"I feel like that's a lil too literal," Malachi says politely. "What about #WeAintLeaving? Straight to the point."

"How about #Rooted?" I offer, desperately trying to shake off my genuine shock that Auntie somehow knows that we're behind SOSI. "Because 'rooted' is like, 'we're not going anywhere'?"

"'Rooted,'" Auntie says slowly. "I love it. You may have a future in branding and marketing, sweet thing." She gives me a wink that affirms what I already suspected: although Auntie may know what's up, that doesn't mean she's going to snitch on us.

Zeke bursts through the doors of Colony Cantina and joins us at last. "Whose idea was it to make people do labor for money? Can we time-travel and tell them that sucks?" He sinks onto the patch of grass beside us and dramatically rolls onto his back. "Minimum wage is a scam."

"Yes, but we're so proud of you! Out here making money for yourself, that's good. Colleges will like that," Auntie encourages.

Zeke rolls over onto his stomach and groans. "I don't want to sit on a bus for eight hoursssssss."

Auntie laughs. "Now why would you do that?"

Malachi explains our beach plans, and how Lacy and Camesha can't drive us. "Hah! Those girls ain't busy, they're lazy. They've been sitting on my couch watching reruns of *Pose* for almost ten hours straight."

We try to stop her, but it's too late: Auntie calls up Camesha to guilt her into giving us a ride. Though it'd be sick to not take the bus, we all know better than to tear the girls away from their TV binges. But Auntie clicks her phone and places it back in her purse with a smug grin. "They'll be here in twenty minutes."

I text Marley and Lou to get over here ASAP while Auntie stands up, her statuesque figure towering over us all. "Well, I've got to get going. I'm hosting a fundraiser tonight for a friend's surgery and have to make a hundred vegan cake pops."

"Do you need any help?" I ask.

"With the cake pops, no. But you can read this." From her purse, she pulls out a thin purple book titled *Beyond the Gender Binary*. "Pass it around. Talk about it. Do some internal work. That's always helpful."

Zeke tries to intercept the book from me, but Malachi lunges forward, calling first dibs. Auntie laughs and we beg her to stay longer, for no reason other than we like having her around. Whatever suspicion I know I should have about her just won't stick. She's like sage plants in that she brings a grounding yet clarifying energy into whatever space she enters.

Auntie indulges us for a few minutes while Zeke catches her up about his fight with Lou and how Lou rescued him from what would have surely turned into a full-blown ass kicking at the roller rink. She listens thoughtfully and asks for more details like how she always does, making whatever story you're telling feel like the most captivating thing that she's ever heard.

Once she's up to speed, she tells Zeke to come by one day next week for a "recap" of some of the things that they talked about a while ago. I don't know what she's talking about at first, but from the way that Zeke blushes, I figure it's about safe sex.

"Don't rush things, baby," she says as she hugs him. "And more importantly, be safe. In all areas." She gives him a firm squeeze that communicates that she's not just talking about hookups anymore. Zeke searches her face for details, but she just motions toward us. I mouth to Zeke: *I'll tell you later.*

I feel a text come in and expect to see Marley saying that she needs more time to get ready, but it's not from her. The sender's number is blocked: UNKNOWN ID. I almost rage-delete it, assuming it's another spam text from that one time I signed up for a raffle like four years ago, but then I see the preview.

It's a screenshot of an argument on the Community Safety subzeggit. Users are debating whether SOSI really killed the DWG, or if this is just another instance of lazy detective work. I almost smirk, assuming this is from someone in the crew, until I keep reading.

My eyes skim over the words, sending my brain into a spiral. The trails of my own breath form a lump in my lungs that suffocates me from the inside.

Below the photo, there's a message, loud and clear:

SEE WHAT YOU STARTED, RHEA?

SOSI KILLED VIC.

LEAVE IT ALONE.

STAY THE FUCK OUT OF THIS OR YOU'RE NEXT.

TWENTY-SEVEN

The hand holding my phone goes limp with that type of stinging numbness as if my whole body's been plunged into a bucket of ice.

OR YOU'RE NEXT.

OR YOU'RE NEXT.

OR YOU'RE NEXT.

The final words of the text ring in my head. I hear it first as a furious shout, then as a menacing, nearly silent whisper. I imagine the threat in a variety of world accents, then it comes to me playing over the soundtrack from *The Shining.*

OR YOU'RE NEXT.

How the hell does this person have my number? And how the fuck do they know my *name*?

Clearly, it's SemiCharmed87 from Zeggit. That I'm sure of. This person has had it out for me ever since my first post after the murder, but still—*why?* I don't think this is a regular troll. SemiCharmed87, Unknown, whoever they hell they are—they know something about Vic's murder. And they must know that I'm onto them.

"What's going on?" Malachi's voice cuts through the million thoughts racing through my brain like cars speeding around the swirly interchanges of the 110 and 10 freeways. His eyes ignite with concern. When I still don't speak, he moves to look at my screen, and I snap out of it. I force out a laugh and tuck my phone away, out of his reach.

"I thought I finally won this lottery. False alarm." I eke out one more laugh and step backward, putting both physical and emotional space between me and Malachi. Zeke looks over at me and frowns, worry lines burying into his forehead.

They don't need to know about this text. It would only upset them. And the last thing I need is either of them telling the others, then Lou will return to his "dump SOSI" soapbox and then we'll be back to Square One with stopping the evictions. If the DWG's real killer, or at least someone who *knows* who the real killer is, sent me this message, and if they believe SOSI is real, then that's . . . well, it's confusing, but I don't think it's bad.

Plus, the way they're commanding me to let SOSI take the fall feels desperate. Almost begging, even. And the "me next" bit, well, they must be trying to scare me. They can't be serious, right? I don't know how seriously I should take a text message threat with impeccable grammar. So, yeah, this message is evidence that I'm on the right track. That I'm asking the right questions. And I just have to—

A car horn blares, announcing Lacy and Camesha's arrival.

"Let's go!" I say to the boys, trying to sound as chipper as humanly possible. I run to the car before they can ask any more questions.

I'm in control of the situation. My plan is solid. I'm strong. The text is one little secret that I can carry all on my own.

———

Even with the extra seat in her third-generation hand-me-down station wagon, we're all crammed into Lacy's car tighter than a LykLuv model's hips in her jeans. My thighs stick to the faded leather seats as I'm smushed in the back with Marley, Malachi, and Zeke. Lou's leaning out the shotgun window, trying not to freak out from claustrophobia, while Camesha's in the extra seat next to the driver.

"We better not get pulled over for this hoodrat shit," Lacy complains.

"If we do, it's all good. Make Zeke talk to them and use that light-skin privilege," Camesha says with a laugh.

"Me?! But the cops are already looking for me," Zeke says defensively. I poke him in the stomach to remind him not to say too much.

Camesha turns around in her seat to stare down Zeke. "Now why would the cops be looking for *you*?"

"Because I'm"—Zeke looks at Malachi for help but comes up dry—"too cool for school?"

"Booooooooooo!!!" The whole car erupts in relentless jeers.

"I was under pressure!" Zeke rests his head on my shoulder. "Let me be pathetic in peace."

Camesha grabs the aux cord to DJ. She puts on some horn-heavy, funky soul music at max volume. We all start singing along to this psychedelic Brazilian track, pretending to know the words but mostly just hitting the *ooh*s and *aaah*s. The song cuts off when Camesha's phone starts ringing.

"And who might that be?" Zeke leans forward, shamelessly nosy. He brushes her faux locs away to get a clearer look over her shoulder. "Does that say Troy? Like *Troy* Troy?"

"Colony Cantina Troy the Corny Frat Boy?!" Malachi screeches. "Why the hell is he calling you?"

Camesha sends the call to voicemail and rotates to face Zeke, the seat belt pressing into her sunset-orange tube top. "He's not that bad."

"He's a walking cartoon character of a problematic man-child." I gag.

"Also, racist," Marley adds.

"And cringey," Malachi says.

"What happened to the whole no-non-paying-boyfriends-until-you're-a-homeowner thing?" Zeke piles on.

"I came up on some biiig money recently, so I hit my savings goal," Camesha explains. "I got all the down payment money I need now. It's about time that I entertain the idea of a traditional boyfriend again."

"You hit your savings goal already?" The last time we talked about her whole property ownership plan, she was still a solid twenty grand away from meeting her target. I wonder how she came up with that much money so quickly.

Camesha shrugs, her demeanor switching up real quick. "I mean, not really. But, like, almost. I'm close to my goal, I mean."

Nobody else seems to clock the energy shift except for me. Could all this cash that came out of nowhere have something to do with her trip? Something to do with Vic?

"How did you two even meet?" Malachi asks, interrupting my train of thought.

"Lacy introduced us."

Malachi lunges forward to shove a finger in his sister's face. "Traitor!"

"Boy, chill," Lacy says, swatting Malachi's hand. "Y'all are gonna make me crash this damn car." She puts on her turn signal and changes lanes to avoid the onslaught of traffic forming in the right-hand lane of the 10 freeway.

All of us in the back are leaning forward now, staring at Lacy to give us more details. Even Lou is repositioned so that his head isn't totally hanging out the window anymore. Lacy's eyes break from the road for a split second to see us glaring at her. "Y'all are annoying as hell, you know that?" She rolls her eyes and extends her left hand out the window to catch the breeze. "I introduced them at my internship."

Malachi immediately starts laughing. "Since when do you have an *internship*?"

"Your sister got a whole-ass secret life," Camesha says mischievously.

Lacy sucks her teeth. "Don't tell Mom and Dad."

Zeke shimmies his shoulders and taps his fingers together like an evil villain. "Oooooh, I love a good secret."

Lacy changes lanes again and sighs. "You know what, never mind."

The entire car erupts in groans.

"Oh, for crying out loud, she's a cannabis apprentice!" Camesha blurts out.

She says it as if we're supposed to suddenly get what's happening, but I'm still lost. We're all pretty quiet until Lou breaks the silence. "So, you . . . deal drugs?"

Lacy shakes her head. "No. I work at a *legal* growery. They think I'm twenty-one. It's just so that I can learn the industry from the ground up. The regulated cannabis sector

is white as hell even though there are mad Black people still
in jail for that shit. Young kids of color are still getting records
for black-market dealing and possession. Somebody has to
learn the business and work on policy to change that. Might
as well be me."

"She's gonna be like Angela Davis but for weed, y'all,"
Camesha says approvingly.

"That's cool as fuck, but how does this relate to Troy
again?" I press.

"Well, we're a women-owned-and-operated cannabis col-
lective, so Troy buys his weed from us."

"Ugh." Zeke sticks out his tongue. "He probably goes there
just to seem woke."

"Maybe, but does that matter?" Camesha asks. "Money is
money, babe. And he's not that bad. He's an entrepreneur."

"Yeah, so is Jeff Bezos and he's literally the devil," I say.

"Y'all are too hard on people," Camesha says. "I know
Colony Cantina is wack, but has it ever occurred to you that
maybe his intentions are good?"

Honestly, it hadn't. But even so, I'm not sure what having good intentions really means for someone like Troy. At
the end of the day, he got a place for cheap in our neighborhood to lure in more people like him. "Good intentions" aren't
enough to prevent Zeke and his family from being the ones
who have to leave to make space for the newer, paler wave of
people to "discover" the hood.

We pull into the parking lot and pool together just enough
crumpled dollar bills to pay the fee. Lacy pops the trunk and
Zeke pulls out the cooler of snacks that his mom packed for
us: onion dip, Ruffles, and a giant Tupperware container of
watermelon and pineapple cubes with Tajin.

I watch Malachi pick up the towels and remember how nervous I am to shoot my shot with him today. Marley appears at my side just in time to prevent a full-scale meltdown from occurring. "You got this, girl." She takes my arm and marches us onto the sand, following in Lou's massive footsteps. Despite the weather, he's wearing platform leather combat boots.

"Interesting footwear choice," I say to Marley.

"He doesn't fuck with sand," Zeke says, slightly out of breath as he trots to catch up with us. "The boots are high enough that no sand will get in."

The fact that Lou stepped in to save his ass at the roller rink helped melt some of the ice between them, but Zeke's still not totally out of the doghouse for what he said to Lou the other day. Zeke readjusts the bright purple strap of the cooler pressing into his shoulder as he fumbles through the sand. The amount of struggle that it takes for him to carry the food contrasts perfectly with the elegant warriors over-looking Wakanda on his Black Panther T-shirt. He gets the cooler to an angle where he's not totally falling over and takes a deep breath before speeding up to catch Lou. "Wish me luck!"

We find a decent spot on the sand between a group of greased-up older men in Speedos and a family with a million screaming kids. Not the most ideal neighbors, but we're far enough from the boardwalk on a stretch of sand that's surprisingly clean, so we take it. I haven't even finished laying down my bag before Marley has taken off her cover-up and run straight for the waves. An old pang of jealousy about how free she is pokes at my chest, but this time I ignore it.

"Are you swimming too?" Malachi asks, laying his towel dangerously close to mine. He sprays on sunblock, which makes his skin literally glisten like a Calvin Klein model's.

I dig my fingers deep into the hot sand so that I can manage to hold still. "I think I'm good here for now."

He reaches behind his neck to pull his shirt up and over his head. When he leans back onto his elbows, the muscles underneath his skin tense up a bit in a way that makes me want to touch him more than anything else. I sink my fingers deeper and deeper into the sand.

"You're not hot in that?" He motions toward Marley's shirtdress, which I'm wearing over my shorts. It's at least ninety-two degrees out, and to be honest, I'm melting. But do I want to shed layers down to a bikini with *all that* going on right next to me? No, thank you.

"I run cold," I lie. He grabs a fistful of sand and holds it over my thigh, slowly letting the grains trickle from his grip and drip onto my skin. It tickles, and I inhale sharply. He catches my eyes and smiles.

Camesha and Lacy put on their giant sunglasses and adjust the seams of their bathing suits that are extremely sexy, but will no doubt leave crazy tan lines. They announce that they're "going for a walk" and take off in the direction of a group of college guys playing beach volleyball by the lifeguard post.

Once the girls are gone, Lou and Zeke start talking.

"It's not a good look is all I'm saying," Lou says in a hushed tone.

"It's just a coincidence," Zeke says.

"Yeah, well, coming up with a shit ton of money out of nowhere the same weekend that your client is killed and you're conveniently hiding in Vegas sounds sketchy to me," Lou grumbles. "I couldn't even bear sitting next to her."

I figured that he was leaning out the car window because he was uncomfortable being smushed together in the car, not because he was trying to avoid Camesha.

"I've known her my whole life, she doesn't have it in her," Zeke says earnestly.

I look back at Malachi and see that he's eavesdropping too. Malachi whispers to me, "Lou would probably say the same thing about his mom, and she looks as guilty as Camesha in my eyes."

"This is all so fucked." I'm trying to figure out what happened to keep Zeke out of trouble, but I didn't expect so many people close to us to potentially be the ones locked up in his place.

In the distance, a skater pops up out of the concrete bowl in the middle of the sand and lands on the ledge with a loud *crack*. The board flies out from underneath him and his friends pull him up, laughing hysterically. Despite the heat, he's wearing a beanie with swooped hair underneath that reminds me: "We assumed that Diego didn't do it, but what if he did? What if the cops *did* get it right?"

Malachi grits his teeth. "Diego's a punk. All talk. He couldn't hurt anybody."

I consider telling Malachi about what Diego tried to do to Marley but bite my tongue. Why is it that every girl knows someone who's been harassed but, conveniently, no guys know any harassers?

I'm brought out of my mind and into my body when I feel Malachi pouring a hot stream of sand up and down my leg once again. "We'll figure this shit out soon," he says with confidence. And for some reason—despite the overwhelming amount of evidence suggesting that we won't get to the bottom of this without someone we know getting hurt—I let the bass in his voice soothe my nerves. I believe him.

I notice that I can't hear Lou and Zeke's conversation anymore. Zeke's whispering what appears to be a rapid-fire string of apologies. He puts his hands into a prayer position, then presses them against his heart. He passes Lou a tiny, folded piece of paper. Lou opens up the note, written in brightly colored gel pens, and reads it carefully as Zeke trembles by his side. When Lou finishes, he tucks the paper into his pocket and looks back at Zeke. He swipes the back of one hand against Zeke's cheek where a tear was starting to fall. Lou leans in to say something into Zeke's ear, before meeting his lips in a kiss.

Zeke grips the side of Lou's long-sleeved shirt and presses against his chest until they're completely intertwined. I look away and become acutely aware of my own body's proximity to Malachi.

"Come on." Malachi stands and extends his hand toward me. He towers over me, his height and glowing skin so stark that a group of girls passing by do a double take. "Let's give them some time to finish . . . making up."

His eyes flick toward mine, then back at the floor, less confident than before. The hint of shyness reminds me of pre–growth-spurt Malachi, the quiet kid on the school bus who was never the first to speak. His silent phase was short-lived, but still. I feel fondness for all the different stages of Malachi through the years that make the young man standing in front of me now only the more appealing. Although today, staring at his defined abs and the way that his trunks hang loosely around his hips, "appealing" doesn't quite capture the range of new things that I feel for him.

We walk on the sand past the skate park with a backdrop of palm trees and California coastline so gorgeous that it ignites some serious LA pride within me.

"I think there's a smoothie shop right here," Malachi says as we step onto the boardwalk lined with dozens of vendors selling everything from cheap sunglasses to henna tattoos and weed oil. Sure enough, he leads us right to where we want to be.

"How'd you know that?"

"*Grand Theft Auto 5*." He orders us a drink to share and we wander down the boardwalk, dodging shirtless men with dogs on longboards and girls with piercings in places that I didn't even know piercings could go.

The newness of the boardwalk and its distance from our neighborhood—inextricably tied to the history of how our relationship has always been—creates room for me to indulge in the fantasy of a new version of me and Malachi, together. I wonder what it would feel like to be us, elsewhere. I get caught up in this little dream of us on a plane to somewhere on our bucket list. We're the same, but older. A woman sitting across the aisle leans over to say how sweet we look together and asks how we met. He tells her our story as he holds my hand where we share an armrest. I listen and revel in the comfort of him knowing all of the details of my life, all of my quirks, because he was there to witness it all. Meanwhile, the slow burn anticipation kicks in of preparing to experience a new place with someone I love who loves me back. I can see it all so clearly: the plane, the hotel room, the bed . . .

I channel the pep talks that Marley gave me and swallow a giant gulp of frozen strawberry lemonade. *Now or never.* I wipe away the condensation forming on the plastic cup to give my hands something to do as I look at Malachi. "So, uhm, I've thought about what you said and . . . I want to try . . . *different.*"

I wait for him to play games and act like he doesn't know what I'm talking about like every communication-averse, emotionally repressed high school boy, but he doesn't. He makes his stern face that accentuates the hard lines of his jawbone.

"You're not just humoring me, right?" He speaks less steadily than before. His self-doubt is a bit surprising, given that I've literally been ogling his body all afternoon and I could have sworn that he noticed. "You can tell me if you really don't see me that way." His voice lowering to a coarse whisper. "Because honestly, once we start this thing, I know very well how much restraint it would take for me to stop."

I say his name, but my voice comes out hazy—more like a moan than a real word. I grab his hand and squeeze it tightly.

It takes a second for him to react. At first, he just looks at me with his deep eyes in a way that makes me worry whether or not I did something wrong. But then he bites his lip.

He starts to walk fast, his fingers interlaced with mine, and steers us into an alley decorated with Technicolor murals on both sides. He grabs the drink from my hand and tosses it in a recycling bin before pressing me up against the wall. The bricks, having absorbed a whole day's worth of sun, radiate warmth through the fabric of my shirt. He floats his free hand up to my face, and heat moves through my veins like lava. His lips part, and I lean forward to close the space between us.

And then we're kissing. We start off slow at first, the weight of his body pressing against mine in such a way that I feel simultaneously heavy and featherlight. I find myself letting go of his hand to grip the side of his waist right above his shorts, which triggers a low growl in the back of his throat. And I like it. Our lips move heavily now with more urgency as he matches my hand, now tracing those abs that I've been dreaming of all week. His fingertips wander the outline of my rib cage in a way that makes me dizzy. I'm eternally grateful that I'm the one leaning against the wall.

I'd normally be mortified by the thin layer of sweat forming on my stomach, but the sensation of his hands gliding effortlessly across my body quiets any self-consciousness. Malachi slides his tongue against mine and the world goes black, little stars twinkling in the space above my eyebrows. We settle into a rhythm once we realize that there's no need to come up for air. He takes deep inhales through his nose that translate into waves of heavenly pressure against my lips.

We kiss until it stings.

TWENTY-EIGHT

We had decided to let SOSI's social media presence ride itself out for a while, letting the flood of shares and posts from the "shooting" at the Lenway party do the work for us. But now the buzz is starting to slow down, so it's time to make more videos to keep SOSI relevant. Rent day isn't going to stop getting any closer just because there's a local murder investigation going on. No one's bothered Zeke since the roller rink, so until we hear for sure that the evictions are canceled, we gotta keep the heat on high.

Around 9:00 p.m., Malachi and I pull up to the alleyway where we made our first round of clips on the Fourth of July. Minutes later, Marley appears, balancing on the back pegs of her bike while Lou pedals. He's still anti-SOSI, but he agreed to come help tonight on the condition that we make Zeke stay home, just to be safe.

"It's about time," Lou comments when he catches Malachi moving his hand from the small of my back. Marley's eyes glint as she pops off the bike and smiles approvingly. Malachi laughs, bringing his arm back over my shoulder. He leaves it there.

"We all can't go from zero to sixty like you and your man," Malachi says jokingly.

Lou grins as he locks the bike to the post. Under his breath, I catch him whisper, dreamily, "My man . . ."

"All right, all right, let's make these videos and get out of here," I say. It's hard not to feel at least a little shy being official with Malachi all out in the open now, even if it's just Marley and Lou here to witness.

I shoot a blurry video of Lou in a hoodie, pretending to kick the shit out of Malachi, who's in the fetal position so that nobody can see any identifying features. Marley shatters several empty glass Mexican Coke bottles in the background to add a lil extra pizazz. When we're happy with our propaganda masterpiece, I send the video to the girl with the loudest mouth and most active social media presence in our class. Within minutes, she replies with the shocked-screaming emoji and adds the video to her story. Honestly, this part is too easy.

We move to the main street illuminated by flickering streetlights and Lou's the first to break off from the pack.

"Where are you going?" I ask.

"I got a date with Zeke at Colony Cantina," he says with a faint smirk.

I check the time on my phone. "But it's late. Aren't they closed by now?"

Lou raises an eyebrow like he knows something that we don't. "Yes, they are closed, and Zeke's locking up alone tonight . . . which is precisely why he suggested I meet him there." He winks and plunges his hands into his pockets, strolling in the direction of the restaurant.

"I should get going too," Marley says. I start to protest,

genuinely wanting her to stay and not feel like she's third wheeling, but she shakes her head. "I got a date with Jordan Catalano. *My So-Called Life* is streaming now, so I must bid you adieu." And with that, she hops on her bike to head home.

"You're not going to leave me now too, are you?" Malachi asks playfully.

"Not a chance." I grab his shirt and move in for what must be the fortieth kiss today.

The quickness with which I've let myself get caught up with him feels inevitable. When you've loved someone for your entire life, the moment that you let them in, it's not totally brand-new—there is newness, of course, but there's also a familiarity. It's like this documentary that he and I watched once about how in Los Angeles, there are so many lights and cars and planes that you can't see the stars at night. But if you drive just two hours away out into the desert of Joshua Tree, suddenly, the sky is illuminated with more stars and galaxies than you can imagine. It's all right there, and it has *been* there the whole time. All you had to do was step away from the noise of what you've always called your home and realize that *home* is actually a bigger concept than you previously believed.

We walk back to his spot holding hands, switching between whose thumb is in front to figure out our best fit. He takes shorter strides and I move a little quicker until we fall in sync. Malachi's telling me about some prank video when we turn the corner toward his home and see an abandoned skateboard on the front lawn.

"Is that Lacy's?" I take a few steps closer.

"Nah, hers is a pink Proper Gnar one with candy on it." Malachi uses his foot to flip the board upside down to examine its deck. A vintage-looking airplane cuts across a bright orange sky. "This one's Kernshaw Skate Club."

I groan. "Oh, shit."

"Aww, you know me so well." Diego emerges from the side of the house. He's always been thin, but tonight, he looks noticeably skinny. Thinking about how much it probably sucked being held in juvie makes me feel bad for him. "Rhea, Rhea. You still remember all my favorite brands. Your love for me is so sweet."

The pity stops.

"What are you doing here?" I'm trying hard to mask the cataclysmic pounding in my chest. Now that he's out, the cops are probably moving fast to arrest someone else.

"No 'How are you?' No 'We were so worried'?" Diego asks in a wounded, sarcastic voice. He flashes a smug smile as he runs a hand through his hair. The gesture reminds me of the night of the party. Of Marley. The memory of my selfishness makes me want to scream and choke. I can't find the words for how I feel about the choice I made that night, but I know one thing for sure: I don't ever want to be that person again.

I cross my arms. "My question still stands, Diego. Why are you here?"

"I was looking for your novio." Diego approaches and Malachi reluctantly gives him dap. "You got a minute, bro?"

"If this is yet another attempt to bring him in on your bullshit, you can fall back," I say with bite.

Diego laughs at me in a cocky way that feels distinctly sexist. "Apparently a lot has happened since I've been away." He motions at the way that I've positioned myself between him and Malachi. "It took him long enough. Maybe a little too long for someone with legit feelings for you, if you ask me . . ."

"Diego—" Malachi growls.

"Just an opinion," he says, brushing a lock of hair from his face. "Later, though, Malachi. For real." Diego grabs his board and carries it to the sidewalk. "Don't you at least want to hear how I got free?"

I don't want to give him the pleasure of thinking that we're interested in him, but we honestly do need to know what happened. I don't say anything at all, which Diego naturally considers as an invitation to keep speaking.

"They let me out once they realized that dead guy had a lot of beef with people with serious money. My lawyer thinks one of his local business partners got pissed and hired SOSI to make the hit." Diego jumps onto his board. "It's like a fucking novela, huh?"

The streetlight catches Diego's face and I see for the first time that he has a deep cut above his left eyebrow. The stitches are still in. The tiny pang of pity creeps back in.

"What happened there?" I point at the gash.

Diego repositions his hair over the cut. "Nothing," he says curtly, his voice suddenly soft and childlike. He takes off on his board down the street before I can comment on how fucked up it is to lock up minors like that before a trial. I may hate Diego, and he's not a "good guy" by any stretch of the imagination, but he didn't deserve to be held up like that. Nobody does.

"Wait!" I shout at Diego's back before he rides too far away. "Did your lawyer say who exactly the police think pulled the trigger? Do they have a name?"

Diego pops off his board. "Okay, *nosy*," he sneers. "Why are you so interested?"

I shove my hands into my pockets and shrug. "Just am."

"SOSI killed Vic, that's for sure." Diego's eyes scan my face slowly, moving with a level of silent concentration that makes my skin crawl. "Beyond that, though? I'd stay the fuck out of it and mind my own business if I were you."

Mind my own business? Why does he sound like—

"Ay, yo, don't talk to her like that," Malachi seethes, taking a step toward Diego.

Stay the fuck out of it and mind my own business . . .

Sounds a lot like the messages from SemiCharmed87. Too much alike.

"Relax. I'm only givin' ol' girl a bit of advice," Diego says. "I was tryna leave anyway. I have a meeting in the bank parking lot."

The boy just got out and he's already taking "meetings" at 10 p.m.? I'm about to warn him to take it easy, but he's already gone. The steady rhythm of kick-push carries him into the restless summer night, leaving us with more questions than answers.

TWENTY-NINE

"Well, that was . . ." Malachi begins, and waits for me to fill in the blank, but I don't. I've memorized every word of my last threat from SemiCharmed87/Unknown. I play the message over and over in my head in Diego's voice to see if it fits. "Damn, I don't even know," Malachi continues. "This is getting real."

"Has this not already been real?" I say tightly.

"You know what I mean, Rhea."

"I'm going to text Marley," I announce.

"About what?"

"The whole pissed-business-partner thing from Diego's lawyer. They have to be looking at Staples. The DWG's company was working on the charter school expansion. His car's data was deleted on the day of the murder. He might be dangerous."

Malachi grabs my phone from my hands. "Yeah, maybe, but their mom might be too. Either way, why freak them out? There's no evidence yet."

"Well, their mom wouldn't kill them, obviously, but Staples? We don't know anything about that guy." He's creepy enough. I put out my hand for Malachi to give me my phone back.

"Wait, here me out: What if Staples and Ms. Allen did it *together*, though? Like what if they killed that dude in, like, a conspiracy or some shit."

I consider this for a minute before shaking my head. "They don't have a common motive." Plus, the more that I get to know Marley, I don't believe that the woman who raised her and risked so much to save them all would do something so wild to potentially ruin their lives once again.

"We don't know that," Malachi replies. "People can surprise you."

"Fair point." He hands me back my phone and I delete the draft of the text. There's so much to read into after that conversation with Diego, but it's hard to know which leads are legit. Crickets chirp in the background over the low rumble of cars at the busy intersection one block over. I search for any recent news on the investigation.

"There's a new interview with the guy's daughter." I flip my phone sideways so that we can see the video on full screen.

Amelia Reagan, daughter of murdered real estate mogul and developer, announces plan to convert late father's company into a community revitalization organization.

I increase the brightness to get a clearer look at the woman's face. Amelia looks into the camera and says, "This neighborhood has been historically disinvested and is long overdue for some change. I hope to leverage the resources of Becker Real Estate Group to breathe new life into Kofa Park."

"Sounds like classic white savior complex to me," Malachi mumbles. Sometimes when people talk about South LA, they act as if there isn't life here already. We're literally a mecca of hip-hop culture and small-business innovation—not some dusty old, abandoned Mars wasteland. "Should we go inside? We can take a break from SOSI . . . do some other activities . . ."

He tugs the drawstring of my sweatshirt, pressing his lips to mine. I lose myself in the sensation of his fingers grazing my spine. I want to lean into him even farther; the curiosity about all the unexplored territory between us only builds with each kiss. But right now, I can't get Diego out of my head. Not because I have even the slightest interest in that infuriating speck of scum, but because the way he just spoke to me . . . I wonder if he's behind all the crazy threats.

He has my number, and he's enough of a sadistic fuck to scare me for fun. He was in juvenile holding when I got the messages, so I doubt he had his phone there, but I wouldn't put it past him to have snuck in a burner.

I reluctantly pull away from Malachi. "I need to head out actually," I say. There's a nagging voice in my head, telling me to follow Diego to his "meeting," and I can't ignore it. I know which bank he must've been talking about—there's one just a few blocks away with stairs and a railing, so people skate there after hours.

Malachi winces. "I know we're taking things slow. I didn't mean to suggest that we'd—"

"No, no. It's not that." His fear that I'm not thinking about the same things that he's thinking is endearing. I kiss him again so he knows this part of me is telling the truth. "I just need to go home." Malachi doesn't know about the threats, so I can't tell him where I'm going.

He frowns. "You sure?"

"I'll see you tomorrow."

He pauses, seemingly considering whether to say more. "You sure you're not coming back tonight?"

His need to triple-confirm that I'm leaving is cute. "Yes. Good night." I fight the urge to linger. Whether or not Diego's behind SemiCharmed87, he probably knows more than he's let on. Now that he's been released, the clock is ticking.

As I walk, I take my time to gather my thoughts, but also because the air feels cooler tonight than it has in weeks. I let the breeze settle the sweat on my collarbone and guess whether the car radios whizzing by are tuned into KDay or 94.7 The Wave.

When I arrive at Diego's location, I post up behind a silver Honda Civic that looks like it's been around since the '80s. I take comfort in old cars like this—they've seen some shit. Across the parking lot, he and his minions skate around a couple of benches.

Twenty minutes pass and Diego's still just trying to land this one trick that's not even that cool. No "meeting" seems to be happening. Until—

"Yoooooo, finally!!!" Diego's voice booms out over the chatter of his friends. I can't see the new arrival at first—they're facing away from me. But they're tall and young. Dressed in all black from their hoodie to their jeans, down to the backpack.

The boys talk, and I keep my eyes fixed on New Guy. At least this guy had the common sense to wear something to hide his face. When he turns, I notice that the backpack isn't all black, but space-themed. Just like . . .

No.

My heart stops beating.

I click the lock screen on my phone to reveal a picture of

me, Zeke, and Malachi at Lacy's birthday party last year. I'm smiling like a dweeb, Zeke's holding up two peace signs like a tourist, and Malachi's squatting with his hands in the prayer position.

His galaxy-printed JanSport rests against his leg.

THIRTY

The hallway to Zeke's unit is littered with a new batch of eviction notices that have all been ripped and dropped to the floor. Zeke opens the door before I can knock.

"What's going on?!" He pulls my wrist and slams the door behind me.

I said it was an emergency, but I didn't want to text Zeke the full news because I need to tell him in person. I need to watch the betrayal hit someone else in real time. It's cruel, but I can't process Malachi's lying on my own. I start pacing. I'm about to say the words when I see Lou quietly emerge from Zeke's bedroom.

"Oh, hi." It's hard to contain my surprise, and annoyance, to see him right now.

"Lou walked me home from work, so he was already here." It's then that I notice through the crack in Zeke's bedroom door that inside his room, a candle is lit. Slow electronic music wafts from Zeke's iPhone wedged into an empty mug functioning as a makeshift speaker.

"Oh." I blush. "Was tonight, uhm, the Night?" I raise my eyebrows.

Zeke turns bright red. "*Jesus*, Rhea, no, we're not—" He runs his hand over his face. "We're not *there* yet." Over Zeke's shoulder, Lou cracks a sly smile. "What's the emergency you mentioned?"

"Malachi is a fucking *liar*." I grab a pillow and throw it against the front door.

"Aaaaand I should go," Lou announces.

"Yeah, *bye*," I say, opening the door for him. This is between the original crew—Lou has no business being here to witness the shitshow that is about to go down. Zeke frowns and nods at Lou as he leaves.

"My god, what is with you, girl?" Zeke asks.

I fill him in on what I saw, straining for a deep breath in between details. Zeke's face falls, little by little, like a sand castle slowly being taken over by a series of small waves.

———

Malachi knocks on the door seconds after my anger manifests as a full-blown ugly cry. I use the sleeve of my sweatshirt to rub away the tears, but it's pointless—the fabric quickly becomes so soaked that it starts to chafe, leaving my skin stinging and raw.

When Malachi sees me, he makes that contorted face—a mix of discomfort, horror, and heartbreak—that guys make when girls cry. He hesitates for a moment before stepping forward to hug me, but I back away, knocking over the lamp on the side table in the process. I didn't say what was up when I told him to get his ass over to Zeke's, so he's just now putting together the pieces; I'm not just mad at something, I'm mad at *him*. He looks at Zeke for answers, but Zeke just winces and plops on the couch.

"Can someone tell me what the hell is happening?" Malachi begs, frazzled. He drapes his hands around his neck, his dark eyes wide with anxiety.

"How long have you been dealing?!" I shout. Zeke shushes me to not wake up Lupe, but I can't bring myself to care about my volume.

Malachi choke-laughs. "What are you talking about?"

"Don't lie. That will only make it worse," Zeke says.

Malachi stares at the floor, seemingly weighing his options before proceeding. He crouches to the floor and sits with his knees tucked into his chest. I consider the possibility that he's making himself small so that we go easier on him, which makes me furious. I grab a pillow from the couch and throw it at his stupid fucking head. "HOW. LONG."

He buries his face into the nook of his elbow. "Not long." I grab another pillow and hurl it at him, this time hitting him in the shin. "Since the day that Marley and Lou were out of town. When Lupe got that shrimp on sale and made us lunch."

I'm transported back to that moment when Malachi and Diego disappeared behind the building right as I pulled up to Zeke's. His and Diego's beef being so casually set aside just to exchange a boring video game was suspicious—part of me knew that even then. For our entire lives, Malachi has been stubborn, but never has he been this stupid.

"Why the fuck would you get involved in that? You know that now you've committed a *real* crime, you could do *real* time," Zeke whisper-shouts.

"Bro, I'm doing this for you!" Malachi raises his head. "I've saved *every penny* just in case our plan didn't work. You know that this month alone, I've made—"

"I don't want to hear it," I interrupt.

"What about Lacy? Don't you think she'd be—" Zeke begins.

"You can leave Lacy the fuck out of this."

"That'd be convenient for you, wouldn't it?" I say. "To just forget that your actions affect anyone else?"

"You're one to talk," Malachi mumbles.

"What's that supposed to mean?" I bark.

He shakes his head. "Look. It was the right choice. I've made Zeke an emergency fund, and it's been crucial to hype up the gang and give it cred. Do you really think that SOSI is still trending because of the fake videos and shootouts alone? People don't just suspect SOSI is legit, they *believe* it is, and the drugs helped prove it."

All along I've been holding on to this sense of pride that I've managed to pull off SOSI and keep my promise—that it's not real, that it helps the community, and that no one we care about got hurt. But now I know that none of those things are true, and it's fucking embarrassing that I was naive enough to believe any of that in the first place.

"We agreed to start a *fake* gang. That line gets real blurry when you start committing *real* crimes," Zeke says, glancing nervously at the door to Lupe and the kids' bedrooms.

"The line doesn't get 'blurry,' it completely fucking disappears," I say, my voice hoarse. "What happened to our promise that nobody will get hurt?"

"Oh, c'mon, it's just weed, Rhea." Malachi sucks his teeth. "I didn't get into the other shit Diego sells."

"God, that's not the point." I can't believe he doesn't get it.

"You have me out here looking like *an asshole*, defending you and shit, and for what? Just for you to be sneaking behind my back, *lying* to me?! You—" My voice breaks, in part from the anger, but mostly from the embarrassment. I believed him. Even when I saw the signs. I press my hands into my eyes and they're cold. "You promised us that you wouldn't get involved. Where the hell is Mr. Keeps His Promise now?"

Malachi clenches his fists and explodes. "What's the point of keeping promises right now? For our whole damn lives, movies and television and the government promised that we'd get to grow up like happy little teenagers in this land of opportunity who get to spend their time on silly dramas or hijinks or whatever, but guess what? *We don't get to do that.* We have to deal with this shit, like the fact that our entire goddamn neighborhood is falling apart, and half of our family is about to be evicted." He lets go of the tension in his fists and stares at the wall. "I wasn't the first person to break my promise—I just realized that this country broke its promise to us first. I don't owe it to anyone to play fair anymore."

Zeke runs his hands through his hair. "This is over. All of it. The dealing, but also SOSI and trying to chase whoever killed Vic. We're letting all of this go. It's not worth it."

My head starts to throb. "Zeke, no. We can't just give up on everything. We can't—"

"Why not? I'd rather y'all have to visit me out in the middle of nowhere than us having to visit Malachi in juvie."

"Nobody's going to juvie," Malachi says, deflated.

My vocal cords tremble so hard that it hurts to speak. "Malachi, if the cops figure out that you've been dealing and saying you're SOSI affiliated, they one thousand percent will lock you up. And if we give up on trying to figure out who killed Vic, they're going to have no trouble swooping up Zeke too, given that an eyewitness apparently saw him at the crime scene. You two are *known as friends*—this is a slam dunk for the cops." I tug at the collar of my sweatshirt to keep myself from overheating. "We need to figure out who killed Vic to get SOSI's name out of the mix. *Then* we can think of a new plan to keep scaring off the developers. That's the only way we can be sure that both of you will be safe."

"Rhea, no new plans," Zeke says. "This is too much. I'll get a lawyer, or something."

"You think you got lawyer money? And even if you did, you think you'd have the kind of money to buy you a real lawyer that can get your brown ass off the hook for murder in a city known for throwing people of color under the bus to uphold the police state?"

Zeke frowns. "I've made up my mind, Rhea. It's over."

A pained noise from the back of my throat spills out of my mouth. "You guys don't get it." I inhale to catch my breath, but the tears are back again in full force. "We give up now and we don't only lose you, Zeke. If you move away, that means we lose Lupe, Stella, Kiké, Auntie, Camesha. And if all of you are gone, then who knows what will happen with me and Malachi. Like maybe we'll make it as a couple, but maybe we won't—statistically he's just going to keep getting better and better looking and the gap between us is going to get bigger and bigger and high school couples never make it anyway, right? So then we break up and I lose Malachi and there's no Zeke here to keep the friendship alive. That means Lacy, Mrs. and Mr. Reed—all of them are gone too. It's a slippery slope and in the end, guess what happens? I'm completely alone."

"Rhea—" Zeke tries to move closer, but I throw my arm out to keep him away.

"Y'all know that my mom is worn out and I'm the accident that she kept but didn't have the energy to parent. On my own, I can't pull together a new chosen family like the one that we all have right now. I got lucky to be taken in by Dante years ago, and I know that I won't get lucky like that ever again."

When I finish, my throat is dry. I need water, but I can't stay here.

"I'll still be your family—just your family that lives a little bit farther away," Zeke says, wiping away tears of his own.

I look at the photos of the three of us on the wall: posing in front of the Haunted Mansion in third grade, holding a starfish at the aquarium in first grade, hanging off one another while laughing hysterically in front of Lupe's car on our way to the freshman dance last year. There will be no more pictures like this anymore.

I grab my bag and take off for the door. Malachi and Zeke call my name, but I ignore them. In the hallway, I swipe one of the discarded eviction notices from the floor and shove it into my pocket. A memento of the last time that we were still us.

I don't make it past Auntie's house before a muscular hand grabs my shoulder. I had been crying so hard that I couldn't hear anything beyond the ringing in my ears. I get ready to run or fight or do whatever I need to do before I realize that it's no stranger.

"I'm sorry," Malachi says. The streetlight illuminates the misty film over his eyes. He squeezes my shoulder harder, and then some. "I fucked up. I didn't know—I should have known. It was only me and Diego. It all stops right now. I'm so sorry."

The tightness in my chest ramps up to an unbelievably painful level. I press my palm against my collarbone to force myself to breathe. It doesn't work. The world feels lighter and lighter. I start to choke from what feels like a simultaneous overabundance of and complete lack of air. Chills run up and down my spine and I'm freezing cold. The tingling sensation begins at my fingers, then creeps up to my hairline before things go black. I grab Malachi's forearm to prevent myself from falling, but I stumble anyway. He's there to catch me.

The eviction notice tumbles out of my pocket and lands faceup on the sidewalk. A dirty flyer from the now-closed restaurant where I ate on my birthday every single year of my life sticks out from underneath a discarded Starbucks coffee cup inches away. "I can't breathe."

—

I have no sense of time. I don't know how long it takes before my lungs can inhale again, before I can see colors and the world no longer feels like I'm underwater, drowning. I find myself on the floor, seated with my head between my knees. The rhythmic movement of Malachi's hand down my spine rocks me back to consciousness.

I open my mouth to speak, but my throat is so dry that it hurts. I close my mouth to swallow enough spit to dull the pain. "I don't know what happened," I say at last.

"I think that was a panic attack," Malachi replies softly.

That makes sense. I think about apologizing but decide that I don't need to.

Malachi moves his hand from my back to my forearm. I still hold on tight to my knees because I'm not yet convinced that if I let go, I won't fall apart.

"Do you want to talk about it?" he asks.

"No." I really don't. All I want is a glass of water and my bed.

"Well, can I just say one thing?"

I hum until my head stops spinning. I take a deep inhale through my nose and nod.

"I know that I hurt you, and I'm sorry. I never want to play any part in making you feel like this ever again. And I know that this is probably too soon, but I want you to know that I—"

A siren pierces my ears, undoing the progress that I made to dull the sharp throbbing in my brain. Three police cars rip around the corner and pull into the driveway next to us.

The cops jump from their cars and hurl down the hallway of the apartment building. Malachi takes out his phone and starts recording, a learned reflex of staying ready to document any misconduct. Best-case scenario, the footage may save someone's life; worst-case, at the very least, it can be used in a trial. We keep a safe distance but move forward when we hear a woman and children screaming. One of the cops yells at us to stay the fuck back, but we don't listen. I pull out my phone to call Zeke to make sure that they're safe. The phone rings two or three times before I see it.

Two burly officers emerge from the end of the hallway, dragging someone kicking and shouting. Malachi stops recording.

Latino, male, fifteen years old.

I watch one of the cops pull Zeke's phone from his pocket and hand it to his colleague as Lupe follows them, going around the long way to wheel down the ramp faster than I've ever seen her move. I sprint over to Stella and Kiké and hold their hands so that they don't get too close. Malachi starts cussing out the cops, who give him a warning, and then another. All of the neighbors are outside now, yelling from their windows, shouting from their doorsteps: *"He's only fifteen!"* "Let him *go*!" I look up and see Auntie and Camesha standing on their balcony, holding one another and sobbing.

Once Zeke's tossed in the back of the car, a cop shoves a baton between the spokes of Lupe's wheelchair to prevent her from moving. Stella's little fingernails claw at my arm as the arresting officer hangs out the driver's seat window to leave us all with his final words.

"It's not my fault he's a thug."

PART THREE

*So early in my life, I had learned
that if you want something,
you had better make some noise.*
—MALCOLM X

THIRTY–ONE

I set out a bowl of apples in the middle of the table, but then feel silly and put it away. There's nothing I can do to make my house look less cold. It's quiet here and nobody's around, so Malachi, Marley, and Lou are coming over. I run a paper towel along all of the surfaces to wipe up the dust as I wait for them to arrive.

I stayed up all night thinking about lines. Boundaries. What makes anything real or fake. What makes someone innocent or guilty. Who makes that choice. Who bears the consequences.

Zeke is fifteen, going on sixteen. SOSI is fake. The fear is real. Gentrification is real. Zeke is innocent. Kofa Park is innocent. Am . . . am I guilty?

In my dreams, there is no other sound besides the wail of the siren, the bang of the firecrackers. I'm pushed off a cliff, and I brace for the fall. The arresting cop smiled when he threw Zeke into the squad car.

We are only fifteen years old.

Did they really have to use handcuffs?

I'm yanked back into the present by the chime of the doorbell on its second ring.

Malachi shows up first. He's been here before obviously, but it's been a while. He hovers in the doorway for a moment before closing the screen behind him. He's dressed simply today—blue jeans and a plain white T-shirt. None of the colorful jerseys or brands that he typically wears.

After Zeke's arrest last night, Auntie drove me home before we could talk about what happened. I'm not sure where to begin, but he is.

"I'm sorry that I lied to you." Malachi's voice startles me. It's sort of like hearing someone speak in a library—when you're used to the silence, any noise at all seems so loud.

He's waiting for me to meet his eyes, but I don't want to look at him yet. I get myself a glass of water. "It was a dangerous lie," I say with as much bitterness as I can gather. From the corner of my eye, I watch him wince. "And you know what's the most ridiculous part?" I absentmindedly run my finger around the rim of the glass. "All the signs were there that you were involved with Diego. I just chose to ignore them."

Malachi moves to hoist himself up to sit on top of the kitchen island, but then pauses. Instead, he pulls out a chair from the dining table. "Why do you think you ignored the signs?"

"Maybe I had tunnel vision, being so focused on Zeke." I take a sip of water. "Or maybe part of me has some nostalgia for the sanctity of the pinky promises that we'd make when we were little. I guess I didn't want to accept that shit isn't that simple when you get older." Sitting in the aftermath of the loss of Zeke, I'm reminded of the words of the woman from the church bathroom at Dante's funeral all those years ago: *We're not just kids anymore.*

She was right.

Malachi rubs his neck with one hand. "Do you want me to leave?"

Do I really want Malachi gone, too?

A few moments pass before I make my decision.

"No." I sigh and finish my water. "If I lose Zeke, I'm not losing you too."

"That doesn't sound too enthusiastic," he jokes.

"Yeah, well, I'm not too enthusiastic about you right now." It's too soon for laughter. He should know that.

Malachi nods and corrects himself. He drags his deep eyes up from the floor to meet mine. "So, are we okay?"

No wonder he came early before the others. I should've known that he'd ask—not like it'd make any difference, though. I already know my answer.

The words catch in my throat as if they're clinging to me, not wanting to be made real, before I force myself to spit them out. "We're over," I say at last. "I'm at capacity for change right now. You and me . . . this was a mistake."

Malachi heaves like he's been stabbed, but he doesn't protest. I dab the corners of my eyes to keep them dry, waiting for the hurt between us to dull to a manageable level. We don't speak again until the doorbell rings.

Marley rushes in and hugs us both. What really throws me off, though, is Lou. He looks mad, furious even, and the whites of his eyes have turned bright red.

He's been crying too.

"You good?" I point to the faint trace of bruises on his knuckles.

"I'm fine." He moves his hands into his pockets. "The wall of my bedroom, though . . . Less fine."

I see. I motion to the couch, where Malachi and Marley settle in, unpacking last night's horror, but Lou stays frozen by the door. I walk over and lean on the wall next to him. "How are you really feeling?" The words feel ridiculous as soon as they come out. Neither of us is really the type to jump at the opportunity for an emotional check-in, but it's too late now.

Lou shrugs, opens his mouth to speak, then closes it. He looks up at the ceiling and tries again. "Has Zeke ever made you watch the new *Star Trek* movies with him?"

I chuckle. "Yeah, unfortunately."

"Remember that scene early on in the first reboot where the spaceship is attacked? There are a bunch of redshirts running around as all the sirens blare, but then a missile breaks the wall, and everyone is suddenly sucked straight out into open space without any oxygen. They suffocate immediately and everything goes completely silent—you know what I'm talking about?"

I tell him that, weirdly, I actually do.

"Well, that's sort of how I feel right now."

Word. "I hear you."

Lou brushes off his pants. "Let's go figure this shit out."

He and I settle on the floor across from Marley and Malachi, our backs resting against the wooden stand holding up the television that nobody watches. I clear my throat. "We've known that this was a possibility for a while, but now that it's happened, we need to kick things into high gear to clear Zeke's name. We've identified five possible suspects—"

"If we tell the police that SOSI was all just a joke, then they'd have to let Zeke go, right?" Marley interjects. Her eyes sparkle with equal parts anxiety and optimism.

Lou nods. "I said it before, and I'll say it again: we need to call this off."

Maybe Lou was right before. Maybe there was a time when we should've quit, but now is way too late. "From where the detectives are standing, they have a murder on their hands, neighbor testimony about a rise in 'gang' activity in the neighborhood, and a suspect in custody who people apparently say bangs. I don't think an 'LOL, JK' from a bunch of Black teenagers who are friends with the suspect will change their mind."

"Not to mention the fact that Zeke's family are tenants in what used to be the DWG's building. They probably assume that's his motive," Malachi adds, his voice heavy. "He's in deep." We all are.

"Well, even if they don't believe us, maybe we should call off SOSI anyway," Marley says. "This is a lot."

"What would be the point?" We're only seven days away from the eviction. Giving up now means giving up on everyone. "We can still clear Zeke's name without throwing away everything that we've worked for up to this point."

"Jesus, Rhea." Lou clenches his fists, shifting away from me. "Zeke was *arrested*."

I'm freaked out too, but we can't lose sight of the long-term goal. "We can't let go of SOSI until we know that the evictions are off for good. Our plan is *working*. Remember what Auntie said about the volunteers ghosting after they heard about SOSI?"

Marley sighs, but nods.

"And Malachi, you *saw* how scared those architects were. They're probably considering pulling out of the project now as we speak."

"You really don't think that Auntie's protest will work?" Marley asks.

I shake my head. "No. The way to free Zeke is to find the real murderer. And the way to keep him around after that is to maintain the threat of SOSI."

"SOSI doesn't seem to be making anyone around here more *free*," Lou mumbles.

"Not yet, but it will," I insist.

Marley grimaces, but gives in. "You were talking about suspects, Rhea."

Lou casts her a look of disgust and clicks his tongue.

Seriously? "Lou, if you're so against our plan, then why don't you just go?" The last thing we need is his stanky attitude messing everything up.

"And leave Zeke's fate up to the three of you?" Lou scoffs. "No way. Somebody who *actually* cares about him needs to be here."

Every muscle in my body clenches, then explodes. "Yo, you got some fucking nerve. I *do* care about *my* friends."

Lou rises to his feet. "Like how you 'cared' about my sister enough to leave her with Diego at the party?"

An icy silence whips through the air. Lou's blow hits like I've been slammed in the stomach with a ninety-mile-per-hour dodgeball.

"We're all worried about Zeke, we're all stressed," Marley says in the trained voice of a hostage negotiator. "Let's settle down. . . ."

Lou points at me, hand shaking with anger. "You say that you're doing everything for your friends, but really you're pushing this for yourself."

I laugh at the absurdity of his accusation. "Why the hell would I do that?"

"So you don't lose control. So you don't end up alone. I don't know, you tell me—it's *The Rhea Show*, isn't it?"

That's it. Fuck this. Fuck *him*. I don't care that Zeke's obsessed with him. The fact that Lou has the audacity to claim that he's more invested than *me* while he wants to give up on the plan? No way.

I take a step toward him, closer than I should. "Don't come at me acting like you've earned the right to say shit about what's best for Zeke when you're just his basic-ass summer fling. You're a cheap novelty to him now, but he'll be over your bullshit soon enough."

Lou's eyes go wide, then narrow into a tight glare. "Forty-eight hours," he barks.

"What?"

"You have forty-eight hours to solve the case. And if you don't, I'm coming clean about SOSI to the police myself."

White rage thuds against my temples. "You selfish traitor snitch—"

"Every second that Zeke spends locked up because of your ludicrous plan makes *you* the traitor, not me. We can cope with the eviction. I'll save up for a car, drive to see him wherever he moves, do whatever it takes. I just want him safe, now. And you should too."

I do want Zeke safe, but it's not that fucking simple. So many people's lives are on the line. Our home is in danger, and this first wave of evictions won't be the last. If we give up now, this will have all been for nothing. I owe it to Zeke, to everyone, to finish what I started. I won't let the new guy ruin everything.

I flip Lou off, and the undertones of his skin turn a copper red. "I'm out." The door slams. He's gone.

I angrily fasten the bolt behind him, accidentally ripping out the chain in the process. I throw it in the corner. Useless piece of—

"What happened the night of the party?" Malachi asks cautiously.

Marley's quick to shut him down. "It's private." Her voice melts my frustration, morphing it into something else entirely.

I shove Malachi aside to join her on the couch and grasp her hand. "I'm so sorry." I don't think I'll ever stop being sorry.

Marley squeezes me back. "I know, Rhea."

Silence creeps back in, the absence of Zeke and now Lou sinking in deeper.

This isn't how I wanted any of this to go.

"You think Lou's serious about the forty-eight-hour thing?" Malachi asks Marley.

"Lou's always serious."

If she's right, then we got work to do, and fast.

Malachi massages his temples and releases a strained sigh. "So, what were you saying, Rhea? About the suspects?" I don't know what I did to stop Malachi and Marley from jumping ship with Lou, but I'm grateful for them both to keep the ball rolling.

"Right," I try again. "Five potential suspects: Staples, Camesha, Auntie, Diego, and, uhm . . ." I trail off to try to find the right way to say it.

"My mother," Marley deadpans.

I grit my teeth and nod.

"I obviously don't think that she did it, but it's okay—we need to explore every possible option."

"Of course," I say, relieved at the level of chill she's exhibiting about her mom being considered for murder. "And for the record, I don't think Camesha did it either."

"Auntie also seems super unlikely to me," Malachi joins in. "She didn't even know Camesha was missing yet when the guy was killed, so I doubt she would have been amped up enough to pop off like that."

"I adore Auntie, but I wouldn't be too quick to eliminate her. She's protective as hell and definitely did not like how the DWG creeped on Camesha. Plus the whole gas station thing. And Camesha's whole story for why she disappeared for a couple days and suddenly came up on enough money to stop sugar dating—there's something off there," Marley says.

Malachi hunches his shoulders. "I feel like we can all say for sure, though, that Staples is one sketchy-ass nigga."

We sound off in agreement.

"I have an idea," Marley says. "All we know about the DWG is stuff that we've gathered from people who either knew or worked with him in some capacity. But his daughter, Amelia, has been all over the news coverage. She seems to be enjoying her thirty seconds of fame, and she's without a doubt the closest person to him that we can identify. It doesn't sound like he had a wife or any other kids. Maybe there's something that we can learn by checking up on her. She's running his company now, isn't she?"

I'm almost jealous that I didn't think of this myself. Amelia made a big deal about the transition to becoming a community development organization, so she must've had concerns with the way that the company was being run before she inherited it.

Malachi's phone vibrates. "Camesha says Auntie's out running errands but should be back soon," he announces.

"Should we start with the daughter, then?" I suggest.

Marley raises her hand as if we're in class. "I found the address of the real estate company. It's not far—fifteen minutes on the bus. It says that they're open."

Marley and Malachi start messing around, throwing fake karate punches at one another, but I rush straight for the door. I remember the stitches across Diego's eyebrows after he got released. I think of Zeke and my throat clenches.

There's no time to waste.

THIRTY-TWO

The Becker Real Estate Group has one of those cheap signs on the front entryway that looks more like a bus advertisement than an introduction to a place that actually makes money. The office is in a strip mall wedged between a Subway and a bail-bond dealer.

"Anyone tryna split a five-dollar footlong after this?" Malachi asks.

I almost poke him in the side, but catch myself, remembering that it's probably best that we reconstruct the Touch Barrier between us.

"It is strange how every single Subway on the planet smells exactly the same," Marley says absentmindedly as she investigates the cars parked in front of the office.

"Let's get in there and see what her deal is," I say impatiently.

"Hold up!" Marley jumps in front of me. The glass door has plastic shutters drawn to block the sun. They're shut right now so we can't see inside, but Marley brings her finger to her mouth to shush us. "Listen."

I lean in and hear two people arguing in those angry yet restrained voices that parents use when they're fighting about something but don't want their kids to hear. One of the people tells the other one to fuck off.

I'd know that voice anywhere. "Yo, that's Auntie."

"This is the last time I'm telling you this: we are *not* calling it off," Auntie says on the other side of the door.

The second voice is the high-pitched tone of Amelia. "Are you sure that this right here wouldn't change your mind? It looks like you need it." She slides something heavy across a table.

"I won't accept that, or any amount." The object slides back. "If you really believed in genuine community revitalization, you wouldn't be trying to kick us all out."

They must be talking about the evictions.

"Look, I'm sorry that my father initiated the evictions. I really am. He lacked vision—he would've turned this place into a sterile, boring shell of a neighborhood. But my plan is different. I'll keep some of the edginess, some of that *grit* that makes the neighborhood cool, and we'll subtly improve things, little by little. Sure, these first evictions are painful, but I believe that I can make the neighborhood better for everyone. Don't you want to stimulate the local economy?"

"That's bullshit and you know it," Auntie spits. "We have a permit. The protest is happening tomorrow whether you like it or not."

"If you could take a second and see that I'm really trying to help here. The protest will confuse people—"

"I think the only confused person here is you," Auntie says. A metal chair screeches across the floor. "I'll see you tomorrow."

As Auntie's heels click against the tile floor toward the door, Marley yanks my arm. "Subway! Hide!"

We scramble away toward the smell of bread and deli meat. We jump inside and freak out the acne-ridden cashier when we pile into the booth in the back of the restaurant. Malachi's begging him to chill out. "Give us a second then we'll buy a meatball marinara or something, I swear." But there's no use.

"Hello, my children." The bell above the door rings as Auntie strides in coolly with her hands on her hips. She takes her time staring at us one by one with that guilt-inducing look that all mother figures master. "Do you need a ride?"

Malachi starts stammering. "Nah, we're just out here—"

"Boy, there is a Subway two blocks from your house, you are not just randomly hanging out here. Do not play with me."

He lowers his head. "Yes, ma'am."

"Now come get in the car." Auntie holds the door open for us as we sulk out of the restaurant. She unlocks the car and turns back to place a dollar bill in the tip jar. I take shotgun and turn on some music. Once settled into the driver's seat, Auntie immediately turns off the radio, which is how you *know* that you're about to get scolded.

She takes her time to back out of the parking space and merge onto the main street in bone-chilling silence. She doesn't speak until we're several blocks away. "So, let me get this straight. Your friend was *arrested* last night in a *murder investigation*, and you three decide to show up at the business of the man who died in *broad daylight* to poke your nappy lil heads around and make *all of you* look suspicious as hell? Is that right?"

Well, when you put it like that . . .

"The plan sounded better in our heads," I admit.

Auntie mumbles "Lord have mercy" under her breath.

"What were you doing there, anyway?" Malachi asks, which is bold as hell given the shade that Auntie's throwing at us right now.

"Grown folks' business." She grips the steering wheel firmly.

Malachi speaks up again. "Will you tell us more if we confess that we were eavesdropping and heard the last minute anyway?"

We hit a stoplight and Auntie whips around to glare at him. "Malachi Samuel Reed, you got some nerve. You're lucky that you're sitting back there and I'm driving this damn car." We all know that Auntie would never really pop off on any of us, but she has been known to flick people in the back of the head (and acrylic nails slamming against your skull hurts more than you'd think).

I lean over the cupholder to get her attention. "Auntie, I mean no disrespect, but we *really* need to know. Is that lady tryna shut down the #Rooted protest tomorrow?"

Auntie groans. "She's trying, but she won't succeed. All of the tenants in my building and in Lupe's are participating. And after last night's events, more people than ever are riled up to put an end to this shit. We want to stay in our homes, and we want to be safe. Nobody can stop us from exercising our right to fight for that."

"Nobody believes that Zeke did it, right?" Marley says quietly from the back row.

Auntie looks in her rearview window to get a look at Marley's fallen face. Her voice morphs back into the gentle, soothing hum like usual. "Of course not, baby. We all know Zeke is an angel. The cops are just trying to pin this on anyone, and unfortunately Zeke makes an easy target."

"It's not fair," Malachi huffs.

"It isn't, but y'all knew this was a risk when you started SOSI."

I swallow and tense up in my seat. Here it comes.

"Look, babies, we can cut the shit, okay? I may be old, but I have Quipp. Mainstream news doesn't cover shit on South LA, so I use social media to keep tabs on the neighborhood and make sure that all the trans and queer kids are safe." She glances over her shoulder at Malachi. "Plus, I've been to every single one of your school art shows—I'd recognize a tag by you any day." If Malachi's skin wasn't so rich, he'd be blushing hard-core. I shouldn't be surprised that Auntie knows us all better than we think.

She continues. "The cops round here are still recovering from their last scandal when it came out that they falsified evidence to claim that people who they stopped were gang members. The fact that the city's war on gangs has been shown to be a huge racist sham will work in your favor— people will fight for Zeke, even if they do believe that SOSI is real and that he's affiliated. But you have to be prepared for the possibility that if they don't find out who really did it, Zeke may still end up serving some amount of time. It's time to let SOSI go."

"We can't do that," I say firmly.

"I know that you acted out of love and loyalty for your friend, but SOSI isn't without controversy. Gangs are a complicated part of our neighborhood's history, baby girl. They gave some people a sense of belonging during a time of rampant, systemic disinvestment when opportunities of any kind were scarce, but not without a cost. You've been to home-goings." Auntie shakes her head. "I worry that y'all don't know how deep these scars run around here. There are better ways to think of what a future could look like here that includes everyone, without taking advantage of past pain."

I fight the urge to roll my eyes. I'm not looking for a lecture. "We're not 'taking advantage' if our goal is to save the community as a whole."

Auntie reaches over to pat my forearm. "Look, Rhea. You need to focus on helping Zeke get out. The #Rooted protest will take care of the rest."

I dive my hands into my curls in frustration. "But it won't!"

Auntie slows her driving. "And why not, love?"

I hit the dashboard in frustration as the rage in my chest spills out as a growl. "Auntie, we've *been* protesting. The whole entire world watched George Floyd get lynched on video in broad daylight. Everyone everywhere took to the streets, but have the police stopped killing us yet? *No.*" The car falls quiet except for the panting of my breath. "If a protest can't stop them from murdering us, then how can we expect it to stop them from turning us out of our own neighborhoods?"

Auntie draws a heavy inhale. "Your generation has seen a lot of pain. All of us have. But organizing *works*. It might be slow at times, but building community power doesn't always happen overnight."

"I'd rather be feared than have to beg to live." I cross my arms. "I'm not going tomorrow."

The car is dead silent as Auntie pulls into the driveway of Malachi's house. I try to jump out quick, but Auntie grabs my shoulder. "Give it a chance, Rhea. Show up at the protest and pay attention. You may figure out what you need to free Zeke. And, maybe, you'll see that SOSI isn't the only way forward."

I climb out onto the sidewalk and shut the door harder than necessary. Auntie stares at me, eyes full of something stormy that I can't quite read, before she puts her car back into drive.

"Wait!" Marley pleads right before Auntie pulls away. "How can tomorrow help us figure out who did it?"

"That man who died played a complicated role in this neighborhood," Auntie says. She turns back on the radio, catching a Nina Simone song midchorus. "You never know what will come out when shit hits the fan."

THIRTY-THREE

The night before the protest is the hottest it's been since the heat wave began. I sit at the foot of my bed in a worn-out sports bra, lazily catching stale air from the standing fan.

Zeke's locked up; I pushed Malachi away; Lou and I are at war. Marley texted me earlier to check in, but her brother's words about how I did her wrong are still ringing in my ears.

Great job at keeping everyone together, Rhea.

When the doorbell rings, I ignore it. It's 10:47 p.m., too late for anyone to be coming over here. I lie back on my bed and wipe the sweat from my collarbone.

It rings again. Then again.

My mom's home for once, so I listen out for her, but she's in the shower.

"For fuck's sake . . ." I roll out of bed to get the door. I look through the peephole, but no one's there. I slowly crack the door open and a piece of paper floats inside. Had it been wedged between the door and the frame? My hands pick up the note, and I find my name typed in sterile Times New Roman across the top.

I open the note, already knowing and dreading who it's from.

In large black lettering across the page:

FINAL WARNING, RHEA. STAY OUT OF THIS.

So, Unknown knows where I live. Fan-fucking-tastic. A silent scream leaches out as a strained exhale between my gritted teeth.

The texts were one thing, but this is crossing a line altogether. The murder suspect list hasn't changed much and any of those people have access to, or could easily ask around and find out, my address. Plus I seriously doubt that half the names on the list would harass *me* like this. I have no new leads, no new evidence, connecting the dots between any of these people.

I slam my hand against the closed door before heading back to my room. This is all so *frustrating*.

There's the possibility that the killer is someone else entirely—someone not connected to the neighborhood at all—but then again, if that were the case, why would they specifically threaten *me*? I'm just a random kid from the block, who simultaneously knows too much and not enough at all. Unknown is aware of this, which is why they're targeting me. So, it *has* to be someone that I know. That's the only way that this all makes sense.

When the doorbell rings again, I practically lose my shit.

I hear my mom's footsteps shuffle toward the entryway. "Don't get it! They're ding-dong-ditching," I warn her, but she doesn't listen. I know I should get up and try to intercept her from potentially finding another Unknown note, but part of me wants her to find something. Part of me wants to see what she'd do and what questions she'd ask. . . . I want to know if she'd ask me any questions at all.

"So nice to see you!" My mother's voice chimes down the hall.

"Hello, Mrs. Edmunds," the visitor responds.

My heart drops, and I scramble to pull on a faded Dodgers T-shirt.

Malachi.

I frantically throw the clothes on my bed and turn off the melodramatic playlist that I've kept on repeat all night. I crumple the note from Unknown and shove it deep under the weight of my mattress.

"What are you doing here?" I ask when his figure appears in my doorway.

He wastes no time before diving in. "When I lied to you about what I was doing with Diego, I lost your trust. I take full responsibility and I know that it will take time to rebuild that foundation with you."

"Malachi, you don't have to do this," I cut him off. My hands start to quake. I don't want some heartfelt reconciliation. I want to forget.

"No, I do." He closes the door behind him. He keeps his distance, choosing to sit in the chair in the corner. "I won't jeopardize my position in your life ever again, Rhea." He looks older when he's sad. There's no trace of the soft, young energy that normally shines through when he smiles. Right now, his face is all hard lines. "Do you believe me?"

There's a hint of heartbreak and desperation in his voice that makes my chest contract. I count up all our years of friendship and note the absence of even the slightest betrayal until this.

Nearly twelve years isn't nothing.

"I believe you."

For now, at least.

Malachi must sense the trace of doubt in my voice because, although he lets a small smile escape, he stays put several feet away. "About #Rooted tomorrow—"

"You were right when you said that you were done keeping promises—I'm done too," I interrupt. "I'm done playing by their rules. A peaceful protest isn't going to get shit done."

"Maybe. But guess what? Everyone we love is 'bout to be there tomorrow because we care about each other. Even if you don't believe it will work, how does you not showing up for the hood prove anything other than that you're just tryna avoid shit?"

"I'm not trying to avoid it."

"Then what do you call what you're doing right now?"

I don't have a good answer, so I just plop back onto my bed. I stare at the ceiling, searching for an excuse, a comeback—anything at all to justify the space between us.

"How do you think Dante would feel about all of this?" Malachi asks. "Starting SOSI, making people afraid, getting in so deep?"

The question catches me off guard. I tug at a loose string on my blanket and watch the corner come undone. "I don't know." I can't remember how Dante felt about serious stuff. "Did we ever even get to talk about heavy things like this, or were we too young?"

He grasps his elbows. "I guess his death was the first heavy thing to happen to all of us."

I nod. "So then there's no way to know."

He grows quiet again, and I do too.

"I guess I'll head out." He rises slowly from the chair and makes his way toward the door. When he passes by the bed, my muscles buzz. The visceral sensation reminds me of when you try to press two magnets together, but they're of opposite charge, so they hover away from one another, trembling in their struggle not to touch.

I blurt out his name before he reaches the door.

He turns to me, dark eyes waiting patiently.

"It's not about avoiding things for me." I shift to the side to make room for him to join me on the edge of the bed. He raises an eyebrow, but I motion him forward. The mattress creaks from our combined weight. "I just want things to stay the same."

"Yeah, you made that clear already. You're 'at capacity.' I get it."

"I was talking about the protest tomorrow."

"Oh." He blushes. "Well, whatever you want. I'll drop it. The protest. And us."

The invisible magnet within my body flips and I find myself moving toward him, pulled by a force that exists beyond the constraints of my own anxieties and fears.

"With you, though . . . I liked different." I inch my hand toward his thigh but stop short. "I like you, Malachi."

He looks at my hand, then straight at me. He hesitates for just long enough that I start to retreat until he grasps my forearm.

"Can we hug?" His voice is small, timid even.

"Yes."

He closes the distance between us in practically one large swoop. His arms wrap around me as I rest my head against his chest. The touch is soft, cautious, at first, but I find myself looping around him tighter and tighter as the weight of last night sinks in. He squeezes me hard, and I count his heartbeats to distract myself enough to keep from crying. Warmth builds between us in such a way that I can't believe we've spent practically our entire lives together without knowing the comfort of melting into each other's arms.

Tonight, I hang on to him, hard, not knowing what disasters tomorrow holds for us.

THIRTY-FOUR

Zeke has been in custody now for thirty-five hours and twenty-two minutes. I keep compulsively checking our texts, half wishing that there will be an impeccably selected, witty meme from him waiting for me. Something like *Yikes! That was a weird dream, right?* And then I'd wake up and realize that none of this is really happening—that it's all just a heat wave–induced hallucination.

Unfortunately, though, people like us don't get to wake up from nightmares like this.

On the morning of the #Rooted protest, I meet up with Malachi at his place. He comes up behind me and nestles his chin on my shoulder as he loops his arms around my waist. "You ready to fight the power?"

"Don't get too excited," I say. "I agreed to *attend* the protest to support the fam—no more, no less. You won't be catching me with a mic today."

"I'll take what I can get," he says, smile beaming from the nook of my neck.

I give his forearms a squeeze. "Then yes, I'm ready."

"And about Lou—" Malachi begins.

"I have nothing to say to him." Sure, the way that I came

for his neck yesterday was intense. Even for me. But if he's serious about blowing up our plan tomorrow, there's no way in hell I'm apologizing.

Malachi frowns but doesn't press. He calls out to Lacy and Camesha to see if they're good to go. They promptly reply for the third time now that they need five more minutes. "They take forever to get dressed. It's a protest, not Coachella."

Camesha shouts back, "There's no harm in making justice look good!"

"I guess I can't argue with that," Malachi says. And surely he cannot—the boy looks fine as hell today. He's got on a vintage Jackie Robinson baseball jersey, a backward cap, and those Adidas soccer pants with the stripes on the sides. He lets go of my waist and motions toward the living room. "Wanna watch TV while we wait?"

Does he not notice that I've been staring at his mouth all morning? I bite my lip. We both have a lot on our minds today, might as well take one off the list. I tug the bottom of his jersey and pull him close.

I pause for a second, a brief moment of panic doubting whether this first kiss after our first fight would still feel like the ones before. But I don't have time to get caught in my head. His hand brushes my cheek on its way to find the curls dangling over my ear, which he grasps lightly as he presses his lips to mine. He wastes no time before gently nudging my mouth open a little bit wider so that his tongue can flow against mine.

The kiss is deeper than the ones before. The initial excitement has been replaced with a heaviness that feels as though we're creating a new gravity for ourselves. His hands move slowly and deliberately. I shake a little when his lips run down my neck, lightly tugging on my skin. As my thumbs brush his lower back under the cover of his shirt, I can feel that I'm not the only one with goose bumps.

Lacy's voice breaks us out of our trance. "Aight, let's roll!"

I pull back from Malachi but let my hands linger a few seconds longer. "To be continued?"

He flashes a crooked smile that makes his face glow. "Yes, please."

We make it to the protest right on time. Auntie's standing next to Lupe as they distribute signs. There's a local news van where a woman with box braids assembled in an intricate updo points out the things that she wants the cameraman to capture.

I see why Amelia didn't want this to happen. More and more people keep showing up—every single one taking photos and videos of the scene. This will be all over the internet by the end of the day.

Malachi weaves his hand with mine as we walk over to collect a sign from Lupe. She gasps once she sees us holding hands. "Mira, qué es esto?" She starts grinning so hard, I worry that her face may literally fall off. "It's about damn time!" She squeals and brings us both into a hug. "I'm so happy for you two."

I laugh to hide my embarrassment, but it feels good to make the transition from a low-key couple that only your friends know about to a real couple that even parents recognize too.

"Here, take a sign." She hands one to Malachi that says "Fight, Fight, Fight—Housing Is a Human Right." The one for me is inexplicably covered in glitter and reads: "We Out Here. We Been Here. We Ain't Leaving. We Are Loved."

I thank her and gather the courage to bring up Zeke. "How's the, uhm, bail fund coming along?"

She lets out one of those weary sighs specific to single mothers who have to bust their asses to keep everyone around them afloat. "We're working on it, but it's not easy. Since he's been accused of something so violent, they're asking for a lot of money. They want to charge him with felony murder with a gang enhancement, so it's serious."

"Gang enhancement?"

"If you're found guilty of a crime committed in association with a gang, the prosecutors can tack on more time to your jail sentence."

"But they can't even prove that Zeke's in a gang! And even if he was, how . . ."

"In their eyes, anyone with melanin is affiliated. It's their way of making sure that Black and brown people stay locked up for the longest, mija," she says. "Anyway, we're getting help, but not enough yet."

Not exactly the news that I was hoping to hear.

"We got you, Lupe. We're going to figure something out," Malachi says, his voice stern yet cryptic. If Zeke were here, he'd probably tease Malachi for sounding like Batman. The thought makes me smile for a split second, but that's it.

"We've been looking all over for you guys!" Marley squeezes her way through a cluster of very large men in very tight shorts and skips toward us.

Lou follows shortly behind but walks around the group rather than through it. There's a ton of people here and not a lot of personal space—I'm low-key impressed that he showed up. That said, the boy looks *stressed*. He walks carefully as he grips on to his earphones from Zeke. When he crosses his arms, I notice something that momentarily makes it hard for me to stay mad: below his bruised knuckles in intricate, coral-pink letters across a black backdrop, Lou has the words "FREE ZEKE" painted across his nails. We give each other an awkward nod.

"Lupe, our mom is a lawyer, so she wants to talk to you, if that's okay. Just to see if there's anything she can do to help. She's parking right now, but will be here soon," Marley offers.

"That would be wonderful, thank you, chica." A humming noise starts to float through the air followed by the static pop of a microphone being plugged into a speaker. Lupe rolls away to direct the news crew to set up near the front.

"What is up, my people?!" Auntie's voice booms across the crowd that immediately erupts into hoots and cheers. She stands on top of a bright orange beverage crate. "Thank y'all for coming out. As you know, today is about *justice*. Today is about *humanity*. Today is about *our rights* as the residents, the mothers, the fathers, the children, the shop owners, and the culture bearers of this community."

The vibe is straight-up Black church with people shouting "Amen" and "Tell 'em!" between fanning the air and shaking like they're ready to testify. A sign language interpreter communicates animatedly by her side.

"We'll begin with a land acknowledgment, grounding ourselves in appreciation of the Gabrielino and Tongva peoples as the traditional caretakers of the Los Angeles Basin," Auntie explains. She's joined by a protester who speaks on the cruelty of Native people being priced out of their own ancestral land.

"What did we miss?" Lacy whispers in my ear out of nowhere.

"Don't go sneaking up on people like that, damn," I shout as she laughs mischievously. "Where did y'all go?"

"Nowhere," Camesha says in a fake-innocent voice like a movie star from the 1930s. She waves at Troy and Lance, who've just arrived at the edge of the crowd. They're both wearing matching #BlackLivesMatter shirts with their Colony Cantina baseball caps.

Auntie explains the route of the march and announces the various speakers. "And now to kick us off right, please welcome the lead developer of the Bayrex Charter School network, Christopher Staples!"

Staples's bald head shines in the sun like a brown crystal ball as he grabs the mic and takes Auntie's place on the crate. He's wearing a highlighter pink polo with a Bayrex Charter pin. Marley and Lou literally boo him, but they're drowned out by the overwhelming cheers around us.

"Oh my *god*, I hate this man," Marley growls.

Camesha scoffs. "Chris is the fucking worst."

We all whip around. *"Chris?!"*

Camesha freezes, her hands shooting up to cover her mouth.

"Hold up," Malachi says. "You're on first-name basis with this wannabe Keegan-Michael Key nigga?"

"He *seems* like the worst—that's what I meant," Camesha shoots back, defensive as hell. "Look at his shirt. Only an asshole would wear a shirt like that."

She's lying. I *knew* she's been lying.

"Camesha . . ." I begin softly.

"Are you in trouble?" Malachi offers cautiously.

Camesha sucks her teeth impatiently. "See? This is why I don't tell y'all shit. So dramatic."

"If we're so dramatic, then tell us the truth," I say.

She sighs and rolls her shoulders. "Remember I told y'all about the disagreement that I had with Vic the night of the party?" We nod. "Well, maybe it was a bit more than just a disagreement. And maybe Creepy Chris was involved."

A sharp pressure clamps my chest.

"After I got in that car leaving the party, I got a call from Vic that he wanted me to have dinner with his friend before coming to his spot."

"Dinner at midnight?" Malachi asks.

"There's a private restaurant in West Adams that does these super-bougie tasting menus all through the night—there's always lots of people there after clubs start winding down. Anyway, I get to the restaurant and sit with his super-tall, bald friend. It was Chris. We talk and it's normal at first, but then he starts getting touchy. I tell him to cool off and he freaks out, talking crazy about how he knows so-and-so and I should watch my mouth, yada-yada. Classic misogynistic man shit."

"Damn, they never age out of that, huh?" Lacy comments.

"Then what happened?" I ask, steering us back on track rather than down the classic Men-Are-Garbage rabbit hole that these two (rightfully) love to indulge.

"I got up and left, obviously," Camesha says proudly. "I don't play those games. Light-skinned dudes have some next-level nerve."

"And he's been dating my mom all this time. . . ." Marley holds her mouth to prevent herself from gagging.

"He has no business being up there right now," Camesha continues. "When he was wasted, he was bragging about how he could pay me to do anything, because he and Vic struck some deal where Becker Real Estate would sell him land for the school expansion at an inflated price but let him skim some of the money. They were all buddy-buddy after that."

"I bet that's his whole thing," Lacy adds. "He runs these charter schools and gets all this public funding from the county, but takes a personal cut under the table."

"When I called Vic to tell him that Chris was mad disrespectful, I made him promise that he'd never work with him again if he wanted to keep seeing me. Vic said that he'd call off the school deal immediately."

"Camesha, I'm sorry this guy creeped on you," I say. "But I don't get why you didn't just tell us the truth in the first place."

"Well, because before I took off, I threatened to tell a journalist that Bayrex Charter leadership tried to get handsy with an eighteen-year-old alum." She shrugs. "Let's just say that I got my reparations from him for making me feel unsafe."

So that's where that last chunk of money for her house fund came from. No wonder she didn't want to tell us right away; she can rightfully call it reparations, but others might call it blackmail. Who am I to judge?

Marley clears her throat and pulls us back on track. "So, let's get this straight. The night that man died, he had just called off a major deal with a Chris 'Corruption' Staples. . . ."

"And the DWG had dirt on Staples that he was stealing money *and* that he was creepy with Camesha," I complete her thought.

"Sounds like Staples had one hell of a motive," Malachi says, dismayed.

We all stand quietly and tune back into Staples's speech. He hits all the buzzwords: resilience, #KnowJusticeKnowPeace, empowerment. But none of that's real to him. The blood rushing in my ears makes his voice sound distant and distorted, like he's preaching from underwater.

"We have to warn our mom," Lou says at last. He and Marley whip out their phones.

"There are too many people here, I don't have any service," Marley whimpers. I look around and see how the protest has grown—I can't see where the crowd begins or ends. There must be at least 250 people in attendance.

We start weaving through the crowd, dodging amped-up protesters holding signs and fists proudly in the air. Every age group is out here, from little kids in baby Jordans and chanclas to elders with kente cloths and peach seeds around their necks. There are people communicating in Spanish, Tagalog, Patois, and Amharic. When Kofa Park turns out, goddamn are we beautiful.

"There she is!" Marley points at a silver afro poof that no doubt belongs to her mother. Marley holds her arms out wide and mows through the crowd, paving the way for Lou to follow closely behind, skillfully dodging strangers. Ms. Allen stands on the edge of the crowd next to the area sectioned off with blue tape for attendees with special needs.

Once we reach her, we see that she's talking to Lupe, who looks upset.

"Zeke," I assume. "Should we give them a minute?"

"We don't have a minute to waste," Lou says, pressing forward.

We follow his lead and reach the mothers as Lupe asks Ms. Allen, "Are you sure? Because Ms. Amelia said—"

"Well, I'm not a housing expert, but it sounds like Amelia lied. Think it over, then give me a call, okay?" Ms. Allen whips out a sleek, black business card and hands it to Lupe.

From the corner of my eye, I see the DWG's daughter passing out T-shirts that read "Community Revitalization, Now!" written in African-influenced colors.

"Oh, no she is not," I say in sheer disbelief. Everyone follows my gaze and sees Amelia chatting at a group of people around our age.

"This bitch . . ." Lupe takes off faster than any of us can blink. We run after her, but there's a slight downhill, so Lupe's wheels have the advantage. "How dare you show your face here today. Are these T-shirts a joke? Community revitalization for *who*?"

A few heads turn our way as Lupe slams to a halt right at Amelia's feet. "I'm sorry, do I know you?" she asks, her voice polite, yet bored.

"I live in the building near the park."

Amelia's eyes widen, then narrow. She looks Lupe up and down, then leans over. "Why does it matter? Rent is due August first, and you can't pay. I'm afraid you'll be gone soon anyway." She rests her elbows on the armrests of Lupe's chair and whispers, "Oh, and I heard the news the other night. Great job raising that young gangbanger of yours. Zeke, is it, right?"

And this is when, as Auntie predicted it might, shit hits the fan.

Lupe snatches that white lady's hair so quick like it's her *job*. More heads turn, and everything escalates fast. People start yelling. The kids who've been watching this whole exchange grab the attention of the newscaster and tell her about Zeke's violent arrest. A chant demanding safe housing and community control begins. I grab Malachi's hand so that we don't get separated while Marley ushers Lou to the side.

Camesha and Lacy trail behind us as we dive out of the circle forming around Lupe.

"Where did Mom go?" Marley whips around in place several times to no luck.

Lou steps onto the bus-stop bench to get a better view. "She's heading that way with Staples."

The protest has grown too big, and the energy is too amped up for us to move effectively as a group. "We need to split up," Malachi declares. He lets go of my arm. "You go with Marley and Lou; I'll go with my sister and Camesha." I try to disagree, but he stops me. "You and I are the ones who started this whole thing. We have to be the ones to end it." He kisses my forehead, then slips away with the girls through an opening in the crowd.

"You heard him!" Marley shouts as she grabs my hand. We take off running with Lou by her side. On the speaker, Auntie's voice leads a chant: *"Tenants united, will never be divided!"* We sprint in the direction of where Lou saw his mom with Staples, but don't see her anywhere. We pause for a minute to catch our breath and strategize. I let my body hang over itself and hold on to my knees for support.

Across the crowd, I catch a glimpse of Jamal walking with his brother. He looks cute today in his school's football warm-up shirt and cuffed jeans. An airplane flies overhead and I can't help but laugh remembering how he thought that the plane was some big clue back at Colony Cantina. That and the barking dog, and the . . . space car.

The space car.

I whip around to the fake twins. "Remember when we interviewed Jamal and Jabron at Colony Cantina? What was their description of the person they saw in the alley? The one waiting in the fancy car?"

"Tall and bald," Lou says without skipping a beat.

That's what I thought. My palms start to sweat like crazy. "If Jamal was calling the Tesla a 'space car,' and if he spotted a tall, bald guy driving it . . ."

"It was Staples!" Marley screams. "They saw Staples at the crime scene!"

"But why would he stick around after Vic was already dead?" Lou asks. "Do you think he was waiting for something?"

No.

I think he was waiting for *someone*.

THIRTY—FIVE

"I don't feel well. I'm sorry, but I—" Lou forces his earphones deeper into his head, but even I know that it's pointless: there are people screaming from megaphones in every direction with protest songs, African drums, and car horns on top of it all. "This is overwhelming." He winces.

Lou's hands tremble as he shuts his eyes and starts humming to himself. His breathing grows more and more erratic.

The phantom pain of my own panic attack the other night resurges in my chest as I watch him start to unravel. It's not like we're on great terms, but the look on his face . . . Zeke wouldn't want me to leave him hanging. I sigh, forcing myself to look beyond my own tunnel vision and turn to Lou. "We have to get you out of here."

"We can't split up again," Marley pleads. "We're never going to find each other."

She has a point, but when I look over at Lou and see that his eyes are clenched shut with so much strain that it looks like his soul is being sucked out of his body by a Dementor, I stand my ground.

"Marley, you find your mom while Lou and I go somewhere

quiet. I've met your mom a few times, but her daughter's much more likely to pick her out of a crowd than I am."

Marley frowns because she knows that I'm right. She cups her hands around her mouth to speak to Lou, loudly enough that he can hear her through the earphones. "Breathe. You did great today. I love you."

I wish her luck, and then she's gone.

Disagreements aside, Lou and I haven't necessarily bonded independent of the group. I try to shake off the slight discomfort that this is our first time alone together. His breathing is unsteady. I copy Marley and cup my mouth. *"Follow me."*

I can see from the veins twitching in his neck that it takes a Herculean effort to pull his eyes open, but he does it anyway.

We need to get somewhere inside that's quiet, preferably with air-conditioning. All of the nearby businesses are packed with people on their way to or from the protest, except one: right on the other side of the underpass, Colony Cantina sits completely empty.

—

I try the front door of the restaurant, but it's locked. A handwritten sign hangs behind the glass: *Closed in solidarity with the #Rooted protest.* Feels a bit ironic to me.

"The back door," Lou murmurs. "Zeke said that Lance and Troy always forget to lock the door where the kitchen staff comes in and out."

We circle around back and sure enough, it opens. Lou immediately shuts off the lights and sinks to the ground. He brings his knees into his chest and rocks steadily. The air-conditioning makes me shiver and I realize how much I've been sweating. I take a seat opposite of him and savor the silence. The pounding in my head slows to a dull throb.

I try not to look at Lou to give him some privacy, but there's not much else here to distract myself. In the dark, windowless room, I can only make out the edges and shadows of the cooking equipment around us. I can tell, though, that while Lance and Troy clearly invested in renovating the front of the restaurant for themselves, their cheap asses didn't bother to make the back area where their employees work anything nicer than the bare minimum needed to pass a health inspection. I pick at a chipped piece of paint on the wall to my side and a giant chunk falls right off.

"Rhea?" Lou asks, his head still bowed, facing the floor.

"Sorry. I was playing with this thing and—" I don't know why I'm explaining myself. "It's nothing. I'll be quiet."

"Can you do me a favor?" he asks in a strained voice.

"Sure." I try not to sound as apprehensive as I feel.

"At home, I have a weighted blanket that helps calm me down, but I can't seem to level out right now. I don't want to make you uncomfortable, but can you, like . . ." He pauses to catch his breath. ". . . hug me?"

We aren't exactly friends, so I don't think a touch from me would be particularly comforting. "You sure about that?"

"Some pressure would be nice. It helps me from disconnecting." He sounds just as unenthused as I am. But he also sounds desperate.

I set aside my frustration with him and ignore the twinge of awkwardness as I move closer to wrap my arms around him. "Like this?"

"Tighter."

I squeeze more.

"Sorry, but tighter."

I reposition my hands so that I'm grabbing my own wrists, pulling as hard as I can.

"There," Lou says, his voice finally sounding a bit less strained. We sit like this for several minutes until Lou releases a genuine exhale of relief. "Thank you." He unravels from the little ball that he's been tucked into and releases my grip.

"Yeah, no problem." My arms feel like noodles after letting go of the pressure. "Look, I'm sorry about yesterday."

"We were all under a lot of pressure. Still are."

"I should've listened to what you had to say, though," I admit.

"Obviously."

Damn. Well, that's one way to accept an apology.

"But you did have a point," he continues. "We shouldn't give up on stopping the evictions. This protest might help, but I have my own reservations." He looks across the grimy kitchen and frowns.

"Ah, a fellow cynic," I say.

"Not all of us are made of sunshine." His smirk tugs at the corner of his mouth, revealing a deep dimple. "I didn't mean what I said before. I know that you care about all of us, and I know that you love Zeke." He pauses to buff out a scratch on his boot. "But I love him too."

I think about how hard today must have been for him— being trapped in a chaotic crowd of people with no personal space was probably his worst nightmare, but he did it anyway. He did it for Zeke.

"I know you do, Lou." Ever since losing Dante, I've always been afraid that something, or someone, would tear the rest of us apart. But even more than that, there's this fear that

Zeke, Malachi, and I would simply meet new friends, new lovers, and drift apart. It's hard to look at Lou, and the hazy-warm way that he and Zeke look at each other, and not feel a tiny, selfish pang that this person might grow with Zeke in ways that challenge our friendship. It's intimidating, especially when we disagree, but I remind myself it's not lethal. There's enough room for us both.

"I've never seen Zeke's goofy ass so happy," I say to Lou. And I mean it. His eyes brighten as he casts me one of those subtle, crooked grins that Zeke adores, and it's settled: truce.

I pick at a dried stain on the floor. "You know, I was really pissed that Marley liked this restaurant so much."

"Yeah, you weren't good at hiding it," he says with a laugh. "She was so embarrassed. It took her a while to rebalance."

"Rebalance?"

"Marley is one of those people who really wants to do no harm. But the way our world is set up, that's impossible. There are all these things happening—messy things like gentrification—and she feels like she's forced to be complicit in the suffering. And I feel it too. Especially given that now Zeke's . . ." He trails off.

"He'll be okay."

Lou nods and continues. "Like, Marley's fifteen, I'm sixteen—we didn't get to choose where we moved. Even if we're not as bad as the owners of this place, complicity still doesn't feel good, you know?"

"I don't want you guys to feel guilty—"

"It's okay to sit with the guilt for a minute. But Marley's all about getting to a balanced place of gratitude for what and who is still here. Like you should've *seen* how hype she was to help Lupe with the protest signs last night." I should've known that the hint of glitter on my sign wasn't Lupe's doing. "Anyway," Lou continues, "Marley said that she likes this tacky place, but what she meant was that we like being here with you guys."

We look at each other and smile, but our Hallmark moment is cut short by the sound of keys jangling on the other side of the wall. Sloppy, uneven footsteps stumble around until someone slams against what sounds like a door. They press it open and moan theatrically as they plop onto what must be a rolling chair. Little wheels trace the floor while Lou and I crawl closer to the door that connects the kitchen to the rest of the building.

What's going on? I mouth to Lou. He shrugs right as Snoop Dogg's music suddenly starts blaring from the speakers everywhere.

"WOOOOOOOHOOOOOOOOOOO!!!"

Of course.

It's Troy.

"From the depths of the sea, back to the—the block, yo." Troy fumbles as he attempts to rap alongside the music, slurring every word and stopping to gulp air between lines.

"He's higher than LeBron James's former hairline," Lou deadpans. I hold my hands over my mouth to capture a laugh.

"Neither of our phones is working, but this guy probably has Verizon or some fancy shit. Maybe he'll let us use his phone to call Marley?" I suggest.

"Not a bad idea." We get up and open the kitchen door. There's a little in-between space separating us from the dining area. The music flows from a room to our left that can't be seen from the public-facing front. "Must be an office."

Who knew this place was so big? We knock first, but Troy

can't hear us over Snoop Dogg's izzles and drizzles. I nudge the door open. "Hellooo?"

"WHOA." I feel Lou tense up next to me as we take in the sight of piles upon piles of cash strewn across the room. There's money on the desk, money on the floor—easily over a hundred grand laid out alone, not to mention however much is stacked up in the open safe embedded in the side wall.

"What the fuck?" Troy barks. He wobbles up from the office chair. "Who let you in here?" His neck rolls like a bobblehead as he speaks.

"I am so sorry, we didn't mean to interrupt," I say, backing out of the room.

"Where the fuck d-d-do you think you're going now?" Troy jumps onto the chair knees first and whizzes toward us, slamming the door. "You came all this way just to leave like that?" I can smell the booze on his breath. His eyes are bright red, unnervingly accentuating the amber in his beard. I've never seen anyone so crossfaded.

"You two look *so* surprised. Guess you didn't think I was a baller, huh? Living this *gangsta* life? This *thug* life?" Troy raises his hands in a ridiculous attempt at a gang sign, but he can't seem to coordinate his body enough to actually bring his fingers together. Normally, this would be sort of funny, but there's a level of contempt in his voice that makes me nervous.

"Everybody around here was soooo quick to write me off, but guess what?" Troy grabs a stack of dollar bills and throws it in the air. "I'm the realest *nigg-a* out here."

His unironic use of the N-word makes me flinch. I inch closer to the exit, but he slams his foot against the door. "Tsk, tsk, tsk." His face breaks into a sleazy smile though his eyes seem distant. He must be blacked out right now. "Don't you want to know how I got all this money? How I'm rolling in more cash than you've ever seen?"

Lou glances at me, then at the stapler on Troy's desk. If he won't let us out, we might have to make him. My stomach turns at the thought.

Troy burps. "I did a little deal with a real estate developer. You know him, right? The guy who died? It's been all over the news?" He snorts. "Well, we met up late night at the park basketball courts and I took out a 'loan' from him for 'the restaurant.' Then, when he least expected it . . ." He raises his hands in the shape of a gun. *"Pow pow pow!"* Troy laughs maniacally as we back away, our backs pressed firmly against the wall. "I took his phone and keys to make it look like a robbery. When you get a cash loan from a single guy, it's almost too easy to clock him and clear your debt. Two can keep a secret if one of them is dead, am I right?"

Troy sits properly in the chair and spins so that his back is pressed against the door. His #BlackLivesMatter shirt faces us head-on.

"Thank god the cops are lazy enough to blame that new gang. God bless the USA."

If Troy needed SOSI to take the fall for killing Vic, that must mean that he's the one behind the threats I've been getting. But then again, if he's the one who didn't want me to find out the truth, why would he spill everything now? I take my chances and ask. "Are you SemiCharmed87? From Zeggit?"

He looks at me, dumbfounded, like I'm speaking Latin. "Am I Demi Alarmed who?"

"You've been texting me, right?"

"Hah. You wish. You're a little young for my taste." He

laughs and coughs again, harder this time. He shuts his eyes, but they don't reopen.

I freeze. A minute passes, and Troy begins to snore. He's out cold.

What did this dude take?

Lou nudges Troy's chair blocking the door to roll him over an inch. We brace for Troy's reaction, but his neck just bobs to the opposite shoulder. Guttural gurgles rise and fall from his throat.

Lou counts off to three on his fingers before fully pushing Troy away from the exit. Once we get the door open, we almost make a run for it, but I hesitate.

Troy is fast asleep.

And the safe in the corner is wide open.

Lou glares at me like I'm crazy, but I remember Diego's stitches. I'm not letting Troy's bullshit keep Zeke in jail for even a second longer. Plus, there's no telling that the cops will believe us anyway when we go to them with the truth. I run to the safe and grab as many stacks of cash as I can carry. I clear out a good chunk of money and creep back toward the door.

And then I hear it: the unmistakable sound of a gun's bullets being clicked into place.

"Whoa-ho-ho! Looks like somebody's tryna *come up*, huh?" Troy laughs menacingly as he waves the gun in our direction.

I forget how to breathe and focus on Lou to remember, only to discover that he's frozen too: not a single breath in, not one breath out. Suddenly, though, the sight of the gun sparks a thought. "Wait, Troy . . ." The place where he shot Vic is really far from where Vic's body was found. Like, at least a mile, far. "If you shot Vic at the park, how'd you get his body all the way to El Pollo Loco?"

"Eh, I blacked out at that point, but I must've carried him. Ya boy's been hitting the gym. We got a double Gun Show goin' on here!" He flexes, slapping the limp muscle of his freckled bicep. I recoil, and he laughs. "Let's just put the money down, though, okay?"

"Zeke is in jail for what *you* did," I say firmly. "He needs this money to meet bail."

Troy's voice comes out in a low slur. "Don't make me ask twice, kid."

Reluctantly, I let the cash trickle to the floor like heavy rain.

Troy wipes his nose with the gun. "Good girl."

My throat clenches, unsure of our next move. But then Lou does something so out of character—he lightly brushes my hand. The signal is clear: we break for the door.

The horrific noise is so abrupt that for a moment, I can't tell which came first: the shot or the deafening ringing in my ears. My chest pounds as Lou and I stare at the door in disbelief. The bullet ripped straight through, scattering little splinters of wood everywhere.

Troy hollers. "Didn't think I'd do it, huh?!"

His eyes widen, and all I see is the red.

Maybe it's residual trauma or maybe it's true intuition, but I've never been able to imagine myself growing old. I've had dreams where it was me who died at that track meet, not Dante. I've been forgotten by my mother to the point that when she comes home, she's so shocked to see me standing there that she looks at me as though I am a ghost. I wonder if these have been signs all along that I too would die young.

"Don't worry, I only have to shoot one of you to keep the other quiet." Troy cackles and waves the gun back and forth between us. His hand shakes from the drugs, not nerves. An Ice Cube hit bobs in the background as Troy nods to the beat. He grabs his chest. "This is my anthem." But before he can start laughing again, he drops to the floor. I think it's an act . . . until his eyes roll back and his head bucks.

He flinches two, three times, then falls still.

He's not shaking anymore.

Lou and I make a run for it, dodging the stiff frame of Troy as he lies contorted on the floor, surrounded by dollar bills.

We bust through the front door, and I gasp for air, shocked to still be breathing. We get to the bottom of the entryway stairs when Lou freezes. I whip around, worried that Troy woke up and is right behind us.

Lou trembles, frozen to the railing. "What if he dies?"

"The ambulance can handle it," I say curtly.

"Shouldn't we try CPR? Shouldn't we do *something*?"

"Why the hell would we try to save the man who just threatened to shoot us?"

"So, we leave him for dead? Just like how they do us?"

I try to bargain with him, but he takes off running back into the restaurant. I follow, begging him to stay back. "But he has a gun!"

"What damage can he do if he's having a medical emergency?" He breaks ahead up the stairs. "We need to help him."

I guess Marley's vexing sense of compassion runs in the family. "Nigga, if your empathy gets us killed, I swear to god . . ."

We run back in and fling open the door to the office.

But Troy is no longer alone.

I notice the gun in her hand before I take in her face.

"Hello there."

THIRTY-SIX

Vic's daughter smiles at us over her shoulder as she calmly places stack after stack of money into a duffel bag like she's a 1950s housewife and we just walked in on her baking a cake. She's wearing one of the "Community Revitalization Now!" T-shirts from earlier over a pair of tight jeans, cropped at the ankle above Steve Madden boots. The gun in her hand reflects the light from the fluorescent ceiling bulbs.

She points at us, making the tiny gold chain around her wrist jingle. "So, you two were the voices that I heard?"

Troy's body lies cold, splayed out on the floor between us. "Don't worry," Amelia says when she catches me staring. "He brought this on himself. He'll take any pill he can get his hands on, especially when it comes from a pretty woman." Amelia winks, and my skin crawls.

We attempt to back out of the door, but Amelia shakes her head condescendingly. "Don't look so upset. I did this for my safety, and for yours too."

"What do you mean?" I ask, my voice small.

"Troy thought that he was some mastermind, but he was just an idiot. He had this big dream of being some white gangster and 'running the neighborhood,' but what he didn't realize is that gangsters don't run neighborhoods—" She grabs a bundle of bills and grins. "The asset holders do."

I examine the gunshot damage on the door and shudder at the thought of what a bullet would do to a body. A Dr. Dre song begins overhead and Amelia snatches Troy's phone from the desk to shut off the music.

"Like I was saying." She clears her throat. "The people who own the real estate, who lend the money, who know the other developers and the politicians—*those* are the people who run a neighborhood." She takes on the tone of a run-of-the-mill TED Talk speaker, reciting a rehearsed speech. "Kofa Park is flipping faster than that new high-speed train line being constructed down the street. Someone needs to step up and steer the ship. And I just so happen to be the right woman for the job. In six years, this area will be the new Williamsburg, Brooklyn." A hipster bubble of no affordable housing that displaced most of the people of color that made the area cool in the first place? No thank you.

"Fuck that," I hiss, trembling with rage.

"Look, we all benefit from redevelopment. Under my vision, I'm going to push out the liquor banks, smoke shops, and fast food, and turn those into businesses that better the neighborhood. I'll get public grants to build a dog park, yoga studios—if we're lucky, we can even get a Whole Foods to move in for the health of the community."

I scoff. "Your 'vision' isn't for the health of the community here right now—it's for whatever richer, whiter people these initiatives will bring in to displace everyone's who's been here for decades."

"We won't scrub *all* of the 'color' away." She draws air

quotes around the word. "The people moving into this neighborhood like the idea of diversity—"

"The *idea*?" Right, yeah, because that's all we are: an *idea* for white people.

"Look, kid. Real estate is real estate. People with money want to live in the heart of the city, but they want to live in places that embody a predictable, upper-middle-class standard of living."

She doesn't get it. There are different (and better) ways to live—ways that are based in community support, not the cold, corporate sameness and isolation of existence that people in segregated suburbs find so comforting. She doesn't get that what we have here—the interconnectedness, the intimacy, the life-affirming safety of walking down the street and knowing that when people see my black skin, they think "my neighbor"/"my cousin"/"my friend" and not "criminal"—is something much more sacred than anything that a franchise SoulCycle studio could bring.

"I don't see what all of this has to do with Troy," Lou says.

Good point. I glance at the wannabe thug on the floor between us, then back at Amelia. "Troy kills your father and now you're here for revenge and . . . this?" I motion at the little piles of bills scattered around the room.

"More like tying up loose ends. Troy and I were working together. We connected through Becker Real Estate. My dad owned this building, and for whatever reason, he met this idiot and decided to invest in his tacky restaurant. You know how men are—always giving each other chances, even when they're completely unqualified."

She's not wrong there.

"I've been wanting to kick my dad out of the business for a while. Troy watched one too many mafia movies as a kid, so after we met, he was more than happy to help me blackmail my father. His business partners wouldn't have been happy to know that he'd been spending all his money creeping on one of his eighteen-year-old tenants."

Camesha. While I didn't love the idea of her spending time with Vic, Amelia and Troy attempting to use her choices as leverage to exploit Vic is what's really sickening.

"The plan was for Troy to confront my dad and get a ton of cash out of him. Then I'd use the missing money as an excuse to cut him out of the business and take over for good. It was supposed to be a win-win for me and Troy."

This woman must really believe that we pose absolutely no threat to her to be so casually sharing this. You've gotta have an extremely inflated ego and demented sense of white privilege to move through the world like this. It's like the college admissions scandal from a while ago when all those famous white-lady celebrities bribed universities, blatantly committing sloppy fraud over *email* without a care in the world. I guess if I was a pretty white woman with money and connections, I wouldn't worry about getting caught either.

"But if you were just going to blackmail Vic, why'd he have to die?" Lou asks.

Amelia rolls her eyes. "Obviously that was not part of the plan. That was all Trigger-Happy Troy's fault. Luckily, I know how to fix a narrative in my favor."

Amelia raises the gun at us with one hand and uses the other to grab a spray can from the duffel bag. She keeps her eyes on us as she draws a sloppy SOSI tag on the wall.

The pieces fall together. When I mentioned the text threats

to Troy, he was clueless. If Amelia was pissed at him for messing up their plan and desperate to gain control of Vic's company, that must mean she's the one behind the messages. She could use her fancy tech people at the company to figure out my Zeggit username, and one call to her dad's BFF business partner, Staples, and she'd have access to my phone number, address, my name through Bayrex's records. . . . I suck my teeth, overwhelmed by the audacity of everyone involved in this mess.

Amelia tosses the spray can back in the duffel bag. "Now that I've handled Troy, it's time to handle this protest down the street." Amelia waves goodbye as she makes her way out into the main dining hall.

"Handle?" Against my best judgment, I follow her, eyes fixed on the gun. The gears in my head turn and lock. "You're going to shoot someone?!"

Amelia's laugh is wild and free. "I won't have to." She shifts her voice down an octave, mimicking a newscaster. "'Shots fired at riot attended by local gang members. Meanwhile, a local business is robbed, its owner caught in the crossfire.'" She shoots the glass window, shattering it to pieces. Lou winces by my side, slamming his hands against his ears. "That's all the headline I need. The cops will eat it up."

Over her shoulder, I can see the booth where we all sat and complained about the soggy Sriracha tacos. My mind goes back even further, bringing up a memory of the fried fish restaurant that was here before Colony Cantina moved into the neighborhood. I used to love that place. . . .

Lou's voice yanks me back to the current moment. "If you're tryna get rich off of the development around here, isn't SOSI bad for you?" he challenges Amelia.

"Quite the opposite. The only reason why Troy shooting Vic didn't totally screw things up is because SOSI's new gang presence has been perfect to convince even more investors to funnel cash into my Community Revitalization plan."

Marley's words from our stunt at the Lenway party flood back to me: *But the fear is real.* My head swims with defeat as the room goes hazy. The very logic that propelled my own plan, now co-opted by the very person I'm trying to keep away.

"None of this will ever work," Lou says, his voice faltering. "We know your plan now, and we'll never let you get away with it."

"Well, if that's how you feel . . ." Amelia smirks as she cocks the gun and nods toward the office where Troy's body lies cold on the floor. "I have alternative options."

A pained gasp chokes out from my throat as Amelia places her hand on the trigger.

A loud bang rips the breath from my chest.

THIRTY—SEVEN

When Nipsey Hussle's voice starts wafting through the air, I black out for a second, assuming that Amelia fired the gun and I am the one who died.

But then I see her pink face shrivel up into a contorted snarl.

The door from the kitchen has been kicked wide open. An artificially bright light shines on Amelia, accentuating the clumps in her black mascara.

"Oof, girl. That's *real* cute. Did you practice this speech in the shower?" Camesha holds her phone up to Amelia's washed-out face. Her shimmery case twinkles as she performs some legit cinematography, circling Amelia like a shark.

Lacy emerges at Camesha's side, holding Troy's phone. She cranks up the volume of the music so loud that I can feel the sound vibrating through the floor.

"Get the fuck out of here!" Amelia shrieks, pointing the gun at Camesha's forehead, tastefully adorned with elegant swoops of baby hair styled like a natural crown.

"Bravo!" Lacy laughs wildly as Camesha zooms in on the gun. "You're like a white Viola Davis, you know that? Stellar performance. One hundred percent certified fresh."

"Give me that!" Amelia snarls as she lunges for the phone.

"That won't do shit." Camesha grins. "Ever heard of LykLuv LIVE? Smile to the world, bitch. We got over four hundred thousand of BF4U's most loyal followers and their friends tuned in. We got your lil evil villain monologue on camera, baby."

Amelia lets out a feral scream and takes off running through the front door of the restaurant. The sirens are at a full-blown howl now.

She's gone.

But she won't get far.

Lou folds into himself, melting onto the cool tile floor. Camesha pivots the camera back on herself. She brushes her immaculately groomed eyebrows into shape.

"Aight, y'all. We gotta go sort this shit out. But Imma leave you with this: *white girls really be doin' too much sometimes*. This is why y'all gotta invite all ya friends to follow Black Feminism 4 U & Me and educate themselves so they don't end up like Gentrification Becky over here, ya feel me?" She blows a kiss to her followers, but I stop her before she can sign off.

"Wait!" I scramble over, my legs still shaking from the residual terror. "How much of Amelia's monologue did you catch?"

"Just the end," Camesha says. "We came in after we heard her shoot the window."

That's what I thought. My stomach tightens, begging me to let it go, but I can't. "Keep recording."

Camesha raises her eyebrows and flips the camera on me. "It's all you, baby girl."

I gulp and stare straight into the camera.

"SOSI is fake."

"Rhea," Lou whisper-shouts from the floor. "It's over now. They'll catch her. You don't have to do this."

"They may catch Amelia, but that won't stop the next Amelia, or the next Vic, or the next Troy from filling her place." I pull the strings on my hoodie tight to keep myself from falling apart. "Amelia and her network were always one step ahead of us with SOSI. They *been* co-opting the gang for their own benefit—getting rich while blaming us for their bullshit, all while calling us thugs and pretending that we don't deserve to shape the future of our own hood." I move my hands into my pocket to form a fist. "It's time to end this shit."

I take a deep breath in and face the camera.

"Aight, I know how it looks—bad—but I can tell you for damn sure we didn't do it. . . ."

THIRTY—EIGHT

When I finish Camesha's livestream, I practically fall against the counter, collapsing under the weight of the afternoon.

"I'm sure Auntie will appreciate the #Rooted plug once she sees the video," Lacy says. She takes a seat on the floor so that the first responders that just arrived can examine her.

I hope she's right.

"Damn, I got twenty thousand new followers already," Camesha muses at her phone. She gives Lacy a high five before bringing me a cold glass of water. "Ain't social media a trip?"

I take a sip and stumble behind the cash register. I grab one of the Colony Cantina caps from the shelf and press it on, even though it's too small to fully contain my hair. I sink onto the floor and pull out my phone to open Quipp. Someone has already retweeted Camesha's livestream with the hashtags #FireFireGentrifier and #FreeZeke.

. . . And #SosiScam, too.

I go to settings and delete my account.

It's a fucking trip indeed.

Everyone around me is celebrating. Marley and Malachi ran straight over when they saw Camesha's livestream.

They're hyped up, riding the adrenaline of it all. But when I finally stand after the cop takes my official statement, I'm dizzy.

"Whoa there," Marley says, swooping an arm around my rib cage. "You don't look good, girl."

"I'm just tired," I say. *Understatement of the year.* I've never been so exhausted in my life.

Marley nods with mom-like understanding. "Want me to walk you home?"

Part of me wants the company, but the other part wants to enjoy the blissful relief of not talking to anyone for a few hours. Today, this week, this *month*, has been a lot—I'm overdue for a mental recharge. "Thanks, but I need a minute by myself."

Malachi walks over, rubbing the back of his neck. "You sure I can't change your mind about that?"

His smile is infectious. I can't resist grinning back. "You probably could, but I'd rather you didn't." Marley lets go of me and steps aside to make room for Malachi. "Give me a couple hours to nap. I'll meet up with y'all later."

Skimming my cheekbone, his fingers are careful as he plants a soft kiss on my temple. "I won't push then."

I kiss him back, gently, and head out.

"Text me when you get home, okay?" Marley shouts at my back.

I wave her off and walk home, the solidarity chants from the protest still echoing in my ears.

—

I enter my house, half hoping that my mom heard the news and will be there to greet me. But it's empty, as always. One afternoon can't change everything.

My head is pounding by the time it hits my pillow, but before I knock out, I send one last message to the person who's been on my mind every second, every minute, every day of this crazy month.

> I know u won't get this until later but just know that I love u.

See you soon, Zeke.

THIRTY-NINE

Whoever thought of the phrase "tossing and turning" to describe insomnia was really on some true poetry shit. I check to see how long my mind's been racing instead of welcoming the rest that I desperately need. My clock stares back at me: Too long, sis.

This afternoon marks the end of an era: SOSI is dead. Fin. Case closed. Yet I can't sleep because I'm waiting. Waiting for the reality that everything is over to hit at last.

For the past few weeks, I had been imagining the scene when we solve the murder, when we clear Zeke's name, as this grand moment of relief. Like the shock of an icy mountain waterfall cascading over me, followed by the relaxing glow of a hot shower. I'd feel calm. Accomplished. Grounded. But now that I'm here, I feel none of that. It all just feels as it did before: unsatisfying.

A few days ago, Malachi said to me, *People can surprise you.* His words have proven true a thousand times over this summer, both in good ways and in bad. But there were no surprises this afternoon. Sure, I might not have seen it coming, but looking back, it's so clear that Troy and Amelia would be behind all the violence. Gentrification triggered the need to start SOSI to save Zeke, and Troy and Amelia are practically the patron saints of unabashed greed and megalomania. At the end of the day, everything feels so . . . neat. Too neat.

I pull out my phone and reread the texts from Unknown/ SemiCharmed87. Troy said he didn't send the messages, and miraculously, I believe him. When I confronted him, he was ready—giddy, even—to admit all that he had done. Then there's Amelia. She's evil, for sure, but it feels like something is missing from her story.

I recite the messages out loud, first in Troy's voice, then Amelia's. No matter how hard I try to distort the tone, it just doesn't fit. I can feel the anxiety, the fear, radiating in each line of these messages begging me to let SOSI take the fall. But Troy was proud of shooting Vic, and Amelia never considered that she'd ever get caught. These texts, though—there's a panicked, almost-pathetic level of urgency here. It just doesn't make sense. . . .

Unless someone else sent the texts. Someone afraid, someone desperate to cover their tracks. . . .

Because they're the one who *really* killed Vic.

I bolt up from bed and start to pace. It would all make sense now—how Vic's body ended up so far from where Troy shot him, Amelia's calm confidence that SOSI would take the fall for her crimes. The amount of pit sweat that I produce in the nanoseconds it takes for my brain to connect the dots is a world record. This is it. This is huge.

Two. Different. Assailants. Troy—aka the idiot who *thought* he killed Vic—and then whoever else finished the job.

Whoever was fucking with me is still out there.

I look at the suspect list with fresh eyes. Who's been around this whole time? Who's creepy *and* tech-savvy? The person must be connected to Vic and know enough about SOSI to harass me specifically.

Shit. That could still be several people. I tap my phone against my forehead, brainstorming what else I know about Unknown/SemiCharmed87. The threats started on Zeggit before they moved to text. Who could have known that I was behind ConcernedCitizn? A number is easy enough to get, but my username? I created it as a ghost account just for SOSI stuff. So, whoever knew must've had access to my phone at some point to see my log-ins. Except that's impossible because I always have my phone on me. I never lose it. Except when . . .

My lungs contract with a gasp so sharp that it hurts.

Mental screenshots of the threats that I've received flash across my mind with a blinding glare. The Zeggit DMs from SemiCharmed87. The texts from Unknown. All the curses, all the attempts at intimidation.

I don't know how. I don't why. But I know who really killed Vic.

I have to tell everyone.

I open my phone to text the group chat, but there's a knock on the door. "Beat me to it," I half laugh, half sigh under my breath. I forgot to check in with Marley that I made it home safe, so that's probably her. I toss my phone on the bed and rehearse the big reveal in my head.

I fling open the door, beaming. "Guess. What!"

Time stops. My heart rate accelerates, the force of my pulse wreaking havoc through my contracting muscles.

No. No. No.

The spit in my mouth dries as the words choke out of my mouth as the real killer stands before me. "H-hey."

Lance stands shakily just beyond the threshold. He's

wearing a Supreme hat paired with a canvas tote bag urging us all to "Support Public Radio!" He waves at me, which is weird, because we're standing two feet apart. I wave back because I don't know what to do, or why he's here, or whether he's aware that I know he's guilty. All I know is that this man is dangerous.

Over Lance's shoulder, I see one of those undignified, derpy electric scooters that litter the sidewalks of millennial-dominated neighborhoods. I imagine Lance's ridiculously tall stature hunched over the embarrassing contraption, squealing in delight as he zips through the streets, noise-canceling Air Pods in place, marveling about how cool and brave and cutting-edge he is to live here.

Then I imagine the same scene, drenched in blood.

"Can I come in?" he asks, voice urgent.

I stare at the floor. "I don't think that's a good idea." I try to play ignorant, keep it light. "Shouldn't you be—"

And then it happens.

I stumble backward, heels digging into the carpet to prevent myself from falling. My sense of control disappears as Lance shoves me through the doorway, forcing himself indoors.

"Wh-why are you here?" My voice keeps itself small while it waits for my brain to piece together what the hell is happening.

"I saw your little SOSI confessional video." He sniffles as he shuts the door behind him.

Shit.

"I told you to stay out of this, Rhea." He clenches his fists so hard that the skin on his knuckles turns from beige to pink to a bloodless white. "I explained that SOSI had to take the fall. I warned you to mind your own business. I tried to avoid this situation altogether."

Shit. Shit. Shit.

"My mom will be home any minute," I lie.

"I've driven by here a lot recently. Her car's never in the driveway during the day, and you're always with your little friends all afternoon." He coughs into his elbow. "I know you're all by yourself."

His harsh words echo. I hate that he's right.

In the dimly lit foyer of my home, we face each other, alone.

I shut my eyes, furious that I couldn't figure him out earlier—couldn't protect myself from whatever's to come. "How'd you find out about me and SOSI?"

"You guys are loud, you know that? And if you hadn't noticed, we never had many customers. I heard everything during your little scheming sessions in that corner booth."

It's humiliating to have believed that we were so in control, that *we* were the ones spying on *them*, when Lance had been spying right back.

"I didn't care at first," Lance continues. "I thought it was kind of funny. Plus, you guys were our only returning customers and I didn't want to scare you away. But then when everything happened with Vic . . ." He swallows his spit, trembling. "I needed the gang to be real."

"You looked through my phone when I forgot it by the counter, didn't you?" If only I had put these pieces together days ago instead of just moments before he showed up.

"I had to figure out how much you knew. Zeggit was one of your recently opened apps. Your phone number is linked to Apple Pay. Later, it was easy enough to get your address from

Zeke's phone when he was spinning the sign, and now . . ."

"Here we are," I say, finishing his sentence.

He takes another step toward me. "Here we are."

I debate whether to dash for my phone in the other room or try to escape past Lance out the front door. I keep up the conversation to distract him, waiting for the right moment to make a move. "If Troy shot Vic, why'd you get involved?"

He grits his teeth. "Troy told me that he was going to meet Vic, but when he came home, he said he shot him. He was *bragging* about it. So, I thought to myself: What kind of person would I be if I left Vic to die? Like, what if he was still alive, bleeding out? Or what if he was dead, but the next day some kids find a body and are traumatized for life?"

"How heroic," I mumble.

If he heard me, he ignores me. "When I got to the park, Vic wasn't there. I drove around until I found him near the entrance, not far from where he met Troy. He was trying to wave down help. I had to convince him that I was nothing like Troy. That I wanted to take him to the hospital."

I knew there was no way that Troy transported Vic's body a mile away to El Pollo Loco while blackout drunk.

"Vic was fine at first," Lance continues. "But then he started yelling. Saying 'Fuck Troy' and that he was going to end our lease and sell Colony Cantina so that someone could build some luxury coworking space there instead."

"Troy made the mess, then you just *had* to clean it up, huh?" White masculinity is one hell of a drug. Men will perform the wildest mental gymnastics to avoid ever seeing anything as their fault.

"Exactly!" Lance doesn't pick up on my sarcasm. "Troy knew that the restaurant was in financial trouble, but he didn't care. He was always going on and on about the restaurant as just 'a means to an end' for him. How he was destined to 'live that baller life.' I knew he was going to get money from Vic, and I knew it meant trouble, but I thought I could convince him to use some of it to help the restaurant. Fucking Trust Fund Kid.

"But me? I put the last of the last of the money my parents gave me into Colony Cantina. I have student loans. I *needed* the restaurant to work. I couldn't let Vic shut us down." The tears that have been building in the corners of his eyes finally fall. "When Vic freaked out, he was already weak from losing so much blood. So, I did what I had to do." He sniffles and uses the back of his free hand to wipe his nose. "I pulled over and smothered him until he stopped breathing. I had an Anti-Gang Community Task Force flyer in my car, so I left it in Vic's pocket to point the cops in the right direction when I dumped his body."

There it is: the full confession.

I have to get the hell out of here.

"Lance, if you let me go, I swear I won't say anything to the cops," I bargain. "Troy's dead, Amelia's arrested. For better or worse, I think you got away with this. You don't need me or SOSI."

Lance sighs. "Troy isn't dead."

Whoa. This catches me off guard. It did not look like that dude was breathing.

"Whatever Amelia slipped him knocked him out, but he's stable in the hospital," Lance says. "He'll wake up soon. And when he does, his parents will hire a lawyer. Even if Troy and Amelia admit to the blackmail, they'll never let Troy confess to shooting Vic."

"But he told me!" I yell. "I know the truth." That should matter, right?

"Your story is just hearsay. So, when Troy's fancy Ivy League attorney starts digging around, they're going to realize that the parking lot where they found Vic is far from the park." Lance is reeeally talking up the abilities of Troy's imaginary lawyer, but I solved this shit without even a high school diploma. Lance's sentences pick up speed. "Troy will explain that I knew about his meeting with Vic. Then they'll discover the restaurant's financial trouble. Then they'll realize I don't have an alibi—" The emotion behind his tears morphs from self-pity to anger. "And that's where you come in, Rhea."

He grits his teeth, shaking his head. "So long as SOSI existed, the cops would blame the gang and ignore me. Their theory that Vic was robbed and murdered by the gang still fits, even if Troy is found guilty of blackmail."

Understanding sinks in. "Because why would LAPD look at the nice white guy when a gang of dangerous Black and brown kids exists, right?"

Lance makes that indignant expression that all white people do when you call them out on their racism. "It's not like that."

"It's *exactly* like that." I give the slinky of a man in front of me a disdainful up-down.

A gurgled cry leaches out from his throat. "I never wanted anyone to get hurt." The guy is on the brink of full sobs, and I have no space to deal with the burden of his white guilt or white grief or whatever white emotion coming my way. When he pauses to fish for a napkin in his bag, I take my chance.

I lunge the full weight of my body at Lance's side that's been guarding the door. He fumbles sideways, and I feel the cool brass of the doorknob graze my palm. I turn, yanking the exit open. If I can just get up quick enough, I can—

The door slams as Lance kicks it shut with startling force, sending shock waves through the wood. I try not to cry as my best shot at a quick escape vanishes.

"Let me *go*." Fury takes over as I scramble to my feet. But the curses boiling on the tip of my tongue evaporate when he reaches into his tote bag and pulls out a butcher knife.

Fifteen years living in South LA—a place that racists have historically over-characterized as violent and disturbed—and I've had not one, but *two* weapons pulled on me in twenty-four hours, all by white people. What a sick joke.

"Over there," Lance barks. He points the long knife at my chest, gesturing me toward the kitchen island. I do as I'm told. "This is the plan: you're going to get on camera and tell everyone that your SOSI confessional video was a lie. You're going to explain that you were scared about your friend, so you said SOSI was fake to free him, but SOSI is real. And you're not going to keep their secrets anymore."

"And my best friend stays locked up?"

"He'll be fine. Zack is a nice kid—"

"*Zeke.* His name is *Zeke.*" This fool can't even remember our names. We're not real to him. "You get away with everything, and me, my friends, and my neighborhood are left worse off?"

"Vic dying benefits you too," Lance says.

"*Hah.* How?"

"Amelia's Community Revitalization Plan is much better."

"Better how? Because a cute white girl is curating it? Because a community of color can't possibly be trusted to direct its own development, right?"

"Enough." He takes a step forward, closing the gap between us so that it's just the length of his arm, the knife, and a single inch of air between us. "It's time to record."

"And what if I say no?"

He hovers the sharp blade above his forearm. "Then I'll cut myself and say that you stabbed me. That when I tried to tell the police that SOSI is real and Zeke really is the killer, you threatened me because you're one of them. It'll be your word versus mine."

He doesn't have to spell it out any clearer: a Black teenager versus a white hipster who owns a new local business and votes blue. He smirks, knowing that he was born with the trump card. I swallow my spit, and nod. Lance starts recording.

"Earlier today, I made a video about SOSI. I am here now to clarify—"

A knock at the door interrupts my monologue. Years and years of barely any visitors, now my house is bumping. Lance holds the knife steady, bringing the hand with his iPhone to his lips to shush me.

There's another knock and then a voice.

"I know you said you wanted to be alone, but I don't want you to be *alone* alone. So, I'm going to sit with my book, and you can pretend I'm not here. But I feel like our relationship has hit the point where I can, and should, just pop by to check on you, because . . . because I love you, Rhea."

I don't hear those three words a lot, and never before from them. My eyes water and I thank the universe for bringing us together.

I love you too, Marley.

Of course, she came for me.

402

Lance's face shape-shifts into a mask of panic. Dude did *not* think this through.

"Aight, stubborn. I'm coming iiiinn!" The knob turns. "Girl, why you leave your door unlocked? We're not in the suburbs."

Marley takes one look at the scene: me backed against the kitchen counter, Lance wielding the knife, and her jaw drops. I worry that she's going to freeze up. Instead, she cranks her arm behind her head like the young starting pitcher on the Dodgers and hurls her phone at full force toward Lance's egg-shaped head. The hard edge of the phone slams into his bobbing Adam's apple.

"Knife!" I shout to Marley. We lock eyes and form a plan without any further words.

While Lance gasps for air like a beached angler fish, I rush forward and knock the baseball cap off his head. Instinctively, his hands shoot up to cover his balding temples. Marley jumps on his back, and they stumble together like drunk Cirque du Soleil performers. She tangles herself around him like a vine, trying to seize the weapon from his hands. "I got him! Call for help!"

My phone's still on my bed, so I glance at Marley's on the floor. As soon as I lunge for it, Lance stomps down, shattering its screen.

Great. *My phone it is.*

Marley's wrestled Lance into a jujitsu neck-grabby move, so when I see that she has the upper hand, I dash toward my room. I'm almost there when a high-pitched yelp pulls my focus back to their struggle.

"I don't want to hurt you, but I will," he spits through gritted teeth. I rush forward, plotting a swift kick to his balls, but I'm too late.

Marley wails as Lance hurls her off his back. My stomach lurches as she lands facedown on the floor. Lance steadies the knife and moves it deliberately toward the small of her back. *"Final warning!"*

SOSI is my fault—Marley can't get hurt because of me and my dumb idea. I catapult my hand to intercept the knife from entering the soft flesh surrounding her spine. She screams my name. I shut my eyes and brace for pain.

Lance hesitates.

"Do it, you fucking coward." I spit on his Converse high-tops. Sweat gathers on his brow as his blue eyes narrow. He hovers the blade centimeters from my skin. At first, I think he's just trying to build suspense, but then a new theory forms.

The blade glints beneath the light, but his wavering makes me wonder . . .

If I'm wrong, this will have been the dumbest thing I've ever done in my life.

I hold my breath and curl my hand up, gripping the blade head on. I wait for sharp pain to slice through my palm.

But the blood never comes.

No way . . .

I let out a full body laugh as Marley turns beneath me. Her eyes dash in horror to my hand squeezing the knife. Lance's face turns a violent shade of pink that makes his splotchy complexion look more like a tongue than skin.

The gang is fake, but the fear is real.

The weapon's "steel" blade is nothing but plastic.

"You done fucked up, dude," I say to Lance as relief floods in. I toss the prop weapon across the room.

"Wait. None of this is my fault," he begs. The venom of his previous threats slips away into pitiful cries for mercy. "I'm also a victim. Vic was trying to push me out too. I was just trying to stop my business from going under. No different than the protest."

"We were fighting for our community. You were trying to save your own ass," Marley says as she stands. She saunters over to her phone, cracked and vibrating, a few feet away.

"Look, I'm from San Francisco, I can't afford to live there anymore, I get it. Please. We're in this together."

I save my breath because he isn't worth another second of my time. He tried to weaponize the anti-Blackness that he and the police feel to use the gang to cover up his own crimes. When his business was in danger, he killed a man, then justified his actions by siding with a white woman's vision for change that would sacrifice the rest of us. We are not the same.

I watch this Swiss-cheese slice of a white man melt before me. Lance sinks onto his knees, begging for forgiveness. Pleading for sympathy. Advocating for his innocence. Shouting his entitlement. But there's not a shred of sincerity in it at all. Throughout his life, he's been taught that his passions, his concerns, his good deeds, his word, matter more than anyone else's. All my life, mainstream society has tried to ground me into believing that he's right.

Fucking nonsense.

With each second, Lance's performance becomes more and more boring. I take Marley by the arm and lead her outside, where we wait for help to arrive on the splintered steps of the front entryway. Lance's cries echo against our backs, but then a lowrider cruises by blasting Kendrick Lamar. We wave at the couple in the car, umber skin shining beneath the late-afternoon sun, and they wave back. My neighbor pulls into her driveway and unloads several bags of groceries, asking me how my summer is going, and if I've finished that book I was reading yet. Auntie shows up alongside the mental health crisis team that she called when she heard the news. Malachi follows shortly after, folding me into a hug that doesn't end. I exhale.

I feel safe.

This is home.

EPILOGUE

TWO WEEKS LATER

"Easy, easy, go slow." Malachi wraps his hand around mine and applies just the right amount of pressure to the spray can, releasing a steady stream of paint. "Like this, see?"

"This is much harder than it looks," I admit. I let our arms relax and take a few steps back. Malachi circles his arms around my waist as we lean against the light pole, admiring our work. On the wall of Genie Theater in bright yellow paint and West Coast Gothic font, Malachi painted the phrase *"Gentrification is . . ."* with all of our answers below.

> <u>Not</u> revitalization.—Lou
>
> Collective trauma. —Marley
>
> Bad speculative fiction framed as redevelopment.—Zeke
>
> Weaponized against low-income communities of color.—Malachi
>
> Bullshit.—Rhea

Lou sets up the rack of spray cans against the wall for passersby to add their own thoughts to as part of #Rooted's visual protest campaign.

"Can I add the glitter now?!" Marley asks.

I laugh and wave her on. "Go for it."

"Yeeee!" She dips the paint roller into the bucket of clear glue and spreads it across the wall before she and Zeke start throwing handfuls of rainbow confetti. Lou perches on the fire hydrant, watching them go wild with a smile.

"I couldn't think of a better reason to reemerge from hiding," Zeke says.

It's been two weeks since the whole #Rooted protest shitshow. It didn't take long for authorities to release Zeke after Camesha's video went viral, but since West Coast news outlets are still covering the "Sosi Scam" story, Lupe's been mad protective of Zeke. Today's the first day that she finally let us take him out, which is great. Except for the fact that she still won't look me in the eyes.

This morning, though, she sent Zeke with a Tupperware of flan and five spoons: one for Zeke, Malachi, Lou, Marley . . . and me too. It's a small gesture, but I'm glad I made the cut.

There's a lot to celebrate: Zeke's a free man and Auntie Inga's tenant organizing worked. The #Rooted protest ended up going strong for seventy hours straight. The news coverage of the movement was enough to get local politicians to enact an emergency policy restricting landlords' ability to spike rent prices for the next year. Plus, nobody in either Zeke's nor Auntie's apartment buildings needs to pay rent until Amelia and the other landlords are fully investigated for foul play. Lupe and Auntie are tag-teaming the effort to push the politicians even further to give all long-term, low-income residents an annual credit to stay in the neighborhood.

After dumping Staples (who, in addition to being a complete asshole, was most definitely cheating on her), Ms. Allen has been working closely with Auntie too. She's helping provide guidance on potential litigation strategies to sue the city for racist zoning policies that encourage gentrification and reduce the amount of affordable housing in the county. There are even talks about starting a grant program to build community ownership of land and help create more local worker-owned co-ops. Some say it's a long shot, but Lupe says that *impossible* isn't a word in our community's culture.

In terms of the other suspects, turns out Staples is a piece of shit, just not a murdering piece of shit. After Camesha blew up on him, he called Vic to convince him not to pull out of their deal and asked to meet up. Vic was already on his way to see Troy, but he said he'd meet up before heading to Vegas if Staples would wait nearby. On their dinner date earlier, Ms. Allen told Staples that Lou and Marley accused him of cheating on her. He realized his navigational system would look suspicious, showing the fancy restaurant he went to with Camesha later that very evening, so he deleted all the data from that day to cover his tracks.

Anyway, when Vic never showed up for their meeting, he started driving around looking for him. He didn't see what happened, but he saw the body in the parking lot. Apparently, rather than calling the cops, he stuck around to see if he could gather any dirt that he could use against someone later. He was hoping for someone powerful to walk into his blackmail trap, but when he saw Zeke, he settled for trying to punish the boyfriend of his girlfriend's son. Luckily there are laws against leaving false information for police officers, so his ass is in big-time trouble.

And Diego, well, he's still a piece of shit too. But at least he's innocent of murder.

"Yo, have y'all seen the line over at Colony Cantina?" Camesha shouts. She leans out the car window as Lacy pulls up to the curb to park. "There's at least thirty people sweating outside, waiting to get in."

"White Americans really do love a line," Lou says.

Colony Cantina's been mad popular ever since the murder stuff went viral, and the two new white boys running the place while Lance and Troy figure out their legal situation don't seem too mad about it.

"I heard they started selling a new taco called the 'Poblano Escobar,'" Malachi says.

I roll my eyes. Not only is that a tasteless and low-key offensive nod at the crime scene, but it's literally not even culturally correct. But then again, what can you expect?

A #BlackLivesMatter sign still hangs over their front door.

"I bet the place is haunted now, though, so whatever. Let their greedy asses get cursed," Lacy says as she hops out of the car. She sways over to the spray cans and adds her line with Camesha's. *"Gentrification is . . ."*

Erasing the heart of a community.—Lacy

Putting economic growth over the well-being of residents.—Camesha

Apparently Camesha and Lacy had been keeping close tabs on Troy for weeks. Camesha was never really interested in dating him, but she wanted to earn his trust after their initial meeting at Lacy's cannabis growery gig. He made a comment that didn't sit right with the girls—something about how he wants to get in on a cash-only business so that he could "level up" in the neighborhood. They suspected that he was involved in some shady shit, and Lacy wasn't tryna let some random guy mess up all the work that she put in to make sure that the new weed industry wouldn't turn into an exclusive white-led mafia sort of thing.

Turns out, she wasn't that far off.

"Y'all are coming to my housewarming next month, right?" Camesha asks us for the fourth time in the past forty-eight hours. With Auntie Inga's help, she was able to make a successful bid on a cute one-bedroom condo, right here in the neighborhood. "The theme will be 'Buy Black the Block,' so be sure to wear all black."

"And look cute because I will be taking pictures for her blog!" Lacy adds, beaming with pride.

In the end, we did find out what Auntie and Vic were fighting about at the gas station: Auntie asked Vic to stop seeing Camesha. Auntie lied about it because she didn't want Camesha to think she was butting in. Auntie's usually so good about letting young people make their own choices, but she admitted that with Camesha it's harder for her because she truly sees her as a daughter. Auntie apologized to Camesha for overstepping, Camesha thanked her for caring.

"Ay, yo, Malachi!" The door to the theater swings open as the owner waves him over. "Come here for a second, brother."

Malachi gives my shoulder a squeeze. "I'll be right back."

As he walks away, Zeke rushes to my side. "I can't believe this is happening," he says.

"I know. It's crazy that after everything that went down, the neighborhood is—"

"Oh my god, Rhea, no. I mean, yeah, that's real, but I mean this." Zeke nods his head over at Malachi, arms crossed and smiling as the theater owner compliments the mural. "I can't believe that it took starting a goddamn gang for you two to finally get your shit together. Ridiculous. Truly ridiculous."

I catch Malachi's eyes for a second and the butterflies go wild.

It wasn't SOSI that did it, though, really. When you grow up lonely, it's so easy to fall into a false scarcity mindset about love: that there can only be so much of it and only so many people can share it. I guess it was realizing how far I'd go to support Zeke and letting Marley and Lou into the crew that taught me to embrace abundance. Zeke's sentimental ass doesn't need to know all that, though, so I just link my arm with his and lean onto his shoulder, letting the soft vibration of his laughter lull me into a state of complete and total relaxation.

The *wee-woo* sound of a police siren cuts through my calm. Two cops pull up right behind Lacy's ride. They roll down their window, but before they can say anything, Malachi shouts from the corner, "We have a permit!"

I can tell the cop has more questions, but an old married couple walking by intervenes without a blink. "Read the damn wall!"

The cop scans the mural and fixes her expression into an awkward grimace before nodding at her partner, who takes the hint and keeps driving.

Even though everyone now knows the gang was fake, ever since the SOSI shit went down, the increased police presence around here has been wild. It feels like there are new cops on every corner these days.

"This isn't your fault," Zeke whispers.

"Feels like it is," I mumble.

He gives me a sympathetic shrug before turning to the rest of the crew. "Aight, it's too hot. Can we go inside now?"

"We'll take over from here," Lacy offers. She and Camesha take out their phones to snap pics of the wall as Zeke, Lou, Marley, Malachi, and I head inside the theater.

Marley picks the movie today. She originally wanted us to go to a special summer showing of *Get Out*, but then we all agreed that felt too real right now. She settles on a raunchy, R-rated comedy, so we sneak in after the previews. We snag a large Icee with five straws and take over an empty row in the way, way back, passing the snacks between us.

"So, can we get matching tattoos when we turn eighteen? Something to commemorate this summer?" Marley asks as she settles into a seat in the center of our group.

She kicks her Doc Martens up onto the back of the empty seat in front of her. She helped me pick out a pair for myself that we ordered online—they're bright yellow with matching laces. They'll be here next week.

"Cornyyyyyyyy," Lou groans as he weaves his hand with Zeke's.

"I'm pro–squad tattoo," Malachi says. "Should we all get Troy's face on our necks?"

"Too soon," I say with a laugh. "Give me four more years with my new therapist before I can handle that."

"As you wish." Malachi chuckles and plants a kiss on my cheek.

"Maybe we'll all get chest tats of the entire neighborhood," I joke.

"You know, I thought about that," Zeke says with a laugh. But then his voice becomes serious. "I've always thought that after growing up in South LA, one day maybe I'll have kids or nieces or nephews whatever running around here and I'd be able to point at a building and say, 'Yo, when I was your age, my friends and I were here, and we did so-and-so.'" He pauses as another crew our age creeps up the aisle to hide from the security guard. "But the way that things are changing, I don't know if my stories will make sense to them." Zeke pulls his hand out of the bag of chips and wipes the salt onto his jeans. "Our hood will probably be completely unrecognizable from theirs one day. I don't think that anything we did will have changed that." He takes a long sip from the almost-empty Slurpee, the sound of the straw scraping the bottom of the cup being the only sound between us.

"It might look different, but still feel the same," Malachi offers.

Maybe, but I know exactly what Zeke means. There has been more change around here in the past three years than in the first twelve years of our lives combined. It's hard to do the math to figure out what that means for the future.

"What do the transplants think?" Malachi says to Lou and Marley.

Lou shakes his head. "I don't know, man, but I do hope to shed the transplant label eventually. I got a feeling that I might grow old here if someone will let me," he says to Zeke more than the rest of us. Beneath the fringe of his hair, Zeke smiles.

"I wasn't here to see the neighborhood before, but I'm

fully committed to pulling a Tupac." She raises her hands and starts shaking her shoulders while singing "To Live and Die in LA." A hipster couple several rows in front of us shushes us, and we shoot back with five artful variations of theatrically giving them the finger.

I feel the rest of the crew look at me to wait for my hot take, but for once in my life, my big mouth doesn't have one. I shrug and am saved by the faint vibration that hits all our pockets at the same time. It's a text from Auntie asking if we've figured out our talking points for the next #Rooted meeting.

After everything that happened with Zeke, the next action is criminal (in)justice reform. LA County still has the largest prison system in the world, but we're tryna abolish that shit. Lacy and Camesha immediately text back that they're almost done with their part. Lupe gives each message a heart followed by an unintelligible string of very mom-esque emojis. She's been connecting with other parents of incarcerated teens—talking about creating more youth jobs and youth centers, but most of all, ending "gang enhancements" for everybody.

To be honest, I don't know what I'll say at the meeting yet, but I'm hoping that it'll come to me in the moment. And if it doesn't, that's okay. There will be another meeting and another action and another campaign, and #Rooted will just keep getting bigger and bigger.

Anyway, we don't have to figure it all out now because today is August 1 . . . Rent Day.

But guess what?

Nobody's going anywhere.

THE END.

DEAR READER,

If you haven't realized it by now, here's my not-so-hot take: gentrification sucks.

It sucks because communities of color are the culture-bearers of many cities, yet we are currently facing the threat of displacement.

It sucks because gentrification undervalues and discredits this cultural labor while simultaneously exploiting and promoting its product.

It sucks because it destabilizes the fragile ecosystems of human connection that not only make diverse neighborhoods so special, but also make life worth living.

My own home in South LA is one of such communities undergoing tremendous change. It's home to West Coast hip hop, Black Hollywood landmarks, lowrider shows, and some of the best damn pupusas in the country. It's a culturally and socioeconomically diverse place where many people feel rooted because of their connections to neighbors, local businesses, and loved ones that share the block. Yet gentrification brings many challenges, including but not limited to loss of social capital, increased police presence in public spaces, and heightened mental health challenges to the communities that have been there long before.[1] Thus, this novel seeks to put names and faces to the human cost of gentrification without losing sight of the creativity of those resisting the tidal waves of erasure.

Although There Goes the Neighborhood *is inspired by the love for my own community in Los Angeles, it is a work of fiction and I have taken a great deal of creative liberty. I chose to create the fictionalized neighborhood of Kofa Park to highlight how the issues that the characters face relate to people in cities across the United States, as well as the world. By no means is Kofa Park intended to be representative of all communities facing gentrification today.*

Having grown up in a historic Black and brown community that is currently facing gentrification, I've long thought a lot about how real estate developers market certain neighborhoods. The idea for the teens to start a fake gang in the book emerged from my own experience observing how anti-Black narratives are used to justify the displacement and erasure of communities of color. The characters' neighborhood being advertised as the "first frontier" for gentrification—because it's Black/brown, yet perceived as "not as dangerous" as other places—produces the central conflict of the book: how white people can simultaneously look at a historically Black neighborhood as ripe for economic exploitation, while still maintaining a deep-seated fear of Black people and connecting their image of people of color to violence. This very tension is what the characters explore and exploit with their bold, though problematic, scheme.

For those of you who may still be wondering why I chose to tell this story through a comedic lens, I'll respond by asking you: Why the hell not? *While growing up, my friends and I dealt with racism, of course, but we also laughed. A lot. We were, in essence, wild fools running around, sneaking into movies, thriving alongside our found family, falling in love, and being absolutely ridiculous. I wanted the same for my characters in this book. There's always been play, mischief, and joy in the way that Black people cope with the pressures that this country has imposed on us. I wanted to share a story that finds the silliness within the absurdities of capitalism and asks:* How can we grapple with the systemic racisms that shape our lives while still centering the joy of being young and Black, the warmth of feeling held by your community, the euphoria of a first kiss at the weekly drum circle with the flavor of a mango paleta still lingering on your lips?

My dream for you, reader, is to walk away from this book reflecting on how change shapes our lives and our connections to one another. Thank you for coming along for this ride with me.

In solidarity,
JADE ADIA

Work Cited:
(1) Bethany Y. Li, "Now Is the Time!: Challenging Resegregation and Displacement in the Age of Hypergentrification," 85 Fordham L. Rev. 1189 (2016)

ACKNOWLEDGMENTS

This is a book about community, inspired by the love that I hold for the irreplaceable people in my life. Leslie Ivy Noble, thank you for being my mother and working so hard to protect our family, no matter what. I'll love you forever, I'll like you for always. To my ancestor-grandparents Norma Jean and Gil, thank you for making me noble and strong. To my sisters, Jasmin Ayana and Jordan Adero, home wouldn't be anything without you. And to my nephews, Jah and Yasir, thank you for lighting my heart on fire with each smile.

Jim McCarthy, my unbelievable agent, thank you for being a grounding presence on this journey from the start. In an era when so much of working life feels rushed and harsh, you move with patience, intentionality, and kindness. Massive appreciation to everyone at Dystel, Goderich & Bourret for cheering us both on.

Rebecca Kuss! My effervescent editor! Thank you for your constant honesty, vulnerability, encouragement, and wisdom. You and Ashley I. Fields helped me whip this book into something that I will be proud of for the rest of my life. I appreciate everyone at Disney-Hyperion who read this wild story and believed that there is magic in these pages.

To the geniuses behind my gorgeous cover: Zareen Johnson and Shane Ramos. Zareen, your design vision is incredible. Shane, you are truly a phenomenal artist. You captured all the love, chaos, and euphoria of this book and its setting so beautifully—I'm grateful to be connected through this incredible work of art.

Danielle Parker, my fellow author, my critique partner, my pseudo-therapist: thank you for dreaming and scheming with me every day. Monumental thanks as well to my literal therapist who shall remain unnamed, but just know: you're a real one.

Thank you to the generous people who guided me through early revisions: Zan Romanoff, Micah Mingo, Max Mendelsohn, J. Elle, and Emily Bowie. Thank you Baridilo Dube for being my brilliant first reader. I am forever grateful to the amazing young beta readers who provided feedback on this story when it was still a flaming pile of garbage: Daksha, Kayjah, Lucinda, and Lucas.

English teachers are amazing. Anne Fadiman, you encouraged me to be vulnerable on the page. Amanda Chicago Lewis, your mentorship is a gift. Your classroom was my refuge in high school, and you've looked out for me at every stage of my education and career ever since. I'm a better writer because of you both.

To my chosen sisters, Blair Thompson and Alixx Lucas, we've been awkward, spastic geeks together since childhood and I wouldn't have had it any other way. Whenever I write about what it feels like to love your best friends so fiercely and so protectively, I think of you two.

Thank you to the friends who I confided in that I was

secretly writing a novel and didn't blink twice: Latrel Powell, Dianne Kaiyoorawongs, Cameron Walker, Phaedra Frampton, Márk Fedronic, Myles Gaines, and Paula Gaither (the Alexander the Great story is all you!). Shoutout to The Nigglets group chat: who knew that wandering around the neighborhood, sneaking into movies at Magic and eating Krispy Kreme donuts for all those years would lead to this? I'm grateful for the memories and the constant support from y'all over the decades.

Devin Page, you read and watched every single major YA franchise with me for fourteen years. Every moment of this book that celebrates the sheer silliness and chaos of being an awkward Black kid is intertwined with the legacy of you and our friendship. Rest in peace, gorgeous.

To The Village—my found family of neighbors, aunties, uncles, play cousins, and friends—I'm proud to have been raised by and alongside you all. Thank you for teaching me what it means to be part of a community that's worth fighting for. Much love to my OG godmother, Roxan Humes; my fairy godmother, Marchelle Bailey Barnes; and my forever friend, Sarita Barnes.

To my readers, thank you for engaging with this story and for giving me a chance. Also, please search online: "LASD gangs."

And finally, to all my South LA folks, I love you. Our communities are sacred.

Bless this block.

CREDITS

There Goes the Neighborhood was created with help and collaboration from the following people:

EDITORIAL DIRECTOR
Kieran Viola

EDITOR
Rebecca Kuss

ASSISTANT EDITOR
Ashley I. Fields

DESIGNER
Zareen Johnson

MANAGING EDITOR
Sara Liebling

COPY CHIEF
Guy Cunningham

PRODUCTION MANAGER
Jerry Gonzalez

MARKETING DIRECTOR
Matt Schweitzer

SENIOR MARKETING MANAGER
Holly Nagel

MARKETING MANAGERS
Danielle DiMartino
& Tim Retzlaff

SENIOR MARKETING MANAGER, SCHOOL & LIBRARY
Dina Sherman

MARKETING COORDINATOR, SCHOOL & LIBRARY
Bekka Mills

PUBLICITY DIRECTOR
Ann Day

PR MANAGER
Crystal McCoy

SALES
Monique Diman & team

DYSTEL, GODERICH & BOURRET
Jim McCarthy